CRAZY LOVE

THE SINGLE DAD PLAYBOOK
BOOK 5

WILLOW ASTER

All rights reserved.
No part of this book may be reproduced in any form or by any electronic or mechanical means, including information storage and retrieval systems, without written permission from the author, except for the use of brief quotations in a book review.

Willow Aster
www.willowaster.com

Copyright © 2025 by Willow Aster
ISBN-13: 978-1-964527-06-2

Cover by Emily Wittig Designs
Photo: Wander Aguiar Photography
Map by Kess Fennell
Editing by Christine Estevez

NOTE TO READERS

A list of content warnings are on the next page, so skip that page if you'd rather not see them.

CONTENT WARNINGS

The content warnings for *Crazy Love* are sexual content, profanity, foster care, adoption and child abuse (off page).

PROLOGUE
SCREECHING HALT

PENN

February

The sun is just starting to set over the turquoise waters of the Bahamas and I'm trying not to freak out over this ceremony. I'm officiating the wedding of one of my best friends tomorrow—Bowie Fox. I technically married him and Poppy in their hospital room while they were giving birth to their baby, but this is the polished-up, beautiful version. The pressure is on. I've gotta get this right.

I try out a few lines under my breath as I stare out at the water, willing it to calm me. "Marriage is like the ocean—vast, mysterious, and full of surprises." I wince. "Nope. Too deep. Literally."

"You might want to avoid ocean metaphors unless you're comparing love to a hurricane…which *has* been done, I suppose."

My thoughts halt like a record scratch when I look over and see an impossibly gorgeous woman staring out pensively at the ocean. Her long, black hair cascades down her back and her skin looks bronzed in this light. She's wearing a white tank top and *short* white shorts and she is wearing them *well*.

When her eyes meet mine, she gives me an amused smirk and I get this weird ping in my gut. Like I just went skydiving and lost my stomach.

"Caught me practicing," I say sheepishly. "I'm marrying my friends tomorrow."

Her eyebrows lift. "You're marrying your friends…"

"I mean, I'm officiating…" I tug on my shirt, feeling hot all of a sudden.

"And you're nervous?" Her gaze drifts over my face and I swallow hard but then try to play it off.

"I-no. Not really. I—" I run my hands through my hair and laugh. "Well, yeah. I am. Words matter, you know? I love my friends and they're trusting me to set the tone for their wedding…and the rest of their lives. No pressure or anything."

Her smirk widens into a smile and I'm done. Sign me up. I'm in.

"Well, Preacher Man, I think you'll be just fine."

"Preacher Man?" I volley, a grin taking over my entire face.

Damn, she's pretty.

"Sounds like it fits." She gives a slight shrug and my eyes drop to her delicate shoulder. Her skin looks so soft and it takes effort to drag my eyes away from her body, but her big brown eyes and pouty lips are oh so alluring, so the payoff is still huge when I do.

"Trust me, I am not…holy."

There's a beat where we stare at each other. My eyes drop to her mouth and stay fixated there for a few seconds. God, I've never wanted to kiss someone so badly in all my life. Not after just meeting, for Christ's sake, and honestly…kissing isn't really my thing. I find kissing way more intimate than sex.

"I have just the thing to help you relax," she says.

"Oh…*really*." I have to say I'm surprised that she's going there so soon, but you won't find me complaining.

"Yes, follow me." She turns and walks toward the resort, turning once to look at me over her shoulder. She smiles when she sees that I'm following, and my stomach does that free-fall again…it's the weirdest thing.

I'm not sure where this girl is leading me, but I'm beyond caring. I take her hand and let her guide me through the sandy paths of the resort.

"Where are you taking me?" I ask.

"Patience is a virtue," she teases.

"Virtue is overrated."

"Says the preacher man."

I laugh. "Right. Preacher Man. Name's actually Penn. What's yours?"

"Addy."

The path opens up and there's a secluded section of the beach that wasn't visible before, and a group of people are stretching.

"What—" I gasp when a group of flamingos move between the people. Some might think they're beautiful, and I guess they are in an odd, gangly, *terrifying* way.

"Yoga with flamingos," Addy announces, like it's a perfectly normal thing to do…ever. "This will help you relax for sure."

"I assure you it will not," I say under my breath. Louder, I say, "Yoga with that?" I point to a flamingo that has locked eyes with me, its head tilted as if to say, *You lookin' at me?*

She laughs, and fuck me, if my dick doesn't respond in spite of the flamingo staring me down like a mob boss.

"You're not scared of flamingos, are you?" she asks.

"Are you sure this is a good idea?" I back up a step. "That one is looking at me funny."

She glances at the bird, her grin widening. "You'll be fine. Look, they're used to people." She points at another bird being petted by a guest. That one does look sweeter, far less Al Capone. "Besides, don't you want to try something new? Live a little?"

"I was thinking more along the lines of a cocktail I haven't tried before…with a gorgeous woman…whose name starts with an A."

One of her shoulders lifts and she bats her eyelashes. "Aw, thank you." Her smile deepens and she gives me a pointed look. "Maybe we can have that cocktail after the yoga."

"Fine," I mutter. "But if I get pecked to death, I'm haunting you."

She laughs and I'd appreciate that it sounds like music if I wasn't worried for my life.

We join the group and I do my best to focus on the instructor's overly serene voice instead of Capone the flamingo, who seems *very* interested in my mat. It begins innocently enough—stretching, deep breaths, the usual yoga stuff. But then, as I'm stretched into what the instructor calls Warrior II, Capone decides to move in closer. As in, absolutely no respect for my personal boundaries whatsoever.

"Hey, dude. Back off," I say between my teeth.

He waddles closer and pecks at my foot.

"Hey!" I yelp.

The bastard stands on my mat, staring me down like I owe him something.

"What do you want from me?" I ask, trying to give it the evil eye.

Addy bursts out laughing. "I think she likes you!"

"There's no way this one is a female. He's sizing me up for dinner," I mutter. When it steps closer, I try to shoo it away. The flamingo responds by flapping its wings and letting out an ear-splitting squawk that startles me so much, I trip over my own feet and fall flat on my back.

The instructor gasps and hurries over when the flamingo's face dips closer to mine. I hear a camera click from a person nearby and cover my face to avoid being pecked to death. It's not fun to be under a pileup on the football field by a three-hundred-pound freight train, but this flamingo right now with that sharp, hooked beak that's deceptively precise and those beady little eyes that scream chaos? That's a fucking horror show.

Instead of the peck of death, I feel a soft hand on my arm and peek between my hands. Addy is laughing so hard, she's clutching her side, but with the other hand, she tries to pull me up.

"Okay," she says between laughing. "Maybe yoga with flamingos isn't your thing."

"It's so not," I tell her, scrambling to my feet. "Let's get out of here before he calls for backup."

We bolt from the beach, and now that I have some distance from the claws of Satan, I can see a little bit of the humor in the situation. We end up at the tiki bar. Addy leans into me, still laughing, her eyes sparkling in the sunset.

I put my arms around her, leaning in to whisper, "We survived. Barely."

"I'll buy you a drink to make up for it," she says softly.

"Oh no. I'm buying you a drink. I need to make sure you stick around long enough for me to recover my dignity."

She giggles. "It will be hard to get that image of you dominated by the flamingo out of my head, Preacher Man."

I turn to face her, my hands going to either side of her face, as I dip down, eyes level with hers. "Tell me what I have to do," I say huskily.

She bites her lower lip to keep from laughing and I struggle to keep from laughing myself, but this close to her, barely a breath between us…it's intoxicating.

"Give me a new memory," she whispers.

The air between us is charged. I feel her warmth, her breath mingling with mine, the faintest scent of her perfume. She isn't just beautiful, she's magnetic—a force pulling me in until the distance becomes unbearable.

There's nothing left to do but close the distance between us. It's a *need*.

My thumb trails the curve of her jaw and her eyes are steady and unflinching, like she can see straight into the part of me I don't show anyone.

And just like that, I give in.

When our lips meet, it isn't fireworks—it's a detonation. A deep, bone-shaking, soul-rattling detonation that shatters me into pieces and rebuilds me in the same instant. Her lips are so soft, but the kiss isn't. It's raw, consuming. It's a thousand unspoken words all pouring out at once.

Time stops. The noise in the bar falls away. There's no past, no future, only this moment with her.

She kisses me back with the same abandon I feel. It's intense, the way we crash into each other with everything in us.

When we finally break apart, my forehead rests against hers, both of us breathing hard.

"That was…the best thing I've ever felt," I say.

"Yeah," she says breathlessly.

Just then, an annoying sound erupts from my phone. Dammit. My alarm. I'd forgotten I'd even set it, but it's a good thing or I think I would've remained in this stunned stupor for a while.

"I can't believe this. I've gotta go. The rehearsal dinner. Come with me? My friends won't mind."

She wrinkles her nose. "Oh, no. I couldn't."

"Really, it'll be okay." My face falls when she shakes her head. "Okay, meet me afterward? Right here? I'll be back by nine."

She lifts her chin, eyes dancing with amusement. "You sure you can pull that off?"

I smile. "I'm determined."

She studies me for a second before nodding. "Okay, I'll be here."

The second I walk in, I spot her. I'm conflicted about leaving Bowie's rehearsal dinner until I see Addy sitting at a high-top table in a dark corner, twisting the stem of her martini glass between her fingers. She's the kind of girl who owns the room without even trying.

I walk over, slipping onto the stool next to her. "Told you I'd be here, beautiful."

She doesn't look at me right away, just takes a slow sip of her drink. "Right on time too."

"You thought I wouldn't show?"

She tilts her head toward me, her lips curving up. "I considered it."

"You wound me."

"Do I?" she asks, playfully.

"Deeply." I place a hand over my heart and lean in. "Tell me what's on your mind."

I never ask women this because that's a minefield waiting to explode, but I genuinely want to know with her.

Her eyes narrow.

"Uh-oh." I laugh when she doesn't say anything, just studies me. "You're plotting something. Based on previous experience, when you get that look, it means trouble. No more flamingos tonight." I lift my hands up.

She exhales dramatically. "Dammit. You catch on way too fast."

I smirk. "What are you scheming?"

"Not so fast. How was the rehearsal dinner?"

"It was great. Good food. Everyone's so happy to be here, happy to be together…"

Her nose crinkles up. "I feel bad for taking you away from your friends."

I shake my head. "We have fun whenever we're together. You should meet them. Tomorrow?" I ask hopefully.

She grins and gets that mischievous look again.

"So, what were you thinking about when I got here?" I take her hand and thread my fingers in hers.

She turns in her seat, facing me. "Whether or not I should kiss you again."

Heat licks up my spine. "And?"

"I mean, the first kiss was good…"

"Good?" I scoff. "Addy, that kiss deserved a standing O."

She lifts a shoulder. "Eh. Seven out of ten."

"Seven? Why does that crush my ego into dust?"

She bites her lip to keep from laughing. "Okay, eight."

"Unbelievable," I mutter. "You *loved* it."

She leans in, close enough that I smell the soft vanilla and coconut scent of her skin. "Maybe you should remind me," she whispers.

That's all the invitation I need.

I kiss her, slow and deep, letting it build. And holy hell, it's even better than the first time. The way she melts into me after luring me in with her sexy mouth—I'm gone.

She lets out a small, satisfied hum against my lips, and I smile against her mouth. "Still an eight?"

"Nine," she says, breathless. "But if we keep going, I *might* consider a ten."

"Let's test that theory."

I stand up and hold out my hand, and she takes it, smiling up at me. I lead her to the elevators, both of us buzzing with anticipation. By the time we reach my room, we barely make it inside before my hands are on her waist, her fingers threading through my hair. It's ridiculous how fucking good this feels with her.

She presses against me, her breath warm against my jaw. "You always move this fast?"

I chuckle, brushing my lips against her ear. "I could kiss

you all night long and die happy…and no, I do *not* always work like that."

Her breath hitches. "You like kissing me?"

"More than I should," I admit, my voice rough.

She pulls me down for another kiss, and I swear, I could get lost in her mouth forever.

And then—

My phone rings.

I groan against her lips and consider ignoring the call, but when I see Rhodes' name on the screen, I exhale sharply. "I have to take this."

She steps back and nods. "It's okay. Go ahead."

I answer. "Rhodes?"

"Hey, man. I haven't seen you in a while and need a favor. Some of Poppy's friends had a little too much to drink and Elle and I are going to take them to their rooms. Any chance you could help us handle them? We're still at the restaurant. It's like herding elephants over here."

I crinkle up my face, giving Addy an apologetic look. "Yeah, I'll be right there."

When I hang up, I turn to Addy, brushing my fingers along her jaw before kissing her softly. I just can't resist those lips. She is a taste that leaves me feeling both sated and hungry. I drag myself away and stare at her.

"You're so beautiful, Addy."

Her cheeks flame and I can't stop smiling.

"Don't move," I tell her. "I'll be right back. I need to help wrangle some people back to their hotel rooms."

She smiles, giving me one more quick kiss. "Hurry back."

I walk backwards, still staring at her like I've been struck by lightning because that's how I feel. "I promise you, I will be so fast."

"Go, go." She laughs.

I grin and bolt out of the door, already desperate to get back to her.

Of course it takes longer than expected. Poppy's friends are nice and so happy to be on a tropical getaway, but they are hard to finagle drunk. Fifteen minutes stretches into thirty and I'm sweating by the time I reach my door.

When I walk into my hotel room…she's gone.

CHAPTER ONE

ALL I'VE GOT

PENN

July

The bell over the door chimes as I step into Luminary Coffeehouse, the familiar hum of conversation and the hiss of the espresso machine welcoming me like a massive heated blanket. Clara stands behind the counter, grinning with her eyebrows raised, waiting for me to bust a move.

"Don't think you're getting coffee without dancing, Penn."

I groan. Normally, I'd play along. Hell, I was here the day she started this whole dancing-for-coffee tradition, and I'd like to think I've displayed some of my best moves right here on this coffee shop floor. But today, my feet feel like lead, and my mood isn't much lighter.

"Half a dance, Clara," I say. "That's all I've got in me today."

"Half a dance?" she repeats, feigning shock. "Who are you, and what have you done with Penn Hudson?"

I shuffle halfheartedly to some pop song playing over the speakers. It's more of a tragic sway, but Clara smiles at me sympathetically and hands me my caramel macchiato.

"Here's a sweet to sweeten your day," she says.

"Thanks, Clara. You're the best."

The low rumble of Marv and Walter's bickering back and forth as I walk past their table makes me pause. They're mid-rant, per usual—the two old men are here every time I set foot in Luminary, and I can always count on them to be arguing.

"And another thing," Marv says, his voice sharp. "You can't call it a tackle if the guy practically hugs him first. It's football, not a slow dance!"

Walter shakes his head. "Back in my day, we didn't even have these cushy helmets. We played with grit! Not like these wimps who need a commercial break every five minutes."

I smirk as I approach, but before I can pass, Marv's eyes lock onto me. "Well, look who it is. We saw some footage of you guys at training camp on the news last night. You care to explain why everyone's forgotten how to tackle?"

Walter jumps in before I can reply. "Or why they're tripping on their shoelaces out there? Are you clowns gonna be ready when the season starts?"

I chuckle, pausing at their table. I don't bother to correct them. Training camp hasn't officially started, but our workouts have increased and the news team came out while we were messing around yesterday.

"Good morning to you too, gentlemen. I assure you, we will be more than ready when the time comes."

Marv snorts, pointing a gnarled finger at me. "You better be. We want you back in the Super Bowl this year."

"I want that too, trust me."

"Do it while you've got knees that still work, Penn," Walter says, leaning back in his chair.

"*My* knees still work," Marv says. "Maybe not out on a football field anymore, but these knees smoked you at bowling last week." He points at Walter, who's shaking his head and waving him off.

"Bowling doesn't count," Walter mutters.

I tap the table and point at Walter. "Bowling totally counts, and I'll take your words under advisement. Super Bowl, while the knees work, no hugging tackles," I tick off the list.

I think I might see a crack of a smile from Marv as I head back to our private room, where the guys are already waiting. My best friends and teammates. The Single Dad Players. I've given them so much crap for calling themselves that. Rhodes, Henley, and Bowie were single dads who started getting together to talk about their kids and fatherhood, and Weston and I looked up to them so much that we started showing up at their little meetings.

I'm happy to be playing the field…in all the ways. But it's starting to feel strange to be the odd man out. The only non-dad. The only single one. Once upon a time, we were in the same boat together. Now they've all gone and gotten themselves hitched and procreated.

Henley's the veteran of the group, balancing his podcast and his job as a football commentator with fatherhood like some kind of superhero. He has four daughters now—three from his first marriage…Cassidy, Audrey, and Gracie—and a new baby girl, Avery, with Tru, the love of his life.

Weston has Caleb, his mini-me, and he's so far gone over Sadie, it's almost comical. The man glows when she walks into the room. It's sickeningly sweet, but I can't give him too much grief for it because they're actually perfect together.

Rhodes has the funniest little dude, Levi, and he finally wised up and married Elle, his best friend. Let's face it, she's the only person who could put up with him long term. We all saw the writing on the wall and knew they were meant to be together, but it took them a hell of a long time to get there. It's only a matter of time before they announce a baby's on the way, I just know it.

And then there's Bowie. My last hope. The one I thought would hold the line with me in singledom forever. But nope. Bowie's daughter Becca is almost ten and I think she knew before anyone that Poppy and Bowie should be together. Now Bowie and Poppy have a seven-month-old son, Jonas. And in case that wasn't a shocker enough, Poppy's pregnant *again*. The guy who never dated anyone is now a walking diaper commercial.

It's like some cosmic joke. I've been thinking there's something in the water, but now? I'm convinced it's the coffee. Whatever Clara's brewing in this place, it's turning these guys into Hallmark movie dads…with filthier mouths, of course.

When I open the door to the smaller room at the back of

Luminary, they're deep in conversation, but the moment I walk in, their attention shifts to me.

"What's up with the sad vibes?" Henley asks when I sit down. "You're usually the one bringing the energy."

When I don't say anything right away, Weston's eyes narrow. "You've been off for months. What's going on, Penn? Spill."

I hesitate, staring into my coffee. The truth is, I haven't brought it up lately because I feel like a hypocrite. I've spent years teasing them about being lovesick fools, and now here I am—moody, distracted, and hung up on a girl I kissed... months ago.

It's absolutely ridiculous is what it is.

"Penn," Rhodes says, snapping his fingers in front of my face. "Fess up."

"Okay, fine." I sigh. "You want the truth?"

"Always," Bowie says.

"I can't stop thinking about that girl." I've already told them about her, but I definitely downplayed what I felt. "In the Bahamas, the night before Bowie and Poppy's wedding..." I look around the table and they all lean in, clearly intrigued. "I met Addy," I admit. "We talked. It was easy and fun. She was beautiful and hilarious and so fucking charming. We kissed, and...it was...I can't stop thinking about her."

Weston's eyebrows shoot up. "You're still hung up on that girl? And you didn't tell us sooner because...?"

"Because I felt so stupid," I say, running a hand through my hair. "I've given all of you so much grief, and here I am, wrecked over a girl I'll never see again. And why her? Why the hell can I not forget her?"

Rhodes smirks. "So the pretty boy's got a heart after all."

If they only knew. It was embarrassing how hard I looked

for her that night. Begged the front desk to let me know who she was, looked at the bar and the beach and the pool and the restaurant…and then finally, I came to terms with the fact that she'd left my room…*on purpose*…and she hadn't come back.

"Very funny," I mutter. "We had this connection…I thought. And then…she left. We were about to…well, I don't know how far it would've gone, but I left to help Poppy's friends…" I nod at Rhodes and he winces. "And when I got back, she was gone. Just disappeared." I sag against my chair. "I think I've lost my touch. Definitely lost my mojo."

The guys laugh, thinking I'm joking, because 99.9% of the time, I *am* joking. The table goes quiet, the guys exchanging glances before Henley says, "You? Lose your mojo? Not possible."

"I'm actually getting tired of the clubbing scene," I add.

They stare at me like they don't recognize me. Hell, I don't recognize myself.

Henley gives me a shit-eating grin. "It had to happen at some point." He pounds my back.

I roll my eyes. "Let's not get ahead of ourselves."

"Oh, we're gonna have the best time with this," Rhodes says. His smirk is at an all-time high.

"Maybe she had a reason for not showing," Bowie says.

"Yeah, something out of her control," Weston adds.

"Or maybe she just wasn't as into me as I thought," I say, the words hurting as much now as they did when I looked for her. "Either way, it doesn't matter. I need to forget about her. It's not like I can find her."

I've tried and come up empty.

Before anyone can respond, my phone buzzes on the table. I glance at the screen and pick it up. "It's Sam. I better take this." I click the screen. "Hey, Sam. What's up?"

The sound of his voice hits me like a punch in the gut and

my chest tightens. He's crying—something I've never heard him do in the years I've been mentoring him. He's tough, tougher than most eleven-year-olds have any right to be, but right now, he sounds broken.

"Penn," he chokes out. "I...I need you."

"Hey, hey," I say quickly, my heart pounding. "I'm here, buddy. Take a deep breath. What's going on?"

He sniffles and the line is quiet for a moment before he speaks again. "I-I messed up. I'm in trouble."

I stand up, already moving toward the door. "Where are you, Sam? I'm coming to you."

The guys are watching with concern, but I don't have time to explain. All I can think about is Sam, how he hasn't been himself lately either, but I haven't been able to get to the bottom of it. I haven't spent as much time with him as normal because I've been gearing up for training camp, which starts soon, but we try to FaceTime every day. Now, hearing the fear in his voice, I know I've been right to be concerned.

"I'm at the police station. They said I could call you."

"The police station?"

"Yeah," his voice cracks.

"Okay, I'll be right there. Less than ten minutes, okay?"

"Okay. Thank you," he says, and I hear him sniffling again before he ends the call.

"You need help?" Rhodes asks.

"I'm not sure yet. He's at the police station."

"Let us know," Henley says.

"I can go with you," Weston says.

"That's okay. I'll see what's up first and then let you know," I say.

He nods and Bowie squeezes my shoulder. "We'll be there in a heartbeat if you need us."

"Thanks, guys." I go out the door, zigzagging through the coffee shop and rush to my SUV.

The fluorescent lights buzz as I walk into the police station, my stomach already in knots. Bill Shockley stands near the front desk, his large frame looming over a small, hunched figure. Sam. His shoulders are slumped, his face a mask of shame.

"Penn," Bill says, his usual gruffness softened slightly. His firm voice feels almost for show, like he's acting tough with Sam watching.

"Bill," I reply, my eyes locking with Sam's. "What's going on here?"

Bill gestures at Sam. "Caught this guy stealing over at Aurora's."

My brows furrow, and I bend in front of Sam, meeting his eyes. "Stealing? That's not like you. What did you take?"

He reluctantly meets my eyes, and they're full of tears that he's trying hard not to let fall. "Some granola bars and peanut butter," he says, his voice barely above a whisper. "I was hungry."

The words hit me like a baseball bat.

"Sam," I say, my voice cracking. "I will feed you every day of the week if you're hungry. I didn't know…I'm so sorry."

He collapses in my arms, and I hug him tight, my throat burning. Over his shoulder, I look at Bill, my jaw clenched. "I need to talk to child services."

Bill's face softens more, but his voice stays professional. "Penn, you know it's not that simple."

"How is this happening?" I ask, trying to keep my voice

steady. "Why is he in a foster home where he's not getting enough to eat? I want to take him home. I can take care of him."

Bill sighs, crossing his arms. "Look, I get it. But you'll have to talk to CPS to see what you can do. It's not just about feeding him."

"I can do better for him than what he's getting right now," I snap. "Look at him, Bill. He's stealing food because he's hungry. How is that okay? How can we just let that slide?"

I've been worried about him losing weight for months and brought food to him regularly, but are his foster parents not letting him have it? What's going on here?

Bill's tough facade cracks. "I'll make some calls. But Penn, these things take time. You can't just…take him home tonight."

I look down at Sam, his small frame trembling against me, and feel a surge of helplessness like I've never known. He needs me and I want him to know I will fight for him, no matter what it takes.

"It's been almost three months now, since I started the process to become his foster parent. It's been tedious. I've done the background check, the interviews, the home visits… all I'm waiting for is the approval and the license. This is crazy that there can be people willing to help and they're turned down. "Make the calls," I say, my voice steel. "I'll order some food to be delivered while we wait. I'm not going anywhere until I know Sam's taken care of."

CHAPTER TWO

HOME AGAIN

ADELINE

It feels great to be back in Silver Hills. Strange, too. I almost feel like a stranger as I drive down Jupiter Lane and see all the new faces and shops, but I'll acclimate quickly. I've been back often to visit Mom and Dad, but there's just something different about *living* here again. The big city wasn't for me.

"There you are," Dad says, holding his arms out for me as I step into Starlight Cafe.

I walk into his hug and inhale his aftershave. "Hi, Dad."

"I'm so happy you're home," he says, smiling down at me. We walk back to a booth near the window and sit down. "Well, kind of home. Are you sure Mom and I can't change your mind about moving back in? There's so much room."

I shake my head as I smile down at the menu. "I haven't lived at home since before college. I love you and Mom dearly, but I need my own space."

He sighs, looking both proud and exasperated. "Well, I don't see why you need to pay for some fancy condo when you can just—"

"I'm happy where I am," I cut in. "Besides, it's not that fancy. It's just…nice. Quiet."

Dad doesn't push it further. He switches topics to something he's excited about. "I want to be the one to bring you in on your first day," he says, his chest puffing out slightly. "Introduce you to everyone in the office…you've met a lot of the staff over the years, but not everyone."

"I don't need to make an entrance," I say nervously.

My dad might have had a say in getting me hired, but I've proven myself in my field and feel like I'm more than able to hold my own. If I can make it in California as a registered dietitian, I can survive anywhere. Still, I don't want a big production. A proud dad hauling me in before my peers doesn't seem like it'll win me any friends.

"Adeline, I'm telling you, this is going to be great. They're going to love you."

"Thanks, Dad. I hope so."

Lunch is easy and fun, the way it always is with my dad, and after we finish, I decide to take a stroll down the street before heading home. The bright sunshine and warm breeze are a nice distraction—until I see him.

Penn.

He's coming out of the police station, a boy walking next

to him. Penn's head is down and his expression is stormy. Even from a distance, I can see the tension in his shoulders, the way his jaw is set like he's trying to hold himself together. My heart thuds against my ribs, and instinctively, I duck behind a parked car, hoping he doesn't see me.

Why am I hiding? It's not like I've done anything wrong…until now. But seeing him again stirs up so much—too much. Memories of our night together in the Bahamas rushes back, the way he made me laugh, the way he kissed me like it meant everything, and then the way I disappeared without a word.

It was for the best that I left. I honestly don't know what I'd been thinking, starting a conversation with him in the first place. I'm going to rack it up to being on vacation for the first time in years and letting my guard down.

Big mistake.

I peek around the car, my pulse racing. He looks so different now…so serious, so weighed down. I want to rush toward him, ask if he's okay, but what would I even say? Instead, I'm frozen, watching as he gets in his SUV and drives away. The guilt that's been simmering since I left him that night boils to the surface. I'd told myself it was for the best, that I'd tell him who I was eventually, but seeing him now, I'm reminded of how just being in his presence is so heady.

If anything more had happened between us, I probably would've made more of a mess of things and fallen even deeper for the guy.

And that just can't happen.

Once he's gone, I let out a shaky breath. This job is supposed to be a fresh start, but right now, I'm not sure I'll be able to accomplish that.

As soon as I left Penn that night in the Bahamas, regret

settled in like a storm cloud I couldn't shake. I hadn't planned any of it—the spark, the pull, the way he made me feel like the only person in the world. I'd told myself I'd stay under the radar, enjoy the free vacation my parents had brought me on while they went to Bowie Fox's wedding, and I'd finally recoup from my exhausting job before starting a new one.

But then I met him, and he was like a beacon in the dark night. Gorgeous, hilarious, and a strange combination of cocky and self-deprecating that just worked for me. I couldn't ignore the pull to him. And I haven't been able to stop thinking about him ever since.

I'd expected all the guests to already be caught up in the wedding activities when I ventured out at the resort, not to stumble straight into Penn Hudson. I thought maybe he'd recognize me, but when it became clear he had no idea who I was, I let myself enjoy the flirting.

I wasn't immune to Penn's good looks—is anyone? But it wasn't just his looks. It was the way he carried himself, the easy humor in his voice, the way we laughed so much…the way I forgot why I was trying so hard to keep my guard up. The chemistry between us was undeniable. For those few hours, it felt like we were in our own little bubble, separate from reality.

And then we kissed. It was…well, I'm still getting heart palpitations after all this time, just thinking about it, so that says a lot.

I'd be lying to myself if I didn't acknowledge that I've had a massive crush on Penn Hudson since the day he joined the Mustangs…despite never meeting him in person until that night in the Bahamas. He did not disappoint; in fact, he was even better than I'd imagined.

But the second I walked away, I knew I'd let it go too far. And I'd made it so much worse by not telling him who I was.

I told myself I'd fix it. But I never got the chance.

Goldie, my college roommate and one of my closest friends, got in a car accident. When I got the call, there was no question. I packed my bags and flew to Minnesota, where she's from, to be with her, leaving Penn without an explanation.

There's no more avoiding him. I know that. Still, I'd like to stretch out running into him for as long as possible. Just a few more days to settle in, to prepare myself and pretend that I'm fine, that nothing from my time with Penn Hudson lingers.

But who am I kidding? It lingers.

Kissing him is something I've revisited daily since it happened. Something I don't think I'll be able to forget.

CHAPTER THREE

TIRED

PENN

A few days later, Sam sits next to me in the SUV, staring out the window. He's been quiet this week despite my texts asking if he's okay and for him to please talk to me. I've spoken to his social worker, who assures me she's going to look into the food situation, and I've dropped off meals at his house twice this week. I don't know what to do.

I've let Sam know that I want him to live with me, but that I have to go through the process of getting a license. I've wondered if it's a good idea that I told him because it's taking so damn long.

He fiddles with the frayed edge of his hoodie sleeve.

"Top Golf sound good?" I ask, trying to sound upbeat.

He shrugs. "Yeah, I guess."

We have to drive to Denver, and the whole way there, I try to get Sam engaged in conversation. He's never like this—usually, he doesn't *stop* talking when we're together. I grip the steering wheel tighter. My chest has ached since I got the call from the station. I can't stand the thought of him being hungry. Not Sam. Not any kid. But especially not this one that I love and can do something about.

We pull into the parking lot and I nudge his shoulder gently. "Come on, buddy. Let's see if you can finally beat me."

His lips twitch like he wants to smile but can't quite manage it. "I'm already better than you," he mutters.

"Prove it," I say, grinning like the cocky son of a bitch I am, but inside I'm thrilled that my favorite kid hasn't lost his fire.

Inside, the familiar sounds of clinking clubs and loud laughter almost feels too bright after our quiet ride here. But I get us set up, and for a while, I let Sam focus on the game. He swings half-heartedly at first, but slowly, he loosens up. By the time he smacks a ball that sails straight into the farthest target, he's smiling.

"See? Told you I was better than you," he says, his voice lighter now.

"Okay, okay," I say, holding up my hands. "We're not done yet."

He smirks and for a moment, it feels normal. Easy. Like everything's fine. But when we sit down to eat later, I can see the weight creeping back in. Sam finishes his burger before I've eaten half of mine and I'm not slow.

"You okay?" I ask, keeping my tone casual.

He shrugs. "About the food…at Aurora's." His voice is quiet, and he doesn't look up. "I'm sorry. I wasn't trying to—"

"Sam," I cut in when he leaves it hanging. "You don't need to apologize to me, okay? But I do need you to talk to me. Tell me what's going on."

He hesitates, picking at his napkin. "Does me stealing mean…you won't want me anymore? To live with you?"

Just when I think my heart can't break any more. "No, it doesn't mean that, Sam. I want you to live with me like…a year ago."

His lips lift a little.

"I don't want you to steal anymore though, okay? I want you to tell me when you need something…anything."

"It's just…things have been rough," he admits finally. "At the house."

My stomach tightens. "What do you mean by rough?"

"They're just…mean sometimes," he says, his voice barely above a whisper. "To me. To everyone. I stayed because of Jesse and Winnie. They're younger, and I didn't want them to feel like I abandoned them. But Jesse's not there anymore…I hope Winnie won't be much longer, even though I'd really miss her. She deserves a good home."

I nod slowly, trying to let him get it out at his own pace. "When did Jesse leave?"

"Day before yesterday. Hopefully he was moved to a better place. I don't know."

"When you say they're mean to you? How exactly?"

"They yell at me. Tell me I can't have dinner if I haven't

done my chores the right way." He looks at me. "I try to do them the right way, I really do."

Fuck me. My heart cracks a little deeper.

"Have you told Mrs. Murphy everything?"

He swallows and shakes his head. "Not yet. She came out the night before Jesse was moved, but I didn't want to leave him. I didn't know he was moving. I'm just..." He stares at his plate and I reach out and put my hand on his shoulder.

"What, Sam? You can tell me."

When his eyes meet mine, he looks way older than he should. Like he's lived too much life. "I'm just so tired. Tired of moving. Tired of everything."

His words hit me like a punch in the gut. This kid has been through so much already, and he shouldn't have to feel like this.

"Have they been feeding you this week? Did you get the food I brought?"

He looks away, watching the family next to us. "Yeah, I think it made them nervous that I'd get taken away, so they've been feeding me and acting nicer."

I sigh and lean back in the booth, taking a deep breath. "Sam," I lean in again, "you don't have to handle this alone. I'm here for you, okay? We're going to figure something out."

He nods, but the weariness in his eyes doesn't go away. It kills me. We hit a few more balls, and by the time I drop him off, he looks a little better than when we started, like the time out may have helped. But it's not enough.

I sit in the SUV after he goes inside, staring at my phone. I'm annoyed that I haven't heard more from Mrs. Murphy this week. She heard me out and assured me she'd look into things, but I expected more communication.

I decide to call her yet again.

"Penn," she answers, sounding cautious. "What's going on?"

"I've just dropped Sam off. He's not okay. What more can I do to have him stay with me?"

There's a pause on the other end, and I already know she's gearing up to put me off longer. I get it, she can only do so much.

"Penn," she says gently, and my fists ball up at her placating tone. "I know you care about Sam, but you should be prepared for the fact that the court might not think you're a viable option. You travel for work. You're not consistently home. And…you're not part of a family unit. Foster care prioritizes stability, and—"

"I can give him stability," I cut in, unable to hide my frustration. "I can do better for him than what he's getting now. A lot better. They yell at him. They withhold food from him as punishment. I'd think foster care would also prioritize feeding a hungry child!"

"I know you mean well, but these situations are complicated. I've looked into what's going on at the foster home and have no reason to believe he's not being fed. I questioned the other kids there, and no one had any complaints. Perhaps Sam is just trying to get your attention."

I scoff. "He's had my attention. There's no reason for him to work hard to get it, he already has it. And maybe the other kids didn't say anything because they were scared if they did, nothing would fix it. Sam said himself that he didn't want to say too much in case he was moved from Jesse and Winnie… and that backfired on him because Jesse ended up being the one who was moved."

"Okay, I'll make another visit over there, but we did get some good news. The grocery store didn't press charges." She pauses and clears her throat. "Penn…often, these kids will act out. It's not uncommon for them to steal food. I'm sure there's more to this than you know. But I'll keep an eye on things and continue looking into it, I promise you that."

"If you don't see this as a cry for help, then I don't even know what to say." I end the call, anger and helplessness twisting in my chest.

I promised Sam I'd figure this out, but the system is stacked against us. I get that I travel for work, but I own my home, have no debt, and make millions of dollars a year. Why the hell can't he live with me? As I sit in the dark, I become more determined than ever to figure this out. I refuse to let Sam down.

When I get home, my phone is blowing up with texts from the guys.

> RHODES
> How did it go with Sam?
>
> WESTON
> Yeah, man, you okay? Let us know.
>
> BOWIE
> Poppy's ready to go primal on his foster family.
>
> HENLEY
> You don't mess with a pregnant woman.

He admitted tonight that they've been rough on him. You know he doesn't usually say much about his foster home, but he said enough tonight to concern me more than I already was. Jesse, the younger kid Sam looked out for, got moved this week, and I think Sam is just...done. He said he's tired. Tired of moving, tired of everything.

RHODES

That fucking kills me.

> Me too.

HENLEY

Shit. That's heavy.

WESTON

What do we do? What's the plan?

> I called his social worker again tonight. She shut me down again. Says the powers that be might not think I'm a viable option. I travel too much. I'm not a "family unit."

WESTON

Fuck that. You'd do anything for that kid.

> Doesn't matter what I do. I mean, I'd go through all the red tape all over again if someone would just tell me what I need to do to fix this. Everyone has a job. I can work out childcare when I'm out of town.

HENLEY

He can stay with our family when you're traveling.

RHODES

Elle says he could stay with her too when we're at away games. Or just anytime! We'd love to have him around here.

WESTON

Sadie's saying the same thing.

BOWIE

As I said, Poppy's primal about it. She's in.

> Thanks, guys.

RHODES

What about filing a complaint against the foster home?

> Mrs. Murphy said she's looking into it. But you know how slow that process is. Meanwhile, Sam's stuck.

HENLEY

What about temporarily? Can he stay with you while they figure it out?

> I asked. Same answer.

WESTON

This is so messed up. A kid shouldn't have to stay in a bad situation just because of red tape.

RHODES

Maybe there's a way around it. We just need to figure out what that is.

HENLEY

In the meantime, we're here.

BOWIE

If you need someone to write a character reference or show up at a meeting or hearing, I'm there.

WESTON

Same. Whatever it takes.

> I appreciate it. Seriously, thanks, guys.

CHAPTER FOUR

I'M A SURVIVOR

ADELINE

"What do you mean, you're not coming to the family picnic?" Dad asks, sounding so hurt.

"I just...I'm still unpacking and trying to be ready for Monday."

"This is important. You have plenty of time to unpack. And I know you, sweetheart—you've been ready for Monday for weeks."

He's not wrong. I already have a full presentation ready to

go for Monday. I know it backwards and forwards and all I need to work on before Monday is finding my nerve.

"I'll be by to pick you up in an hour," Dad says and he hangs up.

"Ugh," I yell, tossing my phone on the bed.

And then I get up and scramble to get ready.

My parents are so pleased I'm here, and I'd be happy to be too, if I wasn't a nervous wreck. Every year before training camp, the entire Mustangs team and staff meet at one of the coach's houses for a huge party. This year it wasn't at my parents' house, so I thought I could get out of attending, but here I am at Coach Crawford's large estate, stuck under the bright afternoon sun, pretending to enjoy myself as my eyes scan the crowd.

Please don't let Penn be here. Please let him have better things to do today. *Please.*

"Come on, sweetheart," my dad calls, gesturing for me to follow him toward a cluster of people.

I force a smile and trail behind him. I'll need to remind my dad not to call me sweetheart at work events. We chat for a few minutes before I'm taken to the next group of people.

And then I see him.

My stomach twists, my breath catches, all those things I thought I might be imagining after so much time has passed come rushing back with a vengeance. No, it's all still there.

He turns just as I try to move away, and our eyes meet. His whole face lights up. Sunshine breaking through the clouds.

"Addy?"

I freeze. He's already walking toward me, that familiar

swagger in his step. His grin stretches wide, so genuine it makes my heart hurt just a little. The rest of me is so happy to see him though. So happy.

"I can't believe you're here," he says, stopping in front of me. "What are you doing here?" His voice is warm, happy, *relieved*. Not a trace of anger for me bailing on him.

It's more than I deserve.

Before I can answer, my dad's booming voice cuts through the air. "Everyone, can I have your attention?"

I sigh, glancing at Penn, and his eyes are steady on mine as the crowd quietens.

"I'd like to introduce someone special to the team," my dad announces, clapping a hand on my shoulder. "My daughter, Adeline Evans. While some of you may remember her from when she was younger, a lot of you probably haven't gotten to know her yet. She's back from California and has decided to join the Mustang family. We are so excited that she's the Mustangs' new registered dietitian. Lorelai, our director of nutrition, will have more to say about Adeline on Monday, but I wanted to be the first to introduce her to you all today. Make her feel welcome…but I am looking at all you single players—don't even think of making a move on my little girl. Got it?" He laughs and *I. Am. Mortified.*

His words hang in the air like a grenade. There's a loud cheer, but the only thing that registers for me is Penn's face. His smile vanishes, his face going blank and then falling as the realization hits.

"Thanks, everyone!" I say, waving and forcing a smile. "I'm looking forward to working with all of you!"

Bright, cheery, and true, but I've never felt more fake than right now.

"Penn," I start, but before I can say another word, he turns and walks away.

My heart sinks. I move to follow him, but my dad catches my arm.

"Adeline, come meet a few more people," he says, steering me toward yet another group.

"I just need to catch someone," I tell him.

My eyes dart to Penn, and my dad turns to see who I'm looking at. "Penn? Penn Hudson? What would you want with him?" His eyes narrow on me. "Don't waste your time on him, sweetheart. He's a manwhore and lots of trouble that you do not want to get involved in. Trust me on this."

"You shouldn't talk about one of your players like that," I say under my breath.

I smile bright and keep the conversation brief before taking off in the direction Penn went. Weaving through people, I apologize as I rush by.

When I see him, I call his name, but he doesn't slow down. His long strides put more distance between us, and these sandals are not the best for chasing someone with legs as long as his.

Finally, I catch up with him as he nears his SUV.

"Penn!" I say again, breathless.

He stops abruptly and turns, his expression a mix of disbelief and frustration. "Adeline Evans," he says, his voice low but sharp.

I flinch. I deserve his tone, but it still stings. "Can you please…not go?"

His jaw clenches, and he crosses his arms over his chest, looking down at me. "Why not?"

I swallow hard. "I didn't mean to—"

"You didn't mean to what?" he cuts in, when I don't say anything else. "You didn't mean to kiss me the way you did and then disappear on me?"

"I didn't mean to ghost you," I say quickly, my voice barely above a whisper.

"Well…you did."

Guilt twists in my chest, but I feel a little defensive too. I step closer. "You don't know what was going on, Penn. You don't know why I left."

"I'm listening." His tone is clipped, but his eyes don't look as cold.

Maybe that's just hopeful thinking.

"I wanted to spend more time with you. Even though I shouldn't have. Kissing you…scared me."

He blinks, clearly not expecting that. His eyes soften. "It scared you?"

"Yes. For a lot of reasons…one being because I was considering coming to work for the Mustangs…"

His shoulders sag a little with that.

"And you were this…surprise I didn't expect. I wasn't ready for you."

He doesn't look as angry, but the hurt is still there. "You could've told me that."

"I wanted to. But then my friend got in a car accident, and I had to leave. I left in a hurry and didn't have your number…"

He gives me a look and I sigh.

"I know I could've gotten it, but…from my dad? And the more time passed, along with the fact that I did take the job—surprise!" I hold up my hands and his lips pucker with his effort to not smile. "I just…"

He stares at me for a long moment, the tension between us thick. "How is your friend?"

"She's good. Had a bad concussion and has to go to the chiropractor often, but it could've been so much worse."

He nods and then runs his hands through his perfect hair.

It falls back into place in a way that I'm jealous of. "You lied to me, Addy...Adeline. When were you going to tell me you're Coach Evans' daughter?"

I make a face and sag against his car. "I didn't lie. I just... didn't tell you everything."

"Same thing."

"Not exactly."

He shoots me another look but sags against his car next to me. "Is that why you said your name was Addy? You were afraid I'd know?"

"I go by both. But...maybe." I shrug. "I really liked the way you looked at me when you didn't know."

He stares at me and a chill skitters over my arms. And then he shakes his head and a choked laugh comes out of him.

"I can't believe you're Coach Evans' daughter. I have so much respect for that man and his coaching, but...yeah...he does not care for me too much."

I frown. "Why is that?"

He shakes his head. "I wish I knew. It's kind of been that way since I joined the team."

That doesn't sound like my dad, but he did warn me about Penn. I wonder why. Penn might be a player, but a player probably wouldn't be this disappointed in me. Would he?

"Well...I'm glad I had a chance to talk to you before running into you at the training facility. Training starts on Monday, right?"

He blows out a long breath. "Yeah. It does."

"I hope we can put this behind us," I say. "I'm sorry I didn't tell you right away who I was. Sorry for leaving and not saying goodbye..." My face scrunches up. "Sorry about all of it."

"Don't be sorry about all of it," he says. He lifts off of the vehicle. "That would mean you regretted the kiss."

I want to tell him I could never regret that, but he speaks before I can, and it's probably for the best.

"I'll see you around, *Adeline* Evans." His voice is distant and he gives me a little salute before moving to his car door.

I step away and watch as he drives away, lifting my hand in a wave when he glances at me one more time.

Damn. I just thought this was going to be hard. Now that I've seen him, I don't know how I'm going to survive.

CHAPTER FIVE

SIGNS

PENN

I don't know how I drive away from Addy, because the last thing I want to do is leave her after I've just found her, but holy fuck. What the hell just happened? The girl I've been pining over is Adeline Evans?

My pulse is hammering. My brain keeps replaying the moment—her standing there staring back at me, finding out who she was…and realizing she knew who I was all along.

She knew. The whole time.

I don't even realize I've driven to the Mustangs training facility until I'm there. I park and exhale sharply, then pull out my phone and open the group chat.

> Emergency Single Dad Players meeting. Whenever you're able.

HENLEY

Uh...what? You all right? Are you still at the picnic? Looking for you.

> No, I left.

WESTON

Oh shit. Sam? Is he okay?

RHODES

Be there in ten.

BOWIE

Where?

> Gym. Place is empty because everyone is at the picnic.

HENLEY

On my way.

They all hurry, no doubt assuming this is about Sam. I feel bad for leaving that hanging, but this is another kind of dire situation that has me in distress.

It only takes them fifteen minutes to get here, which is impressive since they'd all been at the picnic, even Henley. They all file into the gym. Henley is in a polo, Weston's wearing a backward cap like he's fifteen, Rhodes looks suspicious...like he's expecting me to drop something insane on them—which, fair—and Bowie just levels me with a look.

"What's going on?" Weston asks, breathing hard like he sprinted here. "Is it Sam?"

I rub my face. "I wish I had an update on Sam. But this is about Addy."

They exchange glances, still catching their breath.

"Addy?" Henley repeats.

"The girl I'm so hung up on…you guys met her today," I say, the words feeling surreal as they leave my mouth. "All of you. At the picnic."

They look at each other and then back at me, not following.

"What do you mean?" Rhodes asks.

I brace myself. "Addy is *Adeline Evans*."

Silence.

Then—

"Shut the fuck up," Rhodes yells.

"No freaking way." Weston throws his hat on the ground dramatically.

Henley just stares at me like I've told him I'm quitting football to become a monk, which now that I think about it, might be a good idea since *I kissed Coach's daughter.* "Hold on, hold on. Adeline, Coach Evans' daughter, is the girl from the Bahamas?"

"Yes."

Rhodes lets out a low whistle. "*Damn.* I don't even know what to say."

Bowie pinches the bridge of his nose. "You're fucked," he says.

"This whole time you've thought she was this unattainable mystery woman and it's Adeline? I've met her before. Have you never met her?" Weston asks.

"No," I say, feeling defensive that I missed out on that.

"I've never even seen her until the night before Bowie's wedding. I would've remembered, trust me."

"It's a sign." Rhodes grins. "You're meant to be together."

"Rhodes," I groan.

"No, listen. You don't just accidentally kiss someone in the Bahamas and then find out she's tied to your life in a permanent way. That's fate."

"Fate?" I scoff. "Or some cosmic joke? If Evans finds out I'm into his daughter, I'll be shipped off to the next team so fast I can't blink."

"Shit. Yeah. He's really hard on you already…this would not fly," Weston says.

I wince, rubbing the pain in my chest that's been there since I figured out who Addy is.

Henley leans back against the treadmill. "What are you gonna do?"

I exhale, shaking my head. "I don't know. She followed me after the announcement. Tried to explain. She was scared of what we had…because she knew who I was the whole time." I shake my head again. "And her college roommate got in an accident and that's why she had to leave."

"So she didn't just ghost you for no reason," Rhodes says, folding his arms.

I sigh. "No."

Weston spreads his arms. "Bro. This is your second chance. Don't blow it."

"What am I supposed to do? I can't pursue her," I grumble. "You heard Coach today. *All you single players*…and you know I'm not high on his list to begin with."

"You can't miss this opportunity," Rhodes says.

"Agreed," Henley says, smirking.

"Prove yourself to her dad," Bowie says.

"I've been trying to for years now!" I say, louder than I intended.

"And don't be a bonehead," Rhodes says.

"I'm not being a bonehead," I mutter.

"Keep it that way," Rhodes adds, pointing at me. "Now is not the time to dive back into your player ways. You said yourself that you're tired of the clubbing. Prove it."

I glare at him, glare at all of them. "Is it even allowed for me to ask her out?" I ask. "Elle wasn't allowed to date Rhodes when she was a cheerleader. It's probably against the rules for us to date too."

"But you *want* to date her?" Weston asks, grinning.

"Have you not been listening?" I yell, flinging out my arm.

His smile just grows. "I gotta say, I love seeing you like this."

"It is pretty great," Bowie says, chuckling.

"Third best day of my life after having Levi and marrying Elle." Rhodes smirks.

"I thought you said that about me and Tru," Henley teases.

"Yeah, I think I was one of the best days in there too, with Sadie," Weston adds.

"Same." Bowie nods.

Rhodes waves them off. "Focus, people."

"We knew the day would come, pretty boy," Henley adds smugly.

I roll my eyes. "I hate you all."

"You love us, and we're gonna help you," Rhodes says. "Where is Project Woo when we need it?"

I throw my head back, groaning at the ceiling. "No. This is not the time for Project Woo. She's off-limits! No-go. This cannot happen!"

"Dude. It's already happened," Weston says. "She cast the net and you didn't just get ensnared…you dove right in. She has caught you— hook, line, and sinker."

I scowl at my favorite people on Earth besides my family…hell, these guys *are* my family. "No, she didn't," I grumble.

"Beg to differ," Weston says.

"How 'bout we go out tonight? It's our last weekend before training camp starts. Not super late, just a little outing with the girls. They can help with this," Rhodes says, nodding *yes* when I shake my head *no*.

"I do not want them involved in this. I'm staying in my lane," I say, giving my hair a tug. "I am," I insist, trying to sound more determined. And then a beat later, I add, "Maybe going out is a good idea. Otherwise, my thoughts will drive me crazy."

"Texting Elle right now," Rhodes says. "I'll see if she can gather up the crew. I think they were going to Twinkle Tales after the picnic, so maybe they can meet up with us in a few hours. What if we go eat at Whitman's in Denver?"

Everyone nods. We all love that place.

"Okay, let's do it. Meet at Whitman's at seven?" Henley asks, checking his watch.

I lift off of the wall. "Sounds good. I need to go shower and change."

"Same," Weston says.

On the way home, my mom calls.

"Hey, Mom," I say.

"Hey," her voice fills the SUV. "Calling to see if there's an update on Sam."

"Not yet. I'm supposed to meet with the social worker again this Tuesday."

"Have they come up with a plan?"

"Not that I know of. But I think I've bugged her enough this week that she knows I'm not backing down."

"Good. Don't give up," she says.

"I won't."

"And tell them your parents would be happy to move closer to help out."

My eyes widen. "You'd seriously move to Silver Hills?" My parents live in Arizona and have never talked about moving here.

"Well, we don't really want to leave your grandparents, but we could come for a while. We could stay during the football season to help out with Sam."

I sigh, feeling emotional. "That's…you're the best, Mom. Thank you. I'd love to have you here, but I don't want to take you from your home, and Papa and Nana need you."

She snorts. "We hardly see them these days! They're playing pickleball all the time. Nana won second place in the little competition thing they had last weekend."

I chuckle. "Go, Nana."

Mom laughs. "They have more energy than I do these days. And I would love to spend more time with you, honey. I miss you."

"I miss you too," I say, and a wave of homesickness hits me harder than it has in years.

I miss my parents all the time, but we see each other often and I've learned to deal with it, but during weeks like this, I'd give just about anything to go hang out with them.

"You know what? Yes. Please come," I say. "It would really help."

"We'll get to work on that right away, honey."

CHAPTER SIX

IT'S GOOD TO BE HOME

ADELINE

Twinkle Tales is exactly the kind of bookstore I'd dream of owning if my life had gone a different way. I'm happy with my choices, but this…it's magical. Cozy and charming, with that comforting scent of books and coffee and candles. Growing up, I came here often, and even during school breaks, I'd stop in, but I haven't been in since Calista took over the shop from her aunt. I loved it before, but it's even better now.

A massive orange tabby meows and swirls its tail against my leg, and I bend down to pet the beauty. "Hello. You're so pretty," I whisper.

I spot Elle, Tru, Poppy, and Sadie near a display of romance novels, all of them mid-laugh. They're the wives of some of the Mustangs' best players. I've met Elle before, but I'm not sure she'd remember me. I'm younger than her and Calista but remember what a good dancer Elle was when we'd go to the high school games. She'd graduated by the time I got there, but they talked about her on the cheer team because she'd gone on to be a cheerleader at Stanford, which was a big deal in our little town. I knew Calista better because I loved coming to Twinkle Tales even when her aunt owned it, and Calista was often here, working behind the counter or stocking the shelves. As far as the rest of the group, I've heard about them from my parents. My mom has enjoyed getting to know them at the family events, and I met them briefly at the picnic earlier. They were the bright spot in my anxiety-filled day.

"Adeline!" Elle calls, waving me over. "Good to see you. We're probably being so loud." She laughs.

"Sounds like you're having fun." I grin, stepping into their little circle. "I heard you laughing from outside."

They crack up even harder at that, and my shoulders relax another degree.

"Guilty," Elle says unapologetically.

"These girls know how to have a good time," Calista says. "Hey, Adeline! It's been a long time since I've seen you. You look great. And looks like you met Hank."

"I know. It's been forever. Twinkle Tales looks amazing." I look at where Calista is pointing and Hank the cat is sitting at my feet.

"I was wondering what his name was. Hank, I love it," I say, leaning down to pet him again. "Yes, we met. He's gorgeous."

"So you're the team's new dietitian, I hear?" Calista asks.

"Yes, I'm the new RD. Back from California finally and ready to get to work." I smile at her and then get distracted by a little squeak coming from one of the babies.

Both Poppy and Tru have their babies in little slings across their chests, looking like the most fashionable moms I've ever seen.

"Cutest babies ever," I tell them both.

"Aw, thank you. Jonas is exhausted from missing his nap at the picnic. He was too interested in everything to settle down," Poppy says, shifting so I can see him better.

"Oh," I coo, when I get a better look. "Total baby envy right now."

Tru smiles when I look at her little one. "This is Avery, and she's pretty dreamy…until she's hangry and then her face turns the brightest shade of pink. Even that's cute though," she says, and we all laugh.

"We're getting our baby fix through them," Sadie says.

"You don't have baby envy yet?" Tru asks her, eyebrows lifted.

"Okay, yes. I do have baby envy. Caleb would love a little brother or sister…I'm maybe ready to start trying soon," she admits.

"Ahh, best news ever!" Tru says and then looks at Elle.

"Don't look at me," Elle says, laughing. "I'm so glad you're here, Adeline. *Save me*." Her eyes meet mine and I laugh at the mischievous glint in her eyes.

"I'm happy to get the baby talk off of you anytime," I say, and she squeezes my arm.

"Thank you," she whispers dramatically.

"You need to be initiated," Sadie says, giving me a once-over. "And by that, I mean, you need to hear us lose our minds over Elle's book being made into a movie. Excuse me...*Zoey's* book." Her eyes narrow on me. "Have you read Zoey Archer's books, by any chance? Did you know you're in the presence of greatness?" She holds her arm out toward Elle like she's a game show host and Elle groans, glancing at me apologetically.

"Ignore them. They don't get out much," Elle says, and they laugh at that while also pretending to be offended.

"Beg to differ," Tru says. "I did two extra things today that weren't related to being a milk cow. One of them includes being here." She snorts. "I think that constitutes a very busy woman."

"I'm totally kidding," Elle says, looking at me. "These women are the great ones."

"Aww," Tru says, leaning her head on Elle's shoulder.

"I have read your books," I tell Elle. "I loved both of them!"

"Thanks so much!" she says.

"Did you know her book's being made into a movie?" Poppy asks. "We're trying to get her to tell us all the details."

I lean in, intrigued. "A movie? That's huge!"

"And she won't tell her best friends anything!" Tru frowns and shakes her head, but in the next second, she's smiling.

Elle groans. "I swear, I don't know! They barely tell me anything."

"That's not what I heard," Calista chimes in with a smirk. "Word is they've already got a director, and the casting rumors are *delicious*."

Elle shakes her head. "You can't believe everything you

see online. I know a little…and what's online is mostly gossip. They're keeping everything under wraps for now."

"Don't secrets leak sometimes?" Sadie asks hopefully.

Elle smirks. "So far I haven't seen anyone with the right information."

Tru gasps. "So you *do* know something."

"I promise when I know anything solid, you'll be the first to know," Elle promises. "Well, after Rhodes, of course… because he's the nosiest human on the planet."

The conversation turns animated, bouncing between book-to-movie adaptations, our favorite actors, and which of Elle's characters would translate best on screen. Before I know it, they're talking me into joining them for dinner.

"You don't even have to drive," Poppy says. "Just ride with us. We're taking two vehicles just to handle all of us and the car seats."

"And you're in too, right, Calista?" Elle asks.

She nods. "I'm not sure yet. I'll close up and see if Javi can pull it off."

Normally, I'd hesitate around new people, but something about them makes me want to say yes. So, I do. And within minutes, I'm crammed into Elle's SUV, listening to these women laugh and talk to me like they've known me forever.

By the time we arrive at the restaurant, I'm in an even better mood. Especially when I see Camden Whitman. I hurry toward him before he even spots me. "Cam!"

His head snaps up, and a slow grin spreads across his face. "Adeline?"

He opens his arms and I wrap my arms around him, squeezing him tight.

"I came with friends and didn't even realize we were coming to your restaurant! I've been dying to come see you since I moved back."

"Looks better since the last time you were here, right?" He looks around proudly.

"It's gorgeous, Camden. Really beautiful."

"Goldie is going to be so jealous that we're seeing each other without her," he says, laughing.

"Tough luck. Tell your sister she needs to come see both of us sooner rather than later."

He shakes his head. "You'll probably talk to her before I do, but I'll try."

I laugh. "You're probably right. She seems nervous to travel since the car accident, but she's doing so much better, right?"

"Yes. Everyone's assured me that she's fine. I had to see for myself like you when it first happened, but since then, this place has taken over every brain cell I have. I call to check on her, but then ask everyone else to tell me if she's telling the truth or not."

I sigh. My best friend doesn't love everyone fussing over her. "I've done the same thing, calling your dad when I don't hear back from Goldie as soon as usual. It's driving Goldie nuts."

He snorts. "She can just deal with it. We all love her. What's the crime in that?"

"Exactly."

"It's so good to see you. I better get back in the kitchen. You staying for dinner?"

"Yep, with some new friends. I'll come find you before I leave though."

"You better. And your meal's on me."

"Absolutely not," I argue, but he just winks before heading toward the kitchen.

Still smiling, I turn to join the girls at the table—only for my stomach to drop. Because sitting there, surrounded by my new friends and their partners…is *Penn*.

Dammit.

I had no idea he'd be here!

And from the look on his face?

He is *not* happy to see me.

CHAPTER SEVEN

THE LAYERS OF HUGS

PENN

I start to relax when we get to the restaurant, excited to see the girls. I didn't get enough time with them today at the picnic, since I hightailed it out of there when I saw Adeline Evans. They've become my best friends too and I need a night out with my friends. I called Sam on the way over here to see if he could come to dinner with us and he had homework to finish, so it looks like I won't be seeing him this weekend. He's been to a lot of the family events with me and I missed having him there today. The family he's with doesn't allow me to see him as much as the last one, and it's just another reason that I'm anxious for the meeting on Tuesday with the social worker.

When we walk in, the chef and owner of the restaurant, Camden Whitman, walks out to greet us. He's a class-act dude, and we love everything he makes, so ever since we found out about this place recently, we've been looking for excuses to come back.

"It's great to see you guys again," he says, standing at the head of the table.

"Great to see you," Henley says. "Thanks for fitting us in at such short notice."

"I'll always try my best," he says, smiling around the table. "I hope you're not too cramped here. You're expecting more, I see. Can I get you started on appetizers?"

"Our wives will be here shortly," Weston says. "And I'm starving. Should we do one of each of the appetizers?"

"Yes, two of the salmon tartare," Rhodes says.

"*Yes*," I jump in. "I don't know what you put in that thing, but it's amazing."

"I appreciate that, man," Camden says. He looks up when the server walks to the table, poised to take our order. He nods at her and glances at us once more. "I'll leave Josie to it. She's the best."

"That's what he says about all of us," Josie teases.

"It's true, I do," he says, laughing. "But it's also true." He tilts his face and gives her a playful look. "Just let me know if you need anything. I want to make my favorite players happy."

Such a cool guy. He makes what must be an insanely

stressful job look effortless. He taps the back of the chair and walks away, while Josie takes our drink orders.

"Sorry, Josie, we're boring tonight. Practice starts on Monday, so there will be no alcohol in our future for some time."

"Not a problem. Pellegrino with lime?" she asks.

"That will be perfect," Rhodes says, and the rest of us chime in.

And then, freaking Addy walks into the restaurant. My entire body locks up. I don't know whether to be excited or terrified. Probably both.

Fate is just screwing with me at this point.

I tell myself to stay cool, to just let it be. But then I watch her.

And son of a dickless man, she lights up when she sees Camden Whitman.

And then she hugs him.

Not just a friendly, *hey-good-to-see-ya* hug. No, this is a lingering, *arms-tight-around-his-neck* kind of hug. A *wide-smile, eyes-sparkling* kind of hug. And when they start talking, she's using that same damn flirty smile she used on me.

Is this just...what she does? Does she make every guy feel like the center of her universe?

My jaw clenches as I watch her laugh, all easy-breezy, while I sit here at the table like an absolute numb nugget.

"What's with you?" Rhodes asks, giving me a weird look.

"Nothing," I mutter, reluctantly dragging my gaze away from Addy.

Weston leans in. "That is the most *not* nothing tone I've ever heard in my life."

I grab my water and take a long, unnecessary sip. "I just didn't expect to see her here."

Bowie raises an eyebrow. "Who?" And then he brightens up when he sees Poppy. "Hey!"

There are hugs all around, and the girls start making introductions—until they realize that they're missing their friend.

"Where did she go?" Elle asks, glancing around.

Tru follows her gaze. "She was right behind us…"

Sadie leans back. "Oh, she's over there. With Camden Whitman."

Henley snorts. "She lost interest in us fast."

"Can't blame her." Rhodes laughs. "Camden's a good-looking dude."

I whip my head toward him. "He's not *that* good-looking."

Now that I think about it, it's not like he's all that nice either.

"Uh, have you looked at him?" Rhodes says. "Dude's prettier than me."

"Not possible," Elle says, kissing his cheek.

"Elle love, you know how to make a man feel good," he says, catching her lips and kissing her soundly.

I groan.

"Oh, I see the problem now," Weston says, looking in the direction of Addy and Camden.

"Mm-hmm," Bowie says.

"Now you have me curious." Henley cranes his neck to look for Camden and his eyes widen when he sees Addy talking to him. "Well, look at that. It's Adeline Evans."

"You okay there, Penn?" Rhodes asks when he finally comes up for air.

"I'm fine," I grumble.

And as if this day is not bad enough, Addy makes her way over to *our* table and slides into the empty seat across from me, still smiling like she hasn't completely ruined my night.

"Sorry," she says, adjusting her napkin on her lap. "It's been a while since I've seen Camden."

I let out a low, unimpressed hum. "Clearly."

The girls turn to me with various levels of frowny faces. I start pulling a roll apart.

Addy glances up, giving me an unsettling smile and then looks around the table. "This is a nice surprise, seeing all of you twice in one day. I hope you don't mind me intruding on your dinner."

Henley clears his throat. "We're so happy you could join us. I hear you go by Addy too? Is that right?"

Weston choke-laughs.

She looks at me and her cheeks bloom into red. "Penn must have told you we met." She bites the inside of her lip and I wish I could do that.

The girls immediately perk up.

"Wait, you know Penn?" Tru asks.

"How do you two know each other?" Sadie asks.

Addy and I are doing a staredown and I take a small amount of pleasure in the fact that she folds first. She blinks and tilts her head, a small smile playing at her lips, like she's daring me to answer.

I sigh, scrubbing a hand down my face. "It's…a long story."

Elle leans in, practically vibrating with curiosity. "We love long stories."

Rhodes shakes his head, biting back a laugh. "This is gonna be good."

I shoot him a glare, but I can already see it happening—the matchmaking, the scheming. These women love to meddle, and most of the time I love them for it, especially when it's not *my* business they're dipping into. They already look way too invested in this, and the guys are enjoying my misery too much.

And Addy? She just sits there, looking beautiful and somewhat pleased with herself, while I try to figure out how the hell I'm going to survive this dinner.

And okay, I'll admit it: I'm still stewing over Camden.

"So, are you dating Camden?" I ask, with an air of complete nonchalance. Because despite my insides doing 360s, I know how to maintain an outward calm.

I can Jason Bourne with the best of them.

Her jaw tightens and her eyes narrow on mine. "No. I'm best friends with his sister, Goldie."

"Aw! Best friend's brother! I love that trope!" Elle says happily.

I glare at her. "This is not about Camden," I snap.

"But you *just* asked her if she was dating Camden," Elle says, confused.

"And she said she's not," I say, glancing back at Addy.

"You best take that sassy tone elsewhere, pretty boy," Rhodes murmurs under his breath.

I shoot Elle an apologetic look and she smiles but looks confused. Damn. Maybe I'm not pulling the outward calm vibe off very well.

"Do you *wish* you were dating him?" Fuck me, that growl in my tone kind of sounds like Bowie on a normal day.

Addy sits up straighter and her cheeks get fiery again. Her eyes narrow again and my dick stands at attention. *Yes, ma'am, whatever you say, ma'am.* That's what *he* says, not me, because *I* am in control of this situation, *not* her *nor* my dick.

And I don't think I've ever thought or said the word *nor*, in my head or otherwise, but it just feels fitting right now.

"I've never really thought about it, *Penn*." The way she says *Penn* sounds like a curse word.

Is she *mad* at me right now? I don't *think* so.

"But maybe I should. Camden is great," she adds.

I tap the table. "Maybe you should. I just hope he's okay with you disappearing out of thin air."

She tosses her napkin on the table and leans in. "He would be, because he's an *adult* who listens and understands when an explanation is given." She turns and looks at the rest of the table, and they're all staring at us in shock. She stands up. "I'm sorry to cut this evening short. Thanks so much for the invitation. Maybe we can try again sometime, girls. And I'll see you guys on Monday."

"But," Sadie stands up, "you rode with us. Come on, stay." She glares over at me. "We'll behave, I promise."

"I'm exhausted from the move. We'll do it again. I'll get an Uber back, don't worry." She hugs Sadie and the rest of the girls and walks away.

Every eye zeroes in on me.

"What the hell was that?" Elle says between her teeth.

"*Penn Hudson!*" Tru says and I flinch.

I've never been on the wrong side of Tru. Never been on the wrong side of any of them really, but now they're looking at me like I ran over a kitten.

"You go and make that right immediately," Sadie says. "She is lovely and she is Coach Evans' daughter. You were such a jerk to her."

"She's the girl I met in the Bahamas," I say.

Rhodes nods as the girls freak out over that little tidbit. "I hadn't had a chance to tell you," he says to Elle. "We just found out before this and didn't know you were bringing her to dinner."

"Ooo," Elle winces. "Sorry, friend." She shoots me an apologetic look. "But...I still think you should go apologize."

"What even was that?" I ask, yanking on my hair. "I don't know what came over me. I couldn't stop."

"*That*, my friend, was *jealousy*," Henley says, and then they all freaking laugh.

Well, fuck.

I've never been a jealous person in my life and I fucking hate it.

CHAPTER EIGHT

THE PLAN

ADELINE

The moment I walked in and saw that hot man who knows how to get my pulse flaring, I should have turned right back around, thanked the girls for the invite, and faked a stomach virus. But no. Instead, I sat here with Penn shooting me furious looks and having an attitude with me.

Nope, not putting up with that.

I walk outside, stepping onto the quiet sidewalk as I dig in my purse for my phone. I just need to call a ride, get home, and pretend this night never happened.

But life just can't be easy. The door swings open behind me.

"Addy."

I close my eyes for a brief second. *Keep walking. Maybe he'll be the one to disappear this time.*

"Addy," Penn says again, his footsteps heavy as he catches up to me.

Dammit.

I whirl around, arms crossed. "What?"

He hesitates for half a second, like he wasn't expecting me to actually turn around. "I—uh—" He exhales roughly, raking a hand through his hair. "I'm sorry, okay?"

I narrow my eyes. "Sorry for what, exactly?"

His jaw ticks. "For being a jerk."

I lift an eyebrow.

"A total ridiculous jerk," he adds.

I tap my chin. "I don't know. Jerk feels a little…soft. Maybe go with *asshat*?"

His lips twitch, but he fights it. "Fine. I'm sorry for being an asshat."

"Good. Because you *were* an asshat."

"Right." He nods, like he's determined to be mature about this. "Glad we agree."

"Great. Now that we've established that, I'll be going."

I turn back to look at my phone.

"Wait a minute. You were kind of an asshat, too."

I freeze before turning back slowly. "*Excuse* me?"

Penn folds his arms over his broad chest, and he looks so stinking hot right now, it's completely unfair. "You heard me."

Oh, I don't care how hot he is, this attitude is not working for me.

I scoff. "How do you figure?"

His eyes flash. "Oh, I don't know. You showed up, hugged the chef like he hung the damn moon, then waltzed over to our table all, *oh wow, what a surprise!*, like you were totally fine pretending I don't exist."

I gape at him. "Are you seriously mad that I hugged Camden?"

"Mad?" He snorts. "No. Just very aware that you have a type."

I blink. "A type."

"Yeah." He tilts his head, counting off his fingers. "Tall, good-looking, mega-successful."

"Oh my God," I groan. "You are too much. Get over your dumb, jealous self and go back inside."

He looks momentarily stunned. "I wasn't jealous." His cheeks turn pink when he says it, and I smirk.

We stare at each other until he shifts on his feet. He runs his hand through his hair and exhales like he's defeated.

"Okay, I was totally jealous," he says quietly.

My heart soars at that, but it drops in the next second when he says, "But I'll get over myself. I'm really sorry I'm being so rude. I…I'm not used to…uh, that was crazy in the Bahamas, right? The instant connection between us. At least for me. But I know we'd never work out. Fuck. I'm not even the boyfriend type—what am I saying?" He shakes his head, and I feel the loss when his eyes drift away from mine. "I want us to be comfortable since we'll be around each other all the time with work."

"Right. Yeah. I do too." I'm embarrassed that I thought he could ever want anything more.

You knew this was too complicated, I tell myself. But my heart hasn't quite caught up with reason just yet.

"It was crazy for me too, Penn. It wasn't just you."

His eyes flicker over to me again, his full lips parting slightly. He takes a tiny step forward, and for a second, I think he may close the distance.

But then he puts his hands in his pockets and rocks back on his heels.

"There's no way we could ever be anything more than friends anyway," he adds, "because of your dad."

I make a face. "My dad doesn't get a say in who I go out with…I'm twenty-six years old, and I've lived away from home for years." I laugh under my breath. "He might *think* he gets a say, but no, not happening."

Penn winces. "He'd have a lot to say if he thought you were with me, trust me. I don't think he'd even approve of us being friends."

I frown. "Why do you think that?"

"He seems to think I only exist to party. I'm pretty sure that I shock him every time I come out on the field and play my ass off."

"Your record speaks for itself."

I want to argue that my dad would never treat someone poorly unless they deserve it, but the little Dad has said to me about Penn hasn't been the most positive. I wonder what his deal is.

Penn shrugs and I'm surprised by the level of hurt I see on his face. I'll definitely be asking my dad about this when I get a chance.

Rhodes' voice rings out from the restaurant door. "Hey, lover boy, hope we aren't interrupting a moment. The appetizers are out."

I whip my head toward Rhodes, who's grinning like a complete shit-stirrer. Behind him, Weston and Henley are standing in the doorway, equally entertained.

"Ohh," Henley murmurs. "I think we did interrupt a moment."

Penn groans. "Can you *not*?"

"I just wanted to apologize for our friend's behavior...if he hasn't already apologized himself," Weston says.

"He started out with good intentions, I think, but then he almost blew it." When I say the last few words, the guys laugh.

"He means well," Henley says.

"*He* is right here," Penn says.

"Mm-hmm, and how's that working out for you?" Rhodes says, throwing his arm around Penn. "How you like me now?" he sings.

I press my lips together to keep from laughing.

Rhodes gestures between us. "We're just trying to figure out what's going on here. Enemies? Lovers? Long-lost soulmates? What would Elle call these tropes?"

I nearly snort.

Weston smirks. "Right now, I'd say exes who never actually dated."

I do laugh at that. "You guys are too much."

Penn throws his head back, groaning. "Don't you guys have wives to annoy right now?"

Henley smiles at me. "Sorry, Adeline. This one here has given us hell for years, so we're just having a little fun at his expense." He pounds Penn's back. "I hope you don't take us too seriously. We don't want to scare you off. Penn is a good man...despite his earlier behavior."

"It's true," Rhodes says. "The best guy."

Penn rolls his eyes.

"Absolutely," Weston says. "And Bowie would agree if he were out here…but he's got the baby."

I cover my mouth as I try to rein in the giggles. I was looking forward to getting to know these guys better, but I did not foresee it going this way. They're way funnier than I expected. I've always liked them from afar. I even listen to Henley's podcast now. My dad has given his life to this team, and the love for them has carried over into our family for as long as I can remember.

Penn lets out a rugged exhale. "Just…come back inside. Please. Please don't go."

Those eyes. They're hazel with brown outlining his pupils and then melding into green, with a gold rim around that. I remember them in the sunlight on the beach, the way they looked like a fire being lit.

"Please," he says again. "I'd like a redo."

Still, I hesitate. The smart thing would be to leave, put as much distance between us as possible so my feelings for him don't grow by the second. But then I look at him—the slight uncertainty in his expression, the way his fingers flex at his sides…

I've proven I'm rarely good at doing the smart thing.

"Fine," I say, crossing my arms and giving him a playful look. "But if you say one more rude thing—"

I hear the guys crack up in the background as they move toward the restaurant, and I smirk as I stare at Penn.

"I'll let you insult me freely for the rest of the night," he says.

I lift a brow and smile. "Sounds fair."

Penn clutches his heart, shooting me a relieved smile. He gestures toward the door. "After you, Adeline Evans."

I walk past him, feeling his eyes on me the whole way.

When we get back to the table, the girls are so excited.

"I'm so glad you came back," Sadie says.

They all smile at me warmly.

"We just had a great little chat outside. Didn't we, Preacher Man?"

There's a roar of laughter when I say that.

"I'm loving this so much," Weston says, wiping his eyes.

I sit down, picking up my fork like nothing happened. While we were gone, an array of food arrived. I think they must have ordered every appetizer on the menu.

"Camden really outdid himself tonight," I say, digging in.

Penn mutters something under his breath, and I shoot him a look. He lifts his hands and swallows hard, pointedly focusing on the plate in front of him. Smart man. Except his little jealous bit is making me far happier than it should.

"If this was a rom-com, we'd be seconds away from a make-out scene," Rhodes says.

Penn chokes on his water.

Bowie sighs, shaking his head. "Forgive my friends. They have no manners whatsoever."

The restaurant buzzes with energy as we focus on the food. Laughter rises above the hum of the dinner rush. Penn has been quiet since we came in from outside, but I've been answering questions right and left. When there's a lull after we order, Penn leans in closer.

"So, where have you been the past few years?" he asks. "I've been with the team for quite a while and I would've remembered seeing you."

My romantic heart is flattered by that, but he probably doesn't mean anything by it. I need to keep reminding myself of this, despite the way he looks at me. He said it himself—he's not the boyfriend type.

"I've been at Berkeley. Lots and lots of schooling behind me." I grin and take a sip of water.

"Is nutrition your passion?" His eyes dip down to my lips and I nearly fan my face because I'm suddenly so hot.

"It is." I gulp. Talking about "passion" when he's looking at my mouth this way is challenging. I try to sound professional when I add, "I love finding healthy and inventive ways to help athletes perform at their highest peak. To me, the food goes hand in hand with your workouts and practices."

He grins like he can see right through me.

"I can get behind that," he says. "Tonight, though, can we order a whole cheesecake and pay for the consequences later?" He puts his hands together and pleads.

I laugh. "Pretend I'm not even here."

"Impossible," he says softly.

We stare at each other for a long beat, his eyes drinking me in like they did in the Bahamas. My cheeks burn.

The rest of the table asks me more about my plans for the team and the evening flies by. The cheesecake is divine.

"The team's lucky to have you, Adeline," Henley says, leaning back, appraising me. "God, I miss playing."

"You were such an exceptional player," I tell him. "I really hated to see you get hurt."

"Thank you." He waves me off like it's no big deal, but it's obvious the sport means everything to him.

"I hope to make sure you guys feel your best," I say. "I'm not telling you anything you don't know, but fueling your bodies the right way can make a huge difference."

Elle bumps her shoulder into mine. "And if they don't listen, you can whip them into shape."

"That's the plan."

Weston points at Penn. "This means you can't live on gas station snacks anymore."

Penn groans and looks at me, shaking his head. "Don't listen to him." To Weston, he says, "Dude! Don't be telling my secrets to the lady!"

Laughter erupts around the table and I can't help but grin.

Torturing Penn Hudson sounds like a lot of fun.

When dinner is over, he hangs around. "Can I drive you home?"

Part of me wonders if that's all he's asking, but we chat all the way to my house and when he pulls up to my condo, he turns to look at me and smiles.

"I'm glad you stayed," he says.

"Me too."

The air between us is much lighter than it's been, and I'm really glad I didn't miss out on a chance to hang out with him.

"I'll see you on Monday," he says.

I nod, trying not to be too disappointed.

"Thanks for the ride."

"Night, Adeline."

"Night."

I put my hand on the door and he hops out on his side. "Hold up," he says, jogging around to open my door.

My heart thuds against my rib cage and I stare up at him when I place my feet on the ground.

"Thank you," I whisper.

His eyes are on my lips and he nods, distracted. "Mm-hmm," he says, his voice husky.

He swallows hard and takes a step back, his hand going in his hair as he takes a deep breath. I want him to kiss me more than I want my next breath, but I reach out and squeeze his hand instead. It's enough to give me all the tingles, and I nearly laugh at the insane level of desire I feel for this man. It's crazy. What is it about him that checks all my boxes?

I let go of his hand and hurry past him. *He's not boyfriend material*, I tell myself a dozen times as I go inside and shut the door. When I peek out the window, he's still sitting in his vehicle. I jump back, hoping he didn't see me, and attempt to not obsess over the man all night long.

CHAPTER NINE

SCRITCHY SCRATCHY

PENN

On Monday morning, I can't be still. I'm antsy, restless... wired. I'm not a nervous person, dammit, but my skin prickles with tension. It's ridiculous. I roll my shoulders, crack my knuckles, anything to shake it off as I walk into the training center.

I've been this way since leaving Addy at her door on Saturday night.

The buzz hits me before I even make it to the conference

room. Adeline Evans, the new registered dietitian. Her name floats in the air, passing from one conversation to another.

Great. This tension isn't going anywhere.

There's talk about how hot she is, while I struggle not to lose it on my teammates.

I do not understand what's happened to me.

First, kissing her. Then, thinking about her nonstop. And now? She's in my work environment, where I'm supposed to focus. Those flirty eyes and that mouth—God, that mouth. How the hell am I supposed to do my job with her right here, stirring shit up inside my head?

She's a constant itch under my skin, and I can't scratch her out.

I push open the conference room door, and she's the first one I see. She looks stunning in a skirt that hits her knees, her long legs perfectly shaped, and a red blouse that highlights her amazing body. Her hair catches the light and it's so shiny. I curse under my breath. This is going to be impossible.

Coach Evans introduces her to the team, for all those who missed the announcement at the picnic on Saturday, and she stands there, professional and polished. Everyone's watching her, nodding along as she explains her approach. I should be listening, but I'm trying to get my damn thoughts in order.

Later, she meets with each of us one-on-one to discuss food preferences, goals, and needs. When it's my turn, the air in the room shifts. She's not the same Addy from the restaurant the other night. Adeline is quieter, more reserved…distant.

I hate it.

But then she closes her door and her whole body relaxes. "Hey," she says, smiling warmly.

"Hey." My shoulders loosen as she motions for me to sit across from her. "How's it going so far?"

"Everyone's being really great...willing to try new things and open about hearing my ideas."

"I'm glad."

She smiles, and for a second, we just stare at each other. Damn, when will this feeling of wanting to kiss her senseless go away? My leg starts bouncing.

She glances at her clipboard, smiling down at it. "Okay, let's start with the basics. Any dietary restrictions?"

"No."

She nods, jotting it down. "Food preferences? Things you don't like?"

"I eat what's put in front of me. Not picky. Except I do love a gas station run every now and then."

Her pen pauses mid-note, and her eyes lift to mine, her expression playful. "That's fine if it really is just once in a while."

I exhale through my nose, shifting in my seat when her teeth slide over her bottom lip. I don't think she even realizes she's doing it, but it's making me hard as a rock.

"I'll do whatever you tell me to do, Addy." My voice is raspy and she sits up straighter. "I'll do my job, I'll train hard, and I'll eat whatever you want."

Her grip tightens on the pen, her mouth parting. "So agreeable." Her lips twitch as she tries to hold back her smile and fails. "I'm glad. Because fueling your body properly is very important."

"Teach me your ways," I say, and not gonna lie, the flirtation is as thick as my dick in here.

"Oh, I intend to."

There it is. That flash of sass that is seriously addictive.

She clears her throat. "Well, I'll show you the tentative plan I'd drawn up for you, and we can change anything you'd rather not do. But I'm glad you're trusting me...because we'll be in each other's space all the time. It'll really help if we're...on the same page with all this."

Does she not know that the thought of her in my space all the time is all I want? I want to argue with her and make up and kiss her, kiss her, kiss her. What is this obsession with her mouth? I want to talk to her for hours and hear everything she has to say. She has turned me into someone I don't recognize and I don't know up from down at the moment.

My eyes are fixated on the way she moves her lips so perfectly.

"Penn?" she says, tilting her head.

"Oh, sorry. What did you say?"

"Would you like to see the plan?"

I nod, and when she motions for me to move around to her side of the desk to see her screen, I realize I'm in trouble. The tent in my athletic shorts is not messing around. "Uh..."

She pauses and waits for me to say something.

Not a single useful word comes out of my mouth. I'm like a mass void, except for the very visible, very unfortunate problem bobbing against my shorts, begging to be let out.

"I'll be right there," I say, grabbing one of her folders and trying to move discreetly around to her side of the desk.

"Oh, good. That's your folder. Take a look in there too, and make sure I've got everything right...your BMI, etcetera."

I open the folder and nod. "Mm-hmm. Yes, helpful."

"Penn, it's upside down."

I glance at the folder. Fuck. It is.

Now that I'm over here, it's only getting worse. She smells citrusy, and the way she's leaning forward, from this angle, I can see the tiniest hint of cleavage. Not enough because she's buttoned too high, but—

"You okay?" she asks.

I nod and flip the folder around and fuck me, it slips. I fumble to catch it, but it's too late. It drops. Leaving my dick at her exact eye level.

Her gaze flicks down, her mouth dropping. And I swear on my entire career, time slows to a crawl.

Oh, hell.

She lets out a choked sound, like she's trying to swallow a laugh, but it's not working. I don't blame her. If the roles were reversed, I'd be on the floor.

I hustle to get the folder off the floor, wincing, and hold up the barricade in front of me once again.

The room is silent for a few seconds.

And then…

"You good, Penn?" she asks, her voice a little too innocent.

"Fine," I grit out, willing myself to look away, but I can't. Instead I think about cold showers, tax season, and that time I got food poisoning at training camp. I even think of Martha, Bowie's little scary-ass hairless dog.

She's smiling now and it undoes any progress food poisoning has made. I sigh.

"You sure?" she asks.

Troublemaker.

"Addy." My voice sounds strangled.

Her brows lift. "What?"

"You know what."

She hums, tapping her keyboard, her eyes shining with amusement. "I don't know, maybe I should redo this plan. Looks like you may have some…excess energy to burn."

I groan and clench the folder for dear life. "Oh, if you only knew." My jaw clenches. "Sorry, this is…inappropriate."

"Don't worry," she says. "It happens to everyone. Probably."

I give her the side-eye. "You're enjoying this?"

"Oh, immensely." Her cheeks bloom with color and she looks at her screen, pointing out what she'd like me to look at, and I'm grateful for the redirection.

We manage to get through the meeting without me embarrassing myself any further, and I bolt out of there, thanking her for her time.

I run a few exercises with the team before heading out. Tomorrow will be more intense and I need to sleep tonight. Ever since seeing Addy again, I haven't gotten much.

The next night after practice and a day of staring longingly at Addy—she wears a turquoise jogger suit that makes my pulse skyrocket—I have a meeting with Mrs. Murphy, the social worker. She's more sympathetic this time, but her words still don't offer much in the way of a solution.

"Penn," she says, her voice softer than before, "you have a lot in your favor, but the reality is, the court prefers a two-parent household. Without someone steady at home to help when you're out of town, it doesn't bode well."

I grit my teeth. "I can provide stability. I'm paid very well and can provide Sam with anything. My job is demanding, but I have a strong support system. My friends have already offered their homes for Sam when I'm away. I have a list of their names and references if you'd like to see. My parents have offered to move to Silver Hills to help too. Sam knows and loves them already."

She nods, taking the paper from me and jotting down a few notes. "This is good. Having a network of reliable people helps. But I want to be honest with you—judges tend to look for an environment where the child has someone consistently at home."

I lean forward. "I get that. But there are plenty of single parents out there doing just fine."

"Of course." She offers a small smile. "And you might be one of them. But right now, you're fighting against a system that prioritizes a certain kind of family structure. I'm not saying it's always fair, but it's what we have to work with."

My chest tightens. "So, what am I supposed to do? Just accept that Sam might have to stay where he is forever? He's miserable."

She sighs, setting down her pen. "I'm saying don't lose hope. Keep showing up. Keep proving that you're the best option for Sam. These things take time and persistence. And you've proven you're in it for the long haul. We still just have to wait for the agency to approve."

I nod, the weight in my chest not lifting. I'm not sure it will until Sam is at my house full-time, safe and fed.

"Thanks for being straight with me," I tell her.

"Always. We'll keep pushing forward, Penn. I'm sorry these things take so much time."

I leave the meeting feeling like I'm stuck in the same loop. No matter how much I want this, I can't shake the feeling that it won't be enough.

I won't be enough.

CHAPTER TEN

LEFT FIELD

ADELINE

After a week with the players, I'm beginning to settle in. Everyone's been kind and thoughtful, and they've been super accommodating with my food suggestions. The whole reason I was hired was because the previous dietitian had been too lenient on the players and gave them what they wanted instead of what they needed. And I think it showed in their playing. The years that they won the Super Bowl, they had a top-notch dietitian…who went on leave to take care of her sick mother and never came back.

So, I think they're more than ready to adjust to my methods.

I've heard what they've had to say in our meetings, placed massive food orders, and this morning, one of my shipments came in, so I can start proving that healthy food doesn't have to mean gross food. Besides traveling with the team and providing their meals, it's my responsibility to offer pre and post-workout meals at the training facility. The thought of coming up with creative ways to help the body perform to capacity has excited me since I started learning about it in a nutrition class in high school.

I've arrived every morning at five to get ready for them. We've used up most of what was on hand and this will be the first morning that I can give them my favorite choices—from protein bars and energy drinks to my recipe for salmon and chicken noodle soup that will be on the lunch buffet.

I stir up my special recipe for what I'll call our Mustangs Magic drink and pour it into little cups so they can drink it in two large gulps. I'm excited to see what they think of it. I tested it out in California and heard only positive things. I have that all set up next to the supplements and then they can hit the omelet bar, the waffles, and fresh fruit. There's a carb table full of snacks for them to grab on their way out to practice.

The assistant dietitian, Toby, helps with everything, and Lorelai walks through every now and then to give her stamp of approval. So far, I really like our team. Lorelai's a good leader and Toby takes direction from me well.

Once we're set up, I have only a few minutes to spare before the players start pouring in.

Penn is the first one through the door. It still catches me

by surprise to see him, not because I'm not aware that *I'm working with him*, but because I am so attracted to him. It's like Pop Rocks exploding in my body every time he crosses my path. For the past few days, I have been hyperaware of him.

He's smiled sweetly. Like that guy I met in the Bahamas. Been the perfect gentleman, despite the way his body reacted in my office the other day…which, holy hell, that vision is playing on repeat in *all* my fantasies.

I'm so distracted by him I don't know what to do with myself.

"First one in line, huh?" I tease, handing him a cup of Mustangs Magic.

The drink is neon green and he eyes it for a second and then grins, taking it from me. "What is it?"

"Mustangs Magic."

"Magic, huh? You trying to turn us into superheroes?"

"Something like that. Or, at the very least, keep you from crashing midway through practice."

"Someone's gotta test it out to see if we'll survive this."

I roll my eyes, but I'm grinning, so I can't be taken seriously. "Dramatic much, Preacher Man?"

He smirks and lifts the cup, turning toward the team, filing in behind him. "Gentlemen, today we embark on a journey into the unknown. Will this magic concoction make us stronger? Faster? Will it unlock the secrets to the universe? There's only one way to find out." He nods and leans in, causing my breath to halt. "Watch this, I'll be so convincing they'll be lining up to drink it like it was their idea."

"If you pull that off, I'll owe you," I tell him.

His grin deepens. "I'll keep that in mind."

Laughter ripples through the group as he downs the drink.

He pauses and then nods approvingly, smacking his lips together. "That's actually delicious."

I try to contain my excitement that he likes it.

A few teammates are wary, but then they start grabbing their own cups. One by one, they gulp down the drink and not one of them complains about the taste.

Penn hangs around as the others move on to pile their plates with food.

"Nice work. The preacher man strikes again. You've already got them believing in this magic," I whisper.

He grins. "I can be very convincing when I want to be."

When he walks away, I'm flustered. I'm pretty sure the other day in my office and just now, he was flirting with me.

As soon as they leave, I start snacks and lunch prep. During their break outside, I take out Pedialyte freezer pops and squeezable applesauce. When I reach Penn, his fingers brush against mine as he takes the popsicle from me and I freeze.

He grins and leans in. "What are you doing later?"

I look at him in surprise. "Crashing. I'm exhausted."

"Have dinner with me first?" he asks, his voice husky.

I cross my arms, amused but wary. The things he said about not being able to date and all that. "Penn, what are you doing?"

He grins, tilting his head. "Trying to convince you to have dinner with me. Is it working?"

"Hudson, quit flirting with my daughter and let her work," my dad's voice booms across the field.

My cheeks flame and Penn looks sheepish but undeterred. "Say yes," he whispers.

I run off the field, eager to get back to work on lunch. It's a lot of work to have enough food for these guys and their appetites. They burst through the doors at noon, hungry and sweaty, and I enjoy hearing how much they like the food. When everything wraps up, I go to the kitchen to work on the next round of snacks and to replenish the carb tables. A knock on the door makes me jump and I turn, hand to my chest.

Penn stands there, leaning against the wall, watching me with that infuriating mix of confidence and amusement.

I stop short, narrowing my eyes. "You again?"

He grins. "You say that like you're not thrilled to see me."

I shake my head, exhaling. "It's not that." And then I freeze because I just basically admitted that he's under my skin. "You've been all over the place, Penn. And now you want to go out with me?" I lower my voice. "Aren't you scared of my dad?"

"Terrified," he admits. "But I want to go out with you more than I'm terrified of him."

I laugh and his expression softens, stepping closer. "As friends?"

"I haven't forgotten the Bahamas, Addy." His voice is lower, more serious. "But yeah, as friends."

My stomach flips. *Say no. Keep your guard up and avoid workplace drama*, my inner voice says. But what comes out is, "Okay. I'd like that actually."

His lips quirk up. "You won't regret it."

That night he picks me up, freshly showered, his hair still damp and curling around his ears, and his crisp shirt fitting just right. He looks fan-fucking-tastic, and I hate that he flusters me.

But as I step toward his SUV, I'm met with a surprise. Sitting in the back seat is a boy. He's young, maybe eleven or twelve, with big eyes and a curious expression.

Penn gestures toward him with a warm smile. "We're lucky to have my buddy joining us tonight. Addy, this is Sam. Sam, this is Addy…or Adeline, whichever you prefer." His eyes meet mine.

"I like that you call me Addy," I say softly. "Hi, Sam."

Sam grins up at me and I melt instantly. "Hi!"

"Well, this is fun," I say, grinning over at Penn. This guy is proving that he will keep me on my toes.

"How does Rose & Thorn sound?" Penn asks.

"Suh-wanky!" Sam says.

Penn and I laugh.

"Sounds delicious. I haven't been there in a long time," I say. "Is that a favorite of yours?" I turn back to look at Sam.

"I've never been. Penn and I usually go to Starlight Cafe or Serendipity." His eyes are mischievous as he says, "I think he just wants to impress you."

"Ohhh-kay," Penn says, his eyes cutting over to me. "Didn't we agree not to spill my secrets?"

We all laugh and Sam chats happily as we turn onto Jupiter Lane. The smell of garlic and freshly baked bread fills the air as we walk into Rose & Thorn. We sit in a booth, and I'm surprised again when Penn slides in next to Sam, ruffling his hair before picking up a menu. Sam swats his hand away but grins, eyes lighting up as he scans the choices.

"Anything look good?" Penn asks him.

Sam leans forward, as if contemplating a huge decision. "I'm thinking…lasagna. But I also want spaghetti. And also pizza."

"Ah, classic dilemma," I say, grinning. "All solid choices….with maybe a vegetable or salad thrown in there."

"I like vegetables and salads!" Sam says. "And macaroni and cheese!"

He's so stinking adorable.

"If we get all that food, you might have to roll me out of here," Penn tells him.

He just smirks. "I guess you better keep lifting weights, old man."

I burst out laughing and Penn pretends to be offended, pressing a hand to his chest. "Old man? Excuse me? I'm in my prime."

"Debatable," I tease, sipping my water.

Dinner is full of easy conversation and even easier laughter. Sam is the kind of kid who makes you feel like you've known him forever, quick-witted and effortlessly funny. And Penn—God, Penn is so good with him. Penn listens to him, really listens, and Sam idolizes Penn. He's funny but respectful at the same time. They're easy together, and if Penn is trying to win me over with Sam, it's working. But sadly, it seems like he was serious about the friend thing.

After dinner, we pile into the SUV and head to Serendipity. Sam gets a towering cone of mint chocolate chip in a waffle cone, I opt for a mini cup of salted caramel, and Penn goes for vanilla with rainbow sprinkles on a sugar cone.

Sam side-eyes him hard. "*Vanilla*? With *rainbow sprinkles*?" he asks incredulously.

"Don't judge me," Penn says, taking a bite. "Sometimes you just need to go back to the classics."

"You're a mystery." Sam shakes his head before diving into his ice cream.

"Ain't that the truth," I say.

By the time we drop Sam off, my heart is full. Penn puts his hand on Sam's shoulder and his eyes are serious when he says, "Call me if you need anything. *Anything.* Okay?"

Sam nods and gives Penn a big hug. "Okay. I will. Thanks, Penn."

He hops out of the car and waves before jogging up the

walkway, disappearing inside. As soon as he's gone, I turn to Penn.

"So…what's the story with Sam?"

Penn exhales, rubbing a hand over the back of his neck. "I met him through a tutoring program some of the Mustangs did a few years ago. He was smart as hell but struggling, mostly due to a rough foster home situation. We hit it off, and I started spending more time with him."

I nod, sensing there's more. "And?"

He hesitates before continuing. "He's been in one bad situation after another. I've wished I could have him live with me, but…it's been complicated. I'm young and single and… obviously, I travel a lot." He pulls away and starts driving toward my condo. "I've applied for a foster license recently, and my lawyer is working on paperwork for me to adopt him eventually. The system isn't making it easy."

My chest tightens. "Really? Penn, that's amazing. But it seems like they'd be happy that you'd want to take him. How awful."

He stops at a light and his jaw is tight as he looks out the windshield. "The worst part? Recently he got arrested for stealing food from the grocery store. He was hungry. That's it."

My throat constricts, and before I can stop it, tears are falling down my cheeks. Penn notices and reaches out, taking my hand. It's only for a second before the light turns and he squeezes it before letting go.

The thought of Sam—this bright, funny, incredible kid—having to steal just to eat is too much. I shake my head, wiping at my cheeks. "He's such a sweet kid. It's just not right for any child to be hungry like that."

"I know. This foster home he's in…I don't trust them. Sam says they withhold food from the kids staying there, and

I've tried to get him out of there, but they check out okay when the social worker visits."

Seeing the way he cares about Sam, hearing that he wants to *adopt* him…I don't think my heart can take this.

"What can I do to help?" I ask.

"What do you mean?"

"Can I tell the courts what a good guy I think you are?"

He grins. "But you don't even know me."

"I know enough."

And what I know, I like so much. Too much.

It seems there's no way around falling for the guy.

CHAPTER ELEVEN

FRESH AIR

PENN

After seeing Addy all week at work, I feel like I'm missing out over the weekend. The way she eyed me in her office gets me hot just thinking about it.

I smile, remembering the way she calls me Preacher Man.

No, I will not get distracted by her cute and clever sass.

I check my phone again, hoping for a missed call or a text. Nothing. Just my own reflection staring back at me on the black screen. I'm not even sure she has my number. Oh that's right, she does…I just don't have her number. I wonder how I could get it…

Fuck. It's official. I've lost my shit.

I clearly have no clue what I'm doing. It's like I'm physically drawn to her…*all the time.* I keep telling myself that I'm being her friend. I'm trying to make her adjustment with the job easier, yada yada, but the fact of the matter is, when I'm not with her, I'm thinking up reasons I should be.

It makes no sense.

I call Sam to see if he wants to go to the Pixie Pop-Up Market. He's all for it, so I pick him up within the hour.

"The fresh air will do us good," I tell him, as we drive toward Jupiter Lane. Like that's the reason why I'm crawling out of my skin…not enough fresh air.

Meanwhile, my body's trying to adjust to training camp again after going a little easier on myself this summer. Normally, I'd be happy about this day off.

"This was a mistake," I mutter to myself, rubbing a hand down my face.

"What was a mistake?" Sam asks from the passenger seat.

He stuffs another bite of the granola bar in his mouth. I brought a few snacks to tide him over until we could pick out something better in one of the booths at the market. He's watching me like he can see straight into my soul, which is unnerving.

"Nothing. Forget it."

"You're thinking about Addy, aren't you?" he says, grinning.

I exhale sharply. "Why are you so smart? We're here. Come on."

He just laughs and hops out of the SUV, stretching his arms as if he's been stuck in there for hours instead of just a few minutes. I swear, lately, he's taller every time I see him.

The market is already bustling, tents lining the street, scents of donuts, coffee, bacon, burgers, and fresh flowers all competing with each other.

The priority is feeding Sam and once he has a burger and a donut in his belly, he's happy to just walk around, looking at all the different vendors. We hang out at the petting zoo for a while and then walk back toward the fresh vegetables and fruits, where I pick up a few things for the week.

I'm doing a pretty good job of focusing on Sam and anything but the gnawing feeling in my gut about Addy… until I see her.

She's standing near a stall with a woman and…Camden. Because apparently, my day has to take a nosedive.

I don't know what his deal is, but I think I should find out. Every time I turn around—well, all two times, really—he's there, smiling that effortless smile, standing next to Addy like he belongs there. And maybe he does.

Sam follows my gaze and lets out a low whistle. "Uh-oh."

"No, not uh-oh. It's fine. I'm fine."

His nose crinkles up as he stares at me. "No. You've got that look."

"What look?"

"The look that says you're about to do something dumb."

I glare at him, but he just grins wider. "Since when did you start mouthing off at me like my friends do?"

"I learned from the best," he says, pointing at me.

My mouth drops. "Take that back!"

But before I can stop him, he shouts, "Hey, Addy!"

Perfect.

She turns, eyes widening slightly when she sees me. She smiles and waves at us and then the three of them walk toward us.

"Hey," she says carefully, almost shyly. "I didn't know you'd be here."

"Didn't know you'd be here either," I say.

Why hasn't anyone told me how hard it is to be invested in how a woman I like feels about me? I had no idea.

"Hey man," Camden nods. "Good to see you."

"You too." I hope it sounds convincing because I genuinely like the guy, but damn, I want him to back the fuck off of Addy.

"I'm Goldie," the girl next to Addy says.

"Oh, I'm so sorry, I didn't even introduce you." Addy shakes her head, flustered. "This is Penn."

"Hi, Penn," Goldie says, her grin wide. And something tells me from the look on her face that she knows about me.

That feels promising.

"Hi, it's nice to meet you," I say.

"And this is Sam," Addy says. "Sam, this is my best friend in the whole wide world, Goldie, and her brother, Camden…who's also a great friend." She smiles as she looks over at Camden.

They both say hi to Sam and I stare at Addy.

She shifts, tucking a piece of hair behind her ear. "So… how's your weekend been?"

"Quiet." Too quiet. "You?"

"Good. Goldie came to visit, so it's actually been great. We've just been catching up."

"Where do you live, Goldie?" I ask.

"Minnesota." She smirks. "How is the team treating my bestie so far?" She puts her arm around Addy's shoulder and Addy flushes.

She shoots Goldie a look, but Goldie ignores her, waiting for me to answer.

"Uh, great, hopefully. She'd be the one to ask, but from

what I can tell, everyone's been decent. Especially when we tasted some of the recipes she's come up with."

Addy smiles, looking pleased with my response.

"She's the best, right?" Goldie says. "I wouldn't have survived in school without Addy feeding me."

"You're not a dietitian too?"

"Oh no," she says, shaking her head. "No, no. I wouldn't have had the patience for that. These two are the foodies." She tilts her head toward Addy and Camden.

"Don't let her fool you," Addy says proudly. "Goldie is an amazing artist and has a Bachelor of Arts *and* a Master in Design Studies—"

"She's smarter than all of us," Camden says, laughing. "Not you, Adeline, but our siblings."

Goldie loops her arm through her brother's and wrinkles her nose. "Don't listen to them. I'm here to talk about Addy." She winks at Addy, who looks horrified. "Our girl is pretty great, right?"

Addy's eyes widen as she tries to stare Goldie into silence. I decide then that I think Goldie is fantastic.

"I think she is," I say, nodding as I look at Addy.

Sam, the little traitor, steps forward with a grin. "So, Camden. What do you do?"

"I own a restaurant in Denver. You'll have to come visit sometime. Bring Penn with you. My treat." He smiles at Sam and then me.

"That's so cool," Sam says. "Did you know that Penn has won three Super Bowls, and last year even though his team lost, he was still named the running back to watch?" He looks at me proudly. "On one sports show I saw, they said Penn is on his way to being considered one of the five greatest running backs of all time!"

I put my hand on Sam's shoulder and squeeze it. "And

this right here is why I take this guy everywhere," I say, grinning at Sam. "Thanks, bud."

"Yeah, I think you've got the number one fan spot filled, but I'm right up there with you in the Penn Hudson fan club," Camden says. "All you guys, man. It's been an amazing few seasons."

"Wow. Thank you. I didn't see all this praise coming." I laugh. "Hopefully, we'll make you guys proud this year."

"Well, now that you've got my girl fueling you in the right way, maybe you will!" Goldie says.

"There's just a whole love fest going on here, isn't there?" Addy says pointedly at Goldie, who just smiles innocently.

"Right," I say, clearing my throat. "Well, we should—"

"Join us?" Goldie interrupts, her smile widening. I have to smile back. I think this girl might be Team Penn, but I could be completely wrong here. "We were just about to grab some pastries. You and Sam should come."

Addy's eyes dart to mine, but I can't read anything in them today. Does she want me to say yes?

"Uh," I start, and Sam claps his hand on my shoulder.

"We'd love to!" he says.

CHAPTER TWELVE

EMBARRASSMENTS

ADELINE

When Goldie called to say she had a surprise for me, I wasn't expecting her to show up in Silver Hills first thing yesterday morning. I've never been so happy to see her.

"I've missed you like crazy." We've been saying that to each other over and over.

She's wanted all the details about Penn, and I've been trying not to obsess about Penn, so…it's not going so well. Our little episode in my office hasn't helped, and running into him and Sam at the Pixie Pop-Up Market isn't helping either. Penn, on his own, is enough to make me drool, but seeing how sweet he is with Sam…next level.

I haven't been able to get my mind off of Penn *or* Sam. It seems so obvious to me that Penn should have custody of Sam. Why would anyone keep that from happening? I've obsessed a bit, telling Goldie all about it.

And Goldie is intent on praising me up to Penn, which is making me a nervous wreck. On our walk to Luminary Coffeehouse, I try to subtly tell her to cut it out.

Inside, Clara, the adorable barista, greets us. "Ah, newcomers and regulars alike! Newbies, you're off the hook for today, but for the regulars, you know the drill. You dance, you get coffee."

I glance at Goldie, who raises an eyebrow, intrigued.

"Let's see what you've got," she says.

I do a little hip shake across the floor and turn back to see Penn watching with approval. He nods at me in a way that makes me feel like I've just won a prize and then he turns to Clara.

"Turn up that chorus, please, Clara," he calls.

Bebe Rexha singing "Chase It (Mmm Da Da Da)" blasts through the speakers and Penn and Sam glance at each other, moving to stand side by side. They start twisting their bodies in a way that has me laughing right away and then they shift and do this head-up nod thing in perfect time with the beat *and* with each other. Everyone starts cheering and clapping, and then both of them break out into a full-on hip thrust, booty-shaking dance for a few seconds until the chorus is over, which makes the shop erupt…and then they walk up to the counter like nothing has happened.

Once I've stopped laughing and cheering, I walk up next to them and put my arms on each of their shoulders.

"Oh my God, you guys were so good! Where have you been hiding those dancing skills?" I say, starting to laugh all over again.

"Not hiding it. Are we, Sam?" Penn asks Sam, coolly.

"Nope. Pretty much right out there in the open," Sam says.

I point at him. "How old are you again?" I ask.

"Eleven," he says.

"We'll have to watch this one," I tell Penn. "He'll have the girls lined up."

Penn stares at me for a beat before he says, "Yes, we will. And he already does."

Sam laughs and they high-five each other. I roll my eyes and that makes both of them even happier.

Once we've ordered—The Celestial Donuts that I should have never tried because I'm already addicted—Goldie leans in.

"Seeing Penn on the TV screen is not even close to experiencing him in person. He's *so* hot and so magnetic and he is *all about you*. He's a keeper, Addy. He's crazy about you." She squeezes my arm, as if she's breaking it to me gently.

"I can't *keep* him." I shake my head, trying to play it off. "But how do you know?"

She gives me a dry look. "Have you seen the way he looks at you? That's all I need to know right there. I thought he was going to scorch your clothes right off with those eyes!"

"Goldie! Keep it down," I tell her, looking around to see if anyone heard her.

"Don't worry. I'm the only one who heard that," Camden says. "And I have to agree with my sister."

"That's a first," she teases.

The moment Goldie slides into the chair next to me, eyes

lit up with purpose, I brace myself. I glance across the table at Penn with Sam, looking blissfully unaware of the grilling he's about to endure. Goldie's been dying to interrogate him ever since she arrived in town, and now that she has him cornered, I know she's on a mission.

"Penn Hudson," she begins, leaning forward. "Tell us something important about yourself. Something deep."

Penn, who has just taken a sip of his caramel macchiato, pauses mid-swallow and flicks his gaze to me as if I'll save him. No can do. I'm here for this.

He sets his cup down, eyes narrowing. "Deep like…childhood trauma? Or deep like my thoughts about pineapple on pizza?"

Goldie grins. "Both, please."

Sam laughs next to him, happily chewing on a muffin and fully entertained. Camden is sitting next to Goldie and he groans. "Sorry, man. She's like a chicken pecking for the truth."

Goldie swats his arm. "I am not a chicken."

Penn exhales. "No pineapple on pizza. It's an abomination. That's Rhodes' and Sadie's territory. I'm a purist."

I gasp. "You monster."

Sam fist-bumps Penn. "I'm with you." He gives me an apologetic glance. "Sorry, Addy."

"Okay, so you're not into the sweet and savory pizza," Goldie says. "What about your childhood? Any pets? Tragedies? A schoolyard nemesis?"

He laughs and looks at me like *Is she for real?*

Oh yeah, she's just getting started.

When she just taps the table waiting for his answer, he starts talking. "Uh, I had a dog named Draco Malfoy. No huge tragedies, except for the time I ate a king-sized Snickers bar and threw up in the boys' bathroom at school...in the sink because all the stalls were full."

"Noooo," we all groan.

"Yeah, it was bad. It wouldn't drain..."

We all groan again and Penn shudders with the memory.

"I haven't had a Snickers since," he says sadly.

Goldie nods. "Relatable. What about a nemesis? You're scrappy out on the field...I bet you've been punched in the face a few times off the field too."

"Just once," he says, rubbing his jaw like he can still feel it. "Junior year of high school. Guy thought I was flirting with his girlfriend. I wasn't." He pauses, then smirks. "But she *was* flirting with me."

Camden chuckles under his breath, and I elbow Goldie. "Are you satisfied?"

She doesn't hesitate. "Oh, I have more." She turns back to Penn, crossing her arms. "Do you have any hidden talents? You're quite the dancer. Do you have a stripper past—"

"Goldie!" I gasp.

Penn laughs and his eyes drill into mine when he says, "Wouldn't you like to know..."

The visual burns my eyes and I shake my head, pretending to be grossed out.

"It's time we turn the tables," Penn says, eyeing me.

"Why are you looking at me? She's the one asking all the questions," I blurt out.

"No, you should totally ask her the questions," Goldie says, resting her chin on her hands.

Penn lifts his eyebrows, challenging me.

"I love pineapple on pizza," I say.

His eyes narrow. "I think we've already covered that."

"Okay...I had a dog named Josh that I loved. When we

were moving, my parents said he was going to live at the retirement home and roam the countryside."

They all groan. "No, they didn't," Penn says.

I nod. "I believed them until I went to look up the retirement home and I couldn't find any by that name."

"Brutal," Goldie says.

"What about your most embarrassing moment?" Penn asks.

Without even having to think about it, I say, "Oh, my most embarrassing moment was when my boyfriend asked me to prom and played "Gettin' Some Head" by Lil Wayne in front of everyone…"

"No, he did not!" Penn says.

Everyone's eyes are wide, but then I look at Sam and want to kick myself. Me and my big mouth. Fortunately, he still looks confused.

"I didn't know that!" Goldie gasps.

Penn swipes his hand over his face, laughing. "What did you do?"

"I broke up with him!"

Everyone laughs.

"I don't get it," Sam says.

"It was…nothing. I-I shouldn't have brought it up," I say.

He frowns. "Why?" Then he leans in. "Pretend like I'm not even here."

Penn laughs and slaps his hand on his shoulder. "Impossible." He grins at me and we share a heated look for a moment before looking at Sam again.

"Impossible," I repeat.

"You guys are being weird," Sam says, which makes us all laugh.

Penn's eyes meet mine over Sam's head again and my insides warm.

I have to pull myself out of a Penn stupor, and so I look at Sam and say, "What about you? Any childhood pets?"

A cloud crosses Sam's face. "No, but I want a pet more than anything."

His expression makes my heart pang. "A dog or a cat?"

"Either one. Both!" he says, shrugging. "When I grow up, I want to rescue all the dogs and cats that need a home."

Penn squeezes Sam's shoulder. "I think that's a great idea, buddy."

Gah, my heart just doubled in size.

Later, as we're leaving, there's an awkward moment before we say goodbye. Penn leans in and wraps his arms around me. "Thanks for sharing your childhood traumas," he whispers in my ear.

I laugh and lean up, whispering in his, "Pineapple pizza is superior."

He tickles my side and I jolt in his arms, laughing harder as his fingers dance over my ribs.

"I will never admit that," he says finally. "But I'd be happy to order some for you if you ever want to have pizza together…"

I pull back and give him a coy smile. "Just two friends eating pizza?"

He makes a face and says through gritted teeth, "*Right*. Just two friends eating pizza."

I smirk and move away, missing the loss of his hands on me. When we get in the car, Goldie fans her face.

"The pheromones and the sexual tension and all the *I want you so much* vibes," she says, her hands waving around in the air. She turns to face me. "I think I just got pregnant from the close proximity of all your longing."

"Shut it." I laugh. "You heard him. We're just friends."

"Yeah, and the ocean is pink. I give you two weeks, tops, before you're climbing him like a tree."

"Still here," Camden says from the back seat.

"You can handle it, bro," she says, looking at him over her shoulder. "Don't pretend like you're not Mr. Chef á la mode."

"What does that even mean?" He snorts.

"You know," she taunts, laughing. "But we're not talking about your player ways right now, we're trying to get Adeline to acknowledge that she and Penn are *hot* for each other."

My cheeks flame and I shake my head, trying to act like Goldie couldn't be more wrong.

But I'm pretty sure everyone can see right through me.

The more I'm around Penn, the more I like him.

CHAPTER THIRTEEN

WELCOME HOME

PENN

Over the next few days, I look for every reason to cross paths with Adeline Evans. I linger around longer than necessary at lunchtime and go back for extra snacks. I stop by her office just to say hey and to see if she's busy, and if she's not, I shoot the shit talking about whatever I think will strike her funny. I feel like a junior high kid trying to impress the girl and I can hardly comprehend how fun this is.

I know the guys told me that I would understand one day,

but I truly never believed them. I didn't think I would feel this way about any girl ever. Everything about her is intriguing.

"Penn," Coach barks. "Why do I keep catching you loitering around my daughter's office? Don't you have things to do?"

Addy stands up and frowns. "It's the end of the day, Dad. And he's allowed to talk to me…it's kind of part of my job… that I talk to the players." Her tone is no-nonsense, and he looks chagrined for a moment before he keeps walking.

"I looked pretty good out there today, didn't I?" I say, calling after him. I grin at Addy, waiting for her dad to shoot me down.

He waves his hand over his head and grumbles something.

"I think he's softening toward me," I say and Addy laughs.

A door slams and Peter, one of our security guards, rushes toward us. I'm surprised when he stops in front of me.

"I've got a kid out here. Says he's Sam. He's looking for you. I tried to call you, but—"

"Fuck. My phone's still on silent." I pull it out of my pocket and switch on the sound. "Sam's here?" I glance at Addy for a second and then follow Peter down the hall.

"He's hurt," Peter says.

Addy gasps and rushes to catch up with us.

"What? What do you mean? Where is he?" I ask.

He motions for me to keep following him.

When we reach Sam, I'm horrified when he turns and I see his face. His nose is bloody and his eyes are purple and puffy.

"Sam, what happened?" I rush toward him and pull him in for a hug.

He swallows hard, shaking his head.

"I didn't know what else to do," he says.

"Oh my God, Sam. I'll go get a cold cloth," Addy says, rushing to the bathroom near the main entrance.

"What happened?" I repeat. "Who did this?"

He just shakes his head and stares at me.

"Was it one of your foster parents?" I ask.

He eventually nods.

"Okay, we're going to the hospital."

"I don't need to go to the hospital," he says, "just please don't make me go back there."

Addy rushes out with a cloth and gingerly holds it up to his face.

"You're not going back there, I promise. I don't care what we have to do. I won't let them take you from me this time. But we have to go to the doctor—we need to report this." I glance at Addy and she nods.

"Okay," Sam says, his voice weak. "Thanks, Addy."

"Of course. I wish I could do more," she says.

I squeeze her shoulder, thanking her too.

"How did you get here?" I ask Sam.

"I took the bus and walked."

He leans into me as we walk outside. I can feel him shaking against me and it fucking kills me.

"Oh, my man. I'm so sorry."

"Wait, you're not going without me," Addy calls, rushing behind us.

We get in the SUV, Addy in the back seat and Sam in the front. He's leaning his head back and she's leaning forward, trying to make him more comfortable. She brushes his hair back and sets the tissues near him.

"I should've grabbed ice before we left," she says apologetically.

I keep looking over there to make sure he's okay. Tears

run down his face. But he's quiet, and it cracks my heart wide open. I rush to the ER and as soon as they've taken us back to a room, I walk into the hall to call Mrs. Murphy.

"It's Penn Hudson. I'm with Sam. They hit him…his fucking foster parents hit him," I say. I stare up at the ceiling, trying to rein in the rage. "We're at the hospital. We need your help. Please don't let us down this time."

"I'll be right there," she says.

We hang up and I call David.

We have a lot of great lawyers through the team, but for matters related to Sam, I've been talking to Weston's dad, David. He and his wife, Lane, and Weston's sister, Olivia are all partners at the Law Offices of Shaw & Shaw.

"Whatever it takes," I tell him, "just please help me. I want to adopt him. I don't want there to be any risk of this happening to him again. I can't send him back there."

"No, no, you can't," he says. "I'll get to work on everything."

We're there for a couple of hours and they check everything out. He doesn't have a concussion, and overall, he seems physically okay. Just scarred, traumatized…the things that go deeper than a fist. The things he's seen, the things he's been through…I can't stand to think about it, but it's time we all dealt with it head-on.

My phone buzzes and I open the text thread with the guys.

> WESTON
>
> Sadie and I are grilling tonight. Anyone want in?

> **RHODES**
>
> Hell, yes. Elle and I were just talking about how we didn't feel like cooking tonight. What can we bring?

> Hey guys. I'm at the ER with Sam…and Addy too. Sam was beaten up pretty bad at his foster house today.

> **HENLEY**
>
> Holy fuck. What the hell happened?

> It was his foster dad.

There's a knock on the door and I hurriedly text.

> I need to get off my phone. I'll touch base later.

I turn off my phone and put it in my pocket.

A police officer comes and I can tell Sam's nervous to say anything about his foster parents, but I assure him that he needs to be forthright. Pictures are taken of his injuries, and more than one person asks him questions.

My mom and I text back and forth while we wait. She and Dad will leave first thing in the morning and try to do the drive in one day.

Addy has been amazing. She's distracted Sam with *Would you rather?* questions and let him play games on her phone. She just went down the hall to get drinks for us. Sam's eyes are drifting shut, so maybe he'll rest for a while.

The nurse peeks her head in and whispers that the social worker has arrived. When I walk out to meet Mrs. Murphy, her eyes don't meet mine at first. When they do, her gaze is sorrowful and full of regret.

"He's coming home with me," I say.

She nods. "I was able to get a temporary pass for you, but I don't know how long it'll last."

Addy appears next to me, managing three large drinks. "This is crazy," she says to Mrs. Murphy. "Sam belongs with Penn."

"And you are?" Mrs. Murphy asks, not unkindly.

Addy glances at me and then squares her shoulders, looking back at Mrs. Murphy. "I'm Adeline Evans, Penn's girlfriend."

I try to school the shock from my expression when Mrs. Murphy lifts her eyebrows and tilts her head at me.

"I wasn't aware Mr. Hudson had a girlfriend," she says.

"Well, he does…I am," Addy says. "And we're…very serious."

If the situation weren't so dire, I'd laugh, but as I watch Mrs. Murphy take in the information, nodding as if she's mentally cataloging this, I get emotional. It might not make any difference, but I'm grateful that Addy would try to be helpful.

"Well, this is a nice development," Mrs. Murphy says, smiling at me. "I'll make note of this in your file." And then her smile drops. "But I'm wondering why you didn't disclose this earlier. I'm sure you can understand why we'll need to put Adeline through the same rigorous process you're going through. I'd like to see Sam and then as soon as the hospital clears him to go, you're free to take him home with you."

My shoulders deflate and I reach out and take Addy's hand, needing something to hold onto. "Thank you. It's been a little complicated because Addy works for the Mustangs, but don't worry—we're not breaking protocol or anything like that." I take a deep breath. "I will take such good care of Sam. I swear to you I will not let him down."

Mrs. Murphy gives me a fond look. "He's very lucky to have you."

I smile at her gratefully and motion toward the room. "We're lucky to have each other. He was asleep, but he'll be glad to see you and will be happy for this news."

She nods briskly and walks into Sam's room. Addy and I exchange a loaded look. I want to talk to her about her comment, but now is not the time. Mrs. Murphy isn't with Sam for long and when she comes out, her shoulders are relaxed.

"I'll be checking in tomorrow to see how he's doing," she says.

"Okay. Sounds good." I shake her hand and watch as she walks away, letting out a long exhale.

Sam's nurse walks up and grins. "I think he's ready to go home."

"Really?" I follow her into his room and she walks to his bedside.

"I've got your release papers," she says. "And it sounds like you're going home with this guy." She points at me over her shoulder, and Sam and I grin our faces off.

"You look too happy for someone who's had such a rough day," I tell him after she leaves the room.

"I'm so happy," he says, tears rolling down his face.

I put my arm around him and squeeze lightly, careful not to hurt him.

"We've waited way too long for this," I tell him. "Can't quite believe it's really happening myself." I lean in closer. "I'm so happy too, buddy."

The drive is quiet in comparison to the panic we felt on the way to the hospital.

"Oh, shit. I need to drive you back to the training facility." I glance at Addy when I go in the wrong direction.

She waves me off. "I'll get an Uber home and to work in the morning. Not a big deal. I want to make sure this guy is okay." She turns around to look at him in the back seat.

"I have plenty of guest bedrooms," I tell her. "You can stay the night or I can take you home later."

"I'm not worried about it," she says, smiling at me before she turns to look at Sam again. "How are you doing back there?"

"Pretty good," he says.

"You hungry?" I ask, looking in the rearview mirror.

"Yes," he says emphatically.

It makes me laugh. "I've never been so happy to hear you say that. Means you're feeling better and I can do something about feeding you *right now*. How about I pick up soup and sandwiches from Starlight Cafe?"

"That sounds so good," he says wistfully. "And a Moonlight shake from Serendipity?"

"You got it. Coming right up."

"Now you have me curious about the Moonlight shake," Addy says.

"It's chocolate ice cream with peanut butter chunks and chocolate syrup," he says.

"Sold," she says, laughing.

"That's on a dietitian's approved list?" I tease.

"Chocolate and peanut butter are always on my approved list."

We've missed rush hour, so the drive back to our cute little town is a lot less congested than it usually is on my way back from training camp. Before we reach Starlight Cafe, Tiana is singing on the corner opposite us. I lower my window to hear her better.

"I've missed Silver Hills so much," Addy says.

"Even after living in California?" I ask in surprise.

"I love California, don't get me wrong. I will always wish I was seeing the ocean. But I missed the seasons here, and I missed the slower pace of life. And Tiana, my God. She just doesn't age, does she? What potion is she taking?"

I laugh. "I know. She's a rock star through and through." I pull in front of the cafe and make sure I have their orders right. "Okay, I'll be right back."

"Do you need help getting all that back out?" she asks.

"I can handle it," I say, and the grin she gives me back makes my heart stutter.

I glance at Sam and he's smirking at me from the back seat. I point at him and his smile grows. My little sidekick isn't missing a thing.

When I get back to the SUV, Sam is telling Addy all about the girls at school. Some of the things the guys have said to me about having kids with the women they love comes back to me, because I get a lump in my throat, seeing Sam so happy with Addy.

It's silly though because *of course* I don't love Addy.

Let's not get ahead of ourselves here.

I make one more stop at Serendipity and then drive home. As I help Sam get inside, I'm overwhelmed with gratitude—that he's here, that he's safe, that I can take care of him now in the way I've wanted to for so long.

I glance down at him and despite looking a mess from being hurt, his eyes are peaceful.

"Welcome home," I tell him.

He leans his head into my chest and hugs me. "Thanks, Penn."

I have to swallow down the huge lump in my throat. We've overcome a huge obstacle. Every step feels like a quiet victory…or at least a huge step in the right direction.

I text the guys to let them know Sam is home with me, and they're as happy as I am.

HENLEY

It's about time.

WESTON

So happy for you, man.

RHODES

This was a long time coming. The two of you are meant to be together.

BOWIE

This is the best news. And you'll have to fill us in on how Addy ended up at the hospital.

RHODES

Fuck yeah, you will.

Can't chat now, she's still here.

CHAPTER FOURTEEN

CHECK ON ME

ADELINE

The mood is buoyant as we eat and talk and laugh. Penn and Sam are hilarious together. I can't get enough of them. And despite the awful day Sam has had, it's obvious that he's so relieved and happy to be here with Penn, he's more animated than I've ever seen him. But after he eats, he can't stop yawning.

"All right, little dude. I'm gonna call it. Time for you to shower then go to bed. You need your rest. You don't have to go to school tomorrow. I'll be here with ya in the morning. But you need all the rest you can get to fully recover, okay?" Penn says.

"Okay," Sam nods, fighting another yawn. "Will you get in trouble for missing training camp?"

Penn waves him off, but he doesn't fully answer either. I hope my dad and the other coaches don't give him a hard time about missing. I'll have some serious words with my father if he does.

They go upstairs and I look around the main floor a little bit, appreciating how gorgeous Penn's house is. I don't know what I was expecting, but his house surprises me. There are floor-to-ceiling windows everywhere, and large white, soft couches with deep blue throw pillows and two plush deep blue side chairs are set up comfortably in the living room. Large, colorful artwork dons the white walls, and the bar in the corner has velvet blue stools and colorful glasses. His style is modern but comfortable and quirky. I find myself smiling as I walk through the rooms. His dining room table is surrounded by black and white striped chairs and a fancy clear wine refrigerator looks like artwork in itself with its height and gold handles.

He's gone for a while and then I hear Sam call me. Penn echoes it louder and I find the stairs and go up, following the sounds of their voices. It's beautiful upstairs too, and the room I find them in is gorgeous. Slanted, with a wall of windows, and beautiful woodwork on the ceiling, Sam looks tiny in the king-sized bed. He's propped up on two fluffy pillows, and his dark hair and eyes stand out against the white sheets.

"I just wanted to thank you for everything, Addy," he says.

I think it's cute that he calls me Addy like Penn does.

"You're so welcome. I'm so glad I was able to help, and it was fun hanging out tonight," I tell him.

He smiles and glances at Penn, pointing at him. "Don't do anything to mess it up with her while I'm sleeping."

Penn's mouth drops and he pretends to be offended. "As if I could!" he says. He glances at me, cheeks flushed, and then back at Sam. "I'll do my best."

Sam nods like *that's more like it* and I lean over and kiss him on the forehead. "Night, Sam."

"Night."

Penn reaches over and pats Sam's hand. "Night, buddy. I'll be right here if you need me, okay?"

"Okay."

We walk toward the door and Penn turns out the light.

"Can you…check on me later?" Sam asks. "Just to…I don't know…make sure I'm still here?"

Penn's throat bobs and he swallows hard. "You've got it. I'll check on you lots. And I'll leave this door cracked, okay? Nobody can bother you here, my man. I've got top-of-the-line security, and anyone who comes after you from here on out has got to get through me first. Got it?"

Sam nods, his lips trembling. "Got it," he whispers.

When we leave the room and walk into the hall, Penn leans against the wall and puts his head in his hands. I put my hand on his shoulder and when he lifts his head to look at me, his cheeks are wet.

"I can't let that little boy down again," he says quietly.

I wipe the tears from my face and follow Penn as he moves down the hall. There's an alcove with a couch and bookshelves. Penn motions to the couch.

"You probably have to go, but if you want a glass of wine or anything, I can bring some up here for us. I want to stick close just in case he needs me."

I sit down. "I don't need anything. I'm still full. But I do want to talk to you about something."

Penn tenses and sits down next to me, concern on his face.

I take a deep breath, feeling a bit shaky. "Ever since I met Sam and you told me what's been going on with him, I've been trying to figure out a way to help." I laugh awkwardly. "I've been unable to *stop* thinking about it. I couldn't stand the thought of him going hungry, but today, seeing him in pain…we have to do something. He can't go into another situation that puts him at risk like that."

"Thank you for caring. You just met him and already you care more than a lot of people would. And I agree. I can't stop thinking about it either," Penn says quietly.

"I know what to do," I tell him.

His eyes widen.

"It became clear to me when I told Mrs. Murphy that I'm your girlfriend."

His lips lift a little. "I forgot to thank you…and tease you about that."

I laugh. "Well, you can tease me more soon because…I think we should get married."

He just stares at me.

I wasn't nervous before I said it, but the longer he goes without saying anything, the more nervous I get.

"Penn—" I start but leave it hanging.

He blinks. Then blinks again.

"Did you hear me?" I finally ask.

Still quiet.

And then—

"I heard you, but it can't be right because it sounded like you said we should get married."

"I did."

He sits up straighter. "Oh."

"Hear me out. You saw how she jumped on me being your girlfriend, and you've said she's talked about you not being a family unit…we can fix that easily by getting married. Totally legitimate and noble reasons, but it'll cut through a ton of red tape…"

"Wouldn't that be marriage fraud?"

Now my eyes widen. "What? No! This is the opposite of fraud. This is, like, ethical fraud, I mean, marriage. Ethical marriage, if that's a thing. You want to adopt him one day, right? But you're a single guy with a hectic job and the system doesn't exactly love that. They want stability, a partner, blah, blah, blah…so we get married, they give you custody of him, and it solves everything."

"Married," he echoes. "As in vows, rings, signing legal documents." He makes a face.

"Yes." I scratch the back of my neck. "We wouldn't need to do the whole big wedding thing since it's just for Sam." I grin and hold out a hand. "You can pick out a cake though. I mean, we don't even have to get cake. But we do want to make it look real in every way possible."

"I want cake," he says, turning to face me. "Do you mean it, Addy? You'd really do this for us?"

"Absolutely."

"This is crazy." He laughs.

"I know. But is it a *good* crazy?"

He takes a deep breath and shakes his head. "Why would you do this? Do you realize what it would mean? What you'd be giving up? At least for a little while?"

"It'd be for the best reason."

"It feels like a huge sacrifice on your part," he says.

"One I'm offering to make." I lean in. "At least think about it."

He laughs again. "That's the craziest part. I am thinking about it." He reaches out and brushes the hair out of my eyes. "I can't believe you'd be willing to do this for us." He shifts. "I've never considered myself good marriage material, but there's no one else I could imagine doing this with but you. What about your dad? The team? I don't want to do anything to jeopardize your relationship with your family or your job."

"I think we make sure my dad gets to know Sam. We won't tell anyone what we're doing, but if the truth ever came out, they'd understand why."

"What if you can't stand living with me? There's plenty of room here, but…I really can take care of Sam on my own. We don't have to do it for long, right? A year, maybe two… until everything is finalized."

"I'd love to be part of Sam's life, so count me in on that. As far as everything else, it can just be a marriage on paper." Even as I say the words, my heart is galloping ahead of me, too excited for a marriage on paper. Which is a problem, but one I will deal with later.

"I mean…*yeah*, a marriage on paper." He scoffs, but his lips are twitching. "Marry you? I hardly know you."

My mouth falls open and I laugh. "Oh, Preacher Man. I think it's safe to say we're not strangers. Your lips know me well anyway."

"You're just so forward." He tries to keep a straight face, but when I smack his arm, he starts laughing. "So when do you…propose we do this wedding?"

"This weekend? Or…tomorrow night?"

I can tell he wants to keep teasing me, but he just nods instead. "No one will believe you fell for me this fast," he finally says.

If he only knew.

I lift my shoulder in a shrug. "So we tell everyone we met

in the Bahamas. It was love at first sight, but we went our separate ways…until I showed up here and we just couldn't fight our feelings any longer."

His eyes burn into mine and I have to physically hold onto the couch so I don't jump into his lap instead.

That would not send the right message.

"That could work," he breathes. "Do we tell anyone we're getting married or just go do it?"

"What's that saying about asking for forgiveness later?" I say, laughing. "Not that we need anyone's permission, but I think it'd be easier to just go for it. We could invite friends, but I feel like there's more opportunity for things to go wrong that way. I think we'd have to keep it completely between us and not tell a soul, especially not Sam, what we're doing."

He winces. "I'd feel so bad lying to him though. And my friends."

"Me too. But we wouldn't be doing this if we didn't have to. The system has made this an impossible situation."

He sighs. "You're right. And it would be worth it, knowing we didn't have to worry about losing him ever again." He reaches out and takes my hand, squeezing it. "Thank you, Addy. You should think about it for a few days. Really think it over. Decide if this is something you can do. I'll completely understand if you change your mind."

"I won't change my mind."

"Okay, but promise me you will think about it. And if you still feel this way on Friday, we can move forward."

"By move forward, do you mean get married?" I ask playfully.

He reaches out and tickles my side, which sends me jerking and clamping my hand over my mouth when my laugh is a little too loud.

"So forward," he says, laughing. He looks at me and

shakes his head before starting to laugh again. "I can't believe this. You're serious?"

"Good idea, right?"

"You could've thrown in flowers to really seal the deal," he says.

I give him a flirty grin. "Turns out we didn't even need 'em."

CHAPTER FIFTEEN

WHATEVER YOU WANT

PENN

Well, Sam and I are quite the pair the next morning.

I couldn't sleep due to the fact that Addy had *asked me to marry her*. And Sam looks like he lost a fight with a wrecking ball.

He's doing a hell of a lot better than last night, but his eyes are swollen and edged in black and purple. Every time I look at him, I want to throw someone through the wall for putting him in the ER. But he's chipper, stuffing a waffle in his mouth while wearing my sunglasses and a baseball cap.

"Dude," I say, sitting across from him. "You look like a celebrity avoiding the paparazzi."

He lifts his chin, pushing his sunglasses higher on his nose. "My face looks like a crime scene." He finishes the waffle in three bites, and I slide another on his plate. He looks at me gratefully, taking another huge bite. "I love these waffles. Thanks, Penn."

"Sure thing, bud. What's mine is yours. I appreciate that you're grateful, but you don't have to keep saying thank you. I want you to get comfortable enough around here that you tell me whatever you need. We can go to the grocery store later and you can pick out all the things."

"Really? That would be awesome!" He leans forward. "I like vegetables too. I promise I won't just pick out junk."

"I trust you, little dude."

He grins and then it falters. "I do kinda need one thing… or two."

"What's that?"

"Well, I don't really have my clothes or sneakers. I didn't have many that fit anyway, and they've probably already given them to another kid." He lifts his shoulder in a shrug. "Just something for school tomorrow."

That's all I need to hear. "As soon as you feel up to it, we'll go shopping."

"Today?"

"If you're feeling good enough to go, sure."

He smiles again and I keep being struck by how young he looks when he's happy like this.

"I'm feeling good," he says. "Do you…do you think I'll get to stay? With you?"

"I think I'm going to do whatever it takes to make that happen…even if it takes extreme measures."

His eyes brighten and he nods happily. "Okay. Let's go today then. We can pretend like we're skipping school."

"One of us is skipping school," I tease. "But I did call the school and it's an excused absence."

"Did you get in trouble for missing practice?"

I make a face. "Nah. Coach Evans wanted to give me a hard time, but I told him about what you'd been through and he was really sorry to hear that you'd been hurt. He remembers meeting you at last year's family day and liked you a lot. I hope it's okay that I told him a little about what happened."

He nods. "Anything to stay out of trouble with him. He *is* Addy's dad and you don't want to be on his bad side."

I squeeze his shoulder. "You are wise beyond your years, my man."

We head out, and before Sam knows what's happening, I've bought him several pairs of sneakers, hoodies, jeans, and any T-shirts he checks out for more than a second.

"I only needed one or two things. What is happening?" he says, as we leave the store.

"You deserve good stuff."

"Not *that* much good stuff."

"I beg to differ."

He shakes his head, but he's got a bounce to his step. I catch him sneaking glances inside the bags like he actually loves it.

Next stop: food.

Sam is hesitant when we park in Aurora's parking lot. "I should apologize to the owner. I don't want him to think I'm gonna steal food every time I come in."

"If you're up for it today, sure. We can come back and do it another time too, though."

"I'd like a fresh start," he says. "Let's do it today."

Damn. This kid.

"I get it, bud, and I think it's a great idea. Let's do this."

We go inside and wait about ten minutes before Derek, the manager, is available to chat. Sam gives him a very earnest apology, and Derek is so touched, he looks at me with tears in his eyes. I know. This kid will move anyone to tears.

"You're always welcome here," Derek says as we're walking away. "And for being so honest with me today, I'd like you to pick out whatever candy bar you want, my treat. I'll let the cashier know it's on me."

"You don't have to do that," Sam says.

"I know. I want to," Derek says.

"Thanks, man," I tell Derek as we walk away.

"You handled that flawlessly." I squeeze Sam's shoulder. "You okay to shop?"

He inhales and exhales and then shakes out his hands, nodding. "Yes."

"Okay, grab whatever you want. You crave it, we're getting it."

"Whatever I want?" he asks.

"Go crazy."

He grins and grabs a cart. The first thing he puts in the basket is a big container of mixed greens.

"I've always wanted to get one of these instead of just a ball of lettuce," he says excitedly.

I gulp. I may as well start carrying a life-size package of tissues because this guy is going to make me cry a literal river.

Addy texts as we're shopping.

ADDY
How's Sam?

> Thriving. I told him he could have whatever he wanted from the grocery store—WHATEVER he craved—and so far, he's picked out mixed greens, cucumbers, tomatoes, a huge bag of oranges, and a family pack of chicken breasts.

ADDY

😊 I swear, that boy is golden.

> He really is.

ADDY

Have you thought about what I suggested?

> Only all night and every second since...

ADDY

😊 And?

> I think you're onto something. How are you feeling about it?

ADDY

I think I'm onto something too. I feel really good about it actually.

My heart feels like it's going to rocket right out of my skin. Can this really be happening? I know she's proposing a marriage strictly for the purpose of getting Sam, but my heart is reacting like she's told me she loves me and wants to have my babies. And instead of terrifying me like I would expect it to, I'm excited and hopeful.

> Me too, Addy. I still can't believe you're willing.

When we get in the car, Sam carefully unpeels his Reese's

Peanut Butter Cup and takes a small bite. I lean over and bop his cap.

"I might ask Addy to marry me."

He chokes on the chocolate. "What? Wait. Are you serious?"

I shrug, like this isn't the most important conversation of my life. "Thinking about it. I never told you this part, but… she's the one I met in the Bahamas. Haven't been able to stop thinking about her ever since. I want this."

"Dude!" His whole bruised face lights up. "Are you for real right now? Like, really?"

I nod, and for a second, he just stares at me, then suddenly leans over and wraps me in the most aggressive side hug.

"You have to do it," he says.

I laugh. "You think she'll say yes?"

"I'll be shocked if she doesn't," he says. "She's *way* into you, I can tell."

"Oh yeah?"

"Yeah. When she looks at you, her eyes go like this." He gives me dreamy eyes and I crack up as I start the SUV. "And when you look at her, you're like—" He puts his hand over his heart and he starts panting, his eyes completely deranged.

"Oh God, tell me that isn't what I really look like," I say.

His head falls back as he laughs.

"Should we go pick out a ring?" I ask.

"You mean it?" he asks, all excited.

"Let's go put the groceries away and then we'll run to the jeweler."

"Okay!"

It's the fastest I've ever gotten groceries put away, and Sam is jogging to the garage as soon as he's done.

"Let's do this," he calls.

The moment we step into the jewelry store, Sam gets

completely serious, examining rings like it's a science. When the clerk comes over, asking if he can help, Sam says, "We need something meaningful. Something that says 'Penn is in this for life.'"

The guy gives me a look and I just nod, because Sam isn't wrong.

Then Sam points to a three-diamond ring, eyes lighting up. "What do you think about that one?"

I glance at the ring and then at him. "That's gorgeous, buddy. I didn't know you had stellar taste in jewelry."

"It's one of the most exquisite rings we've ever carried," the clerk says, bringing the ring out of the case to show us. He holds it up into the light, and I curse under my breath. "It represents the past, present, and future."

"Three diamonds," Sam says softly. "Like the three of us."

My throat tightens.

I look at the ring again.

And then at Sam.

And then I buy it.

CHAPTER SIXTEEN

IT'S OFFICIAL

ADELINE

Penn stops by my office the next afternoon.

"Hey, come in." I wave him in and he shuts the door behind him.

"Checking in," he says. He sounds nonchalant, but his shoulders are tense and he's watching me carefully.

"Yeah? How's Sam doing?" I ask.

"He's good. Took him shopping yesterday. That was fun. Then Mrs. Murphy stopped by late in the afternoon, and she asked about you. How long we've been dating, that sort of thing. Made me nervous, but I think she bought the Bahamas story." He lifts his shoulder. "I mean it *is* the truth. Mostly, anyway."

I nod, smiling tentatively.

"My parents got in last night. They'll be staying in the guesthouse…I didn't get a chance to show you that the other night, but it's nice and will give them their own space when they need it."

"They could also use my condo if they wanted…since I won't be living there."

He studies me like he can't believe I'm saying this.

"Thank you. We can let them know that when the time comes. Sam went back to school this morning. He loves my parents, so he'll be fine with them being there when he gets home from school. I'm heading out, but I just wanted to check…we're doing this?"

I tilt my head, my shoulders lifting. "I think we are. I've given it a lot of thought and I don't see a better way. And once Mrs. Murphy sees how Sam flourishes in your house, the rest will all fall into place."

"And you really are sure? I mean, there are a few more days if you need to keep thinking about it."

"I get it, Penn." I grin. "My dating life has been pretty dull anyway, and this is worth it. A year will go by fast, I'm sure." I tap my desk. "I think I'll go look for a dress tonight, something simple."

His eyes light up. "Yeah?"

I nod.

"And where are you landing about people being there?" he asks. "Still keeping it to ourselves?"

"I'll do whatever you want, but I think the fewer people there, the better."

"Okay. Can Sam be there? Just since he'll be in the house with us. I do think…" He looks uncomfortable. "I think we shouldn't tell a soul that it isn't real. Not Sam, not our families or friends…no one. It puts them in a bad position if they're asked any questions."

"I agree."

He looks relieved. "Okay then."

"How about Friday we pick Sam up from school and do it then? That way it's just the three of us."

"He'll love that. Wow. *Addy*. I just can't believe you're doing this for me. For Sam. I'm going to be in shock for a long time."

"Are you gonna marry us, Preacher Man?"

He smirks. "Legally, I could, but just to ensure that no questions are raised about the legitimacy of it, I think we should get married at the courthouse with a justice of the peace."

I hold my hand out. "It's your call. Would've been entertaining to hear what you had to say, but whatevs."

He laughs. "I'd rather stay all built up in your mind."

"Oh, is that what you think you are? On a pedestal in my mind?" Ever since he walked into the room, I haven't been able to stop smiling.

He lifts a shoulder. "It's where you are in mine. Especially now."

My cheeks warm. "You really are very sweet."

He gets a funny expression on his face. "Can't say I've been told that before. Hot, fun…crazy…" His eyes crinkle as he laughs. "Sweet doesn't come up much."

"Well, you are. Sam is really lucky to have you, you know that?"

"I'm the lucky one. He's changed my life for the better. I'm still a selfish bastard, but…I care about him."

"You're not a selfish bastard, Penn. If you were, there's no way you'd be considering any of this."

Why make a big deal out of a dress for a wedding that isn't even real? I don't care about it. No big deal. This is just a formality, something to make Penn's life easier.

Yeah, it might not be a real wedding, but I'm damn sure going to look pretty.

The bridal boutique smells like gardenias and childhood dreams. Brides are in there with their mothers and best friends, giggling as they sip champagne and twirl in front of the wall of mirrors.

I feel conspicuous in my aloneness.

The saleswoman, a woman with short grey hair, approaches me. "Shopping for a special occasion?"

"Yes. I need something simple but elegant. A daytime courthouse wedding."

"I've got the perfect thing." She leads me to a row of sleek dresses, all understated but lovely.

I flip through them, trailing my fingers over satin and intricate beading, everything still feeling like too much. But then I see it. A shimmering white with a low neckline that is still tasteful and a back that dips just enough. The hem hits mid-knee and when I hold it up in the light, I can see that it's perfect.

I walk into the fitting room and slip the dress on, my fingers trembling slightly as I zip it up. I exhale when I turn and look in the mirror. This will do.

It takes extraordinary willpower not to call Goldie and tell her everything, not to run to my parents' house and let them in on the plan.

I'm so afraid that I'll say something that I shouldn't, that I don't leave the house for the next couple of days, except to go to work. And then before I know it, it's Friday.

My wedding day.

I spent a little extra time on my hair this morning and it still looks good by that afternoon. The minute I'm able to leave work, I get out of there, hurrying home. It's the earliest I've left since I started. I rush home and brush my teeth, touch up my makeup, and pin one side of my hair back with a pretty clip.

By the time I put on my dress, my hands are trembling. I glance in the mirror and then the clock. Penn should be here any minute, which makes my stomach churn. When I hear a knock at the door, I grab my clutch and swing the door open. Penn is standing there, looking picture-perfect in his suit. He takes me in and I'm glad I made the effort because he definitely notices.

"You look stunning, Addy," he says.

"Thank you. You're looking pretty stunning too."

A muscle ticks in his jaw as we stare at each other.

"Last chance to get out of this," he says.

"I'm sure about this, Penn. Are you?"

"Yes," he says.

I can tell we're both feeling the weight of the day, and that's not all bad. This is bigger than the two of us. We're doing this for a good reason, and I don't think either of us wants to lose sight of that.

"You ready?" he asks, his eyes searching mine.

"Ready."

We're quiet on the way to Sam's school, nerves thick between us. Penn's fingers tap against the steering wheel. When we pull in front of the school, Sam is walking outside, and when he sees us coming, he grins, jogging toward the SUV.

"Hey," he says, tossing his backpack onto the floorboard as he climbs into the back seat. He leans forward, looking between the two of us. "What's going on?"

Penn and I exchange a quick glance before we both smile back at him, maybe a little too brightly. His eyes narrow. The kid's quick. I don't think there's much that gets past him.

"Hello?" His head veers from Penn to me and back to Penn.

Penn clears his throat and tips his chin toward the garment bag next to Sam. "I brought a suit for you."

Sam blinks. "I don't have a suit."

"You do now." Penn grins. "You can change at the courthouse if you want. We've got a wedding to go to."

Sam's eyes bug out. "We're…getting married today?" His voice lifts in surprise. "I mean, you guys? I get to be there? Is everyone else meeting us there?"

Penn shakes his head. "We're just doing something simple for now." When he glances at me, there's something unreadable in his expression. "Maybe we can do the bigger thing later, but we decided we didn't want a big to-do when Addy's just started working for the Mustangs."

That's a good reason for what we're doing. A logical one. But I can't help but wonder if there's a part of Penn that still isn't sure about this. I'm nervous too, but I haven't changed my mind. I still believe this is the only surefire way to get Sam with Penn, and now that I'm getting to know Sam for myself, I want to be part of his life too.

"That makes sense," Sam says, nodding. "Well, I'm really happy that I get to be there with you."

His voice is so sincere, so full of excitement, that it melts my heart all over again.

The courthouse is quiet when we arrive, the halls nearly empty aside from the occasional person passing by. When Sam comes out of the restroom in his suit, Penn and I both go on about how good he looks until the poor boy's cheeks are bright red. He fidgets with the lapel of his suit jacket while we wait. When we step into a small, unremarkable room, the justice of the peace greets us with a friendly but slightly frazzled smile.

"Are you ready to be married?" he asks.

Penn's eyes are heated as he turns to look at me, and my heart flip-flops. *No, no, heart. Don't get all twisted up in Penn Hudson. This is a business arrangement.*

But the way he's looking at me does not feel at all businessy.

"We are," he says, his voice husky.

I nod. "Yes." It comes out as a squeak and I clear my throat and try again. "Yes."

The justice of the peace clears his throat and begins. "We are gathered here today to unite…uh…Penn Evans and Abeline Hudson in holy—"

"Penn Hudson and Adeline Evans," Penn says softly.

"Right. Penn Hud and Abeline Evans," the man says.

"Adeline," Penn and I say at the same time.

"And Penn Hud*son*," Penn adds.

The justice of the peace gets flustered and chuckles. "Sorry! It's been a long day. Let's start over." He clears his throat again. "We are gathered here today to unite…Perry Hudson and Abeline Evans—oh wait."

Sam lets out a choked laugh, covering his mouth.

Penn shakes his head in amusement. "You know what? Let's just roll with it. Perry…Penn…Abeline…Adeline. As long as it's right on the marriage license, we're golden, right?"

We repeat the vows, the words taking on new meaning as we say them to each other. I don't know what the future holds for us, not even a little bit, but my takeaway so far is that we're going to have each other's backs, no matter what. And more importantly, we're going to have Sam's back together.

I'm in for the surprise of my life when we're asked if we have rings. I shake my head, feeling bad that I didn't think of that, and even more when Penn pulls out three…one for him, and two for me. When he slides a slim band with tiny diamonds on my finger and then another more elaborate ring with three large, beautiful diamonds, also surrounded by tiny diamonds, I gasp.

"Penn! This is beautiful!"

Penn grins and tilts his head toward Sam. "He helped me pick it out."

I look at Sam and reach out to squeeze his hand. "It's perfect. Reminds me of the three of us."

Sam's eyes widen and his mouth drops. He looks at Penn and then back at me. "That's what I thought too!" he says, pure excitement in his voice. "Right, Penn?"

"That's exactly what Sam said." Penn puts his hand on Sam's shoulder and the two of them look like they could be related with their brown wavy hair, full lips, and hazel eyes.

"I love it," I tell them both.

Penn hands me his ring and I slide it on his finger. "I'm sorry I didn't think of this," I whisper.

"It's fine," he whispers back. "Yours is the one meant to shine anyway…"

He glances at his hand with the ring on and takes a deep breath.

"This suddenly feels very real," he says, gulping.

I nod. "I know what you mean."

"I'm so glad you're doing this with me…life. From the

night we met in the Bahamas…it's been an adventure," he says.

I press my lips together and nod. "It sure has. And I think we're about to have more."

His lips lift, his eyes crinkling in the corners. "I think you're right about that," he says, kissing my knuckles. "We're in this together."

"In this together," I echo.

We're pronounced husband and wife. The justice of the peace doesn't bother trying to say our names again.

"You may kiss the bride!"

Penn and I stare at each other awkwardly for a moment and then we both step forward. Penn smiles and closes the distance between us. His kiss is soft and so sweet. It lingers longer than I'm expecting and when we part, we blink at each other like we're both in a fog.

"Woohoo! Perry and Abeline!" Sam says quietly, laughing.

Penn and I crack up and turn to hug him before going over to sign the papers.

"I could've just married us myself with my license, but I thought this route would look more official," Penn says. He grins at me as the justice of the peace fumbles with our paperwork. "Not so sure after all this."

"I'll be going over the paperwork thoroughly, don't worry," I whisper as we step forward and look at the marriage license.

Once we've checked the details, we both sign.

"It's official!" Penn says. "Oh, you're taking my name?"

He's got that sexy smirk again as he looks over at me.

"That okay with you?" I ask.

He reaches for my hand, his fingers lacing with mine. "More than okay, Mrs. Hudson."

CHAPTER SEVENTEEN

VE-NUPTIAL-OUS

PENN

On the way home, I look over at Addy. I feel shy around her right now for some reason, and she's acting the same way. I guess we did just do something monumental. It's probably best that I don't think about it too much or I'll freak out.

"I planned a little something for us at home, just the three of us," I tell her.

"That was thoughtful of you," she says.

She takes my fucking breath away. When I saw her in this

shimmering white dress, the neckline drawing my eyes down for a peek, and her face glowing as she opened the door with a bashful smile…she overwhelmed every single one of my senses.

I am in over my head.

The food arrives not long after we get home, caterers carrying in filet mignon, roasted vegetables, and mashed potatoes. They place the food on the table, and I hold out a chair for Addy and then light the candles. I want this to be a special night. Not that Addy or Sam expect perfection from me, but I want both of them to know that they're important to me.

When the caterers leave, Addy looks at me. "Penn, this is beautiful. Thank you."

I lift a bottle of red wine and she nods. I pour her a glass and then open the sparkling cider Sam likes. "It's a big night. Felt like we should celebrate."

"So, this is…your honeymoon?" Sam asks, eyes round.

"Uh, technically, yeah, I, uh, I guess it is," I stutter.

He grins at me and I roll my eyes. Nothing like a little tweener making you feel all kinds of exposed.

"We're not doing the typical honeymoon," Addy says, her eyes meeting mine while she tries to cover for me. "I can't take off work so soon after starting my new job, and the preseason starts next weekend…" She grins at me and scrunches her nose. "We didn't plan this wedding very well, did we?" She lifts her shoulder in a shrug.

"I thought it was really nice," Sam says. "You both look really good."

"Thank you, Sam," Addy says. "And you in that suit… you look so handsome."

His cheeks turn pink and he digs into his steak as he mumbles his thanks.

The dinner is nice and easy. Addy asks Sam about school and he talks about a book he's reading. Addy's eyes soften as she watches him, and I swear, I think she's looking at me a little differently tonight. Is that wishful thinking on my part?

After we've eaten warm raspberry cobbler with vanilla ice cream, Sam leans back in his chair. "I have a surprise for you guys."

"You guys are full of surprises tonight," Addy teases.

"Oh, just wait." Sam grins. "Come on, let's go outside."

We follow him into the backyard, past the trees and to the small wooden bridge that goes over the creek. The creek winds its way to the lake and as the sun sets, the night air cool around us, we walk up the bridge and stand in the middle. The view is beautiful from the bridge.

Sam pulls out his phone, pressing something, and suddenly, the speakers blast "Die With a Smile" by Lady Gaga and Bruno Mars at full volume.

I laugh, shaking my head. "Wow, he's going all in."

Addy giggles, and even harder when Sam shouts, "Dance, lovebirds!"

The mood is electric between us. The music, the way the moonlight hits Addy's face, the way my heart kicks up when she steps closer...I feel like my heart is going to pound right out of my chest. I take her hand, pulling her close, and we sway to the beat. It's supposed to be playful, but there's nothing about the way my pulse pounds or how she looks at me, like she's trying to figure me out. Or memorize me. I can't get enough of looking at her.

I lean in, my voice just loud enough for her to hear. "We really should make this look as real as possible."

"Mm-hmm," she murmurs, eyes glinting.

Next, I do the only thing that makes sense. Or maybe it's senseless, I'm not sure which. But I kiss her. Our kiss at the courthouse felt like a tease, and this does even more. I can't get close enough to her. My entire body tightens. She melts into me, and I deepen the kiss. Everything about it is perfect and not enough. When we finally pull back, she looks breathless, and I want nothing more than to kiss her again.

We stare at each other for a moment before Sam shouts, "Woohoo! Nailed it!"

Addy laughs, her forehead resting against mine for a second before we step apart.

"So, how do we tell everyone?" I ask, still a little dazed. "The thread with the guys is going nuts because I've been quieter than usual this week."

She exhales, pushing her hair over her shoulder. "A surprise party tomorrow night? Here at the house, you think?"

"We could start by telling my parents tonight. Your parents too, if you want."

Her eyes widen. "Oh. Wow. Okay. Let's start with yours."

I take her hand, squeezing it. "They're gonna love you."

"They won't be mad that we did this without them?"

"I vote we go with we just couldn't wait. Blame it on how in love we are that we couldn't wait like two rational human beings?"

She giggles again and it goes straight to my dick. Oh, this is so going to be a problem.

"Okay, got it. You just couldn't live without me another day," she says.

"No. *You* were dying to be with *me.*"

"Mm-hmm, keep telling yourself that," she says airily.

We make our way to the cottage, motioning for Sam to follow us as we go, and I knock on the door. My mom answers, eyes going straight to where Addy's hand is linked with mine.

"Well, hello," she says. "You all look so beautiful! What's the occasion?"

My dad walks up behind Mom and he grins at us. "Wow. I feel underdressed. Looking good, you guys."

"Mom, Dad, this is Addy. Adeline Evans...uh—" I freeze when I remember she's Adeline Hudson now. "Addy, meet my parents, Margo and Jeremy Hudson."

Addy lifts her hand in a small, polite wave. "It's really nice to meet you."

Dad leans against the doorway, raising an eyebrow. "Penn hasn't scared you off yet? Impressive."

"Oh, he's trying," Addy deadpans, and my parents burst into laughter.

We step inside, my parents hugging Sam, and then Mom motions for us to sit on the couch.

"I'm so glad you stopped by. Are you on your way out? It's great to meet you, Addy," Mom says. "I could've had dinner ready for us. We've been kind of wiped out from the drive, but we're starting to feel a little perkier tonight."

"We have something to tell you," I jump in, unable to keep holding it back. "We got married. Tonight. Eloped."

Their expressions are stunned and then morph into joy.

"What?" my mom asks. "Oh my goodness!" She gets up and walks across the room to hug us. "Congratulations! This is...I can't believe it!"

My dad comes over and hugs us too. "I have to confess that I sometimes wondered if it would ever happen for you, son!" he says. "I know you must have wanted to marry her *bad* for you to elope," he teases. He points his thumb toward me. "This guy likes to make a splash, Addy, as I'm sure you're aware."

Her eyes are dancing as she looks at me and laughs.

"Well, he does want to throw a surprise party tomorrow night where we can announce it to everyone."

"That's a great idea!" Mom says. She tilts her head. "You did pick a crazy time to do this, so I suppose a honeymoon is out of the question." She laughs and shakes her head. "Married!" She pats my cheek, beaming up at me. "So happy for you, son." She looks at Addy and squeezes her hand. "I already know you're really special. He's never been one to even bring a girl home for dinner, so this is just…the best news."

Addy's shoulders relax and she laughs when my dad says, "We were starting to think he'd never settle down."

"What do you think about all this, Sam?" Mom asks.

Sam is next to me on the couch and he leans forward so he can see both me and Addy. "All the girls like Penn, but I've never seen him look all dopey at one like he does at you, Addy."

My mouth drops as the room erupts in laughter.

"Dude," I say, nudging Sam.

He lifts a shoulder. "Just calling it like I see it."

We hang out another half hour or so and then I stand, saying we should probably let them rest. My parents are the ones giving dopey expressions like *sure, that's why you're leaving, so* we *can rest.* I roll my eyes at them and hugs are shared all around.

"Let us know what we can do to help," Mom says.

"Will do," I say. "Love you guys."

On the walk back to my house, I pull out my phone and type out a group text to the guys.

> Party at my house tomorrow night. Be there. Please.

HENLEY

Why does this sound like an intervention?

BOWIE

I need more details before I commit.

RHODES

We'll be there. That goes for you too, Bowie. Should I bring snacks?

WESTON

We grilling?

> Sounds good to me. And no need for snacks. I'll provide everything. Just be there. Please..

RHODES

It's the second time he's said please, guys. I'm smellin' something serious.

BOWIE

You're not pregnant, are you?

WESTON

I think you're projecting. You and Poppy are the ones who keep popping out babies.

HENLEY

He didn't say no.

> GOODNIGHT.

Sam chats happily about the party. When we step inside the house, he pulls out his phone and shows us the pictures he took of us at the wedding and even a few of us dancing on the bridge.

"These are so good, Sam!" Addy says in surprise.

"Sam's become a great photographer the past couple of years," I say proudly.

"Thanks to this phone you gave me," Sam says.

I study the pictures. "They turned out great, buddy. Thanks for taking these. I think we should frame a few. And why don't we take one of the three of us right here." I place the phone on the fireplace mantel and set the timer, rushing back over to stand by them, Addy front and center. We smile and when we're done, Sam rushes over to see if it's any good.

He smiles and shows us the picture.

"It's perfect," I say, bumping his fist.

"This has been the best night," he says.

I wrap my arm around him and hold my other arm out for Addy. She steps in and hugs him too.

I echo Sam's words and mean them with everything in me. "The very best night."

CHAPTER EIGHTEEN

CONFRONTATIONS AND REVELATIONS

ADELINE

I've felt more relaxed than I expected to…after marrying Penn. Wow. That's going to be weird for a while. I'm Penn Hudson's wife. Crazy.

I'd say the wedding went without a hitch.

Met Penn's parents and that went well.

Sam goes to bed and the house is suddenly quiet. I glance at Penn, more than a little tense for the first time all night.

"How about we go tell my parents tomorrow morning?"

He exhales and nods. "That sounds good to me. I'm nervous about that one."

"Yeah, me too."

"Do you need anything from your condo tonight?"

"No, I brought a little suitcase."

He nods and glances at me, making a face. "Does it make it weird for me to admit I've never had a woman spend the night here?"

"What? You're kidding."

He puts his hand on the back of his head and laughs. "Yeah…no. I…when I'm home, it's my sacred space. I've never wanted anyone coming in and disrupting that."

"This must be so weird for you, having me here."

"It's actually not. And *that* is what's weird for me…how happy I am to have you here, in my space."

"Well, I can totally give you more space." My hand flies out. "You've got a zillion bedrooms and I can even go to my condo if you're needing a break from me altogether."

His head tilts and he shakes his head slightly. "I won't want you to go to your condo. Except just say when you need to go get your things."

"I'll need to get my car and a few boxes while we're out tomorrow."

"Okay. You know…you don't have to keep the condo unless you just want to." He puts his hand on my waist and I go still. "I'll respect whatever you need to do to be comfortable, but like you said, there are a zillion rooms. I thought you'd stay in my room with me…you know, so no one suspects anything." His hand drops like he's suddenly realized he was touching me.

"Right," I say, sounding winded. "Yeah, that would probably make it most convincing."

"I promise I'll be the perfect gentleman," he says.

My teeth scrape over my bottom lip and his gaze drops there.

I'm not sure I want him to be a perfect gentleman. Pretty sure I don't.

I clear my throat. "Okay. Lead the way."

He shows me around some of the rooms upstairs and then opens his door with a flourish.

"Welcome home," he says.

"Your house is really pretty, Penn. I know I told you the other night, but…I love it."

"Thank you. I'm glad you do. I hope you'll be comfortable here."

We sound a little stilted, but when he sets my suitcase down and motions for me to look at the huge his and hers closets, a massive bathroom in the middle, I'm blown away. There's a gorgeous chandelier in my closet, with a big island in the middle with drawers, and all the shelves lining the walls are empty.

"All yours," he says simply.

I peek into the bathroom again. The huge tub is big enough for three or four people, and the exquisite glass shower…the lap of luxury. My parents' house is stunning, but it's not anything close to this. There's a separate small room for the toilet, which I'm happy about.

"You think you can make do with this?" he asks.

"Um, yeah." I laugh.

I get my toiletry bag out of the suitcase, and when I walk into the bathroom, Penn is brushing his teeth, his electric toothbrush buzzing in his hand. I decide to brush mine too, and we stand side by side, brushing away.

I try not to laugh, but it bubbles up anyway. "I can't believe we got married," I mutter.

Penn looks at me in the mirror, a little toothpaste on his lips as he keeps brushing. "This is feeling very domestic."

I laugh harder. "Definitely a first for me too."

"You've never lived with a boyfriend or anything?"

I shake my head. "Never."

"It's like we're virgins or something," he says, snorting before he's gotten it all the way out.

"Not exactly."

"No, not at all." He chuckles and moves toward his closet.

I wash my face, then change into a cute short pajama set. When I walk into the bedroom, Penn is walking out of his closet and he's in pajama pants, no shirt. My mouth goes dry and I try not to look at him, but it's impossible. He is a perfect, ripped, beautiful specimen of a man. He has a sleeve of tattoos and a few on his chest and torso. I drink him in. It'd be a crime not to enjoy the view.

He turns off the main light, so the only light comes from one of the lamps on the bedside table. The house is quiet, much quieter than my condo.

"Do you have a side?" I ask.

"I start out on this one…but I don't always wake up here," he admits sheepishly.

I go to the opposite side and pull back the covers. "Ah, so you're saying you're a restless sleeper?"

"I don't really know. I guess you'll have to tell me. I apologize in advance if I snore. No clue whether I do or not."

"Same," I tell him.

He pulls the covers back on his side and looks at me. I've climbed in and am trying not to drool as I look up at him. My heart gallops so hard, I'm certain he can probably hear it.

When he slides in beside me, his body warm next to mine, I forget to breathe. We lie there for a few moments, silent.

"Well," he says, finally breaking the silence. "This has gotta be the strangest night of my life."

I laugh softly. "One hundred percent. Didn't see myself getting married so soon. Didn't expect just pillow talk on my wedding night. But it's actually pretty nice."

His husky laugh skitters over my skin and I shiver.

"You cold?"

"No, I'm good. You? Is it hitting you yet that we've done this?"

"I think it's starting to. I'm really grateful, you know? Seeing how happy Sam is…that…it means everything, Addy. Thank you."

"Him picking out that song." I giggle. "He told me later that he asked one of his girlfriends at school what the most romantic song is and she said that one."

He swipes his hand down his face, his laugh shaking the bed. "He's the best, isn't he?"

"He really is."

We talk for a while, just random things, nothing too serious. But there's something comforting about the way we talk now, so easy, like we've always done it. I can't imagine falling asleep tonight, my mind buzzing with what we've done, but before I know it, I'm drifting off, lulled by the sound of his deep voice. And then we're both quiet, and it's so peaceful.

For all the warm fuzzies, the lust that takes over my body every time I'm around him, and the way I feel when he looks at me, and how hard he makes my heart pound, the last thought I have before I fall asleep is that maybe Penn and I can do this. Maybe we can be friends and raise this little boy together. Maybe putting Sam first will be the best thing we ever do.

"I'm honored to be part of this," I whisper.

He reaches out and touches his pinkie to mine, linking them together.

When I wake up, the sunlight is streaming through the blinds, and for a moment, everything is fuzzy. Then I realize why I'm so hot. Penn's body is pressed against mine, his chest firm against my back, his arm wrapped around me, hand splayed over my stomach, skin on skin.

I freeze, trying not to move or breathe so I don't wake him up, but then I feel it—how hard he is. My breath catches in my throat. I resist the strong urge to arch into him, but I can't deny the heat spreading through me.

Penn stirs, and I feel him tense against me. Then he grumbles softly, his voice thick with sleep. "I'm making this awkward, huh?"

I can't help it. A little laugh escapes me, too breathy... probably totally confirming how turned on I am. "A little."

"I will slowly back away," he says playfully. He backs away slightly and I miss his warmth, but his hand stays in place, and I'm glad for it. Too glad.

I clear my throat, but my voice comes out a little shaky. "I slept better than I have in a long, long time."

"Honestly, so did I."

"You sound really surprised."

"I am," he says, laughing. "For how much I want you, I can't believe I ever fell asleep with you in my bed." His fingers linger and then gradually slide off of me. "I should probably keep my hands to myself."

I want to say, *don't you dare go anywhere*, but instead, I say, "Are you relieved that we slept?"

"Well, I think maybe it's going to work out after all...but fuck me, it's going to be hard."

It's quiet for a beat, and then I say, "In more ways than one."

We both laugh a little too loudly at that. I glance at him over my shoulder and his eyes drink me in.

"It's hard for me too," I whisper.

His lips lift. "It helps to hear that."

I nod and then turn away from him. It's too tempting to look at him and not climb him. "We should make a fun breakfast for Sam and then go tell my parents."

He groans. "I was hoping you'd forget about telling them just yet."

"Ha. Not possible. Once we tell them, I think I can relax a little more. And telling the team...I'm nervous about that."

He puts his hand on my shoulder. "The team will be fine. They're gonna freak out that I've settled down, but they'll be happy for us. It's your dad I'm worried about."

Now I groan. "Let's go get it over with."

Driving up to my parents' house, I feel queasy. This is ridiculous. I'm reverting to my childhood, that feeling I'd get before knowing I'd be grounded.

My mom answers the door and quickly covers her surprise over seeing Penn, pulling me in for a hug.

"I was so happy when you said you were coming over. It's fun to see you here, Penn," she says, smiling warmly as she hugs him too. "Hello."

"Hello, Mrs. Evans."

"Please, call me Danielle." She laughs.

He nods, his dimple popping out with his smile. My heart does that little flutter.

"Dad's here, right? We were hoping to talk to both of you."

My mom's eyebrows lift. "Yes, he is." She turns and

yells, "Rex! Adeline's here." She motions for us to follow her and we go to the living room. Usually our big hangout is in the oversized kitchen, so my nerves amp up a little more.

I sit stiffly on the couch, my fingers laced so tightly that my knuckles ache. Penn is next to me, his posture tense. He puts his hand on my back and rubs it slightly, until the sound of my dad jogging down the stairs. He leans forward, resting his elbows on his knees. My dad walks in, all smiles…until he sees Penn.

"Hey, baby girl. Penn. What's this about?" he asks.

My parents sit across from us, my dad's face unreadable, and even my mom looks nervous now. I've rehearsed what I would say on the way over here, but now that it's time, my throat feels tight.

"I wanted to tell you in person," I begin, my voice shaky. "Penn and I…we got married."

My mom gasps, bringing a hand to her chest. But it's my dad's reaction that I fear the most. His expression hardens instantly, his eyes snapping to Penn's like a laser.

He leans forward and points at Penn. "You married my daughter," he says, his tone cold. "And you didn't think to ask me first?"

Penn exhales slowly. "You're right. I should've. I know this isn't what you expected, sir. But Addy and I—"

"Dad, it's a whirlwind, we know, but—"

"He is the last person you should've married!" Dad yells, standing up and walking behind the couch.

"Coach, with respect—what is it that you dislike about me so much?" Penn asks. I'm proud of how respectful yet firm he sounds. "I've wondered this for a while now."

My dad's eyes narrow. "You're a player. And I'm not talking football. You're never seen with the same woman twice. You don't take anything seriously. I see what's written about you on social media. And now you think you're ready to settle down with my daughter?"

Penn stiffens next to me. He turns back and looks at me, swallowing hard. I can see the pain in his eyes. He looks at a loss for words. I take his hand, threading our fingers together.

I turn to my mom, hoping she'll understand. "Mom, remember that guy I told you I met in the Bahamas?" My voice is soft and vulnerable. "It was Penn."

Her eyes widen slightly, and she glances at my dad before looking back at me. "You told me he made you laugh," she murmurs. "And that something magical happened in those hours together…"

"We care about each other," I say.

"But is that love, Addy?" Concern laces her words. "Why move so fast? Marriage is a big deal. You hardly know one another."

Before I can answer, Penn speaks up. His voice sounds steadier now, but there's something raw beneath it. "I fell hard for her the night we met. I haven't gone out with another person since then."

I whip my head toward him, blinking in shock. I had no idea.

He turns back to my dad, and his jaw is tight, but his eyes are open and honest. "I love and respect your daughter, and I promise I won't let her down. I'll take care of her and do all I can to make her happy."

My mom swallows hard, emotions flickering across her face.

"I'm not sure you're capable of any of that," Dad says.

"I'm definitely on a learning curve, but I'm quick." Penn smiles at me. "It feels like we're learning as we go, but I believe we've got what it takes."

"I don't love that you're practicing on my daughter," Dad grumbles.

"Dad," I sigh.

"You can straighten me out if I mess up," Penn says earnestly. "Haven't I listened to you out on the field? I'll listen now too."

My dad stares at him. I can see his shoulders relaxing slightly. It's small, but I see him softening the tiniest bit.

"Okay," he says finally. "I'll be watching." His lips twitch like he might be joking, but we all know he's not.

"We love each other," I add, feeling more hopeful now. "And we love Sam, the little boy Penn has mentored for years. He's quickly gotten into my heart too, and you'll love him." I look between them, searching for something—anything that tells me they hear me. "Give Penn a chance, please. You taught me to make smart choices. Trust that I've done the same here. Be happy for us. Please."

The silence that follows is suffocating. My dad's gaze is still sharp, still skeptical. But my mom…she's warming up to the idea. I see it in the way her lips press together, and her eyes shine just a little.

"We're having a party tonight, where we'll tell our friends and the team," I say.

"They don't know yet?" Dad asks.

I shake my head. "No, we wanted to let you know before that."

My dad takes that in and it disarms him somewhat.

"We'd love to have you there," Penn adds.

"You're not pregnant, right?" Dad asks.

"Dad! No," I say, my cheeks flaming.

He scowls. "Well, that's one plus. You can't blame me for wondering, though."

I sigh. "I guess you're right. But I'm not. Please come tonight. It wouldn't be the same without you there."

CHAPTER NINETEEN

THANK GOODNESS THERE'S CRYSTAL

PENN

I've played in front of thousands of screaming fans, pressure so thick it's crushing. But standing in front of my teammates, telling them I got married? Yeah, this might actually kill me. I'm most concerned about telling the Single Dad Players... the name I've mercilessly made fun of and that literally does not fit any of us any longer. They're my best friends and I've avoided talking to them for the first time since we all got close because I knew I wouldn't be able to hold it in, and I didn't want anyone trying to talk me out of it. Or the risk that I'd tell them what's really going on. I trust that they'd have my back and cover for us in any way when it comes to Sam—I just don't want to put them in that position.

So, we're going with the love route. And honestly? It's not that far-fetched. They know more than anyone how far gone I am over Addy.

We have quite a spread, and at the right moment, we'll wheel out a beautiful wedding cake. Addy's in a beautiful red dress that is knocking me sideways, and I've thrown a jacket over a black T-shirt and jeans so I match her a little better. I think it catches everyone off guard that we're dressed up for this impromptu party.

I look around at my teammates. Even Addy's best friend, Goldie, and Cam fucking Whitman are here. I smile smugly at the bastard. I can admit again how fucking handsome he is now that Addy is married to me.

"All right, listen up," I say, clapping my hands together.

I reach out and take Addy's hand, and the room falls to a hush. I smile over at her and everything inside me settles.

"We have an announcement to make," I say, still looking at Addy. "As some of you know, I went to the Bahamas to celebrate with Bowie and Poppy...and I came home thinking about a girl named Addy. I met her and she turned my world upside down. I couldn't forget her...and I couldn't stop wishing for another chance with her. Here we are, months later, and I've been given that chance. I intend to let her know how I feel about her for the rest of our lives." I lift up our hands, holding them up so her rings show, and hold up my other hand, ring finger out. There's an audible gasp across the room. "We got married."

Dead silence.

Someone drops a plate and it clatters, which makes my

lips twitch. Rhodes blinks. Elle puts her hand up to her mouth. Bowie looks like he's seen a ghost, and Poppy clutches her basketball stomach.

Then the freak-out begins.

"*What?*" Henley shouts, rushing toward us. "Are you —HOW?"

"Oh my God," Sadie and Tru say at the same time.

Weston puts his hand on his chest and then staggers over to me. He and Henley hug me, and then we're surrounded, everyone talking at once.

"What were you thinking?"

"Congratulations!"

"Were you drugged?"

That pulls me out of it and I turn to look around for whoever said it. "No, I was not drugged. Relax. I got married. And I'm happy about it."

Weston throws his head back and laughs. "My God," he gasps, wiping his eyes. "Adeline, you got the king of commitment issues to settle down. This is historic."

"It *is* shocking," Henley says. "I need a drink."

"I'm in shock, that's what this is," Rhodes says.

Bowie shakes his head, but he's smiling. The dude has softened so much since meeting Poppy. "I just…have so many questions."

Sam squeezes through and his head pops up between me and the guys. "Isn't it the best news?"

"I mean, yeah. It's phenomenal," Rhodes says. "But you went from not even dating to married? I am shook. So happy, but shooketh."

I rub the back of my neck. "I guess I just hadn't met the right person before."

Weston laughs again. "And you've gone soft, just like that. Happens to the best of us."

"I'm not soft," I argue, even though I know damn well I'm as soft as a marshmallow when it comes to Addy.

"Out of all the women you've ever met, Addy is the one," Henley says, his eyes filling as he looks between the two of us. "Addy, we've always known that when Penn finally fell, he'd fall the hardest, and I have to say, before you ever even came back to Silver Hills, he was pining for the woman he met in the Bahamas. You got in his head from the very start."

My cheeks heat and I look at Addy shyly. She's smiling at me, her gaze not wavering. I reach for her again, needing her to anchor me again. "Yes, she got in my head for sure."

"Pretty boy's in love!" Henley yells. He wipes his eyes. "God, this is making me so emotional."

Everyone laughs, but Rhodes and Weston are wiping their eyes too.

"Well, damn. Adeline Evans, you tamed Penn Hudson," Rhodes says. "How does it feel?"

"Pretty damn great," she says softly. "I couldn't stop thinking about him either."

"This calls for a dance!" Weston yells. "We weren't really prepared, but I think we could manage something, don't you?"

I start laughing. "Shit, you guys. Don't run her off before we're even getting started."

"She married you, she's not going anywhere," Rhodes says, squeezing my shoulder. "Elle baby, find us the right song."

Elle holds up her phone and waves it. "On it!"

The sound of "Womanizer" by Britney Spears blasts through my speakers. I turn to Elle in horror.

"What are you doing?" I ask.

She laughs. "We're saying goodbye to the Womanizer. You-you-you *aren't*, you-you you *aren't*," she sings before the song even gets going. "We'll change it to fit you now. Boys, get in place. Penn, that goes for you too. Does your new bride know you and your boys have a thing for dancing to Britney?"

I glance at Addy and smirk at her incredulous face, kissing her knuckles before going out in the middle of the floor with my boys. Everyone else clears out to the sides to give us our space, and I get in the center, flipping my hair like I'm Britney. The room roars in laughter and a few throw their napkins at me. I shimmy, my eyes never leaving Addy's, and for the next several minutes we shake our asses off. Her head falls back as she laughs at us, and I'm sweating by the time we're done, laughing so hard myself.

I walk over to Addy and she throws her arms around me, still cracking up. "That was the best thing I've ever seen!" she says in my ear.

We hug and when we pull back and look at each other, there's a mass tinkling of the glasses. We stare at each other as the sound gets louder.

"I guess we should give them what they want," I say.

"Yep, I think so." She grins.

I lean in and kiss her and just about lose my mind. She feels so good, tastes so good. The room erupts in cheers and laughter, and Addy and I are laughing too when we finally part. Her eyes are bright when she looks up at me. I'm weak all over as I stare at her, like my legs might give out. It's the weirdest feeling.

When I finally break my gaze from hers, I see her dad glaring at me.

Great, her parents decided to come.

I'm happy they're here, I really am. I don't want to do anything to jeopardize her relationship with them, but holy shit, Coach Evans does not look happy.

Addy's eyes are still dazed when I look at her again and it makes me smile. "How about we go say hi to your parents?"

That seems to clear her fog. "Oh, good idea. Let's take Sam with us."

I laugh. "Even better idea."

Sam's talking with Henley's daughters, Cassidy and Audrey. I go over there and put my arm on his shoulder. "I hate to interrupt, but can we steal you for a few minutes? I'd like you to come say hello to Addy's parents."

Sam manages to tear his eyes away from Cassidy and nods up at me. His cheeks are pink and I want to tease him so bad about his crush on Cassidy, but I resist. It's not the time and I wouldn't do it in front of her anyway, but it's so tempting.

"Yeah, for sure," Sam says, his head bobbing.

I grin at him and am surprised when Addy's fingers thread through mine. I love having reasons to touch each other now. "Let's do this."

We walk toward her parents and when we reach them, Addy hugs them both. And then she puts her hand on Sam's shoulder. "I believe you've met Sam before? Mom, I'm not sure if you have. Sam, this is my mom, Danielle, and my dad, Rex."

"Nice to meet you, Mrs. Danielle." He shakes her hand.

I could not be prouder of him than I am right now. When we first met, he was a great kid—kind and considerate and smart—but the confidence he's gained over the past couple of years has been awesome to see.

I can tell they're impressed too.

"It's so nice to meet you, Sam. You sure look handsome tonight," Danielle says.

"Thank you." He ducks his head but doesn't break eye contact with her. And then he reaches out to shake Coach's hand, meeting his eyes. "And good to see you again, Coach Evans."

"Well, hello, Sam," Coach says. "Yes, I remember you. That's quite the shiner you've got there. You doing okay?"

Sam touches his eye and makes a face. "Much better now."

"You were interested in football, if I remember correctly?" Coach asks.

"Yes, sir. Penn put me in a football camp earlier this summer and he says I'm improving all the time."

"He's a better running back than I was at his age, no question," I say proudly.

Sam's face glows with the praise.

Coach studies me with an unreadable expression before looking back at Sam. "I hope to see you at one of our games this season."

"I can't wait. Addy says that since I'm living here now, I'll get to go to all the home games."

Addy's dad looks between me and his daughter. "He's living with you?"

"I've been trying to get custody of Sam for a long time now." I put my hand on Sam's shoulder and he leans into me. "Unfortunately, it took really awful circumstances for them to okay it, but my lawyer is confident that we'll be able to keep him with us now."

He doesn't say anything, just studies us. I shift uncomfortably and Addy squeezes my hand. I look at her and lift her hand to my lips, unable to resist kissing her soft skin, even in front of her dad. Her cheeks bloom with color and I freaking love it when that happens.

I wave my parents over. "You've met my parents before, I believe?"

My mom smiles warmly at Danielle, and my dad shakes

Coach's hand. I feel better knowing that they're here and they have my back.

"Did you know about all this?" Coach asks my dad.

"Only after the fact, like you," Dad says.

That seems to appease Coach somewhat.

"Should we have cake now?" I ask.

"I'd love cake," Addy says, smiling up at me.

I grin at her, my heart doing its skip over itself. I guess I should be getting used to this feeling now, since it's happening all the time around her, but I'm so not. It's exhilarating and terrifying.

My mom steps out in front of us. "Can I take a few pictures of you outside? The flowers look so pretty out there."

"Sure, Mom." I glance at Addy. "And then cake."

She grins and we step outside. My mom leads us to the flowers and they do look gorgeous.

"Great idea," I tell her.

We pose for a few photos and then my mom grins. "Okay, lighten up, you two. Let's have some fun with this."

Addy laughs nervously. I take my jacket off and toss it on a bench, and then I tug Addy toward me. I twirl her around and then lift her up. Her hands move to my hair and she smiles down at me.

For a few frozen moments, I forget that we have a houseful of people and I stare up at the beautiful woman who agreed to be my wife.

"You're beautiful," I say, looking up at her.

"Oh, that's perfect," my mom says, startling us.

I slowly lower Addy to the ground and kiss her forehead.

"Did you get some good ones?" I ask.

"I did," Mom says. "The two of you are absolutely gorgeous together."

I grin at Addy and her cheeks flush.

"Cake?" I ask her.

She nods, her lips lifting in a shy smile.

We walk to the house and when we walk inside, we stop in front of the beautiful cake. The design was all Addy's idea. It's smooth and has this elaborate beading around the bottom edges that looks like little pearls, but it's all icing. It's entirely too pretty to eat, but having had Greer and Wyndham's cakes before from Serendipity, I know it's going to be delicious… which is all I cared about. But I'm pretty damn impressed about the way it looks too.

We printed the pictures Sam took and have them in frames around the cake.

"Hey, everyone, come to the kitchen," I yell, like I have no care in the world, when all I can think about is *what the fuck is this woman doing to me?*

Our guests trickle into the room, and everyone gathers around us. More pictures are taken as we cut the cake together. I feed Addy's piece to her gently, and I think she's going to do the same with me, but then at the last second, she smooshes it into my face. I stare at her in shock while she laughs her fine ass off, and I tug her toward me.

"Are you going to help me get this off?" I ask, my voice low.

She reaches out for a cloth to wipe my face and I hold onto her wrist, pausing it in place.

"Kiss me first." My tone is playful but demanding, and her body sort of sways against me. I remove some of the frosting with my thumb and swipe it over her lower lip.

Her eyes widen and then dart between mine as she laughs. Her tongue peeks out to lick her bottom lip. I get hard instantly and now there's no way I can back away. Everyone in this room will be aware of my situation.

The tinkling of the crystal amps up and Addy straightens.

I put my hands on her cheeks and she stands on her tiptoes, meeting me the rest of the way. When her lips touch mine, it's like an explosion of color going off behind my closed eyelids. I keep it chaste because I don't want to embarrass her. I've been at weddings before where I saw way more tongue than I wanted to see and I won't do that to Addy, but goddamn, do I want to. I want to pillage her mouth with mine and never come up for air.

Eventually, we break apart and I lean my forehead against hers. "I hope they do that with the glasses all night, so I can keep having an excuse to kiss you."

"Do you need an excuse?" She reaches up to smear off the lipstick she left behind.

I smirk. "If I have your permission, I'll kiss you all night long."

Her hands drop from me and she turns to get our cake plates. And then she looks at me over her shoulder and smirks right back. "You have my permission."

Hot damn. It is on.

CHAPTER TWENTY

HEART TO HEART TO HEART

ADELINE

"What is that?" Sam asks Penn.

Everyone has left and we've spent the past thirty minutes cleaning everything up. Penn's parents and the girls helped a lot before they left, so it wasn't too bad.

"You've never seen this?" Penn lifts the blue notebook he's holding. "I would've thought you'd seen it by now. This is gold right here. It's The Single Dad Playbook."

"Oh, that's the book? I've heard about it. It's looking kinda old."

Penn holds the book up and assesses it. "I guess it has seen better days, hasn't it? We've been writing in it for a few years now and it's been everywhere."

My interest is piqued by now. "Who writes in it?"

"Henley, Weston, Bowie, Rhodes…and me."

"But you're not a dad, and they're not single." I tilt my head and point at him, laughing. "And you aren't either now. How does that work?"

He chuckles. "Right on all accounts. We started writing in this when we were all single, and yeah, technically I had no business being in the group or the book, but I weaseled my way into both." Penn lifts a shoulder and Sam and I laugh at him. "We started it when Weston found out he had a son and it's just continued from there. It's been like therapy for me at times. I love reading what the guys have to say. When I need help with something or have thoughts on life or whatever, I write it in here."

"I love that." I walk over and lean against the chair. "I think that's really sweet."

"Want to see what they said today? They were writing in it before they left."

"If you're comfortable showing us," I say.

"I screened it first," Penn says, laughing.

He flips open the book and goes to a place close to the back.

"It's almost full!" I say.

He nods. "Yeah, we'll have to start a new one pretty soon."

He turns the book so I can see it better and Sam moves next to me so he can see too.

Our pretty boy is all grown up.
A wife! I'd wondered if I'd ever see the day.
I could not be happier for you, Penn.
And having Sam finally…
I know that's what you've wanted for so long.
You just thought you were the shit before.
Having the two of them in your life full-time
has already upped your cool factor by, like…
One hundred percent.
But I'm sure you already knew that.
Love you, man.
This is the best surprise ever.
~Henley

Penn looks up at me and grins when he sees my cheesy smile. "I love your friendships with them."

He nods. "They've made my life better, no question."

I keep reading.

I'm so glad you weren't too proud to give in to love.
I almost was,
And I think about it all the time…
How I almost missed out on what is
the best part of my life.
Loving Poppy, loving Becca and Jonas
and this little baby on the way…
It's happiness like I've never known.
Go in with your eyes and heart wide open.
I get now why the guys were so pro "settling down."
And trust me, you'll get it too, if you haven't already.

~Bowie

I fan my face, feeling like I might cry. "These are the sweetest messages. Man, melt my heart."

He laughs. "Yeah, even the big man Bowie is complete mush now. Never thought I'd see the day."

I can't even be mad that we missed your wedding, Penn.
I'm just so damn happy for you.
You've been the best friend I could ask for,
And this is all I've wanted for you.
When you came back from the Bahamas
talking about Addy,
and still were months later,
I knew you'd been hit with a lightning bolt.
It's probably the only way it would've
worked for you, honestly.
For you to be struck stupid over this woman.
<Insert maniacal laugh here>
You're gonna be a fan-fucking-tastic husband.
And I love that Sam will grow up
having two people who have his back.
He's got all of us,
but living in a home with the two of you loving him,
loving each other…
Damn, now I'm crying.
It's just a beautiful thing.
Love you so much, man.
Enjoy the ride.
~Weston

. . .

I wipe my face as the tears drip down. Sam leans his head over on my shoulder and I put my arm around him.

"I do want you to know we have your back," I tell him. "And these guys all have your back too," I say, pointing at the book.

He nods, his lower lip trembling. "I do know it." He wipes his eye with his fist and Penn gets up and puts his arms around both of us.

"There's one more I haven't read," I say. I move the book closer but don't let go of Sam. Penn's fingers are rubbing small circles on my lower back, and my insides warm, my heart doubling in size.

You're the last man down for the count!
No more singles in The Single Dad Playbook.
One of the next meeting's topics:
Considering what our new name will be
since we can't be the Single Dad Players any longer.
Penn, my man, I know you didn't see this coming,
But I knew love would hunt you down one of these days.
Sorry, not sorry that I will never stop
giving you shit about it.
I mean, think about it, you were adamant
that you wouldn't be going down this path, right?
Love is such a fucking bitch.
And you, my friend,
have been bitch-slapped into the next millennium.
This fact is going to make me belly laugh
for the next year, minimum.
Just making that clear right here, right now.

The way you love Sam,
the way you love your friends, your family...
You deserve every bit of goodness in your life.
And the way you look utterly besotted
when Addy's in the room...
Just go ahead and face the facts,
and I think you have,
or you wouldn't have gotten married,
YOU WILL NEVER BE THE SAME.
Now that you're in love,
Go ahead and embrace it fully.
I, for one, am going to get untold joy
Watching your woman keep you in line.
Sign me up for the front row.
I love you, man.
Congratulations.
~Rhodes

I'm wiping my face again and laughing at the same time. "They're just the best. I love this so much. And now, what? Will you write in there too?"

Penn nods, his expression somewhat shy. "Yeah, I'll go full-on mush too, and then when we get together in person, we'll laugh and talk shit to each other and balance it out a little bit."

I laugh. "So it's not all mush, all the time?"

"No. But I'd say them settling down and getting married has definitely softened them. I'm sure the fact that they were fathers already had softened them somewhat, but when they fell in love, each of them went down hard." He laughs.

"Kind of like you with Addy," Sam says, grinning up at the two of us.

Penn and I smile tentatively, like we're both trying to figure the other one out. I know something is brewing between us. It has been all along. And it might've been crazy to tell him I gave him permission…basically giving him free rein to have his way with me later tonight.

But I don't want to be careful right now.

I want to let myself careen into him.

I think we're both adult enough to handle it if it doesn't go well, and we're committed to making sure Sam is taken care of, so we will do that no matter what. But why not enjoy exploring what this could be? Since the night we met, that's all I've wanted to do.

"It's late. We should probably get to bed," Penn says. He looks at Sam. "Shower and brush teeth?"

Sam yawns. "Okay. Yeah, I'm tired." He leans over and hugs me and then Penn. "It was a fun party."

"Thanks for helping us pull it off, buddy. You were a huge help," Penn tells him.

"Yes, you were," I add. "We did it." I wave one of the napkins as I put them back in place.

Sam smiles at us, and it both melts my heart and makes it hurt, the way any kind of praise makes him so happy. I want to smother him with hugs and validate him every other second, but I settle for patting his cheek and kissing his forehead.

His cheeks flush when I pull back.

"You're a good guy, Sam. Hey, what's your middle name?" I ask. "And is Sam short for something?"

"My full name is Samson Cole Miller."

"That is a great, solid name." I smooth back his hair.

"Thank you." He looks at Penn shyly. "I used to always

ask Penn if I could come stay at his house and he tried so hard. I'm so glad it's finally happened. I love it here with you guys."

Penn pulls him in for a hug. "I love having you here so much. Both of you. And if I have my way, we'll make it permanent legally as soon as possible. It feels like we might finally get our wish." He rests his chin on Sam's head and both of them grin at me.

My ovaries take flight.

"And then I could be Samson Cole Hudson?" Sam asks hopefully.

Penn presses his lips together, his eyes glistening with tears. "I want that more than anything," he says, his voice hoarse.

"Me too," Sam whispers.

"It's going to happen. Now that we're here together, things will start working out. I can feel it." I say, cuddling into Penn's chest and putting my arms around Sam too.

"It's okay with you too, Addy?" Sam asks. "I won't, like, be in the way now that you guys are married?"

"Sam, you were in the equation when I considered marrying Penn. I want to be part of your life too, if you'll let me." I dab the tear that starts to fall down my cheek.

He turns and gives me a big bear hug. "I'd love that."

Penn sniffs. "God, the two of you have me blubbering over here. What the fuck are you doing to my emotions?"

"I feel like I should fuss at you about your language in front of Sam." I laugh.

"Oh, I've heard worse out of him, believe me," Sam says.

Penn gives me a sheepish look. "I'll work on that," he says.

CHAPTER TWENTY-ONE

I DID. I DO.

PENN

The door clicks shut behind us, sealing us in our own little world. The air crackles between Addy and me, more electrified than ever.

We spent the night in the same bed last night. Woke up tangled together, her breath warm against my skin, her fingers curled against my chest like she belonged there. But tonight feels brand new. The kisses at the party changed everything. And maybe the vows we said have something to do with it too. The realization that, for now anyway, in this moment, for this time, we're committed to each other.

I can't begin to know what is next for us.

But a switch flipped tonight between us, and now we stand here, looking at each other in anticipation.

I clear my throat, not sure where to put my hands because I want them all over her more than I want my next breath. "Did you mean what you said about giving me permission?"

She meets my gaze, her lips parting slightly. "I did. I do."

We both acknowledge how fitting her wording is with a smirk.

Relief washes over me so strongly that I almost have to sit down. Because I want her...more than anything. Maybe it's crazy to let this boundary fall, but I can't even bring myself to care right now.

"I do too," I say.

I take a step toward her.

"You look so beautiful tonight," I tell her, my voice hushed in the stillness of the room.

A blush rises in her cheeks, and I hum the melody to "Lady in Red" under my breath. Her lips curve in the faintest of smiles, and I step even closer, lifting my hands to rest on her waist. We move together, a slow, gentle sway, as the moonlight spills through the window, casting a glow over her skin and highlighting the way her eyes shine when she looks at me.

I cup her cheek, brushing my thumb over her skin. She leans into my touch, and that's all it takes. I close the space between us, and it feels so fucking good to kiss her. She sighs against my mouth, and I breathe her in, tasting the sweetness of our wedding cake. I deepen the kiss, my fingers threading through her hair, and she grips the front of my shirt. Time stands still, our bodies drawn together like magnets dying for contact. I feel like a guitar string about to break, the tension so taut in my body that I have to remind myself to relax, slow down…we have all night.

I pull back just enough to see her face, my chest heaving. She watches me, waiting, her eyes lust-drunk. I slide my hands to the straps of her dress, easing them down over her shoulders.

"You still want this?" I ask. "I won't hold you to anything beyond this night, if tonight is all you want. At any point, we can put our focus completely on Sam and the marriage being about that, if that's—" my voice trails off.

She nods. "I want this. I want you. Now."

Relief floods through me.

"Get on the bed," I say, my voice hoarse with craving her. "Let me make you feel good."

Her breath catches, but she doesn't hesitate. She steps back, eyes still on me, and slips out of her dress. Underneath the dress is a red lacy bra and panty combo that is hot as fuck and I tell her so.

"I hoped you might get to see this little ensemble tonight," she says, her voice flirty now.

I groan. "I am beyond grateful right now. And I'm going to make you so happy that you married me, I promise you that." I move toward her and lean down to tongue the lace over her nipple. It pebbles under my tongue and I move to the other side, giving it the same attention.

I look up at her, centering myself in her cleavage, one of the best places on Earth. "Tell me anything you want and it's yours." My tongue licks up the center of her breasts and she shivers. I straighten and run my hands over her arms.

"I want you," she says simply.

She turns and I'm struck senseless with the view of her ass. Every angle of her is like a whiplash to my senses.

I haven't even been with her yet, but I already know once won't be enough.

A night won't be enough.

Is this how people feel when they commit to forever?

Damn. I never dreamed I'd feel this way about someone. But the fact that I feel this way about someone I've never even had sex with? Impossible. Hell, the guys have been trying to tell me, but now, seeing her moving toward my bed —and holy shit, her bra just came off. She tosses it to the side of the bed and her back looks like smooth silk.

It's the combination of who Addy is, the way we talk and laugh together, the way she looks at me, and yes, okay, the way she looks, period…everything about her sends me flying high. Whatever it is about this woman, I *need* her.

And it feels pretty goddamn surreal, because I've never needed anyone.

She smiles at me over her shoulder and then turns around and lies down on the bed. I'm mesmerized by the display of her full, rosy-tipped tits of perfection and put a hand on my dick to steady myself. My dick is straining painfully, desperate to be free, and I don't even know where to start. I want to be in too many places at once.

I take a deep breath, telling myself to just slow down and enjoy every bit of this.

I slowly unbutton my shirt and toss it aside.

"I'm obsessed with your tattoos," she says, her voice husky.

She reaches out to touch the small compass over my heart, and I'm sure she can feel it pounding out of my skin.

"It's a good thing," I say, grinning, "because I have a few."

I lean over her, bending down to kiss her lips first, and then chaste kisses on both of her nipples. She gasps at the feel of my mouth on her skin, and I lift up again, smiling at her as I slide the red lace down her legs until she's fully bare.

"There," I say. "That's exactly how I want you." I take her in, my eyes drinking her up. "Holy hell, Siren, you're luring me out into the deep waters, aren't you?"

"Doing my best," she says, her voice raspy.

I stand back and undress, enjoying the way her eyes light up with interest. She sits up, her fingers tracing the outline of my abs, the V that disappears under my boxer briefs. Her thumb curves over the tip of my dick that's made its way out and now I'm the one hissing back a breath. She licks her lips and pulls the briefs down the rest of the way, leaning in to press a kiss on my tip.

"Fuck." My hand clutches her neck before she can wrap her mouth around the rest of me, and I tilt her face up. "The feel of your lips on me like that is enough to knock me sideways, but there are too many things I want to do to you before that ever happens."

Her lips poke out in a slight pout. "But you look good enough to eat."

My dick bobs between us, all about those words.

"And so do you," I tell her. I slide my hand down my face. "Are you sizing me up like Capone the flamingo?"

She giggles. "Yep," she says, the p popping.

I put my hand on her chest with a slight nudge. She pretends to be annoyed as she falls back on my bed, her dark hair splayed out against my sheets, looking so fucking stunning it takes my breath away. She looks up at me with something like trust in her eyes.

I swallow hard and follow her, moving between her legs and spreading them apart, loving how pretty she is everywhere I look. Her pink slit glistens and I rub my thumb lightly over her, spreading her wetness around.

It's like a match being struck for both of us.

She lets out a little whimper and I lean into her, ignited.

When my tongue makes contact, there's no more holding back, no more boundaries.

Only this moment.

Only us.

I explore her with a greedy mouth, sucking her and exploring her with my tongue. She writhes against the bed, arching into my mouth, and I can't get enough of her. The sweetest taste. My tongue dives into her and then I move back to sucking and let my fingers get in on the action. It's almost too much. I could come just hearing the sounds she's making, feeling the way she's reacting to everything I'm doing, it's all *so fucking good*. When I slide one finger inside her, and then another, and another, she starts chanting my name. It's quiet but fervent, like a prayer...or a plea.

"Penn, Penn, Penn, *Penn*—" an anguished whimper.

I don't tease her for long. My fingers work fast, with the pressure and tempo she wants. My tongue and mouth don't let up either, and her entire body trembles with the buildup. When she freezes, her body going rigid as she leans into me, I feel the rush on my tongue, the flutters of her against me, and I ride it out with her until she collapses into the bed. Her head moves from side to side as she throws her arm over her mouth to stay quiet.

I press one more kiss against her puffy lips with a promise to be back and kiss my way up her torso, stopping for another indulgent exploration of her breasts.

"Are you okay?" I ask, looking up at her as my fingers tweak her nipples.

She presses a hand to her chest and takes a deep breath. "Penn," she says, still breathless. "I've never felt anything like that in all my life."

I perk up. "What do you mean?"

"It felt like there was nothing more important to you than making me come so hard that I saw stars."

I smile against her skin, kissing my way up her neck until I'm hovering over her, my face an inch from hers. "And did you? See stars?"

"I saw whole galaxies."

We stare at each other for a long moment, and God, what is this? Honestly, I feel a little shaken.

When I kiss her, it's sweet and soul-stirring. All these moments with her that make this feel *new*. Which is a mindfuck, if I let myself think about it. It's jarring and unsettling, the way this feels so much *more*...in every way, and yet, I'm not about to pump the brakes.

Her hand wraps around my dick and I feel drunk. Just every sensation that I could possibly feel, *bam*.

"We probably should've talked about birth control before we got this far," she says, fisting around me. I hiss in a breath. "I'm on birth control, clear tests, all that."

"Me too," I say. "Never had sex without a condom, tested regularly, all clear...and I was telling the truth when I said I haven't been with anyone since I met you. I was a little slut before I met you," I admit. She grins and squeezes me tighter and I groan. "But you've got me right in the palm of your hand...literally."

She gives me a smug look, her lips parting as she strokes me up and down.

"You're so beautiful," I tell her.

"You are. I can't believe—I mean, I knew you were because...look at you, but...it's a good thing I didn't know what was underneath your clothes all this time." She giggles and I swell into her hand, so hard I might pass out. She leans up and whispers in my ear. "I kind of love that you've never done it without a condom. Neither have I. And I love it even more that you haven't been with anyone since meeting me." Her lips move to mine and she says, "Neither have I," against my mouth.

"I need to be inside you," I tell her. "Is it too much?"

"I'm dying for you to be inside me," she says.

She guides me to her entrance and when I nudge inside just a little, we both gasp.

"You're like silk and a fever and the best feeling in the world," I tell her, a little too mind-blown to be talking right now.

"You make me crazy," she says. "You feel too good. *We* feel too good. Why is everything so big with us?"

I dip in a little deeper, my eyes never leaving hers. "I know. We do feel too good. And I'm not sure why or how this is happening. I'm…just—" I give up trying to say what I'm feeling because it's like she said, so big.

There's a little crease between her brows every time I slide in more, her tongue pressing against her bottom lip, and then I glance down where I'm sliding into her and groan.

"Oh, you're perfect," I rasp. "I want to draw this out and I want to fuck you so thoroughly you'll feel me for days."

"Both can be true."

She starts to meet my thrusts, trying to get more of me, and I keep holding back, teasing her until she's flushed and greedy and all grabby hands, and I fucking love it more than I thought possible.

When I go deeper, she's relieved and satiated for a second, until I pull back out, and then she's hungry for more. I become addicted to filling her up and hollowing her out and then depriving her, only to do it all over again. We're relentless, our rhythm punishing and profound, like we're the only two people who exist and we exist only to bring each other pleasure.

"I'm so close," she cries out when I go in the deepest yet.

"I feel you clenching around me and I'm right there, Addy. Don't stop. Don't fucking stop."

"Harder," she says. "Don't hold back."

I don't hold back another second. I thrust inside her, all restraint falling away, and when she starts coming, I kiss her, both of us swallowing up each other's cries. Spots dance over my vision when I spill into her, and I'm lightheaded as unreal sensations sweep over me. It's like nothing I've ever experienced.

And I think, *I surrender.*

CHAPTER TWENTY-TWO

THE MORNING AFTER

ADELINE

The morning wakeup is entirely different than yesterday morning. For one thing, we woke each other up all night long. After we had sex the first time, we took a long shower, exploring each other slowly in there, and then we fell asleep talking about how fun the party was, how much we shocked everyone…and I woke up to his mouth between my legs again.

The way this man makes me feel. I should've known he'd

know what he was doing, but HOW COULD I HAVE KNOWN THIS KIND OF MAN EVEN EXISTS?

I was thoroughly loved up last night after the first orgasm and then the second surpassed that. The third one in the shower made my legs give out and he had to hold me up while he gave me a fourth. Then the fifth one, I woke up with him between my legs, and the sixth one when he slipped inside me from the back, as his fingers did lazy circles over my center…it's been the best kind of night.

I don't even know what to think.

I expected to have a good time with Penn. I knew that I liked him too much, that I'm unbelievably attracted to him, that we just seem to mesh *so well* together, but I seriously did not see this coming.

Our bodies are like freaking porn stars together.

I sneak out of bed. We both fell back to sleep after that last time and he looks angelic lying on his side, facing where I was lying, his hand stretched out like he's reaching for me. I wash up and put on a cute, oversized sweatshirt and leggings, pile my hair in a messy bun, and go to the kitchen to make breakfast. It's Sunday morning, and despite the night I just had, I feel energized and want to make sure Sam's taken care of.

What Sam said last night, when he checked to make sure I was okay with this…it endeared me to him even more. I don't have a lot of experience with kids his age, but the few I've been around haven't been so considerate of other people's feelings. That he could go through all he's been through and still be concerned about me at all is just further proof of how special this boy is.

I didn't bring all my clothes or any furniture yet, but I brought my juicer. I get the ingredients together for a green juice I already know Penn likes. It's one of the players' favorites. Then I fill a pan with spicy chicken sausage and turn it on low, beat eggs for a veggie and cheese scramble, and then work on smoothing out the pancake batter. When I hear footsteps upstairs, I turn on the pan for the eggs and dollop out the perfect portion of batter on the griddle. Then I turn the juicer on and have enough for all three of us by the time Sam walks into the kitchen.

He sees all the food going and his eyes widen. "Wow! What are you making?"

"A few things. I figured we'd all be ready for a nice Sunday brunch after sleeping in a little this morning."

He comes over and checks it all out. "Yum. And pancakes too?" He rubs his stomach. "I can't wait. How do you make all this?"

"I used to follow recipes to a T and now it just all kind of lives up here." I tap my head. "I can show you how to make whatever you'd like to cook, if you're interested." I turn the eggs down before taking the pancakes off the griddle and putting a pat of butter on each one. I pile them high and pour another batch on the griddle.

"Totally," he says, excited. "I want to learn how to make all of it."

"All right. It's a deal. I'd love your help." The microwave dings. "Oh, would you grab that? It's our syrup."

"You heat up the syrup?" he asks in wonder.

I grin, loving his enthusiasm so much. "I think it adds a nice touch and keeps the pancakes a little warmer, longer."

"Yeah! I never thought of that." When he gets it out, he takes it to the table and looks around, seeing what else he can do. "Should I set the table?"

"Yes, please. Kinda forgot to do that before I started all this."

"I got it," he says. He already knows where everything is more than I do.

Penn walks in as I'm turning off the eggs and have the last stack of pancakes to carry to the table. His hair is wet and he's got sweats and a white T-shirt on…barefoot. I swoon a little inside and can't wipe the goofy smile off of my face.

It helps that he can't either.

He walks toward me, smiling at me and then over at Sam. "Mornin', you two."

"Mornin'," I say, my shoulder lifting as he nuzzles into my neck, his scruff tickling my skin.

"Mornin'!" Sam calls. "You're not gonna believe what all Addy made." He runs down the list of food. "Come on. It's all ready. You came just in time."

"This looks amazing. Thank you for all this," Penn says, brushing back hair that's fallen in my eye.

"I think I'm going to really love feeding my boys," I say shyly.

Penn stares at me for a long moment, as if he's trying to discern whether I'm just playing a part in front of Sam or if I'm telling the truth.

"I mean it." I lift up to whisper in his ear before I move past him.

He puts his hand on my lower back, following me, and sitting at the head of the table where Sam has the table all set.

"And even my favorite green juice?" Penn says, his eyebrows lifting. "Sam, this is the juice I was telling you about. I think you're going to love it."

"It's very green," Sam says, sounding somewhat nervous.

"Trust me. It's way better than it looks." Penn lifts his glass and then downs it in five seconds.

"*Whoa*," Sam says. He lifts his glass and so do I, tapping our glasses together, and we both drink it. When we come up for air, Sam's grinning. "Wait until I tell Cassidy I did that. She's gonna be so impressed." He leans in. "She's a little pickier than I am."

I lean in, matching his excitement with my own. "Tell me more. Is Cassidy someone you like? Just friends? She's really pretty."

He takes a huge bite of pancakes and smirks over at Penn as he tries to chew with his mouth closed. When he finally finishes, he clears his throat and holds up his finger, pausing another second to take a big drink of water.

"The suspense!" I moan.

He laughs and Penn looks at us, amused.

"I've liked Cassidy for a long time, but she's so like—" he holds up his hand— "up here and I'm so—" he lowers his hand— "down here."

Penn growls. "Not true."

"I know you say that, but it is true. She's just like," he shakes his head in wonder, "she's amazing. There was this other girl at school that was all about me and I thought she was nice. We kissed." He lifts his shoulder up. "But I just always go back to wishing it was Cassidy."

"She *is* a few years older than him," Penn tells me. "Maybe she's your Elle though," Penn says, pointing his fork at Sam. "If you still feel that way when you're eighteen or nineteen, you better be letting her know." He frowns. "Or maybe when you're twenty or twenty-one…whatever you do, just don't wait until you're thirty-one."

We all laugh.

"Is that what Rhodes did with Elle?" I ask.

"Yes," they both groan.

"I don't know anything about love, but even I could see that they belonged together!" Sam says. "Just like you and Penn." His eyes are bright as he looks between the two of us.

Penn glances at me and smiles. "You think so?" he asks Sam, but his eyes quickly find mine again.

"I know so," Sam says. "Every single time we've ever gone out, like to a restaurant or to Top Golf…anywhere… girls will come up to Penn and he used to flirt and get all these numbers thrown at him." He rolls his eyes when Penn tries to protest. "You know it's true." He leans in and grins at me. "But then, when he came back from the Bahamas, he told me about you."

I perk up. "Did he really?"

Penn slides his hand down his face and gives me the side-eye. "I told you—you were on my mind."

"He's never talked to me about any girl. Not a single one. And then when I saw you together, it was like, oh yeah," Sam says, nodding and giving us a cheesy grin.

We both laugh.

"You're killing my intrigue, dude," Penn says.

Sam's hand flies out toward me. "You gotta let her know. She's your wife now. You're telling me all the time that I should tell Cassidy she's pretty, or tell her how I like her hair or something like that…" His head tilts and he looks over at me. "Did he tell you that you look pretty this morning?"

You're so fucking beautiful. Those were the words he chanted as he rode me hard in the wee hours of the morning. I press my cold glass of green juice up to my cheek to cool off.

"He did," I say, somewhat raspy.

Penn nods, his lips tipping up in a closed smile, his eyes dancing with mischief. "I did, didn't I? I'll say it again though, to set a good example. You look really pretty this morning."

My God, these guys are too much. "Thank you. You look really great too. You too, Sam," I throw in there, and Sam eases the tension when he sits up straighter and pushes his hair back.

"Thanks," he says. "I'm trying to get some of Penn's swagger. What do you think?" He runs his hand through his hair and then does an expression that Penn makes when he's about to say something funny or sexy, and it's so fitting, we all crack up.

"I see what it's like. There's going to be a lot of ganging up on me around here, isn't there?" Penn says, when we finally quiet down.

"You are really fun to tease," I tell him.

He sends me a look that sends desire pulsing through me. "I don't mind you teasing me one bit."

I exhale a shaky breath. It's going to be a constant challenge not to kiss his face off.

Somehow, this marriage, for Sam's sake, feels more self-serving than I expected it to. The lines got blurred last night, and I like it that way. I'll just have to stay on top of my feelings a little bit…not let myself get too carried away if we're not on the same page here.

But damn, it's hard to do when he looks at me like he can't wait to get me back in bed.

CHAPTER TWENTY-THREE

NOT SO BLISSFUL

PENN

I don't know how I manage to concentrate on anything but Addy over the next few days, but somehow I do. Sam had football practices over the weekend, and then each day, we get him off to school and then head to the training facility. Our first preseason game is tomorrow night and I think we're ready. My parents pick Sam up from school, and Addy and I have started driving to work together. I work out while she preps food for the day, and then during our practices, she's setting it all up so it's ready when we pile into the cafeteria. Everyone loves her already, and no one has had anything but positive things to say about us being together.

I'm still getting teased a lot for settling down, but that's to be expected.

Sometimes she's done a little earlier than I am and vice versa, but so far, it's been seamless. We've had nice dinners with Sam and last night, my parents joined us. It's fun to see everyone interacting with each other. I'm happy to say that my parents and Addy are hitting it off, and Addy and Sam—they seem connected at the hip more every day.

It's all feeling very domesticated and I'm shocked by how okay I am about all of it. I thought I would have a freak-out by now, and I am floundering a bit to know what comes next, but I'm just trying to be in the moment and enjoy the now. If I think too hard about everything, I might panic a little because it's just all so fucking *great*.

Like, too great for words.

Like, speechless great.

Because after we do all these normal things during the day, then at night, she works me over until I'm senseless in bed. Last night, we had barely shut the bedroom door after telling everyone goodnight and our clothes were off within seconds. I took her against the bedroom wall and then carried her to the bathtub while I ran a hot bath. She stepped into the water and then sat down, spread her legs, and motioned for me to come closer. When I did, she pulled me into the water, and it was the most epic night yet.

I'm ashamed to say that I've wondered how people can just want to be with one person. No one has ever made me want to go back for more, even if the sex between us was a positive experience.

But every time I'm with Addy, I'm already craving her

more. I can't wait for the next time, *while I'm inside her.* It's absolutely insane.

Now, I get the appeal of honeymoons.

Getting back to her in our bed…whoa, did I just say *our*?…is all I think about.

I'm even starting to get the appeal of married life.

Being bare and honest with someone…trusting that person.

Okay, slow down, Penn. Slow down.

I'm surviving on less sleep than usual but energized during the day. Coach Evans is watching me like a hawk, just waiting for me to mess up, but I'm not. He even had me run extra laps since I had the "audacity to marry his daughter," and I did them with a huge smile on my face.

He didn't like that, but it's okay.

Addy is my good luck charm.

And a whole lot more than that.

But again, I'm not going to think too hard about it all.

We're in Addy's car on the way home now. She wanted to drive today because she knew my schedule was extra intense. She surprises me more and more with all the ways she's thoughtful. Her cooking is phenomenal, and I keep insisting that she doesn't have to cook when she's at home since she's doing it all day, but she says she loves it. I had flowers delivered to her office this morning with a note that said,

You're making me so happy, Siren.

Love, Penn

I felt a little ridiculous afterward, overthinking the mush, but she found me when I came back in the building, all sweaty from practice, and she dragged me into her office, kissing me until I was weak in the knees.

She glances over at me and smirks.

"What is it?" I ask.

She just lifts her eyebrow, which makes me suspicious. Her eyes flit to the dashboard and I follow her gaze before bursting out laughing. A little pink plastic flamingo is sitting on the dashboard staring at me.

"Capone," I breathe. "He followed me."

"Capon*a*," she corrects. "She couldn't stand to be away from you another second."

I laugh and pick it up, squeezing it and watching its form go back into shape. When I glance at Addy again, I'm serious and her smile drops.

"Is this going okay for you?" I ask. "Us? The past few days? Anything we need to talk about, or…improve on?"

Her lips twitch and she turns back to the road. "I can't think of a single thing we could improve on at the moment…"

I lean my head against the headrest. "Excellent. So what you're saying is you are happy with the way we are spending our days…and nights?"

"*Especially* the nights." She grins at me. "But the days are pretty fun too."

"Agreed," I say, nodding. "Okay, good. So…just tell me if you need to switch things up at all or…if you see room for improvement."

She frowns slightly. "Are you needing to switch things up?"

"No, uh, not at all." For some reason, I go all stuttery. "Um, as I said in my note, I am so happy and I love what we're doing. I just want you to be feeling good about things too, and well, I didn't expect it to be quite as great as it really is, but I'd understand if you didn't feel as great as I did because…yeah, it's a lot, but—"

She reaches out her hand and puts it on my knee. I place

my hand over hers and trace little lines over her skin, her touch grounding me.

"Penn, I'm happy too. Let's just try to keep communicating about it, okay? Please say the minute you want something different, and I will too."

I nod. "Cool. Yeah, I will."

But inside, I'm thinking, *there's no way I'll want this to end, so I really hope you don't either.*

When we pass the gate and she pulls into our driveway, Mrs. Murphy's car is parked in front of the house.

"Shit, looks like we've got a drop-in visit from the social worker," I tell Addy.

She looks at me with as much dread as I feel. "You think your parents are okay with her right now?"

"I think so, but we better get in there."

We both rush out of the car and go in through the garage. When we walk into the kitchen, Mrs. Murphy is sitting next to Sam at the bar, and my mom is leaning against the kitchen counter. There are chocolate chip cookies on a pretty plate and Sam is in the middle of dunking one in a glass of milk when they notice us.

"Hey, you guys!" Sam says happily. "We heated up the cookies Addy made last night and they're so good!"

I smile at him, pausing to squeeze his shoulder and kiss my mom's cheek before reaching out to shake Mrs. Murphy's hand. My dad walks in then and we all say hello.

"Thought I'd stop by and see how it's going," Mrs. Murphy says. "Sam was telling me about the party you had over the weekend. It sounds like a lot of fun."

Addy and I share a look and nod. Do we look nervous? I think maybe so. I try to relax my shoulders and reach out, taking Addy's hand, hoping that I made that look casual too.

Fuck. Why am I so bad at this? Where is this swagger that Sam was talking about? *That I've always been known for?*

"We had such a fun night," Addy says, smiling up at me. "Sam helped a lot with everything too. And it was great having our family and friends with us."

"Seems like everything moved really fast," she says.

I think I audibly hear both of us gulp and can't look at Addy right now or I'll surely look like a deer in the headlights.

"We thought so too!" My mom laughs. "But we'd heard about her months ago, and that was unusual…for our boy to be talking about a woman he met at all is not the typical." She laughs and glances at my dad.

He nods too. "Yep, it was a first for sure."

"And then we saw the two of them together and," my mom shakes her head, smiling dreamily, "it just all felt meant to be." She lifts her shoulder and glances at Mrs. Murphy. "Jeremy and I only dated a month before we eloped, so it wasn't that far-fetched to us, that they'd do the same thing. The fact that she's his coach's daughter makes it a little more complicated…" My mom's eyes crinkle as she beams at Addy and me.

Mrs. Murphy turns to look at us. "Oh, I didn't realize that. What's the connection there?"

"My dad is one of the coaches for the Mustangs, so he works closely with Penn. That's kind of how we met. I went with my parents to the Bahamas when they went for a player's wedding, and I enjoyed a mini vacation while they did the wedding activities."

"And I was the officiant for the wedding and practicing what I'd say at the ceremony when we met by the beach." I smile at Addy.

Her eyes never leave mine and it feels like we're back on

that beach, consumed with each other the way we were that night. "He was so nervous about the wedding that I took him to flamingo yoga to try to calm him down, but that didn't work."

I hold up the little flamingo she just gave me. "One of the flamingos—Capone or Capona, depending on who you ask—took a hatred or a liking, again, depending on who you ask, to me, and we ended up running for our lives."

Addy snorts and Sam cracks up. "Capon*a* just wanted to give you a little kiss," she says.

"You didn't tell me this part!" Sam says, handing me a cookie.

I hold it up and pause before taking a bite. "Because I wanted to scream like a baby when that thing stood over me. Something I'd rather forget."

Sam loves that. "Lost your cool in front of the girl. That should've been the sign right there that you were hopeless over Addy."

I point my cookie at him and then glance at Addy. "He's not wrong." I take a bite of the cookie and can't resist groaning. "And she makes the best cookies. The best everything."

She leans into me and it feels natural to wrap her back against my chest, so I do.

But then I'm thrown when Mrs. Murphy says, "Well, Sam, I have another foster family who is interested in taking you. How would you feel about that?"

Sam shoots an incredulous look at me. "I'd feel terrible about that. I want to stay here. Why do you keep trying to keep me from Penn?" His voice cracks at the end and I move closer to him. Addy comes with me, and we both hover next to his chair.

"It isn't that I'm trying to keep you from him." Her tone

is apologetic. "I just want you to be in the best possible home."

"This *is* the best possible home. I don't know why you're being so hard on Penn." Tears fall down his cheeks and he brushes them away angrily with his fists.

"Hey, buddy, it's okay. I'm not going anywhere." I look at Mrs. Murphy. "Maybe you can tell me what I can do now to improve Sam's situation here. Do you want to check his bedroom again? Hell, you could spend the week with us here and see how we're running the house. But please don't put him somewhere else. I know we're still trying to work things out to make everything permanent, but he belongs with us. He's settled in school and our routine, and coming by here and threatening to move him will only cause more stress."

"I'm not threatening—" she starts.

"I know you're just doing your job and you want to protect him. But it's my job to protect him now too and I'm going to do that, even if it means from you. My lawyer has said things are looking good. I have a friend who's a judge in Landmark Mountain that I'll reach out to as well, to see if we can make this come together even faster. I want to adopt Sam and I don't want the two of us looking over our shoulders, afraid that you're gonna come drag him out of here."

"Don't you mean the three of you?" she asks. She dips her head toward Addy.

"Yes, of course. The three of us. We're all in this together," I say, feeling defeated.

Addy reaches out and rubs my arm.

Mrs. Murphy writes a few things in her notebook. "Thanks for your hospitality," she says, standing up. "I'll be in touch."

We see her to the door and I put my hands on Sam's shoulders as we watch her pull away.

"I'm going to fix this," I say, but it sounds hollow.

I'm afraid Mrs. Murphy isn't buying into this with Addy and me, and I can't blame her.

Later, after Sam is in bed, I call Sutton Landmark, Weston's brother-in-law. He's a judge in Landmark Mountain, and he promises to put in a good word for me.

"From what I can see, things are lining up in your favor," he says. "I hear congratulations are in order, man. I'm happy for you. And it's an added benefit—being married will only help."

That's what we were hoping, I think.

But all I say is, "Thank you. And I really appreciate your help."

"Sam is a good kid and he's crazy about you. I want to see you guys together. I promise, Penn, I'll be all over it."

"Thank you. Really. That means a lot."

CHAPTER TWENTY-FOUR

GAME TIME

ADELINE

Penn is on edge when we get to our room that night.

"Is Mrs. Murphy always so intense?" I ask.

He nods grimly. "Pretty much. She's nice, and yet I'm beginning to feel like she's looking for a way to catch me in a lie…or to come up with another reason Sam can't be with me."

"Maybe that's your guilty conscience about the whole fake wedding thing we've got going here."

"Good point." He makes a face. "It's obvious he's so happy here. I don't understand why it's still an issue. But Sutton, the judge I was talking about, he reassured me. He looked at the papers David has drawn up and he seems to think we can make this move quickly. Once it's official, she won't have a say in any of this anymore."

I put my hands on his waist and he leans his forehead on mine.

"I can't wait for that day," he says.

My hands move up his arms and to his shoulders. I frown when I feel how tight they are and start massaging them. "I think we should take a bath."

"Yeah?" he says, starting to grin.

I back away and hold up my hand. "A relaxing bath. With bath oil and a little massage…"

"Now we're talking. I love the sound of that."

I shake my head, moving past him. "I think you're hearing something I'm not saying."

"We'll see about that."

I snort and go into the bathroom, running the water and adding the drops of oil that I love. My favorite has hints of vanilla and citrus. It's not too sweet but just enough to feel comforting and indulgent. Any time I use it, Penn mentions how delicious I smell and how soft I feel.

I light a few candles and dim the lights. When I turn the water off, Penn walks in behind me.

"You getting in, or are you just gonna stand there brooding?" I ask.

His mouth twitches, the smallest hint of a smile before he shakes his head. "I don't brood."

"You totally brood." I flick a bit of water in his direction. "I feel like brooding after that surprise visit myself. I think we'll have to intentionally unbrood ourselves." I pull my shirt over my head and his eyes light with interest. "Strip."

"Yes, ma'am."

He watches me as he slowly pulls his shirt over his head. As he exhales, and I see some of the tension already leaving his body, mine tightens up in anticipation. The way his muscles shift as he steps out of his pants…he is the most beautiful man. His chest is sculpted with precision, his arms are lined with muscle, his tattoos are beautiful, his skin sun-kissed, and his abs are cut with deep lines, a testament to the work he's put into his body. His waist is lean and his thighs are thick and powerful, and even when he's still, there's an energy about him, like he's about to spring into action. And his face…I love his face so much. So masculine and yet beautiful, a rugged charm despite his pretty eyes and full lips. His eyes are full of mischief, like he knows the effect he has on people. I'm pretty sure he knows the effect he has on me. And when I see the stubble on his face, I imagine the scrape of it between my legs.

When he finally tugs his boxer briefs down, a quick intake of breath escapes my lips. He's long and hard and thick and he absolutely knows how to use what he's been given. He smirks before turning around and I admire his ass. There really is no place on his body that isn't perfect.

He steps into the tub, the heat of the water making him groan low in his throat. He lowers himself into the water and looks up at me. "Okay. This was the perfect idea."

I grin smugly.

He points at me. "Your turn. You didn't finish stripping for me. And I'm not taking this bath alone."

I'm not as deliberate with my striptease, hurriedly getting out of my clothes, but he watches like I am putting on a delicious show. When I'm completely undressed, he holds out his hand and I take it as I step into the bath. I sit in front of him, and his arms come around my waist, his chest pressing against my back.

I hum in approval. "Told you."

His lips brush against my shoulder, warm and lazy. "You like telling me you're right…"

"I really do." I lean back against him, letting my head rest on his shoulder. "You okay?"

"I will be." His fingers trace light patterns along my hip under the water. "It's just…I want this to all work out so much. I want Sam to be okay, I want you to be okay…"

"I'm okay." I turn slightly, enough that I can see the edge of his jaw and the way his gaze is fixed on my chest as he reaches up to cup my breast. "And we're figuring it out together. You don't have to carry this by yourself anymore."

He gives my nipple a slight pinch and my head falls back again. "I'm really glad you're here."

I shift, turning fully so I can straddle his lap, and the water sloshes with the movement. His eyes lift to mine and they soften.

I smile, cupping his face in my hands. "You know what helps?"

He leans close and wraps his mouth around my bud. His tongue swirls around the peak. "What?" he asks.

My lips brush against his head as I whisper, "Distraction."

I feel his lips lift against my skin and his voice is playful. "Is that so?"

He's so hard underneath me and it's hitting me just right. I lean into him.

"Mm-hmm." I press a kiss on his cheek and then a light, lingering kiss on his lips. "You, me, a hot bath…seems like the perfect opportunity for a little stress relief."

His hands slide up my back, pulling me flush against him. "I think I might like unbrooding."

"See? I can be very persuasive."

"I love it when you use your powers for good," he says.

I laugh against his lips and then he kisses me, deep and slow, stealing the breath right from my lungs.

We make very good use out of the bathtub.

His fingers slide under the water and between my legs and when I'm squirming and desperate for him, he seats himself into me so deep, there's no space whatsoever between us.

"God, you're the best thing I've ever felt," he groans.

"Can't possibly be any better than how you feel," I shudder against him.

My phone starts dinging like crazy the next day, mid-morning. I glance down and grin when I see a text thread going on with the girls. We exchanged numbers the other night at the party.

> **SADIE**
>
> We've tried to give you a little time since technically you're on your honeymoon. But it's killing us. LOL
>
> **TRU**
>
> ^Truth! We're dying to hear more deets than what we got at the party the other night! I propose a girls' night out.

POPPY

I'd LOVE a girls' night out. I'm getting bigger by the second and Jonas is into everything! The thought of chatting with you girls without interruption for more than five minutes sounds like a dream.

> I'd love this more than anything!

I can't stop grinning, as I watch more texts pop up.

SADIE

I don't know what your schedule is like during the game, but if you get a chance, come say hi! Or it might be easier if we come to you.

ELLE

It would definitely be easier if we went to her. Are you working your head off, Addy?

> Totally. But we've been working toward today all week, so I'm happy that it's finally here. I'll be going pretty much nonstop during the game, but afterward, if you want to, meet me in the family area. There will be plenty of food there and we could celebrate the Mustangs' win.

ELLE

YES. I love that positivity. Okay, we'll see you then! And maybe a little before the game too, just for a quick hug.

TRU

Oh, and Sadie gave me a great tip when I started dating Henley. If you have Penn's jersey…let's just say, good things tend to happen when they see their jerseys on the woman they love.

I put my hand on my hot cheek.

> Jersey, check. Consider it done. Thank you for the tip.

ELLE

That's what she said. Sorry, channeling my husband.

> LOL

SADIE

See you tonight!

TRU

POPPY

Can't wait.

It's cutting it close, but since I worked hard to prepare everything before, Toby goes to the stadium ahead of me and I'm able to pick up Sam from school so he won't miss anything. It's the most hyper I've seen him; he chats nonstop the whole drive to the stadium. Right before we arrive, I tell him what we'll need to do to have everything ready for the team.

"I'm excited to help," he says, as we're walking inside.

"You need to do homework first, so it's done."

"I already finished it at school."

I glance at him suspiciously and he laughs.

"I promise!" he says. "You think I'd miss out on any of

this? I've been waiting for this day for *months*. And I didn't even know I'd get to be here! This is the best. I've gotten to go to a lot of Penn's games, but this is my first preseason game."

His excitement is contagious. Toby's still lining food up in the cafeteria, and Sam and I each lug huge coolers into the locker room so we can replenish those refrigerators. I take a little note out of my pocket when I pass Penn's locker and slip it on his top shelf.

Play hard, Preacher Man.
   I'll be cheering you on.
   XX,
   Siren

Sam notices and grins at me, happy to be in on the secret.

"Whoa, I've never seen so many Uncrustables ever!" Sam says when we get back to the cafeteria. "And bananas! So much of everything!"

"These players have huge appetites," I tell him. His eyes are round as he stares at all we still have to set up. "There's plenty. If you're hungry, help yourself."

"Thank you, Addy," he says. He picks up a package of Uncrustables and carefully unwraps it, nodding happily as he eats it. "That's really good."

"You've never had one?"

He shakes his head.

"Well, you're not the only one who likes them. I can't keep enough of them around here! Here's the smoothie stuff too, if you want any of that." I point out the smoothie station that Toby's working on, and Sam jogs over there to help him.

From there, he meticulously arranges the protein bars on the table, while I make the Mustangs Magic.

"I love this job," he calls, glancing over at me. "What are you doing?"

"Making my secret concoction."

"Ooo, does it make the players really strong?" He jogs over to see what I'm doing. I wink at him when I pour certain things in and his eyes crinkle as he grins up at me.

Then I show him my notebook of all the guys' requests. What they want before the game, what they want brought out to them during the game, what they want afterward, and Toby, Sam, and I prepare all that as best we can. And then we start on the hot dishes. Once things are close, I pull Sam aside and take him to the room where I've set our things.

I hold up our jerseys, both with Hudson #1 on the back.

"Oh man, Penn's gonna love seeing you in that," Sam says, laughing. "Sometimes I've worn Rhodes' or Weston's jersey just to irritate him."

We're both laughing now. "I'm sure that goes over really well," I snort.

He slips the jersey over his head and smooths it out. "I think he still knows he's my favorite, don't you?"

I wrap my arm around his shoulder and nod. "I think he does. If he doesn't, this should help tonight. That boy's so vain, his head is gonna blow up when he sees us both wearing his jersey," I tease.

"Penn says, 'If you've got it, there's no need to hide it…'" He tilts his head. "I'm not sure what *it* is, but…I think Penn's got whatever it is."

I crack up and nuzzle his head for a second before I let go to tighten my ponytail. "You are so right, my man. And you know what? You've got it too. *It,*" I draw the word out, "is charisma and magnetism, and you have got it in spades."

Sam's posture straightens and he gets taller right before my eyes. "You think so?"

"I know so."

"Well, Penn was right when he said you're the prettiest woman on Earth. But I like that you're nice too."

I swear, I think this boy has made my eyes well up at least once a day, if not more, since I met him.

"Thank you, Mister Samson Cole. You sure know how to make a girl's day."

He sighs. "Tell that to Cassidy. She ignored me today. We passed in the hall and she acted like she didn't even see me."

"Ugh. What are we gonna do about that? Maybe she *didn't* see you. I bet that's it."

He brightens. "Do you think she'll be here tonight?"

"I'm not sure, but I'll show you where she'll probably be, if so. You can sit there if you want."

His shoulders sag slightly. "You don't want me to keep helping?"

"Well, I thought you'd probably want to see the game."

"If I help you carry stuff out to the players during the game, I'll be seeing the game *and* helping…" He waggles his eyebrows.

I put the lid on the massive pile of chicken breasts and laugh under my breath. "One day, I have no doubt you'll be out on the sidelines if that's what you want to do. For today, you'll have to stay back here with me or sit in that area I'm talking about…"

"You don't get to see the game?"

"I'll watch some of it from the TV there," I point at the TV on the wall, "and I'll be running back and forth the rest of the time."

I glance over at Toby, who's deep into getting the post-game meal ready for the players.

"How are you doing over there, Toby?" I call.

He lifts both hands in the air, doing a little booty shake. "We are slaying," he says. "Sam, can you come help every time?"

Sam beams proudly. "Absolutely."

"Amazing," Toby says. "Then we'll be golden."

The way Penn's eyes glisten with lust when he sees me in his jersey.

One hundred percent worth the time it took me to find it.

While Sam is busy chatting with Cassidy and her sisters, Penn tugs me into the kitchen and then into the little closet off to the side.

"Great game. I knew you'd win."

He grins and his eyes rake up and down me.

"What are we doing in here?" I ask, breathless.

"Couldn't wait until we got home to do this," he says, kissing me until my toes curl.

I lift to my tiptoes and kiss him back, and then we're a tangle of arms and clothes tugged down, just enough so he slides my underwear to the side and impales me. So deep, I gasp and whimper his name.

"So good," I whisper.

"Were you ready for me all night or was it just that kiss?" he asks, thrusting hard and fast.

"I've been ready for you since the minute you pulled out of me this morning."

He moans. "I love that answer."

He picks up the tempo and I hold on for the ride as he lifts me until my legs are wrapped around his waist. His hands hold onto my hips, slamming me down, and I see stars.

"Touch yourself," he says. "Touch yourself, Addy. I'll take my time with you later, but I need you to come now."

He doesn't have to ask twice. We both groan when my fingers circle faster and faster, and we both sag into each other as we fall apart.

When our heartbeats slow, he gives me a languid kiss and places me carefully on the ground.

"I'll see you at home, Mrs. Hudson."

"Can't wait, Mr. Hudson."

CHAPTER TWENTY-FIVE

THERE'S MORE

PENN

It's been a damn good few days. The win last week was huge—clutch catch, game-sealing touchdown—the kind of play I dream about. My phone's been blowing up with texts, media coverage, even a few new endorsement inquiries. But none of it touches the high of coming home and finding Sam curled up on the couch with Addy, the two of them trying to decide between a *Spider-Man* movie or one of the *Jurassic Park* movies.

My life has been full of good plays lately. It's like…I don't know…like the universe decided to hand me all the wins at once.

So when Coach calls me into his office after practice, I'm feeling relaxed, despite the tension still between us. I'm a little tired from the workout but still riding that post-win high even days later.

"Take a seat," Coach says, nodding toward the chair across from his desk.

I sit, expecting a breakdown of my performance or some strategy talk about this week's game, but he just leans back in his chair, steepling his fingers. He has a weird little smile that makes my stomach tighten.

"Been thinking about a few things," he says, his voice deceptively casual. "The timing of things…with this marriage."

Oh.

Oh shit.

His smile sharpens. "Yeah. The timing. Sam hanging around the facility. Cute kid. I like the guy." He shakes his head, looking out his window as if he's thinking fondly of Sam. But then his eyes are back on me and they're not so friendly. "Addy's been looking happy too." His gaze narrows. "Almost too happy."

My pulse kicks up. "Well…married life has been good. Honeymoon phase and all that," I say, shrugging like it's the most normal thing in the world.

Inside, I'm flipping the fuck out because what guy talks about the honeymoon phase with his father-in-law?

Shit, shit, shit.

Coach Evans raises an eyebrow. "That's what I'm wondering about. See, Penn, guys don't just get married overnight unless there's a reason. Especially not guys like you."

My mouth goes dry.

"You're young. Rich. I've been watching you hit the party circuit the past few years and now you expect me to believe you're signing up for the PTA and school drop-offs?"

"I'm not really a PTA person, no, but drop-offs are—"

"Want to tell me what game you're playing at, Penn? And how you managed to convince my daughter to play it with you?" He leans in and nudges his index finger into his desk with his next words. "Because I've listened to her talk about a wedding by the water with lots of flowers and how pretty ice sculptures are, and you name it, and you know what wasn't in the picture at all?"

I shake my head.

"Eloping with a guy she barely knows."

A bead of sweat creeps down the back of my neck, nausea making my stomach turn over.

"I'm not playing a game," I say, but even to my own ears, it sounds weak.

He puts his elbows on his desk. "I've loved that girl since before she even entered the world. So I'll ask again. What are you getting out of this?"

I feel the guilt like a gut punch. Because the truth is—it did start as a game in a way. Not with Addy's heart, never that. But with the idea of creating a secure environment for Sam. Making the foster board happy. Bucking the system. Giving Sam a stable home so they would stop throwing up roadblocks for us at every turn.

But now...

It's not that simple.

I clear my throat. "I'm in this. Addy and I are in this

together. And yes, Sam is part of the equation, but it's not all about him."

He watches me closely, and it's like he can see right through me.

I swallow hard. Married life has been pretty fucking great. Coming home to Addy. Waking up next to her. Finding Sam at the table with bedhead. Talking about his homework. All of it…it's been so much better than I imagined it could be. But how do I even begin expressing that when I don't know how to define it myself yet?

It's silent for a few moments as he studies me. Then he leans back in his chair. "I'm watching you, Penn. And if you hurt her…" His jaw tightens. "I will hunt you down and make your life a living hell."

"I know," I say quietly. "I never want to hurt Addy, I promise you that."

He kind of snorts like he doesn't believe me but nods. "Get outta here."

I stand, muscles tight as I head for the door. My heart's still hammering, but it eases up when I step into the hallway and take a deep breath.

That feeling doesn't last long.

When I get home, Sam is waiting by the window. His face is pale, his arms wrapped tight around his knees. He looks up when I walk in.

"Hey, buddy," I say, walking over.

Addy walks in with a tray of celery covered with peanut butter and raisins and I give her a quick kiss after she sets it in front of Sam. Her eyes are sad too.

"What's going on?" I ask.

Sam's jaw clenches. "It's Winnie."

My stomach drops. Winnie is one of the little girls who lived in his foster home. "What happened?"

"She was hurt. I didn't see her, but I heard she had a black eye like I had and that she fell down the stairs..." His chin wobbles and he wipes his nose on his shirt. "She's five, but she's not clumsy. I don't think she fell at all. Penn...I think she's still in that house. Why would they leave her there when they know what's happened with me?"

My whole body stiffens. "No. No way. That can't be right."

Fuck.

I pull out my phone and dial Mrs. Murphy's number. It rings four times before she answers.

"Hello, Penn."

"Why the hell is Winnie still in that house?" I bark.

She sighs. "Penn—"

"No. Don't start with me. You told me you'd keep an eye on things. Every child should've been moved from that house the second Sam got hurt. And now, that little girl is hurt."

"Where did you hear that?"

"Sam heard it today at school. And it's really sad that he would be privy to that information before you are."

"There's a process—"

"Fuck the process!" I yell. "Get her out of there. Immediately. Every child in that house better be out. They can come here if there aren't enough places for them to go. I'll make calls, pull strings, whatever I have to do, but goddammit, you need to make this right, Mrs. Murphy!"

She exhales. "Yes, yes. I will."

"You'd better," I say as I hang up.

When I'm off, I call David and Sutton and then stalk the floor, still raging. Until I realize Sam is still curled up on the couch, his whole body tense. I sit down and pull him into my arms.

"I'm sorry. I need to calm down. I just want to fix this and I will." I press my chin to the top of his head. "I promise."

He clings to me, his voice breaking again. "Okay."

For the first time in days, I don't feel like I'm winning anymore.

The phone rings an hour later. Mrs. Murphy. I put her on speakerphone.

"Did you mean what you said about taking in Winnie?" she asks.

I glance at Addy and she nods.

"Absolutely," I say.

"I will be bringing her in about two hours. She's being evaluated by the doctor now. It looks like she's bruised up and has a black eye, but there are no broken bones. If you're agreeable to this, I'd like her to stay with you for a few days until I can find a new placement."

"She can stay here indefinitely, as long as she needs," I say.

Sam sniffles and hugs me again.

"Thank you," he whispers.

Winnie is a five-year-old little girl with wild blonde curls and the biggest green eyes.

When she looks up at me, her fingers nervously clutching a ratty blanket, my heart tumbles over itself. That pang of expansion that I'm only now learning to recognize. Who knew a heart could keep filling up with more people to love?

Addy and these kids are going to sink my heart until all that's left is goo.

I surrender.

CHAPTER TWENTY-SIX

A WHOLE NEW WAY OF LIFE

ADELINE

I'm on my knees, searching for Sam's missing sneaker under the couch, when I hear Penn say softly, "Hey there, sweetheart."

I sit back on my heels and turn toward the door. And there she is.

Winnie.

She's so small, delicate as a bird, with pale blonde curls that frame her face and wide green eyes that don't blink enough. Her expression is a mix of uncertainty and quiet bravery, like she's scared but determined not to show it.

"Hi, Winnie," I say softly.

Her gaze darts from Penn to me to Sam, and when she sees Sam, she runs to him. He catches her in his arms and lifts her up, hugging her tight. Even Mrs. Murphy looks emotional when she sees the two of them interact with each other.

"I'm so glad you're here," he says. "You'll love it here. Penn and Addy are the best and you'll have a nice bed with warm clothes…and Addy makes the best food you've ever tasted. Penn's parents are great, and Addy's are super nice too."

She looks up at him and nods, not speaking. And then she turns back and looks at Penn and me and swallows hard.

"Trust me," Sam says. "This is the best possible place to be."

"We're really happy you're here too," Penn says. "Would you like to take a look around? Are you hungry?"

She nods and lifts the blanket she's been holding up to her face. I want to give it—and her—a good washing, but first things first.

"Sam and I can show you around. And I was thinking about having breakfast for dinner," I tell her. "Do you like pancakes or waffles?"

She stares at me, unblinking, then looks at Sam and nods.

"Great," I say, grinning. "Maybe you and Sam can help me in the kitchen while Penn talks with Mrs. Murphy."

I'm not sure if Mrs. Murphy will be agreeable to that or not, or if she'll want me to be part of the conversation, but I want to surround these kids with normality as quickly as possible. The last thing they need to hear is the adults talking about all the horrible things they've been enduring in the foster home.

Sam tries to get Winnie talking and she smiles a few times at him, but otherwise, she's quiet and doesn't leave his side. We walk upstairs and I show her the room next to Sam's.

"Look at this big bed!" Sam says. "And my room is just next door. Penn and Addy are in that room there." He points to the room at the end of the hall. "You even have a bathroom in your room. Crazy, right?"

She takes it all in. By now, Sam has set her down and she's holding his hand as we walk through the rooms.

"If you tell me what color you like, we can fix your bedroom to look more like you," I tell her. "Something fun. When I was little, I had a bunch of rainbow pillows on my bed. I also really loved unicorns and Belle from *Beauty and the Beast*."

Her eyes flicker with interest, but I still haven't heard her make a peep.

Sam points at her and grins, "You love *Beauty and the Beast* too, right? And Elsa." He looks at me and nods. "She *loves* Elsa."

"Oh, I love Elsa too and Anna and Olaf…maybe we can turn on that movie after dinner." I lift my shoulder and her eyes brighten, but she sticks her thumb into her mouth and looks at Sam.

"I think she'd like that," he says quietly.

"Great. You can pick out another movie if you're not feeling that tonight, but let's get started on dinner. I'm hungry. How about you?"

"So hungry!" Sam says.

We go back downstairs and I can hear Penn and Mrs. Murphy still talking in the living room. We move into the kitchen and I pull out the ingredients. I hadn't really planned on this for dinner, but it feels like a safe bet for tonight. I'll cut up lots of fruit and focus on more vegetables tomorrow. Tonight, we just want to make this little girl comfortable.

"Sam, can you get the turkey bacon out of the fridge too?" I ask.

I start whipping up the batter and then show Winnie all the toppings. Sam tries to figure out what she wants. She nods yes to chocolate chips in her pancakes and also to whipped cream on top. And she looks the most excited when she sees strawberries and bananas.

Penn walks in about fifteen minutes later and I have a huge pile of pancakes ready. Still flipping another batch of some without the chocolate chips.

"I'm excited about this. Didn't know I was getting your pancakes tonight," he says, coming over to kiss me on the cheek.

Then he walks over to where Winnie and Sam are sitting on stools near me and leans on the island next to Winnie. She tenses and Penn shifts so he's closer to Sam. She takes it in when Sam tilts his head over on Penn's chest and Penn ruffles Sam's hair. Her thumb goes back into her mouth. She's the absolute cutest.

"Okay, let's get these in our bellies!" I say.

I place the platter of pancakes near the toppings and Sam has already set the plates nearby.

"How about we put whatever we want on top and then eat them over there." I point at the table behind us.

"Sounds good. Thank you, Addy," Sam says.

"Yes, thank you," Penn whispers. He puts his hands on my hips and nuzzles into my neck, and when he pulls away, his eyes are searching mine, trying to assess if I'm really okay with all of this.

I smile at him and then move closer to the island to see if Winnie needs help with her plate.

Sam has put a couple pancakes on there and lifts each topping, waiting to see if she'll nod or not. So far, she's got a pretty great combo going.

"I asked my parents to come meet Winnie too," Penn says. "And then we can talk to them after the kids go to bed," he adds softly. "Has she said anything yet?"

I shake my head.

We keep up the chatter during dinner, especially Sam. A few times, there's a twitch of a smile from Winnie and it bolsters Sam up to keep going. He's doing an amazing job of helping her relax. And the little thing can put away the pancakes. She finishes up her plate and I ask her if she wants more. This time, she doesn't look at Sam but nods at me. It feels like a win.

Margo and Jeremy come and meet her and I can tell they're just as taken with her as we are. There's something so fragile about her.

After dinner, we turn on *Frozen* and Winnie falls asleep watching it. When it's time for Sam to go to bed, he carries her upstairs and we go with him, tucking her in.

"Tomorrow, we'll tackle a bath," I say.

"She's normally really chatty," Sam says sadly.

"It might take time for her to get used to us," Penn says.

Sam nods, and I leave the bathroom light on so the glow is faint in her bedroom. We leave her bedroom door slightly ajar and hug Sam goodnight in the hall.

"Thank you for doing this," he says, before he goes into his room. "Um, you guys…I'm big and I'll be okay. If you're only able to keep one of us…I think you should keep her."

Penn and I are struck speechless at first and then we both surround him again.

"I'm not sure yet what's going to happen with Winnie, Sam," Penn says. "The little Addy and I have been able to talk about it, we've agreed that as long as the court allows us to keep her, we will. I have some calls to make tonight, and we need to talk to my parents, just to make sure we can cover all the bases. But Sam, you are still our priority."

Sam looks down at his feet. "I just think it's more important that she's taken care of. You see how small she is. Pretty soon, I'll be old enough to live on my own. I can handle a few more years doing what I've been doing." His shoulders straighten and he looks at us. "I'll be okay."

Penn puts his hands on his shoulders and ducks to meet his eyes. "How about you let me worry about all this, okay? I'm not abandoning you, buddy. Not a chance. It's important to me that you're taken care of, and now that I've met Winnie, I want to make sure she is too." He studies Sam for a moment. "Okay?"

"Yeah." Sam swallows. He nods when Penn lifts his eyebrows, checking that he means it. "Okay."

He sounds tired and I reach over and hug him again. "Get some sleep. We'll be working on all this. Don't worry."

He nods and goes into his room.

"He's too young to carry all of this on his shoulders," Penn says.

"I completely agree." I sigh.

We go downstairs and sit with Penn's parents, trying to figure out a plan. They are so in, it's almost overwhelming. Margo starts talking about helping with meal prep and then goes into school drops-off and even bedtime routines. Jeremy offers to be part of all that too, adding that he can look into some fun after-school activities for them to do together.

"This is a big deal, you guys," Jeremy says. "You've jumped from marriage to a preteen and a five-year-old practically overnight. Are you sure you're not taking on too much?"

"Well…it's why we really need your help too," Penn says sheepishly. "But I feel like I'm asking way too much from all of you."

"We're all in, Penn," Margo says. "We wouldn't be here if we didn't believe this is what we should be doing. I encourage you and Addy to really discuss it, though, because the first year of marriage is already an adjustment. It doesn't help that we're going into football season, and Addy, you're also adjusting to a new job. I don't want you to get burned out and your relationship to suffer."

"It is a lot," I agree, "but this is where I want to be."

I look at Penn when I say it and he exhales and then reaches out to take my hand.

"Thank you," he says. "Seriously, all of you…I know this is a lot, and well, I'm just so grateful."

We discuss the logistics of the next few days a little longer and then say goodnight, promising to keep talking about it tomorrow. Penn calls David and Sutton again, and I get ready for bed, taking a shower and checking on Sam and Winnie again before crawling into Penn's huge bed. I sigh when I lie down, exhaustion warring with my racing thoughts. When Penn comes in a while later, we face each other.

"This is kind of chaos, isn't it?" Penn says.

"Yeah, but it feels like it's chaos with a purpose. I feel good about what we're doing."

"Me too. This is just…more than you agreed to."

"I don't regret my decision," I tell him. "Not even a little bit."

He reaches out and touches my face and then kisses me. Things escalate quickly, but then I hear crying in the next room. I lean back and then jump out of bed, rushing to Winnie's room. She's sitting up, clutching her blanket.

"Winnie, it's me, Addy," I say. "Can I sit next to you?" I ask, pointing to the bed.

She sniffles and nods, still gasping to catch her breath. I grab a tissue from the side of the bed and wipe her face carefully. When she's cleaned up a little, I put my arm around her and she leans her head against my shoulder, her hiccups breaking my heart.

Instead of trying to talk, I start singing one of the songs we heard on *Frozen* earlier, and her breathing slows. I see Penn standing in the doorway, watching us, his eyes full of concern. When she falls asleep, he moves to the side of the bed and sits on the floor, and we watch her breathe for a long time.

The next morning is rough, with all of us exhausted and trying to hurry with a little girl who still won't talk. But after last night, she's sticking a little closer to me, so I make the executive decision to take her to work with me instead of sending her to school. I can tell she's still sore from the way she moves gingerly, and the black and blue around her eye looks even worse. While I'm giving her a bath, Penn sticks her blanket in the wash and it's ready in time to go to work with us.

Sam is still the champion, so careful and gentle with Winnie, putting scrambled eggs and fruit on her plate, and setting a stuffed bear next to her.

"Thought you might like this guy," he says. "I've had him a while and he always makes me feel better."

Winnie picks up the teddy bear and holds it while she eats. Penn's parents take Sam to school, and on the way to the training facility, Penn and I discuss what we'll do with Winnie all day.

"Well, she has to be with me...the only time I could use your help is when I'm doing lunch. The rest of the time, she can help or I can set her up with my iPad." I make a face. "Not that I want to immediately get her on screens, but—"

"Today, it might help here and there," Penn agrees.

We figure out a time we can probably leave, and it's not a perfect plan, but I think it will work.

And it does. Mostly.

It's just extra exhausting, making sure she's okay at all times. She helps me with laying out the granola bars and fruit and I keep her on a steady stream of healthy snacks. The thought of how hungry she must have been is horrifying. We get through the lunch rush, Penn coming to sit next to her while I hustle around. Once that's done, I guide her down the hall toward my office, pulling out my iPad to find a show for her while I have a Zoom meeting.

That's when I hear my dad's voice behind me. "Who's this?"

My whole body tenses, and I turn around slowly.

He's standing there, mouth tight with disapproval? Concern? I'm not sure what's going on in his mind. I'm not used to being at odds with my dad and I really don't like it.

"Hey, Dad." I look down at Winnie and smile at her, swinging her hand slightly. "Winnie, this is my dad, Rex. Dad, this is Winnie."

"Hello, Winnie," he says, smiling sweetly at her. He motions to the Uncrustables she's holding in the other hand. "Ahh, those are my favorite."

She tucks herself behind my leg, clutching my pants in her small fists. I rest a hand on her back.

"Here, why don't we go in here?" I suggest. "I thought you could watch a movie for a little bit while I'm on a video chat."

We walk into my office and I set her up in the chair next to me. She looks like a little queen when I'm done: the blanket, Sam's bear, and iPad on her lap, and snacks and drinks within easy reach.

"You okay?" I ask.

She nods.

My dad has watched me this whole time and I go to the doorway.

"What's the story there?" he asks softly. "Who did that to her?" He looks back in my office, his shoulders sagging.

He might be overly protective of me, but he's not cold-hearted. He wouldn't be on board with the way Penn and I are going about this whole situation, but he also would never want to see a child suffer.

"She was in Sam's foster home and they hurt her the same way they did Sam," I whisper.

He shakes his head. "Why are people so awful?" His eyes are sorrowful when they meet mine. "You've already got a lot on your plate, sweetheart. Between Sam and this…are you sure this isn't too much?"

"I can handle it," I say, my voice too sharp.

His eyes darken. "Are you sure? Because from where I'm standing, it looks like you could be letting this…situation interfere with your career. I really hope you're not planning on bailing on the Mustangs so soon."

I wince. "I'm not bailing."

He reaches out and puts his hand on my shoulder, squeezing it. "Just make sure you're taking care of yourself too. Okay? At least promise me that."

"I will, Dad." I take a deep breath and motion toward my computer. "I need to get to this Zoom meeting."

"Love you, Adeline. Why don't you come over for dinner this weekend?"

"I love you too. Me and Penn and the kids?"

His jaw tightens and he slowly nods. "You and Penn and the kids."

"Okay, I'll see what we can do. That…that sounds nice, Dad."

He knocks on the doorjamb. "Bye, Winnie. It was nice to meet you."

He grins when he sees that she's just taken a big bite of her sandwich and then walks away.

That went better than I expected.

CHAPTER TWENTY-SEVEN

THE NEW ME

PENN

The days fly by in a blur of noise and quiet. A strange contradiction that somehow makes sense. The house is always full—full of noise when Sam and Addy and my parents are around, full of silence when Winnie is playing nearby. Sometimes it feels like Addy and I are barely holding it together with Scotch tape and stubborn will, desperate to keep things from unraveling with one wrong move.

Mrs. Murphy let us know that Sam and Winnie can stay

with us for now, so we don't disrupt their routine. It still feels shaky and like the bottom could drop out from beneath us at any time.

We fall into bed each night, exhausted and hollow-eyed. We fall into each other, and it's always good—more than good. It's meaningful. Grounding. When everything else disappears and it's just us. Sometimes we fall asleep before we can escape into each other, and I'll drift off with her head on my chest, feeling the warmth of her skin against mine, and that alone also feels meaningful and grounding.

Winnie still hasn't spoken. To any of us. It distresses Sam because he knows what she was like before she was hurt, but we all make note of the improvements, smiling at each other when she sits on the counter while Addy's cooking and draws with her crayons, or when she comes over and sits next to me on the couch. We all want so badly to make things better for her, but we know we can't force it. Her nightmares are infrequent now, which is a relief. And her bedspread is lavender with unicorns and teddy bears covering the surface. We might've gotten a little carried away. She clicks her rainbow nightlight on every night before we take turns reading her stories.

Addy and I haven't wanted to overwhelm Winnie, but we also want her to see how great the people in our lives are. Sam wants her to meet the kids too. He tells her about them and how much she'll like everyone. And our friends are starting to push to get to know her better.

> **WESTON**
> When do we get to officially meet Winnie?
>
> **HENLEY**
> I've nearly texted that every day this week.

BOWIE

We're trying not to overwhelm you guys, but we'd really like to get to know her.

RHODES

And we miss you, man.

> I miss you too. I seriously don't know how you guys have been pulling all of this off for all this time.

HENLEY

Well, you've gotten a crash course in fast forward. We all had time to ease into this. I'm so fucking impressed with the way you and Addy have adapted so quickly.

BOWIE

How is Addy?

> She's so great. But I'm worried about her. She's exhausted, but she never ever complains. You know what? Let's get together. Can we do something Tuesday?

WESTON

It's the only day we could do something.

HENLEY

Same.

BOWIE

We're in.

RHODES

Us too.

I just thought we were living in chaos before.

Henley and Tru are the first to show up, Tru carrying a giant salad and macaroni and cheese, and Henley balancing drinks and Avery on his hip. Weston and Sadie come next with Caleb, who tears through the house like he's been mainlining sugar. Rhodes and Elle follow with Levi and their bulldog, Bogey, Elle toting an oversized bag of snacks that she insists are "healthy-ish." Bowie and Poppy arrive last, Bowie carrying Jonas and Poppy's belly being all she needs to carry right now. Becca's carrying their Chinese crested dog, Martha, and it's hard not to laugh every time I see that pup's crazy hair.

It's an instant party. The best kind.

Until Bogey starts chasing Levi and Caleb, and Martha barks at the commotion. My knee bounces as I stand next to Addy, both of us watching Winnie.

"Was this a bad idea?" I murmur. "Too much, too soon?"

Addy squeezes my hand. "I think she'll be okay.

Just then, Martha plops down at Winnie's feet and bends down to lick her bare toes. To our shock and utter delight, Winnie's head falls back and she laughs. Out loud.

Addy, Sam, and I exchange shocked looks. Addy covers her mouth with her hand, her eyes filling with tears. I clear my throat, trying to dislodge the lump that's forming. I had no idea I was going to turn into such a ball of emotions.

We introduce everyone and they all greet Winnie. She looks up shyly, taking it all in and laughs again when Bogey comes over to say hello too. Gracie, Henley's youngest daughter, tugs Winnie's hand, asking her to come play with them, and Addy and I share an excited look when she follows.

Later, when everyone's packing up, I stand by the door with Rhodes and Weston. Henley's trying to corral his girls, who are still running around with Sam and Winnie, and Bowie's walking out with a sleeping Jonas in his arms as Poppy and Becca hug us goodbye.

Just then, Winnie runs over and hands me a flower she picked from the yard.

I take it and lean down, kissing her on the cheek. "Thank you," I tell her.

She grins up at me and then runs off to join the kids again.

"This was good," Rhodes says, clapping me on the back. "She's coming out of her shell."

"Yeah," I say, feeling kind of stunned. "She is."

"I left The Single Dad Playbook on the island," Weston says.

I nod. "Can't wait to catch up in there."

After the last car pulls away and the house finally settles down, I sink onto the couch. Addy joins me, curling into my side. Winnie and Sam are already out cold in their rooms.

I pick up the book and open it up. Last time I read it, those guys were light-years ahead of me in the whole dad department. They always will be. I'm still barely figuring out how to make sure everyone is fed three meals a day without forgetting one, and that's mostly thanks to Addy.

I flip to the new entries.

Penn, you are showing up in a way that has me in awe.
Damn, it is incredible to see you sacrificing
everything for these kids.
You're not messing around.
Once you decided you were going to be a dad,
YOU WENT FOR IT.
Absolutely incredible.

~Bowie

That's how I feel about Bowie. He was always an exceptional dad to his daughter Becca. She has Down Syndrome and for the first nine years of her life, he raised her alone, like a true superhero. And now he loves Poppy and has Jonas and another baby on the way, and he's so happy. I was so resistant to being in a relationship like that, even with seeing how my friends' lives were changed for the better when they fell in love.

Now, I'm not so sure why I resisted for so long.

I hereby bequeath Penn Father of the Year.
~Weston

I chuckle and shake my head. Addy's reading the entries along with me and she smiles up at me.

"It's true, you know. You are."

"I have no fucking clue what I'm doing."

She leans her chin on my shoulder. "Did you hear the way she laughed tonight? Did you see the way Sam never stopped smiling?" She places a kiss on my chin. "You may not have a clue, but you're still getting the job done."

"Thanks to you," I say, leaning in closer to kiss her.

We get lost in that for a few minutes and then she taps the book.

"There were more," she says. "And then I vote we go to bed."

"Yeah?" I say, eyes brightening. "Race you there?"

She laughs and then gasps.

I look down to where she's pointing.

Our pretty boy has finally grown up.
He didn't even announce it when he won
the Sexiest Man Alive title!
~Rhodes

"Why didn't you tell me?" she says.

I lift a shoulder. "I've been too busy to think about it between practice and the kids." I laugh and swipe my hand down my face. "I can't believe how much my life has changed. I used to care about the stupidest things."

"It's not stupid. It's fun and well-earned and *true*."

I wave her off. "I like this life a lot better."

"I like it a lot too," she whispers.

I stand and reach down, picking her up. She laughs as I jog her up the stairs.

"I wasn't done reading," she says, giggling into my neck.

"That can wait. Let me show you just how much I like this life…with *you*," I tell her when I have her laid out on our bed.

I kiss my way down her body and make sure she has no doubts.

The Mustangs have won all their preseason games. We've finally found our groove again and it's great. But it feels a little surreal that things are clicking so well on the field when everything off the field feels like sludging uphill in muddy water.

Tonight is our first game of the season and we win the game. 38-0.

"You're playing better than you ever have," Rhodes tells me as we're walking to the family area afterward.

"You think so? Thanks, man," I say, bumping his fist.

When we reach the room, I see Addy hustling to make sure all the bagged lunches are ready for the players and Winnie's standing close to my mom's side, her head tipped back as my mom talks to her. My dad and Sam are reenacting a play from the game and both are beaming.

Addy walks over when she sees me. "Such a great game!" she says excitedly.

I lean in and kiss her, something I can't resist doing anymore, no matter who's around. Never thought I'd be that man either, but her fucking lips are like a lifeline.

"Thank you, Siren," I whisper.

I crouch down in front of Winnie and smile. "Did you like the game?"

She hesitates for a second, her green eyes flicking to mine.

Then she says, so quietly that I almost think I've imagined it, "Yes."

You'd think she'd just quoted the periodic table from the way we all react. My mom gasps. My dad lets out a loud laugh. Sam's eyes widen as he rushes toward her. Addy's hand flies to her mouth.

"You liked it?" I repeat, just to see if she'll say it again.

She bobs her head quickly.

"That's awesome," I say, my throat tight.

I reach out and squeeze her hand gently. She smiles at me and I have to blink really fast.

Addy slides her hand into my free hand. I glance over and see tears in her eyes, her lips trembling.

Winnie's first word. After all this time. A small win, maybe, but it feels huge. Like we've just scaled the first ledge of a mountain.

Sam throws his arms around Winnie. "Told you it was fun!" he says, and she doesn't pull away. He leans his head against hers. "I've missed hearing your voice, Winnie." His eyes are glassy when he looks up at me, and God, I love that kid.

I'm still flying high when we get home. It was a Sunday afternoon game, so there's still time in the day to hang out. We walk inside and Winnie practically skips through the door, her curls bouncing as she pauses to hang her backpack on the hook. I watch her flop onto the carpet, reaching for the basket of coloring books and markers that Addy bought for her. She starts coloring without hesitation, her tongue peeking out at the corner of her mouth in concentration.

I sit down next to her, legs crossed. "Hey, Winnie?"

She looks up at me, her big eyes trusting. Her cheeks are rosier and more filled out than when she first came.

"Do you like it here?" I ask. "With us?" My voice feels too thick, like it's stuck in a well.

She nods without hesitation. "I love it," she says.

My throat tightens as her answer hits me square in the chest. My eyes burn and I swallow hard, trying to keep it together. "Yeah? That makes me really happy."

She nods again, like it's an obvious deduction, and gets lost in her coloring book again.

Later that night, when the kids are asleep and Addy and I have made up for some lost time this week by having sex in the shower and the bed afterward, she lies with her head on my chest, our fingers laced together. She fits against me, like she's always belonged here.

"Addy?" I say quietly, in case she's already asleep.

"Yeah?"

"I know all of this has gotten way bigger than when we started." My thumb runs over her knuckles. "But where are you with things?"

She swallows hard. I feel her tense against me before her shoulders relax again. "It's been really hard and challenging, and I'm more exhausted than I've ever been." She pulls back just enough to look at me, and her eyes are big and honest and absolutely gorgeous. "But, Penn…" Her voice shakes a little. "I'm kind of loving this life we're creating together."

I freeze.

"Really?" My voice cracks and my heart slams against my ribs.

She gives me that smile that always levels me. "Really." And then she says, "What do you think about us committing to this long-term? You and me…and we try to adopt both of them?"

I swear I stop breathing.

The old me would have run. Hell, I would've never been here in the first place.

But this me, the one who's won a game and done homework at the kitchen table all in the same day, the one who's learning how to French braid hair even though I still suck…I want this more than I can explain.

"I…" My chest feels too full. "I'm kind of loving this life we're creating together too."

Her eyes gleam in the moonlight.

"And…" My throat works as I lift her hand to my mouth and kiss her fingers. "I'm kind of really loving you."

Her breath stutters, and she launches herself at me, her arms tight around my neck as I bury my face in her shoulder.

"Me too," she whispers. "Me too."

"I love you," I tell her.

"I love you too, Penn."

I hold her tighter against me, feeling like maybe this is the life I was meant to have all along.

CHAPTER TWENTY-EIGHT

GOLDEN BOY

ADELINE

"Are you ready for your *golden* birthday party?" I ask Sam at breakfast.

It's September twelfth and Sam is twelve today.

"I can't believe you're twelve," Penn says wistfully.

"I'm ready," Sam says, stuffing his face with scrambled eggs and then barely swallowing before he takes a huge bite of waffle. I swear it's like I can see him growing taller right before my eyes.

"What if we go out for a little while?" Penn suggests. "Lunch at Starlight Cafe? Or at least a stop into Serendipity? It's such a nice day out."

"That sounds good to me," Sam says.

"Can I have a strawberry shake?" Winnie asks.

There's still a giddy feeling in the air when Winnie speaks, even though she's been doing it for a while now.

"Absolutely," Penn says, reaching out to bop her nose.

She giggles and it's the best sound in the world. Watching her personality break out more all the time is one of the most fulfilling things I've experienced.

"Isn't the Pop-Up Market going on this weekend?" I ask.

"Oh yeah, you're right. Even better." Penn grins at me. "How soon can we go?"

Sam starts eating faster and I laugh. "There's time to chew your food. I think as soon as we're done eating and brushing teeth, we can go…"

Silver Hills is buzzing when we park and walk down Jupiter Lane. The Pixie Pop-Up Market is in full swing, and everyone is out and about, laughing and chatting on the sidewalks instead of hanging out inside the shops.

Clara's standing outside Luminary Coffeehouse and waves when she sees us coming.

"There's the perfect family to start off the dancing," she calls.

"Are we sure about that?" Penn asks. "We might cause too much of a commotion."

"Like you would ever mind that," she says, laughing.

Penn's smile grows. "Guess you've got a point there. And it's Sam's birthday, so I think it's the best day for a little dancing."

Clara cues up "Uptown Funk" by Mark Ronson and

Bruno Mars on her phone, and the second that familiar beat hits, we all spring into action. Even Winnie.

Sam holds out his hand to her and spins her around and her head falls back as she laughs. Penn busts out a smooth shoulder roll thing that makes me stop mid-step because he is *still* managing to surprise me with his moves. Sam grins from ear to ear, and when Penn does a high kick that almost takes Clara's head off, Sam bursts out laughing. I join in, stepping in sync with Penn and Winnie, until we're all moving together in a weird little flash mob. At the end, Penn lowers me in a dramatic dip, low enough that I'm clutching his shirt to keep from tipping over. We're all out of breath when Clara raises her hands over her head and cheers with the rest of the crowd who's gathered.

"That was perfect," Clara sings. "You guys win."

"What did we win?" Sam asks excitedly.

"Free drinks."

"Come on, Clara. We'll pay," Penn says, handing her the cash. "But I am proud of that high kick."

Winnie giggles and we all grin at her.

"And how about our Winnie dancing her little heart out?" Penn says.

She wraps her arms around his waist and looks up at him. Yeah, she's managed to fall madly in love with Penn too. She reaches out her hand to me and I go over there and hug them both, tugging Sam into the fold.

"Such a beautiful family," Clara says, sniffling. She clears her throat and waves a hand over her eyes. "Goodness, it's windy out here."

We sip our coffees and hot chocolates as we drift through the market, picking up a few trinkets—a beaded bracelet for Winnie, a cool wooden carving of a dog for Sam, and a gorgeous kite that Sam says will be *legendary* by the water.

Eventually we end up at Serendipity's booth for shakes and Greer and Wyndham burst into song when they see Sam.

"How does everyone know it's my birthday?" Sam laughs, his cheeks pink.

"It's big news around here," Penn says, shrugging. "Our boy is *twelve*."

Every time he says it, he looks like he might cry, but he snaps out of it.

Greer and Wyndham give Sam an enormous chocolate shake with whipped cream, sprinkles, and sparklers sticking out of the top, and Winnie is happy with her strawberry shake with fresh strawberries and whipped cream.

A little bit later when we pass Pet Galaxy, Sam's eyes light up. "Oh! Can we go in?"

Penn and I exchange a tentative look. Every time we're around our friends and their pets, Sam and Winnie are in heaven. They *love* animals.

"This is dangerous territory," Penn whispers.

"Yeah, it's all fun and games until someone falls in love with a creature," I whisper back.

But Sam's already looking at us with those big eyes, and Winnie's pressing her hands together under her chin like a cartoon princess.

"Okay," Penn says. "But we're not leaving with any animals."

"Mm-hmm," I chime in.

Famous last words.

We picked the worst time to stop in…well, depending on who you ask. Because it's pet adoption day at Pet Galaxy, which means there are dogs wagging their tails in crates, and cats lounging on plush beds or chasing each other. Jerry, the guy who's been at Pet Galaxy for as long as I can remember, is chatting with all the customers. Sam and

Winnie walk toward the pen of kittens when suddenly Sam stops short.

When Penn sees what he's looking at, he lets out a terrified, "Ahhh!" He shakes his head. "No. What is that?"

Big ears. Wrinkled, hairless body. One green eye and one blue eye.

"I've never seen a Sphynx cat in real life," Sam breathes.

"Oh, hell no," Penn says.

"She's *beautiful*," Winnie whispers in awe.

"She's terrifying," Penn argues, shuddering.

Jerry ambles over, smiling at us. "I see you're admiring our majestic Jezebel."

I laugh at the name.

"She's been here a few weeks." Jerry shakes his head sadly. "No one seems to want her."

"Nobody wants her?" Sam repeats, his eyes going wide.

My heart clenches. Oh no.

"Aww," Winnie says, stepping closer. "I want her."

"Me too," Sam says softly.

"Aw, hell," Penn mutters. He looks at me, resigned. "That'd be crazy, right?"

I laugh. "Completely. But we seem to be all about the crazy."

He leans in. "I've never seen anything scarier looking than that thing." He stares at the cat like it might launch itself at his throat.

"It's hard to not be wanted," Sam says quietly.

Penn curses under his breath. "Yank my heartstrings into a fist, why don't you?"

Jerry opens the pen, and the cat stretches lazily before hopping out and walking straight toward Sam and Winnie. Sam sits on the floor, and the cat climbs into his lap without hesitation, curling up like she was always meant to be there. Winnie strokes her back, and the cat starts to purr.

"Oh no," Penn says.

"Oh yes," I reply, smiling as I watch Sam's face soften.

Penn sighs deeply, rubbing the back of his neck. "Guess we're getting a cat."

Sam and Winnie cheer. Jezebel looks up at them coolly and lets out a long, contented sigh before nestling back into Sam's arms.

"Welcome to the family," I say, reaching out to pet Jezebel. My nose scrunches when I feel her. It'll take time to get used to her wrinkly skin.

But what else is new with us? Every day feels like we're diving into a new adventure.

Penn eyes the cat with a mix of fear and reluctance. Sam stands up and holds Jezebel within reach of Penn.

"Pet her," he says. "She feels so weird, but it's awesome."

Penn reluctantly pets her and shudders again. "Ohhh, I don't know about this," he groans.

We all laugh at him and he jumps when the cat nuzzles into his hand. He puts his other hand on his heart and exhales.

"Not gonna need to work out with this lady around. She's got my heart rate pumping."

Sam's birthday party is in full swing, and I'm leaning against Penn's chest as we watch Sam. He's got that big, easy smile on his face, the one that makes my chest feel like it's about to crack open. Obviously, he has us both wrapped around his little finger. Penn has been doing jump scares every time he sees Jezebel in the house, and it's freaking hilarious.

Sam is holding a football and throws a spiral at Cassidy

like it's nothing. She's giving Sam her undivided attention and he can't stop smiling.

"I think Cassidy is looking at Sam a little differently today," Penn says, tipping his head toward them.

"Isn't she a few years older than him? I mean that'd be so cute, but..." I smile up at Penn. "Who knows? Maybe they'll date when they're older."

"Oh, I think it's guaranteed," Penn says, smirking. "He's got charm." He sighs. "I've taught him well."

I roll my eyes. "Good thing I'm around to balance him out."

"What are we talking about over here?" Elle steps up and takes a bite of her cupcake.

"We're watching Sam and Cassidy together and wondering if they'll ever sneak out and date," I fill her in.

"I can see it." She nods. "Childhood friends-to-lovers, and she's the grump to his sunshine. *And* age gap. *Or...*" she draws it out. "He could surprise us all and end up with Audrey." She waves her hand. "Plot twist. Sister's ex-boyfriend. Oh! Or Gracie! Oh my God, what if it's Gracie!"

I clutch my heart. "That's so Laurie and Amy from *Little Women*! I don't know if my heart could take it."

Penn laughs. "Should we be worried that Elle is scripting our children's future romantic drama?"

My heart warms when he says *our children*. "Absolutely," I say without hesitation.

She loves that, her shoulders shaking as she laughs. "What can I say? It's in my blood." She takes a bite of her cupcake and eyes Sam and Cassidy again. "They've got good chemistry. But," she points at Gracie, who is leaping in the air catching bubbles nearby, "honestly, I think Gracie's the wild card."

"Interesting," Penn says. He points at Elle. "Your mind is a scary and informative place."

She winks and points back at him. "Don't you forget it."

The house is finally quiet. I'm standing at the sink in my tank and shorts, rinsing the last of the dishes with Penn, when he turns off the water and moves behind me.

"Hey," I murmur, drying my hands.

"Hey." His voice is soft and warm, and threaded with something deeper.

His hands slide under my shirt, palms gliding up my skin until they reach my breasts.

I turn to face him and he leans his forehead against mine.

"It was a good day," he says.

"A great day. Sam was so happy."

"Yeah, I love seeing him like this. Winnie too."

"It's really hot when you're in full dad-mode."

He pulls my shirt over my head and bends down to tongue my nipple over the lace. "Yeah? You like dad-mode?"

"Very much," I gasp.

He puts his hands on my hips and lifts me, kissing me as my legs wind around his waist. I tug at his shirt, pulling it off. He leans me against the wall, kissing me deeper. My head tips back and his mouth trails down my neck, tasting the skin there. My breath hitches.

"Penn," I breathe, nails scraping lightly against the back of his neck.

"I've been wanting to do this all day," he says, pressing against me. I tighten my legs around him and drag my nails down his stomach.

"Bedroom?" I ask, my mouth against his ear.

"How about here and then bedroom?"

I whimper and our bodies tangle together, fevered and rushed. I grip his shoulders as he tugs down my shorts, and when he slides his fingers between my thighs, he pulls back to stare at me.

"I love how you feel."

I arch against him.

"My favorite place," he says, as he slides a finger inside. "You. Are. My. Favorite. Place."

My head drops back against the wall, and he watches as he works me slowly, teasing me toward the edge with another finger.

My eyes flutter closed, but when his thumb rubs circles against me too, I struggle to open them. He watches me with full concentration, his body attuned to mine. Just as I'm getting so close, he pulls his hand away, and I let out a frustrated sound, which makes him grin.

Cocky bastard.

He slides his sweats down and lifts me higher as he lines us up.

My eyes go wide when he sinks into me. "Oh, God—"

He has every right to be a cocky bastard. The guy has awakened my body like no one ever before. There's just no comparison to be made.

"I needed to feel that pussy so bad," he says, his voice going raspy as he thrusts into me, slow and deep.

My legs shake, and my nails drag down his back. He buries his face in my neck, holding me steady.

"Penn," his name spills from my mouth, breathy.

I tug his hair hard enough to make him groan and he presses me harder into the wall, angling deeper, encouraging me when I tighten around him.

"That's it. I want to feel everything when you fall apart," he says. "You're so good, Addy. So perfect."

I tremble, my body tensing as I shatter around him, and it pulls him over the edge right after me. He buries so deep inside, and the aftershocks burn through me.

Our breaths are shaky as we stare at each other.

"I don't want to ever let you go," he says.

"Please don't," I whisper.

"Do you mean it?" His eyes search mine and I nod.

"With all my heart."

"I love you," he whispers. "God, I can't believe that I found you and that I love you so goddamn much."

I grin. "You weren't expecting me?"

He shakes his head. "I never saw you coming." He leans in and gives me a long, scorching kiss. When we pull apart, he looks dazed. "I've never been so happy to be proven wrong."

Eventually, we gather our clothes and put them back on before quietly going upstairs. We check on the kids and when we peek in Sam's room, Penn clamps his hand over his mouth to shush the yelp that came out of him when he sees Jezebel lying on Sam's bed, staring up at us in the dark.

"*Fuck,* that cat is going to make me old before my time." He backs out of the room quickly, and I try not to wake the kids up with how hard I'm laughing.

CHAPTER TWENTY-NINE

FLOUNDERING

PENN

It might be strange to some that before I met Sam, I never gave any thought to being a dad. It felt too out of reach, just not my thing. I was good at football and charming women, and that's about all I cared to pursue.

Meeting Sam changed everything. And then meeting Addy in the Bahamas sent me on another tailspin. I hardly recognize myself these days.

We're in David's office at Shaw & Shaw, waiting for him

and Sutton to walk in. Sutton's married to David's daughter, Felicity, and it's evident the two men have a lot of respect for each other. Felicity lived with Weston briefly and I was around to see some of Felicity's relationship with Sutton develop. It's another example of how far we've *all* come.

Addy's hand rests on my thigh, and I stop bouncing my leg. She's calm and steady. The opposite of how I feel. She's in a fitted navy dress and high heels. She looks smoking hot. But her outfit also screams responsible adult in capital letters. Her eyes have that edge of sharpness they get when she's trying to hide her nerves.

It's also one of the busiest weeks we've ever had, but we've both managed to fit this in, despite it all.

"You okay?" I ask under my breath.

She smiles faintly. "Doing all right. How about you?"

Absolutely not.

Before I can answer, the door opens and in walks David Shaw. Since getting close to Weston, I've loved getting to know his family too, and David is such a smart, kind man. He's not a big talker, but when he speaks, you listen. Sutton walks in with him and there are hugs all around. I'm man enough to say that Sutton Landmark is a smokeshow, and I've heard the girls talk about him enough to know they are in full agreement.

"I'm really grateful you came all this way," I tell him.

"For you, anything. And hey, your playing this season... insane. You guys are *back,* and my brothers and I have specifically talked about how your game has gone next level. Love must suit you." He grins at Addy.

"Thanks, man. I really appreciate that. And I think you're right." I glance at Addy and smile when I see her pink cheeks.

"Penn, Adeline, it's good to see you both." David's voice

is warm as he closes the door behind him. He drops a leather folder onto the table and then settles into the seat across from us. "We've had the word out for almost two months now, looking for any biological family members for Winnie who might step forward. So far, no one has. No challenges, no disputes."

My chest aches. I squeeze Addy's hand.

"And Sam?" I ask, though I already know the answer.

"No surprises there either," David says. "We've known for a long time that no one from Sam's biological family would challenge the adoption. It's been more a matter of Penn, and now the two of you, being approved." He grins at us. "And we're getting closer to it every day." He glances at Sutton.

"It's all looking good," Sutton agrees. "The paperwork is straightforward from here. If there are no objections, you could have a final ruling within a few months. Since it's all going through the Denver courts, it could be a little longer, but I've been putting in a good word for you guys." He grins.

"A few months." I sit back, my hand sliding over my face. I let out a relieved laugh. "Wow. That's...incredible."

I look at Addy and she's lifting her hand up to wipe away a tear. I put my arm around her and scoot closer.

Sutton's smile grows. "I don't think you'll find a judge in this state who would deny it. Especially with how involved you've been in both Sam and Winnie's lives. In Sam's case, Penn, you've been there for years. The stability you've provided, the love..." He glances at Addy. "You've done everything right."

Addy gives him a tremulous smile and when she looks at me, I can tell how hard she's working to stay calm.

"Thank you," she says softly. "For everything."

"I'll file the last round of paperwork this week," David

says. "If you don't hear from me, don't worry. It means everything's progressing as expected."

We talk for another half hour about what to expect and then about how everyone in Landmark Mountain is doing. When the meeting comes to a close, we thank them again and walk out into the bright afternoon sunlight.

Addy sighs, her hand linked with mine. "That went well...right?"

"Really well. For the first time, I'm letting myself hope. Like...really hope." I take a deep breath, my thoughts whirling.

This is happening. We're going to be a family. For real.

Addy rests her head briefly against my shoulder as we walk to the SUV. "Penn? Do you ever feel like things are going *too* well?"

Her words make the hair on the back of my neck rise. "I do know that feeling. But I think we've earned some good." I brush a kiss against her temple.

She nods and smiles, but it's tentative and distracted.

That weekend we travel for a game, and it's really hard telling the kids bye. Winnie clings to Addy's legs and Addy bawls when we get in the car to go to the training facility.

"How can I leave her when she's so terrified of being left?" she cries.

My heart is heavy too. I hold her hand and my other is clenched around the steering wheel. "She loves being with my parents, and Sam will make sure she's okay too."

"He shouldn't have to carry that," she says.

She seems off the whole weekend. She still puts on a smile and does her job, working her ass off to make everything perfect for the team, but I catch her crying more than once, and her eyes have dark circles under them. I try to talk her into coming to my room, but she insists on letting me rest before the game. I miss having her next to me so much that it's unsettling.

When we get back home, the kids are asleep. We go into their rooms and kiss their foreheads. This time I was bracing myself for Jezebel, so she doesn't give me a heart attack when I see her nestled against Sam's legs.

Sam's eyes open, and he whispers, "Hey, you're back," before falling back to sleep.

We go to our room and get ready for bed, and Addy presses her fingers to her temples like she has a headache.

"You okay?" I ask.

"Just tired," she says, flashing me a quick smile as she grabs her toothbrush.

The following week, she's still quiet, and I can't ignore it anymore.

We're on the couch and her head is resting against the back. She looks exhausted.

"Addy," I say, leaning over to kiss her shoulder. "Hey. Talk to me."

Her eyes flutter shut. "I just…" she pauses. "It's a lot. You know?"

It's like a flood of ice-cold water pours through my body.

"You mean the adoption?"

Her eyes snap open. "No." She sits up. "Yes. I don't know."

"You're having second thoughts?"

Her eyes widen. "No! Penn, no. It's not that."

"Then what?"

She shakes her head. "I don't know how to explain what I'm feeling."

"Try me, Addy. I really want to know."

She leans forward, covering her face with her hands. Her voice is barely above a whisper. "What if I screw it up?"

"Addy...not possible."

"I mean it, Penn." Her eyes are shiny when she looks at me. "I want this. I want this so much it scares me. But what if I'm not what they need?"

God. My heart aches at the look on her face.

"You *are*," I tell her. "You're better than good. It's like you know exactly what they need. And you cover for me in all the ways that I'm floundering."

Her laugh is watery. "You're not floundering. You're doing an amazing job. Those kids love you so much."

"They love you too."

"That's the thing...me knowing what they need. I don't know how to not feel like I'm letting them down when I leave."

"Lots of parents have to travel for work."

"And I'm sure it's hard for their kids, but not as hard as it is for kids who have never had a stable home to begin with. Can you imagine what must be going through Winnie's mind? Did you see the way she held onto me and cried?" She puts her head in her hands and I rub her back, feeling helpless.

"I think they'll adjust," I say finally. "We can do this. We *are* doing this."

She lifts her head and wipes her face and then slowly nods. "I hope you're right."

I lay awake long after we've gone upstairs and made love. I hold her against me, listening to her soft breaths and not wanting to let her go. I kiss her hair and can't shake the feeling that something is about to break.

I only hope we'll be strong enough to weather it.

CHAPTER THIRTY

THE ONLY POSITIVE

ADELINE

I'm drowning. Not the dramatic, desperate-to-breathe kind. It's slower, more methodical. Like my limbs just can't tread water anymore. No matter how hard I try to push through it, the weight keeps dragging me down.

It's been a relentless feeling. Work, Penn, Sam, Winnie—it's all good stuff, but every day feels like a hamster wheel I can't stop. I hit the ground running each morning, and by the time I crawl into bed at night, my mind is still spinning. I'm not sleeping well. I can't shut it off.

This weekend isn't helping. Another away game, another stretch of time away from home. When I first took the job, the traveling was exciting. Now it just feels like another thing pulling me away from where I'm needed most.

Is this what being a mom feels like?

Sam's handling it okay. He's tough, resilient in a way that shatters me sometimes. But Winnie…she's starting to crack. She clings to me more lately. Cries as I'm packing for the trip. Cries as I'm leaving.

I've let her know that she's not going to another home, that we're doing everything in our power to keep her and Sam forever, but it's not enough.

This morning, her eyes were wide and her lashes fringed with tears as she whispered, "You'll come back, right?"

That nearly broke me. I told her we'd have tonight together and then Margo and Jeremy would do lots of fun things while Penn and I are gone this weekend. And that Jezebel would be there to play with too, which brightened her smile.

"I love Margo and Jeremy," she said, sighing. "And Jezebel. I just miss you and Penn so bad."

"We miss you too, sweet girl. So, so much."

I leave crying again and then try to suck it up and engross myself in the job. It's the only positive about being away—the job keeps my mind occupied. And Penn.

And that's a bit pathetic, isn't it? That my whole sense of comfort comes down to sneaking into his room just to sleep next to him, because otherwise, I'm stuck inside my head, spiraling over every decision I've made—or haven't made—over the last few months.

I try to resist it and follow the rules. But Penn doesn't make it easy.

Because he knows me too well.

> **PENN**
> Come to my room.

He snuck a key into my pocket when we said goodnight.

> Go to sleep, Penn.

> **PENN**
> I can't sleep without you.

I roll my eyes at that one.

> You've fallen asleep without me just fine for years. You can do it again.

> **PENN**
> These are really the only date nights we get right now…when we're traveling. BTW, I want to change that when we get home.

> You want to date me?

> **PENN**
> Yes.

> You just want me in your bed.

> **PENN**
> I do love having you in my bed. I'll behave. Just come lie down with me.

> If I believed you, maybe I would consider it. But you don't know how to behave.

PENN

😊 Okay, how's this? I promise to only make you come twice.

I snort and cover my face with my pillow. My thumbs hover over my phone for a second before I give in.

Once.

He answers so fast I laugh out loud.

PENN
Deal.

I'm foolish for letting him talk me into this, not to mention, my dad would flip if he knew. Who am I kidding? He probably already knows.

But it's late, and I'm tired, and truthfully, the idea of being close to Penn is too tempting to resist.

When I slip into his room, he's already stretched out across the bed, naked, looking like the man of every single dream I've ever had. He grins and I climb in next to him, pulling the blankets over both of us. His hand slips under my shirt before I can protest, his fingers skimming over my stomach.

"I said once," I remind him.

He nuzzles into my neck, his voice low and dark. "I heard you." He kisses his way down my body and when his tongue skims over my clit, I jerk against his face. I feel his lips lift against my skin, and then he doesn't waste time. He keeps a steady tempo, his fingers spreading me wide, and then he sucks and his fingers dip in. He hums encouragingly when I rock against him, and right as I'm fisting the sheets and falling apart, he leans up and flips me over so I'm on top of him.

I'm so wet that when he lines me up and slides me over his hard length, there's little resistance. He's so big and I'm so full, and the look on his face is enough to make me weak all over.

"I know I promised only once," he says, leaning up to take my nipple in his mouth as he rocks up into me. "And I'd rather have stayed between your legs with my mouth a lot longer, but the need to feel your sweet flutters around my dick won out."

"I love how you feel," I tell him, breathless. "And this is one promise you can go back on."

We do sleep eventually, but he wakes me up early the next morning to start the day the right way.

After a huge win, I'm back in his room, and this time, we don't bother pretending we're going to sleep. We're wrapped up in each other, limbs tangled, our mouths finding each other over and over like we're trying to memorize every kiss, every touch. I wrap my hand around him, stroking up and down, and then I lower myself and hear his breathing sharpen when my tongue circles over him. I want to take my time with him and swallow him whole and when I look up at him, my mouth dipping up and down, he looks down at me with reverence.

"Addy," he rasps. "You have every part of me. You know that, right?"

I take him deeper and his head falls back as he groans. But he can't stop watching, so he lifts his head back up, his hand fisting around my hair.

"Fuck. Fuck, Addy. You're so good. So, so good." He groans when I hum over him, and the next thing I know, he tugs my mouth off of him. "I have to be in you," he says. "I have to." He gets on his knees and moves behind me. "You can stay right here." He sounds playful now and he pulls my ass in the air, his fingers moving between my legs. "Mmm. Just what I was hoping. Did your mouth around my cock get you ready for me, Siren?"

I whimper into the bed as he strokes me, and then gasp when he plunges inside of me. I scream out his name and he spreads my backside, his thrusts going faster and harder. I press back into him, meeting him each time, and when his fingers tap against my clit, little slaps that hit it just right, I lose my mind. We come together, Penn curling his chest against my back as he tells me he loves me over and over.

When we get home, the high from the weekend disappears fast.

"Sam did so amazing at his football game," Margo says, beaming at Sam as we eat dinner together. "He scored twice!"

Penn lights up. "I heard. That's my guy!"

Sam had called to let us know and the joy on his face when Penn told him how proud he was of him—priceless.

"And Winnie..." Margo smiles fondly. "She's been showing us all the moves she learned at dance. She loves Wiggles & Whimsy, don't you?"

Winnie nods excitedly.

Penn's eyes flash toward me and my chest squeezes painfully. He knew I didn't want to miss her first class at Wiggles & Whimsy.

"Will you show us everything you learned after dinner?" I ask Winnie.

She gets up and does a little lopsided twirl, her hair

falling out of her messy bun. Her arms flail slightly, but her smile is so bright it hurts.

"That's amazing," I say, clapping. "You're incredible."

Winnie giggles and rushes toward Penn, grabbing his hand. "Do it with me!"

He humors her immediately, hopping up and taking her hands, spinning her around. She squeals, her face glowing.

"Okay, we better let dinner settle a little before we do too much twirling," I say.

I try to sound lighthearted, but that familiar pressing has slid into my chest again.

Because I'm missing it.

I'm missing all of it.

I didn't even know how badly I wanted this until they came into my life. Some days it blinds me how much I love the people at this table. Not to mention our furless creature. Jezebel is adjusting to home life, and she's just one more in this household for me to love and miss.

We finish dinner and when Winnie starts to yawn, I take her upstairs and help her into bed. I sit beside her, brushing the hair from her face as her eyes start to flutter closed.

I should go to bed too, but I can't seem to move.

I sit there long after she's fallen asleep, tracing the line of her hair, her tiny hand curled against her cheek.

"I'm not going to let you down," I whisper.

She doesn't hear me, but I say it anyway.

"I promise."

CHAPTER THIRTY-ONE

REPUTATIONS AND VILLAGES

PENN

I'm the last one to show up at Luminary, which isn't surprising. Our room is noisy when I walk in, and the guys all stop talking to say hello. Rhodes looks like he could use a nap, and Bowie's already drinking his coffee like it's a lifeline. Weston and Henley are sharing a muffin.

"You can't get your own muffin?" I ask Weston.

He shrugs. "Trying to do what your wife said and cut out some of the sugar."

I grin. Despite my worries lately, it still makes my heart zing when I realize I've got a wife.

It's the weirdest thing.

"All right," Henley says, stretching his shoulders. "What's the emergency?"

"Yeah, we're all wondering, and I am sleepy, so I'm not sure I will have the best tips." Rhodes yawns. "Unless it's to tell you about this move I tried on Elle last night that was—"

"Okay," I hold up my hand, "normally I'd be all about hearing that move, but I don't have long today. I need to get home as soon as I can. I'm worried, guys." I run a hand through my hair and plop in the chair, leaning my elbows on the table. "It's Addy."

Weston frowns. "Is she okay?"

"I don't know." I swallow hard and look up. "I don't think so."

Bowie shifts in his seat. "What's going on?"

"She's tired. Exhausted, really. And distant. I don't know how much longer she can keep going like this." I rub the back of my neck. "Sam and Winnie are amazing, and Addy is just…she's unbelievable with them. She loves them so much. But she's trying to give her all to her job, give her all to our marriage…and give her all to the kids…and—" I shake my head. "I don't know if she's happy. I don't think she can keep going this way. And I don't feel right about her giving up her dream job. My contract will expire before too long. I want to take her into account when I make my decision. I don't have to keep doing this."

Rhodes straightens. "You'd quit football?"

"I've made enough money for us to be set," I say. "I love the game. You know I do. But Addy—she's worked for years to get where she is too. If I can do something to help alleviate the pressure, I feel like I should. And I'm the one who got her into this situation. Two kids overnight?" I groan. "What was I thinking?"

Even though she offered to help me get Sam, we didn't know it would be like this. Winnie is a gift we weren't expecting—the *best* gift—but it's a lot, and I feel like all the pressure is breaking Addy down with each passing day.

And I'm not sure she still feels like she did the right thing.

Henley whistles. "Wow."

Weston leans forward. "Have you talked to her about it?"

I exhale. "I've tried. But right now, I'm scared that if I bring it up, she'll feel like she's failing. Like I think she can't handle it."

"You need to talk to her," Rhodes says firmly. "Let her know you see how hard she's working. And that she doesn't have to do this alone."

"Yes," Weston agrees. "Sadie's mentioned that Addy hasn't been to the last few girls' nights. If she's isolating herself, that's not good."

Bowie nods. "And they'd love to help her. She needs to know there's support. It's hard to become a full-time mom overnight."

Henley puts his hand on my shoulder and squeezes. "It takes a village, remember?"

"What if she says she can't do it anymore?" I pick at the napkin that came with my drink.

"Then you figure it out together," Weston says. "This is probably still just all of you trying to find your equilibrium."

"Yeah." I swallow hard. "Okay. Thanks. This is helping me breathe a little easier."

After I leave the guys, I spot Coach Evans sitting at one of the corner tables. He's alone, his hands wrapped around a mug. I hesitate for half a second before walking over.

"Hey, Coach."

He looks up, surprised, then looks to see if Addy or the kids are with me. "Penn. Sit down?"

"Sure." I sit down across from him and try not to tap my fingers on the table. It drives him crazy when I do that. "How've you been?"

He pauses before taking a drink and then says, "Actually, I'm glad to see you. I've been worried about Addy."

I blink. "Me too."

His eyes sharpen. "She tells you more than she tells me, I guess."

I shift in my seat. "I don't know about that. But I think she's overwhelmed. And honestly..." I rub my jaw and lean in so he's the only one who can hear me. "I've been thinking about quitting football when my contract is up."

His eyes widen. "Quitting?"

The shock in his voice would make me laugh if this weren't so serious.

"Yeah. I don't want her to give up her job because of me and the kids." I keep my voice low. "She's worked so hard for it. If one of us has to step back, it should be me."

He stares at me for several long beats, until I shift uncomfortably in my seat.

"You'd really walk away from football for her?" he asks softly.

"In a heartbeat," I say without hesitation.

He leans back in his chair, his mouth opening and closing. Finally, he rubs a hand down his face. "You know, Penn...I think I may have been wrong about you."

My brow furrows, but I wait to hear what he has to say. I can't tell if he's angry with me or about to cry.

He lets out a soft breath. "I owe you an apology."

Not what I was expecting.

"I've always been hard on you because…well, you remind me of my little brother."

"Really?" Another surprise.

Coach's mouth lifts in a bittersweet smile. "Charismatic, too good-looking for his own good. Sounds like someone else we know, right?" He smirks at me. "He was always riding the next high, always looking for the next party and the prettiest girl in the room to charm." His smile fades. "He died in a car accident during his senior year."

"Oh God," I breathe. "Coach, I'm so sorry."

His gaze is distant. "I thought I saw so much of him in you. But you're not him. He would've never sacrificed his dreams for someone else. Maybe he would've gotten there eventually…we'll never know." He sighs. "But you? I believe you when you say you'd do it."

I nod. "I do mean it. I'm just not sure if it'll be enough to help her."

"The fact that you're willing means a lot to me, kid. Thanks for loving my daughter enough to be willing." He pauses. "I hope she'll talk to me. You know, my wife and I would love to get in on more of that grandkid action."

"We'd love that. I'm sorry we haven't done more to make that happen. We're still trying to figure this all out."

He chuckles. "I can understand that."

An idea strikes me. "How about you come over Monday night when we get back in town? You and Danielle. The kids would love to see you. Maybe we can figure some things out together."

He nods slowly. "I'd like that."

We sit in the quiet for a moment.

"Penn?"

"Yeah?"

His mouth lifts. "You're a good man."

The words catch me off guard. I clear my throat and glance around the coffee shop. "Don't go soft on me now, Coach. I've got a reputation to maintain." But my smile to him is warm, and it's the most relaxed conversation we've ever had.

He chuckles. "I think that reputation might be changing."

When I get home, I see the kids on the way inside and stop to hug them and chat for a few minutes before I go find Addy. She's in the kitchen, placing warm cookies on the counter.

"There she is," I say. "And my favorite cookies too. You're spoiling us."

I come up behind her and kiss her neck, and she leans into me.

"How was your day?" I ask.

"Didn't sit down all day," she says.

"And you're not now either. Why not?"

She turns in my arms and puts her hands in my hair. "Too much to do."

"How about you put your feet up? Don't do anything else tonight. Let me take care of things around here. Let me take care of you."

"You've had a long day too. You're probably exhausted."

I lean in and kiss her. "Let me take care of you," I repeat.

She smiles. "Has anyone ever told you you're sweet, Penn Hudson?"

I frown and pretend to be thinking. "Besides my mother? Nope, don't think so."

She laughs. "Well, you're not fooling anyone."

I lift her and carry her to the couch, placing her carefully there and then putting the blanket over her.

"Hot tea?" I ask.

She blinks and nods slowly. "That sounds nice."

"With cookies?"

"No, I've already had a couple." She laughs.

"So with two cubes of sugar then. Coming right up."

Her eyes shine. "If I didn't know better, I'd think you're paying attention, Preacher Man."

"Oh, I'm not missing a thing about you, Mrs. Hudson."

When I bring her the tea, her eyes open when I place the tea on the coffee table.

"Rest. I'll make you another cup later," I tell her.

"Tell me something I don't know about you yet," she says.

I pause and sit on the couch. "Hmm. Well…I wasn't always this…confident. I was pretty shy as a kid."

"Really? That surprises me. You're so self-assured now."

"I had a growth spurt right between my freshman and sophomore years of high school. And I'd been okay at football before that, but always a little clumsy. It was like everything suddenly started working for me."

She grins and takes my hand, lacing our fingers together. "I bet the girls noticed."

I smile back. "Hell, yeah, they did. That might have helped with the self-esteem just a little bit."

She rolls her eyes and laughs. "Mm-hmm. I'm sure."

"What about you? What were you like back then?"

She lifts her shoulders and yawns. "Not much has changed about me."

"Did you always dream of being a dietitian for the Mustangs?"

Her eyes get a faraway look. "You know what? No, that came much later. I know it's not very progressive of me, but…what I always dreamed of was falling in love, having a family, making our home feel special…" She blinks and her cheeks get pink.

I rub my thumb on her cheek and she leans into my hand.

"Dreams can't be discounted. Ever." I bring her hand to my lips and kiss her knuckles. "You helped make my dream come true, that's for sure…getting Sam into this house finally." I smooth her blanket down before my eyes meet hers again. "But it's turned into so much more. I didn't even dare hope that I could have all of this, Addy. But…you've surpassed every dream I've ever had. I hope…" I clear my throat, needing to get this out, but suddenly a little nervous. "I hope I'm doing the same for you too."

She sits up and winds her hands through my hair, pressing her forehead against mine. "You are. More than I can say."

I exhale, relief spreading through me.

"And it's not just the kids, Penn. Or this house, or all the beautiful things. It's you."

"I didn't know how much I needed to hear that." I pull back, staring at her intently. "It's you for me too. I'm so in love with you, I don't even know up from down anymore."

She laughs and it's the best sound. "I'm right there with you. I love you so much, Penn. What are we gonna do?"

I wrap my arms around her as we laugh. "We're going to enjoy the ride."

CHAPTER THIRTY-TWO

NEW WAYS

ADELINE

It's the day before this week's away game. So much to do. When I get to work, I go to Lorelai's office, feeling like I'm barely hanging by a thread. My talk with Penn helped. I didn't know how much I needed to hear those things either, but I've felt better ever since. I still feel like I have to get things in order though…like maybe I won't be able to rest until I do.

Lorelai looks at me like she knows what's coming. She shuts the door behind me and motions for me to sit down.

"Are you not happy with your position here, Adeline?" she asks.

I let out a sharp breath, pushing my hands through my hair. "I've loved my job. I still feel so lucky to be here. But… so much has changed since I took it…and in such a short amount of time." My throat tightens, and I take a steadying breath. I do not want to cry in front of my boss. "It's not that I don't want to be here. It's just—there's so much going on. Penn and I are trying to adopt Sam and Winnie. And Winnie…she's still crying and asking me if I'm going to come back every time I leave."

Lorelai clutches her heart. "Oh."

"I feel like I'm letting everyone down, no matter where I am."

Her eyes soften. She leans back in her chair, tapping a manicured nail on her desk. "You know," she says thoughtfully, "I used to love traveling with the team before I was the director."

I blink. "Yeah?"

She smiles faintly. "Maybe I could cover some of the away games. You could work on getting ahead with that Mustangs Magic all our guys are addicted to." Her mouth twitches. "And dig into the mound of new products we're being sent all the time. There's lots you could be covering here or at home, and I could feel young again."

My jaw drops. "You'd really be willing to do that?"

Her expression warms. "Adeline, I have a lot of regrets. I missed out on a lot, having kids being a huge one. My marriages suffered, yes, plural. I set myself up to not be needed and it's showing now." Her gaze sharpens. "If you want more time at home, let's figure out how to make that happen. I love having you here. Our players are happy and healthy, and they're winning. I give you credit for being part of making that happen."

My cheeks flush at the praise. I don't know about all that, but I do feel like I've gotten the players on a great trajectory, nutrition-wise.

"I'd rather keep you happy than lose you," she adds.

I exhale shakily, feeling the massive weight that's been smothering me let up just a little bit.

"And besides," she smirks, "Toby is like a robot. That kid gets shit done."

I laugh for the first time in what feels like weeks. "He's amazing. You're serious about this?"

"Absolutely. Let me take this weekend. I didn't have much planned for tomorrow around here anyway. Get me up to speed on the plan."

I walk her through the meal plans for the next couple of days while the team is traveling, and she seems excited at the thought of being *back in the game*, her words not mine.

"Thank you," I tell her again when I leave her office.

She waves me off. "We'll try it and if it doesn't work, we'll try something else."

"You're the best." I smile at her, eyes welling up again.

"Don't you forget it."

Later that night, I tell Penn about it. We're sitting on the couch. Sam is asleep in his room, and Winnie is sleeping curled up on my lap. Penn's arm is stretched behind me, his fingers lazily combing through my hair.

"I talked to Lorelai," I say quietly. "She's going to cover some of the away games. This weekend, in fact."

His hand stills and when I look over at him, his brows lift. "Really?"

I smile. "If it goes well, I'll cover some of her responsibilities here and I'll be home more. For Sam and Winnie." I glance down at her sleeping face and brush her hair away from her cheek.

He doesn't say anything for a moment. His hand slides down the back of my neck, his thumb sweeping over my skin.

"I thought you'd be happy about it," I say carefully.

"I am," he says, but his voice is strained. He looks at me, his gaze intense. "It just worries me."

My stomach twists. "Why?"

His jaw works. "Because you're overwhelmed and I want to help. I'm afraid you're burning out."

I sigh, resting my head on his shoulder. "I'm trying to fix it."

"I know." His arm tightens around me. "I just don't like the idea of you choosing between your job and…everything else."

"I'm not," I whisper. "I'm just trying to find a better balance."

"You know, I've actually thought about quitting football."

I lean back and stare at him in shock. "What are you saying?"

"It's not fair for you to give up a job you love. I've gotten to do this for years now, and I'd be going out on a high note. It's not like we need the money."

"But you love the game so much." I put my hand on his face and he leans into it.

"And you love your job."

Tears fall down my cheeks. "I love you so much right now."

He leans his forehead against mine. "Let me help."

"You're not quitting your job. Not until you're fully ready. Let me try this with Lorelai. It might be awesome."

"Let's keep talking about it," he says. "I don't want things to be distant between us. We're in this together."

"Together," I promise.

The house is quiet without Penn. And we miss him terribly, but things feel lighter.

The kids are so sweet, so happy that I'm home. I yell my head off at Sam's game and take tons of pictures at the game and Winnie's dance class. Winnie's been spinning around the house nonstop, trying to perfect her version of a ballet move.

"I'm gonna be a prima ballerina," she announces as we're about to watch the game. She balances precariously on one foot while holding her stuffed unicorn over her head.

"You can be whatever you want to be," I say, adjusting her headband.

"A ballerina!" she shouts and falls sideways onto the couch, laughing hard.

My insides get all twisty and mushy, tears still all too close to the surface these days, but seeing her so happy, having a moment to breathe…it feels like I'm doing something right.

The girls have been texting me. Penn told me the other night that they really want to hang out and want to help in any way they can. He also mentioned that he ran into my dad and that the conversation between them was surprisingly great. They're coming over for dinner after they're back in town.

My phone lights up and Winnie bounces as she carries it over.

TRU

Addy, are we watching the game together? It's a tradition, you know!

> I'd love that! Wanna come over here?

ELLE

Do you even need to ask?

SADIE

What's the theme? Charcuterie with wine, sushi with champagne, or wings and guac with beer and Coca-Cola?

> Whew. Those are hard choices. I think I need some cheese and chocolate in my life. I've got lots of stuff that will work on a charcuterie board.

TRU

Done. I'll bring the good cheese…and wings for the kids.

ELLE

I'll bring cupcakes and guac.

POPPY

I know this probably only sounds good to me, but I'm craving those ham roll-ups that have cream cheese and pickles.

> My friend Goldie always made those in college! I love those.

POPPY

When is she coming back? I knew she was a good time.

> I wish I knew. I owe her a call, several calls.

I sigh. Everyone in my life has been put on hold while I've tried to get it together. Tomorrow, I'll call Goldie and catch up with her.

SADIE

I'll bring wine, and the only chocolate I have is chocolate-covered pretzels.

> That works for me. And I've got all the drinks the kids could possibly want. Come on over. I can't wait.

By the time they show up for the game, I'm bouncing along with Sam and Winnie, so excited for everyone to get here. We pile onto the couches in front of the TV and the girls dance around the living room. Sam tosses the soft football to Levi and Caleb.

Winnie goes spinning by, giggling until she face-plants onto the rug. I sit up, about to rush to check on her, but she rushes to her feet, arms wide like she's sticking a landing.

"Ten out of ten!" Elle claps.

Winnie beams and launches herself at me, climbing into my lap and resting her head against my chest. My arms tighten around her.

Sadie is curled into the armchair with a glass of wine and she watches us with a soft smile. "She's happy," she says quietly.

"She is," I agree, brushing my fingers through Winnie's curls. "Hopefully we're figuring it out."

"And how are you?" Elle asks, tilting her head as she looks at me.

I let out a long exhale. "I think I'm getting there."

"Well, you're Wonder Woman in our eyes, I hope you know that," Tru says.

"And I hope you know that we are here, *anytime*, for whatever you need," Poppy adds. "You're not alone."

My eyes well up, again, ugh, and I smile around the room. "I can't believe how lucky I am," I say, my voice shaky. "You guys are so great. Thank you."

It's late when my phone buzzes.

The girls left an hour and a half ago, after they helped me clean everything up. The kids are asleep, and the house is a settled, content quiet.

I've just gotten into bed when I see Penn's name flash across the screen. My heart does that ridiculous skip it always does when it's him.

"Hey," I answer, my voice soft.

"Hey, beautiful," His voice is low and rough. He looks tired.

"You were incredible tonight," I tell him.

"You were watching?"

"Of course. Wouldn't miss it. The girls and the kids came over too. It was a lot of fun."

"Tru sent me a picture of Winnie spinning in her ballet shoes." Even if I couldn't see it, I'd be able to hear the smile in his voice.

"She's convinced she's going to be a ballerina."

He chuckles and the sound skitters over my skin like he's sitting right here. "She probably will be. She doesn't do anything halfway."

"Kind of like someone else I know."

He points at me.

I point back at him.

He grins. "I miss you," he says. "Miss my bed." His voice drops lower. "Miss you in it."

I can hear the heat in his tone.

"I miss you too," I admit.

"I love it when you wear that tank top." He pulls the phone closer. "I can see your nipples so well in that one."

I bite back my smile.

"Let me see what you're wearing under that blanket."

I let the blanket slide down, exposing my bare legs. "You already know what I'm wearing."

"Because I'm not there to take them off."

He grins when he sees my black lacy underwear.

"Goddamn," he whispers. "You know what those do to me."

"Yes, I do." My cheeks hurt from smiling so hard.

"Take them off."

My pulse pounds between my legs.

Slowly, I slip them off and toss them aside.

"Touch yourself," he says, his voice strained.

I exhale when I do.

"Are you wet?" he asks.

"Yes," I whisper. I bite my lip and a sharp gasp slips out when my fingers move faster.

He lets out a low, dark sound.

"Fuck, Addy. You're so beautiful. I wish I was there. Wish I could feel you. I'm pretending my hand is your mouth working me over."

"Penn," I cry out. My hips arch slightly off the bed.

"You're close, aren't you?"

I breathe into the phone, my hand moving faster.

"So close."

"Let go," he says, his voice rough. "Let me see you."

My whole body tightens, and my head falls back. I try to stay quiet as I come apart, shuddering.

I hear his breath hitch and a sharp curse. "*Fuck*."

My breath slows, my body going lax. "That was…"

"So fucking hot," he finishes. "I miss you even more though, if that's possible."

I smile, heart thudding again.

"I love you," he says.

"I'll never get tired of hearing you say that. I love you too."

"You look good. Are you okay?" he asks.

"I am," I say, still a little dazed. "We've missed you so much, but it's been a really good weekend."

"I'm glad. So glad." His gaze is so warm it makes my insides melt.

"You okay?"

He chuckles low. "Better than I've been all weekend."

I sigh, a slow smile taking over my face. "Hurry home."

"I'm already counting the hours."

CHAPTER THIRTY-THREE

LITTLE VIXEN

PENN

I'm barely through the door when Jezebel launches at me like a naked demon from the pits of hell.

"Ahh!" I yell, stumbling backward as I try to avoid a full-frontal assault from the hairless cat of my nightmares. Who the hell thinks these things are cute?

I jump as she slinks her body along my legs and try to stand as still as possible.

"Stay calm, stay calm, stay calm," I tell myself.

She does one more swipe of her skin along my legs before walking to the couch. Once she's perched on the back of the couch, she stares at me with those beady alien eyes, her tail whipping behind her like a weapon. The wrinkles on her body glisten in the sunlight. My head tilts. She looks...fuller.

"Hey!" Addy comes up behind me and wraps her arms around my waist, kissing the back of my neck. "Welcome home."

I turn and kiss her. "God, it's good to see you."

She grins up at me and gives me another kiss. "It's good to see you too."

I feel eyes on me and glance at the cat. "Why do I feel like she's flashing me?" I squint at her. "And what's with her...boobs?"

Addy chokes back a laugh. "Penn," she wheezes.

"I'm serious!" I gesture helplessly toward the cat, who stretches out and somehow makes the whole situation worse. "They're huge!" I lean closer and instantly regret it. "And saggy."

Addy snorts. "Don't be hating on my girl's saggy breasts!"

She approaches the couch, crouching down to inspect Jezebel. The cat meows and starts licking her shoulder, completely oblivious to the fact that she's scarring my retinas.

Addy turns to look at me, her eyes wide. "You know... they do look bigger and saggier than when we got her." She tilts her head. "And so does her stomach."

We stare at each other in horror.

"Oh, hell no," I say.

"You don't think she's..."

"No, no, no," I cut in.

Jezebel blinks slowly at me.

"So help me if Jerry didn't tell us this little vixen is about to have offspring," I yell.

Addy bursts out laughing and scoops her off the couch, nuzzling into her.

"I don't understand how you can cuddle with that thing, but you do you," I tell her.

"The kids will be home soon and I'm about to start dinner, but…maybe I should run her to the vet really quick."

"Do we have to know today?" I ask, following her into the kitchen.

"No, but…wouldn't you rather know what we're dealing with?"

"I'm not sure," I admit.

Addy checks the oven. "It's easy to get in and out of Pet Galaxy, right? As long as Dr. Amber isn't too backed up? It used to be anyway."

"I have no idea. I've never had a pregnant naked pet before."

Addy laughs again and shakes her head. "You're hilarious." She leans up to kiss me. "Sorry to leave as soon as you're getting home, but I'll hurry."

"I'll come with you," I sigh. "I was hoping we could bury ourselves under the covers before the kids got home, but…"

"Responsibilities," she finishes.

"Right."

Addy hustles around the kitchen and then the laundry room to get the ridiculous little cat carrier.

"This is unacceptable, Jezebel. We don't condone teenage pregnancy!"

Addy can hardly get Jezebel in the carrier for laughing. "You are too much."

Jezebel yowls like she's wounded once she's in the carrier. I lean down and lock eyes with her.

"I'm judging you," I tell her.

She swipes at the air with her wrinkly paws.

I point at her. "Exactly."

An hour later, we're back from Pet Galaxy. Addy's still laughing. I drop the keys on the counter, and Addy and I look at each other.

"You ready to be a grandpa?" she asks.

"There is no part of that sentence that I'm ready for!"

"At least Jerry offered to take the kittens off our hands once they're old enough." She lets Jezebel out of the carrier and Jezebel skulks off, miffed that she was inconvenienced.

"Really generous of Jerry."

Addy giggles and slides her arms around my waist. "We'll figure it out."

I sigh and pull her close. "Was it good for you to be home this weekend?"

She smiles against my chest. "I loved it. I really needed that. I even got to catch up with Goldie. She says hello, by the way."

"Hello to Goldie. Tell her to come back and visit longer. And I'm so glad you had a good weekend. You seem...happier."

She looks up at me, and her hands wind through my hair. "I'm sorry I've been such a mess. I'm gonna try to do better."

I push her hair back and look at her intently. "There is not a single thing you need to do any better, Addy. This is not on you. I want to talk to your dad tonight about ways I can be home more too. There's not much I can do if I stay with the team, but I've played long enough now that I don't have to be at as much training in the summer...I can streamline the things that I volunteer for…there are tweaks I can make with workouts and such, which would help with being here when the kids are home from school. We'll keep working on this, but it's not on your shoulders." I lean closer, tilting her chin up. "Okay?"

She nods. "Okay."

She kisses me then and lifts up on her tiptoes to get closer. When she pulls away minutes later, breathless, she whispers in my ear, "I think we have time before the kids get home, if we're fast."

"Oh, I will be so fucking fast," I promise, already lifting her over my shoulder. "And so fucking thorough," I add, bolting for the stairs.

The sounds of our laughter fill up the house.

Damn, it's good to be home.

Later that night, Addy is in full domestic goddess mode. She's got an elaborate meal spread out for the six of us. It smells *amazing*.

"This looks stunning, Adeline," her mom says. "What is that salad?"

"Thanks, Mom. I'm so excited you're here. So, we have a pear and gorgonzola salad with candied walnuts. And we have salmon with a lemon-dill yogurt sauce, garlic-roasted Brussels sprouts, and quinoa with sweet potatoes and kale."

"And she made dessert too!" Sam adds happily. "What did you call it?"

"Passionfruit Pavlova," I say, grinning at him.

"Do the two of you eat all this fancy food?" Danielle asks Sam and Winnie.

"Addy is the best cook ever," Sam says.

"Best cook ever," Winnie repeats. "I love Addy's food *so* much."

"Me too." Sam nods.

"Well, you are both remarkable," Danielle says. "Addy always loved any kind of food too." She laughs and looks at Addy fondly. "There were no chicken fingers for you…you were my grilled shrimp and filet mignon child. Expensive tastes."

"I *love* chicken fingers and shrimp and steak," Winnie says.

We all laugh, and the conversation flows into Sam's game over the weekend and our win in Florida. Coach is actually talking to me. Real, genuine conversation, not the awkward grunt-based communication we've had for years.

When pressed, Addy talks a little about how crazy everything's been lately, but she keeps it light while Sam and Winnie are at the table. Winnie ends up on Danielle's lap, and it's evident that both Rex and Danielle are smitten with the kids.

After the kids go to bed, the conversation shifts.

"So…" Rex studies Addy carefully. "How are you really doing?"

She sets down her wine glass. "A little better. A weekend at home helped. I want to keep figuring it out with Lorelai." She glances at me and then back at her dad. "It was actually a lot of fun working on her projects while she was gone. And talking with her today…I think she had even more fun than I did, traveling with the team again."

"You think that's something you'd both consider doing more regularly?" he asks.

"It seems like she's open, which I really appreciate."

He nods. "It sounds like you're finding your rhythm. Let me know if I can do anything to help."

"Thanks, Dad."

"She's a badass," I say proudly, and Addy gives me a sweet smile.

Danielle reaches out and takes Addy's hand. "I'm so proud of you, sweetheart. Proud of both of you." She looks at me fondly. I've always liked Danielle a lot. She's been kind to me since I first signed with the team. "Those kids are so happy. They're absolutely thriving. It's truly remarkable."

"Thanks, Mama," Addy says softly. "I didn't know I could love them so much."

Her eyes meet mine and I see the love shining there. I take her hand, needing to touch her desperately. This woman. How did she become my everything?

When we crawl into bed that night, she snuggles up against me, her hand resting on my chest.

"I think your dad might kind of like me now," I say, chuckling.

"I think you're right. His turnaround is actually shocking. I'm proud of him…and you."

I kiss the top of her head. "Even though our little alien is about to become a single mom?"

She laughs. "Nobody's perfect, Preacher Man."

"No one but you."

CHAPTER THIRTY-FOUR

NOPE, NOT QUALIFIED

ADELINE

Jezebel is massive. It's only been a few weeks since we found out she's pregnant, but apparently each trimester in Sphynx life is twenty days. That's one area where they've lucked out.

Her pink, stretched-out belly drags on the floor when she waddles across the room, looking both smug and fatigued at all times.

It's a Wednesday and we have a game at Clarity Field tomorrow night, so we're enjoying a quiet evening at home.

My job is still in transition, but it's gotten much more manageable now that Lorelai and I are sharing more responsibilities. I'd still like to be home even more, but I want to finish out the year as is and then Lorelai and I can reassess.

I've been watching the kids playing outside, but I run inside to check on Jezebel. I'm surprised to find Penn sitting cross-legged on the floor nearby, looking suspiciously focused on the cat. He's been reading about feline labor for weeks, paranoid that she'll give birth on the couch or somewhere equally awful.

"Here you are," I say.

"Yeah, I came in to go to the bathroom and this arrived." He holds a box up and my eyes narrow.

"What is that?"

"It's a pet birthing kit. I bought it online." He lines up the supplies, studying each item carefully.

I sit down next to him, while Jezebel lounges on her side, her stomach twitching occasionally.

"Could be any day now," he says, his tone *very* serious.

I press my lips together, trying not to giggle. He keeps me laughing about this cat, but now, instead of it being because he's terrified of her, it's how over the top he is with trying to prepare for the kittens. He won't admit it, but I think he's grown rather fond of her.

I've caught him practicing petting her, one finger at a time.

Jezebel flicks her tail and then flinches.

"Yep, you've been saying that every day this week."

"But look at her." He gestures at her belly, which is rippling like there's a dance-off going on inside. "She's ready."

Just then, she lets out an agonized sound. Then another. Penn and I stare at each other.

"Oh my God. Is it happening?" I ask.

"I *knew* it," he whispers.

She stands up—or tries to—and a wave of panic rolls over me because holy shit, this is actually happening. Penn scrambles to his knees as Jezebel circles once, twice, and then dramatically flops over with a heavy plop. Her tail thrashes.

"Okay," Penn says in a gentle tone. He moves toward her carefully and barely shudders when he lifts her. "Let's get you to a soft place, Jezzy."

Jezzy?

Heart, mush.

I follow him as he goes to the laundry room, where he's set up the portable crib he bought for this moment. The side even comes down on one side. He sets her in there like she's so fragile and nods.

"You've got this," he tells her.

Jezebel does not look like she's got this. Her eyes are huge as she lets out a pained sound that makes the hair on the back of my neck stand up.

"I'll be right back," Penn says.

I watch as he rushes back into the living room and grabs the birthing kit.

"Good thing I bought this," he says, grinning at me. And then he's all focus, smoothing out the pad he's put on top of a soft blanket.

"Should we call Dr. Amber?" I ask. "I feel *extremely* underqualified for this situation."

"No, it'll be okay." He grabs a towel and scoots closer to Jezebel. "We just have to stay calm and let her do her thing." His eyes are bright when he looks up at me. "Would you tell Sam I think it's happening? He wanted to see this."

I nod, backing up. "Maybe I'll turn on a movie for Winnie, just in case she doesn't want to see it?"

He grins at me reassuringly. "Sounds good."

"How are you so calm right now?" I ask as I'm leaving the room.

"I have no idea," he says.

When I go outside, Sam is playing tennis with himself against the house as Winnie dances nearby.

"Sam." I motion for him to come closer and he jogs over. "I think Jezebel might be having her kittens."

He gasps. "Is Penn with her?"

"Oh, he's all over it."

We grin at each other. It's been a source of constant amusement for us to tease Penn about Jezebel.

"If you want to come in and watch, I'll set a movie up for Winnie," I tell him.

"Good idea. She does *not* love the sight of blood." He moves toward the house, his level of excitement rivaling Penn's.

I've gotten attached to Jezebel and am excited to see her kittens, but I'm nervous about the delivery part.

Once Winnie is happy with her movie and snacks, I go back to check on Jezebel. When I walk into the room, she's stretched out and her legs are working back and forth as she pushes. Soothing music is playing and Penn is reassuring her.

"You're doing so good," he says.

It makes me emotional, seeing how sweet he's being to her. My lip starts to tremble as I watch him calm her as she struggles and strains.

"It's coming!" Sam's eyes are wild. "I see something!"

It takes some time, but then—oh wow—a tiny, slimy creature slides most of the way out. Penn helps maneuver it the rest of the way with his gloved hands.

"Holy shit!" Penn laughs, holding the little body up for a

second before he sets it in front of Jezebel. "We've got a baby!"

Jezebel immediately starts licking the kitten.

"That's a good mama," Penn coos.

"You did it, Jezebel. You did it," Sam says.

"Whew. That is a *lot* of blood and fluids," I say weakly.

Penn cleans Jezebel's backside with pet wipes as I stare in shock.

"Who even are you right now?" I ask.

He grins like an absolute madman.

"Isn't this the craziest thing you've ever seen?" His brows lift when Jezebel meows and starts shifting her feet. "Oh, I think we've got another one coming."

He moves the kitten out of the way and covers it slightly with the blanket. This time seems a little easier for Jezebel, but she stands and flops to her other side before we see signs of the next kitten. Penn is ready this time. He gently massages Jezebel's belly while she labors and helps the kitten the rest of the way out when it's ready. This one is smaller and wobbly, but Penn's hands are steady as he places it in front of Jezebel.

"You're like a cat doula," I say in awe.

"They're so cute!" Sam says. "Don't you think so?" he asks Penn.

He leans in, as if he doesn't want Jezebel to hear him, and whispers, "I still think they're hideous looking, but there's something very regal about our Jezebel."

She keeps going and Penn stays calm the whole time, Sam too. Penn moves the kittens a little closer to Jezebel and helps them latch on. It takes the second one a little longer to nurse, but they have a few minutes near their mama before she starts shifting again. I watch in awe as the third kitten squirms its way into the world.

We wait for a while and Jezebel stretches out like she's completely spent. When nothing else happens, Penn looks at me.

"I think maybe she's done."

When she doesn't budge, it seems like he's right.

"They're so tiny," I say softly, watching the last one nuzzle into Jezebel's side.

Penn throws his gloves away and scrubs his hands at the sink. As he's drying his hands on a towel, he smiles down at the newborns. Setting the towel aside, he leans down. "You did amazing, Jezzy," he murmurs, stroking her ear.

She's exhausted but purring, and she nuzzles his hand, as if she's thanking him.

He looks up at me, swallowing hard.

"Did you see that?" he asks, his voice raspy.

I lean over and kiss his cheek. "I could not love you more right now."

His face is flushed and his eyes are luminous. "I love *you*. And this thing we're doing…this life we're building…it's fucking intense."

"You think?" I laugh and we hear Sam laughing next to us.

He reaches for Sam's shoulder. "And this guy. Such a trouper."

"So proud of you both," I tell them. "There were a couple of times I thought I might faint."

Sam grins at me. "But you didn't."

I lean over and kiss his forehead. "Nope, I sure didn't. But I couldn't have done what you guys did." I point at Penn. "This guy helping pull those kittens out? No, just no."

Penn looks down at the kittens. "Three of them. That's a lot of mouths to feed."

I lift my hand toward him. "Well...good thing we have a professional Sphynx handler in our midst."

A little later, Penn has moved Jezebel's bed into the living room so we can watch them. I'm on the couch peeking at them next to Winnie, and Sam and Penn are sprawled on the floor nearby.

My phone buzzes and it's Goldie.

"Hey!" I answer.

"Hey." She sounds breathless. "You will not believe what just happened."

"What?"

"So, I'm walking to work and I see this turkey in the middle of the street. Cars are honking—it was by work, so imagine the neighborhood near Lake Nokomis...busy!—and the turkey just nonchalantly meanders across."

"Oh no." I laugh.

"And then..." She lowers her voice dramatically. "The turkey notices the mail carrier walking by and just...loses it."

"What do you mean 'loses it'?"

"It starts *chasing* him!"

I cover my mouth when a loud cackle comes out. I look over to see if it disturbed Jezebel and the kittens, but she's as serene as a floating cloud now that the kittens are here.

"The man was sprinting, Adeline! And the turkey was keeping up."

"Please tell me someone recorded this."

"I wish! It was the funniest thing I've ever seen."

I'm still laughing when Goldie says, "How's our pregnant vixen?"

"Well, I was going to call you in a little bit actually. We have three adorable kittens."

She gasps. "No way!"

"Yep. She had them not too long ago."

"Where are my pictures?"

"I will send some ASAP." I giggle. "I'll send you a video right now."

I send her the video that I've probably watched ten times since recording it. It's of Penn encouraging Jezebel and then helping get the first kitten out. I hear her play the video and gasp.

"Stop!" she shrieks. "Your hottie is a cat midwife too?"

We both cackle and I glance over at Penn, who has fallen asleep on the floor. His hand is on the lowered rail of the crib.

"He's pretty perfect under pressure."

CHAPTER THIRTY-FIVE

LET IT GO

PENN

Halloween is finally here. The day of reckoning. The day that will go down in history as the most humiliating but also possibly the most adorable of my life.

It was a rookie mistake, letting Winnie pick our costumes. We thought we were being good parents, letting her be creative and giving her the power to make a big decision. But then she said the words. The dreaded words.

"We'll be Elsa!"

"You mean you'll be Elsa?" Sam said hopefully.

"No, all of us. *Four* Elsas," she said emphatically.

Sam and I tried everything to change her mind.

How about you're Elsa, Addy's Anna, I'm the Snowman, and Sam's the prince? Or Sam could be the Snowman…

What about pirates or superheroes? Wouldn't you love to be a superhero, Winnie?

Nope, she was set. Addy backed her up, reminding us that we did tell her she could pick. And when I saw how excited she was, how her eyes lit up at the thought of all of us dressed as her favorite character, I knew I was sunk. Sam, to his credit, decided to be the Snowman. He admitted to me that he'd feel dumber dressed like the prince, and the Snowman would feel a little dumb, but at least it'd make Winnie laugh.

That kid, man, he's the best. And he's like the rest of us, he just can't resist Winnie.

So here we are.

I smooth down the sparkling blue dress that barely fits over my shoulders and resist the urge to adjust the platinum blonde wig that's slipping dangerously down my forehead. Sam looks hilarious with his snowman belly bobbing when he walks, and he was right—it does make Winnie laugh.

Winnie and Addy look *perfect*. Like legit, they've walked straight out of the movie. Winnie's version makes her look angelic, and Addy's version is demure and yet she's so fucking hot, I may have to leave her in this get-up as I go down on her tonight.

We take the kids trick-or-treating for a little while, stopping by my parents' cottage first, then going to Rex and Danielle's. We hit a few more houses along the way before going to Henley and Tru's house for the Halloween party. When we arrive, I take one last deep breath before Henley opens the door. He sees Winnie first and tells her how pretty she is, and then he sees Addy and adds how lovely she is too.

The moment the guys see me and Sam, it's over. Scratch that—when they see *me*, it's over. Sam is a charming Snowman. I am a hideous Elsa.

Henley chokes out a laugh so hard he actually stumbles backward. Rhodes doubles over and braces himself against the wall, gasping for breath. Bowie takes one look at me and mutters, "That's your color." Weston's mouth twitches and then he explodes into an outrageous *guffaw*.

I don't think I've ever used that word before, but there's a time and place.

"Hey, assholes," I say in a prissy Elsa voice, which of course, sends them into another fit.

"Hold on," Rhodes manages, lifting his phone. "I've gotta get a picture of this."

"Absolutely not," I say, but Sam is already posing next to me.

If he can do it, so can I.

We pose and then Elle walks up, her eyes lit with amusement. "You're my heroes," she tells me and Sam. "And you, beautiful ladies," she tells Winnie and Addy, "are the prettiest Elsas I've ever seen."

"You're a saint," Poppy adds, winking at me.

Sadie laughs. "You know this is going to be on the group chat forever."

"And all of our Christmas cards," Tru adds, grinning.

"Have you seen yourselves?" I ask, laughing now myself. "You're all actually looking pretty top-tier."

Henley and Tru have gone all in on the *Toy Story* theme. Henley looks hilarious in his Woody costume, and baby Avery is the cutest potato head I've ever seen. Cassidy is rocking the Buzz Lightyear suit, which Sam finds very impressive. Audrey is a gorgeous Bo Peep, and Gracie tries to figure out how to walk while dressed as the slinky dog.

Rhodes is an Oompa Loompa and it's too good. And Levi is slaying as Willy Wonka. Elle goes into full method acting as Violet Beauregarde when she sees us admiring her costume and smacks her gum.

"So good." I try to pull the dress up my shoulder, but it's no use.

I turn to look at Bowie and Poppy and all of them, Becca and Jonas included, are the cutest Dalmatians ever. Jonas howls like a puppy, making everyone laugh.

"And what are you guys?" I ask Weston and Sadie.

They've gone for full drama. Sadie looks like something out of a Tim Burton movie with her ghostly white face and white Victorian dress. Weston leans next to her in an old-fashioned suit, his face also white. Caleb is running around looking like them, except with suspenders.

"We're Victorian ghosts," Sadie says primly before breaking out in a laugh.

We move to the kitchen, filling our plates with food and grabbing drinks while the kids run around. It's loud and fun and chaotic…my kind of party. Then, as it always does when I'm with my guys, the inevitable happens.

"You know what time it is," Henley announces, moving toward the speaker system.

"Oh no," Weston says.

"Oh yes." I smirk.

The opening notes of "Stronger" by Britney Spears start to play. And that's all it takes.

"Penn, I vote you take the lead since you've gone blonde tonight," Elle calls out.

I pretend to be annoyed, but I give my hips an extra sway as I point at her. "This is your fault. You brainwashed us."

Elle is one of the best dancers I know, Tru too, actually. But Elle made Rhodes go over her dance routines in college, so he's passed on his Britney moves to us over the years. I have to say, we're fucking *good*.

Henley rolls his shoulders and we all move into place. Bowie looks around at us.

"If we're going down, we're going down together."

"One hundred percent," Weston says.

I look at Sam and he gives me a thumbs up. Addy winks at me.

We're flawless. We've done this too many times and it's burned into our muscle memory. When we hit the chorus and I lip sync with exaggeration, sliding my hand down my blue dress, the girls die. Poppy's clutching her stomach, crying from laughter. Tru's filming everything. Elle looks like the proud dance mom. Sadie doubles over when Weston twerks near her.

And Addy...she's laughing along with the rest of them, but she's also taking me in. Her eyes and that smile on her face tell me I've already won the night.

I still can't believe she's in my life. God, pinch me.

The song ends and we all collapse onto the couch. Sam leans against me, laughing. Winnie bounces over with excitement.

"You were *so good*!" she cries. "Will you teach me that, Daddy?"

The room quiets to a pin drop and I stare at her, my throat working.

"Yes, I sure can, sweet girl," I tell her, my voice sounding raw.

She hugs me and runs off with Gracie. Rhodes pounds me on the back and Sam wraps his arms around me in a big hug. We exchange a meaningful look.

"Love you, Penn," he says softly.

"I love you, buddy."

"I think of you as my dad too," he whispers.

I tug his head back against my chest and hug him again.

"I'll be whatever you want me to be. All I know is you're mine," I tell him.

His eyes are bright when he gets up to go find everyone else.

I look at Addy and she's wiping tears from her cheeks.

"She called me Daddy." I reach over and hug Addy, unable to fight back all the emotion.

"She sure did," Addy whispers. "That's what you are, you know."

"And did you hear Sam?"

"Yes. Melted my heart."

"How did we get here?" I ask. "You know they love you like that too."

She nods, her eyes spilling over again. "I feel like we're the luckiest people in the world."

There are sniffles around the room and we look around to see our friends wiping their faces too.

"You guys are the cutest," Sadie says, her face scrunching up as she cries harder. "And those kids. I can't take it."

She comes over and hugs us and the rest of them follow, telling us how happy they are for us.

"I will be so glad when it's official," I say, letting out a long exhale as I dry my own damn face. "We're still just holding our breath." I thread my fingers through Addy's.

Her chin wobbles and she nods.

"That has gotta be the most stressful thing," Poppy says, clutching her heart. "Any update on the timeline?"

I shake my head. "No. Nothing for sure. Your dad has been such a huge help though," I tell Weston. "And Sutton…I know he's trying to move it along as much as he can, which is incredible."

"They've both been great," Addy adds.

"Anytime you need to get your mind off of all of it…or to vent about it…we're here, okay?" Henley says.

Everyone else chimes in with their agreement.

"Thanks. You and our families…you're keeping us afloat," I say, looking around the room. Then I put my hand on Addy's chin and kiss her lightly. "And this woman right here. I'd be lost without her."

She waves a hand over her face, shaking her head. "Don't get me crying again," she says.

I kiss her and we all wander back into the kitchen, refreshing our drinks.

Addy stands in the doorway between our bedroom and bathroom, that soft smile still in place.

"You were really good tonight," she says.

"I know," I tease.

She steps closer, fingers trailing up my chest. "You're hot no matter what you do," she whispers. "Singing to Britney. Delivering kittens. Putting the kids to bed. Rocking my world in every single way."

"I want to rock your world right now." I lean down, capturing her mouth in a slow, lazy kiss.

But she pulls back, biting her lip, suddenly shy.

"I have a crazy thought," she says.

I lean in, kissing my way down her neck. "I'm having a crazy thought too."

"I'm scared to even say."

That gets my attention. "Well, now I have to know. You

can tell me all your crazy thoughts." I smile at her and she takes a deep breath.

"What if we go off birth control?" Her words rush out.

I hold onto her arms and pull back to see her face better. "What?"

"I know, I know," she hurries to say. "Forget it. I know it's—" She shakes her head and rolls her eyes.

"But it's not. It's…I love this idea," I say.

I think I've shocked her more than she's shocked me. "You do?"

"Did you see how good both Sam and Winnie were with the little ones tonight?"

She nods. "Yes! And they've both asked me if we'll have babies soon. I'd thought they might not want us to…and I'd never want them to feel like they aren't enough. I don't want to rush it." She sighs. "But they've said multiple times that they really want babies around here. Other than the kittens."

We both laugh softly.

"And I'm finding I do really love being a mom," she says softly.

Everything inside me turns to liquid heat when she says that.

"I never thought I'd be this guy." I tug her closer. "But I'm having the time of my life with you, Addy. A baby…" I say in awe.

"We've lost our minds," she finally says.

"At least we've lost them together."

CHAPTER THIRTY-SIX

WITH GRATITUDE AND TURKEY

ADELINE

It's hard not to let the guilt fester as I work through the insane week leading up to the Thanksgiving Day game. Friendsgiving last week was a nice break—good food, dear friends, and quality time with the kids and kittens. The kittens are the highlight of our lives. It's so funny how you don't even know how much you can love something until you're surrounded by it. I've never even thought of myself as a big animal person, but Jezebel and her babies...*I am in love.*

Sam named the two boys Gizmo and Shadow, and Winnie named the girl Elsa because, yeah…she's still her favorite.

Now, though, I'm slammed. Long hours endlessly on my feet, and so much planning and food prepping that I think I'm doing it in my sleep.

The good part is that I have a plan worked out with Lorelai. Greer and Wyndham agreed to stay at the house to watch the kittens. Since it's a holiday weekend, Serendipity's hours are limited, and they were so generous to do that with their little time off. The whole family and crew—my mom, Penn's parents, Tru, Sadie, Poppy, Elle, all the kids, as well as everyone else's parents—will be flying to Dallas for the game. Lorelai's flying in on gameday, and she'll sit in the box with everyone during the first half. I'll switch places with her during the second half and enjoy the game.

It helps that Winnie is more adjusted now. She doesn't cry when Penn and I leave for the training facility or go on a trip anymore, which is a relief. Last night, she hugged me tight before we left, her little face so sweet.

"I've already got your fun stuff packed," I told her, brushing back her soft curls.

She held Margo's hand as Sam stood by them, grinning.

"I can't wait to see you, Mama!" she squealed.

Yes, she's been calling me Mama. Once she opened the door by calling Penn Daddy, it was the very next day when she tried it out on me. I just *thought* I cried when she did it with him. I didn't think I'd ever get it together when she called me Mama.

"Don't worry. We'll be okay," Sam told me.

God, I love those kids.

I did still cry a little as we drove away, watching them wave as long as we were in sight.

I worked my tail off last night when we arrived at the

AT&T stadium, completely wiped out by the time I crawled into bed next to Penn. I'm not even trying to sneak around anymore. I'm sleeping with my man and I think the whole team knows and is happy about it. Penn's having such a great season that I think the players want us to keep doing whatever we've been doing. They're a superstitious lot, but I grew up with Coach Evans, so that's not exactly news.

This morning when I woke up while it was still dark, Penn rolled over, half-asleep, and patted my butt before mumbling, "Love you," in that low, sleepy voice that always ruins me.

I'm running on fumes by the time I take the world's fastest shower and change into Penn's jersey. When I finally get to the box, I'm exhausted but so excited to see everyone. Sam and Winnie rush toward me, hugging me tight.

"You guys are looking so good in your jerseys," I tell them. I scoop Winnie up and grin at her turkey hat. "And the hat is perfect." I bop her on the nose.

When I set her down, Tru hands me a cocktail, and I gladly take it.

There's a roar of laughter on the other side of the box and Sadie waves us over.

"They're killing it and the commentators are on a roll. Henley is particularly hysterical tonight," she says.

"Would you look at that play! The Mustangs are bucking everyone out of the way!" Henley's voice is thick with amusement.

Daniel, the other commentator, laughs. "Maybe it's Penn Hudson's moniker as the Sexiest Man Alive that has him feeling himself. He's unstoppable."

Melanie snorts. "Whatever it is, it's working."

"Rumor has it that Addy Hudson is part of the reason

Penn's on fire this season," Henley says. "You didn't hear it from me."

I nearly choke on my cocktail and start fanning my face.

"I mean…he's not wrong," Tru says, laughing.

"Keep doing what you're doing, Addy. I know it's a sacrifice," Elle adds.

I snort and shake my head, but I can't wipe the huge smile off my face. "I think we're all doing our part."

They all laugh and Sadie clinks her glass to mine. "Cheers to that."

Penn looks focused and confident out on that field—and absolutely drool-worthy. He glances up at the box like he can feel my eyes on him and gives a nod in my direction. My stomach flips.

Weston makes a long throw across the field and Rhodes somehow leaps through two defenders to make the catch. We jump up and down.

Henley whistles. "Weston launched one that looks like it came from another planet…and did you see Rhodes Archer levitate to catch that thing?"

Daniel chimes in. "I've seen Rhodes jump, but that was more like a controlled flight."

Melanie laughs. "Do we need to test him for wings?"

"I think these guys have evolved past human limitations at this point," Henley says.

"I think we all know you're partial to the Mustangs," Daniel says, "but the way they're playing this year, I know you're not the only one."

"They've made their comeback. And when Weston is on, they're all on. His arm strength is no joke," Henley adds.

"And I'm just going to say it since Melanie won't. The entire Mustangs team is disturbingly attractive," Daniel says.

"You won't get any argument from me there," Melanie says, laughing.

I can't catch my breath, I'm laughing so hard. "Are they actually…flirting with the whole team on national television?"

"They totally are," Sadie says.

Penn receives a handoff from Weston and looks around to pass it, but when he sees an opening, he runs with it and makes a touchdown. The crowd erupts, and I hear Henley again.

"I don't know how they're doing it, but the Mustangs are making this look easy."

I don't sit down for the rest of the game. They make two more touchdowns before winning the game, and I hustle back to help Toby and Lorelai get ready for the players. I prepared huge turkey drumsticks as a little way to celebrate Thanksgiving, and when the team starts trickling in, they're flying high from their win.

Penn finds me right away and I kiss him.

"So proud of you, Preacher Man," I tell him.

"Addy! You are the best!" One of the players holds up the drumstick, and Weston and Penn's eyes go round.

"You didn't," Weston says.

"I did," I say, laughing. "Just a little treat for my guys, playing so hard on Thanksgiving." I grin at Penn. "And maybe there are even a few pies around here somewhere."

Eventually, everyone makes their way into the family area, and I give the kids each a drumstick too. It looks bigger than Winnie's head. Margo and Jeremy linger until Winnie's sleepy, and then they take the kids back to the hotel.

Penn and I make love when we get back to the room, almost too tired to think but too hungry for each other. Always too hungry for each other.

Afterward, he leans his head against mine. "This is the best Thanksgiving I've ever had."

I rub my thumb along his cheek. "Because of the win?"

"Because of you being by my side." His hand slides down my side and his voice gets lower. "And the drumsticks didn't hurt."

I laugh sleepily. "Happy Thanksgiving, Mr. Hudson, aka Preacher Man, sexiest man, and cat doula extraordinaire."

He kisses my forehead and my cheek and then a lingering kiss on my mouth. "Happy Thanksgiving, Mrs. Hudson, aka my Siren, and the love of my life."

"God, I love you," I tell him.

"I love you," he whispers. "More than I ever dreamed possible. And I'm so goddamn happy about it."

We drift off like that, wrapped around each other, sated and so completely happy, and we sleep like the dead.

CHAPTER THIRTY-SEVEN

FESTIVITIES

PENN

It's been a day of Christmas decorating at the house—something I've never done much of—and just like with everything else, Addy's made it so fun.

We've been extremely productive.

Inside, the house is stunning. Classy and completely enchanting.

Outside, our house looks like Buddy the Elf came and worked his magic.

It's me. I'm Buddy.

And I must say, I'm feeling *pre-tty* damn good about myself.

This is a learning curve for me, but once I knew Addy and the kids wanted lights, I went all in. I don't even know how many lights I've strung around the house and trees. So, so many.

And then there are the inflatables.

There's a Santa (15 ft) sitting with his feet dangling from the roof. The sleigh and reindeer (12 ft) are behind him. A Snowman (40 ft) stands on the lawn overseeing the land. Then there's Elsa (15 ft), Mrs. Claus (26 ft), three gingerbread men (12 ft)…and my favorite, the flamingo with a Christmas lei around her neck (40 ft) that I put out by the pool. Not to mention the inflatable candy cane arches everywhere (20 ft each).

And then…the *masterpiece* is the Christmas Ferris Wheel. It's not an inflatable, it's wooden and so stinking cute. Addy and the kids gasp when they see it and then look on in shock as I light everything up.

"What have you done?" Addy asks, eyes wide.

"Pretty damn great, right?" I ask.

"Pretty damn *something*!" she says, laughing.

"I *love* it, Daddy," Winnie gasps dreamily.

Sam fist-bumps me. "This is sick," he says, laughing.

It's such a hit, no one wants to leave the house, but we have to rush off for Winnie's performance in the holiday dance show.

We wind up the mountain, excitement and nerves palpable in the car. When we arrive at the Silver Hills Community Theatre, it feels like there are a thousand people in the parking lot, even though I know it barely seats three hundred. And we're early.

We walk inside, Addy and Winnie holding hands next to me, and Sam on my other side. Holiday garlands and lights cover every surface—although I think it could stand another couple hundred strands of lights—and the chatter of parents and kids running around in costumes rivals the football stadium. My palms are sweating, which is just silly.

Winnie looks adorable in her red tutu and sparkly headband. Her curls are going every direction and her green eyes are bright. She stops suddenly, and we all stop, looking to see if she's okay.

She looks up at us nervously, her free hand twisting around her tutu. I start to lean down to her level to say something encouraging, but Sam beats me to it.

"You've got this," he says, his voice firm.

She looks at him, uncertain. "What if I forget all my moves?"

"Never gonna happen. You've got them *down*," I insist.

"And so what if you forget something?" Sam adds. "I bet no one would be able to tell anyway."

Her lip trembles. "I'm nervous."

"Think about all the stuff you've done, Win," Sam says, taking her hand. "You've survived mean foster parents. Hateful kids. Never having enough food. And you still laughed and played through all that." He leans in. "And your dancing kicks *ass*."

Her eyes get huge and she giggles, clamping her hand over her mouth. She looks around to see if that's gonna get him in trouble, but we're enjoying this too much for that to happen.

"You think so?" she whispers finally.

"I know so. You are *powerful*. You're the toughest girl in the whole wide world, and you're gonna be the cutest, *best* dancer out there tonight," he tells her.

She gulps. "I promise I won't tell Cassidy and Audrey you said that," she says, then nods briskly. "Okay. Okay, I'm ready." She throws her arms around Sam's neck and when she backs away, they high-five hard enough for it to echo.

"Totally got this." Sam grins.

She takes a deep breath and stands taller.

I hear Addy sniffling beside me and she rolls her eyes when I look. "Why are they always making me emotional?"

"Because they're the best little humans…and we are totally soft." I put my arm around her and my hand on Winnie's shoulder. "And I can't wait to see you shine up there, sweet girl." I lean down and kiss her cheek. "Love you."

"Love you, Daddy," she says.

I don't think my heart will ever not drop when she says that.

She looks at Sam. "Love you, Sam."

And then she bounces off with Addy backstage, where they're supposed to be gathering, while Sam and I find our seats.

The first half of the show starts out with the full range of ages—toddlers to teens—and we're laughing our asses off one second and amazed by the talent in the next. The littlest ones are dressed like snowflakes and they scatter in different directions, never quite landing where they're supposed to. A boy dressed as a reindeer hops sideways…instead of staying in line with everyone else, and crashes into an elf. The elf then bursts into tears and looks into the audience for his mom.

We lose it when one of the little girls in Winnie's class does an inappropriate hip thrust during "Jingle Bell Rock."

And then, it's time for the father-daughter dance. The dads file onto the stage and I see our friends out in the audience. I remember how cute it was when Bowie and Rhodes stepped in and danced with Cassidy and Audrey after Henley's injury. Henley's up here now with Cassidy and Audrey flanking him. He winks at me when our eyes meet.

I can't believe I'm here now with a little girl that I want to be my daughter more than anything.

I glance down at Winnie, my hand engulfing her tiny one, and her expression is serene and confident as she smiles up at me. All earlier nerves are gone.

"You ready?" I ask.

"Yes," she says emphatically.

We go full-on cheese with our smiles at each other.

"Okay, little miss. Let's show them how it's done."

After the grand finale, I give her a huge bouquet that I'd kept hidden from The Enchanted Florist, and it's like I've given her a pony or something. She's *thrilled*.

"Flowers?" she gasps. "For *me*? I've never ever had flowers. Oh, I love them so, so much!"

If I could give her the whole world, I would.

Sam plucks one that is dangling loosely and breaks the stem. Winnie beams when he tucks it behind her ear. She shifts on her feet, waiting for our approval.

"Perfect," Addy says.

"You really were the best one out there," I whisper so I don't hurt any other little girls nearby.

We pose for pictures with our friends, cracking up at how we've multiplied over the last couple of years.

"At the rate we're all going, I think we can fill up this theatre on our own next year," Rhodes teases.

"You trying to tell us something?" Bowie asks.

"Nah, I'm letting you be the father of many nations," Rhodes says, shaking Bowie by the shoulder.

Bowie just laughs, completely unperturbed. Honestly, he's

such a good dad, I can imagine him with five kids and still pulling off that stud hair like it's nothing.

We all end up at Serendipity, and Greer and Wyndham go on about how cute Winnie looks in her dance outfit.

"Thank you," Winnie says, twirling. "I think I'm getting a strawberry shake," she declares.

"You always get a strawberry shake," Sam says.

"That's because it's my favorite," she says, her nose scrunching up. But then she sees a banana split at the next table and she hesitates. Her mouth drops a little. "Or maybe that," she says.

We all laugh and she looks around like *what?*

When Greer comes out with the massive thing, sliding it in front of Winnie's awed face, she stares at it. "It's so big," she whispers.

"You think you can handle it?" I ask.

Her chin lifts. "I'm very *powerful*," she says.

Sam looks at me, nodding proudly. "Told you."

We watch as she digs in, taking a huge bite of whipped cream and chocolate and banana all at once. Her whole face lights up.

"*Oh*...I was made for this," she breathes.

CHAPTER THIRTY-EIGHT

WHAT I WANT

ADELINE

I'm sitting in the back of Elle's SUV, listening to Tru and Poppy discussing pregnancy next to me. Sadie's riding shotgun, scrolling on her phone and asking Elle all the questions about her movie premiere. We've got some time yet before that, but we decided that after we get some Christmas shopping done, we'll do a little gown shopping as well.

"Do you have any ideas about what you want to wear yet?" Sadie asks Elle.

Elle squeals, doing a little dance. "Well, I thought I'd wear a Dior dress I've had my eye on, but...Tamara Ralph's people have reached out!"

We all freak out, yelling and waving our hands in the air and pounding the seats.

"You're gonna be styled!" Sadie says, doing a little dance.

"You are *such* a superstar," Poppy says.

"I'm not though! I really liked staying in my little hidey hole and writing away. The way this has all gone is crazy. Is it too soon to say that I'm panicking?" Elle says with a nervous laugh.

"Not about how you're going to look though, right?" Tru asks, leaning forward to put her hand on Elle's shoulder. "Because we all know you're going to look amazing."

"No. I mean, I'm nervous about that too...being seen by all those people. But I'm mostly worried I won't like the movie. Or that everyone else won't. I like what I've seen so far, but I haven't seen it all put together yet. It's hard to tell how it's going to turn out."

"That makes total sense," I tell her. "It must be so exciting to have your characters brought to life, but also, terrifying...because what if they don't capture them how you intended?"

"Exactly. I'm one of those the-book-is-always-better kind of people...unless it's *The Notebook*, and then Ryan Gosling and Rachel McAdams just completely slayed in that movie," she says.

"Agreed," we all chime in.

"Speaking of going all out..." Sadie says, turning around to look at me.

I lift my eyebrows, waiting to see where she's going with this.

"Has Penn added any more Christmas lights outside?"

The laughter in the SUV is loud and I'm laughing right along with them.

"You've seen the lights, huh?" I say.

"Penn told the guys in the group thread that they had to come see the masterpiece he'd created outside, so we drove by last night," she says. "WHOA."

"We drove by too," Tru says. "Unbelievable."

"Us too!" Poppy says. "Becca had to get out and take pictures with Elsa and Mrs. Claus!"

"So cute," Elle says. "Levi is obsessed and a little afraid of the Snowman."

I wipe my eyes, unable to stop laughing. "Yesterday, Penn thought the area around the mailbox needed a little embellishment and the next thing I knew, he was stringing two thousand lights around it and the lamppost."

"Don't forget the ginormous inflatable of Waldo with the stocking hat," Sadie adds. "He was adding that out there when we pulled up."

"Oh my god, you're kidding," Tru says. "I missed the Waldo?"

"That guy," Elle says, shaking her head. "He is a new man with you, Addy. He's always been fun, but the way he is with you and Sam and Winnie..." She sighs. "I just love seeing it so much. Especially because he was so adamant about never getting married, never settling down. He resisted."

"Did he ever," Sadie says.

"But then we all heard about you when we came back from the Bahamas." Tru laughs. "What did you do to him in the Bahamas? I've always been dying to know!"

"I took him to flamingo yoga," I say, which sends us into another round of laughter.

"You guys are perfect for each other," Poppy says.

I grin and look out the window, thinking about the stuffed flamingo with extra-long arms that I surprised him with last night. It's so fun to give him these things. He set it on his nightstand and then took it downstairs this morning, wrapping its arms around the top of his chair at the kitchen table. Winnie and Sam are in on it now, looking for funny flamingos.

"Is that why you have that furry flamingo key chain?" Tru asks.

"Yeah, it's kind of our thing. We surprise each other with flamingos…"

"I love it," she says.

There's a bendable flamingo I've had my eye on for a while now. Maybe for his Christmas stocking. He's given me a cute pajama set with flamingos. I've given him flamingo boxers.

It takes a while to find parking at Cherry Creek North, no small miracle the week before Christmas, and we pile out onto the street. The holiday market is still going on too, and everything is dressed up for the season. Christmas music plays around us and I breathe in the crisp air.

"All right, team," Sadie says, adjusting her purse over her shoulder. "Shall we knock out the Christmas shopping first and then tackle the gowns? Or the other way around?"

"Let's get the shopping done. I don't have much left," Poppy says.

"Me either."

I don't admit that I'm done with the shopping. For the past few months, I've shopped online at night while the kids are watching a movie or after they go to bed. I'm just happy to have a day out with these girls. I love spending time with them. It makes me miss Goldie. I wish she lived closer. She'd be in the big, fat middle of everything and loving every minute.

Two hours later, we're standing in the back of a fancy boutique, the dressing rooms piled with glittering gowns. Poppy's the only one waiting to try anything on because she's about to pop. The rest of us are staring at Elle in a sleek black gown that hugs her figure perfectly.

She tried to resist trying anything on, but since the event is all about her in our eyes, we talked her into it.

"You'll need multiple dresses, probably," Tru says. "So you can still be styled by someone crazy talented, but this one…"

"Exactly. Wow," Poppy breathes.

Elle shakes her head. "I don't know…"

"You don't know?" Sadie looks offended. "You're perfection. You look like you're about to accept an Oscar."

Elle snorts. "It's not too much?"

"It's just enough," Tru says, standing next to me.

"Agreed," I say.

It's evening by the time we pull back into Silver Hills, and Tru's mom, Stephanie, Margo, and my mom meet us at The Fairy Hut. We tried to include all the moms, but the timing didn't work out. My mom and Margo have been welcomed into the fold over the past few months, and it's been fun seeing their friendships grow too.

I sip my Who Let The Frogs Out? cocktail slowly, savoring the perfect blend of flavors. I missed The Fairy Hut's delicious and hilariously-named food and drinks when I lived in California.

"Did you have a successful shopping day?" Stephanie asks.

"Three of us found what we're wearing to Elle's premiere," Sadie says. "I couldn't settle on one."

"And I need this baby out before I can think about a pretty dress," Poppy says.

Margo's sitting next to her and she pats her arm. "You look spectacular. I wish I'd carried a baby the way you do. I puffed out everywhere."

"Oh, same," my mom agrees.

The ones of us who haven't had babies yet take it all in. The unknown. It feels big.

"You okay, sweetheart?" my mom asks quietly.

I turn and smile at her. "I'm good. Really good."

She squeezes my hand. "You look good. Like you're glowing from the inside out."

I lean into her and she puts her arm around me.

"I think I'm going to take a step back. With my job, I mean."

Her eyes widen. "Really?"

"I'm so grateful for my job, and I've truly loved it. But…" I hesitate, searching for the right words. "I feel like Sam and Winnie…they're my calling. I want to devote my energy to them and our family…and maybe a baby even."

Her eyes light up. "A baby!"

"It doesn't feel like giving something up for me. It feels like I'd be missing out if I didn't focus on them while I'm lucky enough to have them. This whole waiting game…I mean, I know we'll most likely get to keep them, but…the what-ifs…it's really made me see what matters most to me."

My mom watches me for a long moment before smiling. "That's not giving up at all," she says. "I admire you so much. And if you ever changed your mind, I'm sure they'd have you back in some capacity or another. That team loves you."

"Yeah, it may not be forever, but for now…I feel like it's what I'm supposed to do."

"Then that's what you should do."

"You're not disappointed or…frustrated?" I ask.

"Why would I be?" She turns to face me fully now.

"Because of all the money you spent on my education… and all the goals and dreams I had."

"You will still put your knowledge about nutrition to good use, and just because you're staying home doesn't mean your goals and dreams die." She smiles when I laugh. "Are you happy?"

"So happy."

"Keep listening to your heart, Addy. I trust you. It won't steer you wrong."

I exhale, feeling something settle inside me. A decision I wasn't one hundred percent certain about until I said it out loud.

"Thanks, Mama," I say softly.

I glance around the table at these beautiful people who have enriched my life in ways I didn't even know I was missing.

My life is so full. This right here, and what I have at home with Penn and the kids…it's exactly what I want.

CHAPTER THIRTY-NINE

A LONG WAY

PENN

"Are you sure we can't just open the presents now?" I ask, following Addy around the house.

She turns and gives me a playful shove and I pretend to be wounded.

"You're worse than the kids!"

"I just can't wait for them to see their presents!" I lean in closer. "They're gonna be so excited about those bikes."

She slaps her hand over my mouth, shushing me. "Do not let them hear you talking about the presents," she hisses.

"Jeez. Where is your Christmas spirit?" I grump. My head falls back and I groan. "This is the longest day ever."

I look at my watch. Our parents won't be here for a few hours yet.

Gizmo nuzzles against my leg and I bend down to pick him up.

"Hey, little guy," I say, kissing his wrinkly forehead.

I've come a long way with Jezebel and the kittens. I'd never let the little dude know that I think he's an alien on short legs. He deserves love. His purr makes me smile and when I look up, Addy's smiling at me.

"We still have surprises to put out tonight, you know. After they go to bed," she whispers.

That lifts my spirits a little. "Right. Okay. What are the kids doing? I haven't seen them for a while."

She lifts her shoulders. "They're working on a surprise...I have no idea."

"Ooo, interesting." I lift my eyebrows and move toward the stairs.

"Do not go and spy on them," she says.

I sigh. I hold Gizmo up and act like he's speaking. "Let the master of Christmas cheer do his thing."

"You did not just call yourself the master."

I peek out from Gizmo. "*No*. He said it."

"Mm-hmm. You're too much," she says, her lips pressing together as she tries not to laugh.

"But just right for you?" I move over and slide one hand around her hip, tugging her against me. Gizmo sighs happily with the increased body heat.

"Just right for me," she says.

"We could have a little one-on-one time in our bedroom…while the kids are busy and all."

She's already shaking her head and backing away. "I have so much to cook still."

"Ruining *all* my fun," I mutter.

I try to help her in the kitchen, but the kittens keep following me around, so Addy shoos us all out. We end up on the couch—Jezebel across my belly, Elsa and Shadow on each leg, and Gizmo curled up in my neck.

I love these hideous things so goddamn much.

My phone buzzes and I try to fish it out of my pocket. Jezebel gives me a look of disdain for waking her up, and I scratch between her ears.

"Sorry, Jezzy. I know your rest is precious."

I glance at the phone. David.

"Hello?"

"Penn! Happy Christmas Eve!" he says.

"Happy Christmas Eve to you!" I say back.

"Are you with Addy and the kids?" he asks.

"I'm actually on cat duty while Addy cooks, and the kids are upstairs working on a surprise."

"Can you put them on the phone with you? Actually…can we make this a FaceTime?"

"Sure," I say slowly.

I sit up and carefully move the cats to the couch, tucking a blanket around them so they go back to sleep.

"Is everything okay?" I ask, as I walk into the kitchen.

"Just wanted to deliver a little Christmas message," he says.

"David's on the phone," I tell Addy. "He wants to give us and the kids a Christmas message."

"Aw. Okay. Let's go get them." She washes her hands really quick and we go upstairs.

I open up the Facetime call and see David's smiling face. I smile back and Addy knocks on Sam's door. We hear whispers and Winnie's giggles, and Sam opens the door, barely creaking it open.

"Can you come out and talk to David for a sec?" I ask.

"Oh," he says, surprised. "Sure. Come on, Winnie," he says over his shoulder.

He closes the door and then they come out a couple of seconds later, shutting the door behind them.

"Okay, we're all here," I tell David. "These kids are being super mysterious," I tease.

"Well, I'm so happy to see all of you. Merry Christmas," David says.

"Merry Christmas!" we all say back.

"And I have the best surprise I could've ever hoped to give you on this Christmas Eve," he adds.

My heart tumbles over itself and I hear Addy gasp.

David's eyes are full of tears when he nods and says, "We have a date with the judge on Monday! How does Monday sound for adoption day?"

"That's perfect," I say, hoarsely.

"Oh my God!" Addy gasps.

"And I have it on good authority…" He leans in and whispers the next part through a big smile, "Sutton spoke with the judge..." He raises his voice again. "And it's just a matter of finalizing everything. Sam and Winnie, the court will issue adoption decrees for both of you, and you'll be given new birth certificates saying that Penn and Addy are your parents…with your new last names and everything. How's that for a Christmas present?"

Sam turns into my chest and starts bawling. I lose it myself. Addy picks Winnie up and we all hug each other, laughing and crying and just so fucking happy. When we finally get our bearings, I steady the phone.

"Thank you, David," I choke out. "This means the world to us. We can't thank you enough for your help. You've made our dream come true."

"You did that," he says shakily. "With the love you've provided each other and the time you've put toward this process…it's all you."

"We couldn't have done it without you," Addy says, wiping her face.

"Thank you, David," Sam says.

"Thank you," Winnie echoes. "Does it mean I'm staying with you forever? Me and Sam?" she asks, looking up at Addy and me.

"Yes, that's exactly what it means," I tell her.

David shakes his head and wipes a stray tear from his cheek. "This has been the most fulfilling case I've had. And Monday, we will celebrate! Heck, I hope you celebrate all weekend long!"

"Oh, we will," I assure him. "Won't we?" I ask the kids.

"Yes, we will!" they yell.

Winnie reaches for me and I take her from Addy's arms, hugging her tight.

"Ahh, this is a good day," David says. "I'll let you get to it. I just couldn't wait to tell you the news."

We all thank him again and when we hang up, we stare at each other for a second before crashing into each other with hugs again. I twirl Winnie around and then keep dancing down the hall. Addy and Sam follow, dancing behind me. The kittens skitter around playfully when they see us, and we have the dance party of all dance parties.

When our parents arrive, Sam and I are wearing sweaters and jeans, and Addy and Winnie are both wearing pretty green dresses.

"Wow, you all look so beautiful," my mom says when she walks in.

"Thanks, Mom. So do you." I kiss her cheek and then Danielle's when she walks in next. "And so do you," I tell her.

Coach even hugs me.

"Hey, Coach," I say, as he pounds me on the back.

"Are you ever gonna call me Rex?"

"Mmm, I'm not sure I can," I say, laughing.

"I can't get over all the decorations out there," I hear Danielle saying to Addy.

"Penn has found a new calling," she says.

"Damn straight!" I call.

I look around at our family and grin. I walk over to Addy and put my arm around her waist.

"Do you mind if we take a family picture before we eat?" I ask. "I put a little something together this morning. It's in the back."

Addy looks at me in surprise. "What did you do? It's not an Incredible Hulk inflatable or something, is it?"

"No, but damn…I missed an opportunity there," I say.

Everyone laughs.

"A family picture sounds great," my mom says.

"Sam and Winnie, can you help me with the kittens?"

"They're gonna be in the picture too?" Coach asks.

"They're family too," I say.

"Not sure how I feel about that," I hear him say as I go into the family room where I left the cats last.

Winnie gasps when she sees them. "Oh, they're so cute!" she coos.

I've got them all dressed in cream sweaters. Jezebel's has a little floofy trim around her neck, and I slide a tutu on her and Elsa, assuring them I'll take the tutus off as soon as the pictures are over.

"Too good." Sam laughs. "You're looking nice, guys," he says, nuzzling Gizmo and Shadow.

Winnie carries Elsa, and I carry the queen, Jezebel, as she looks on serenely.

Addy and the rest of the family lose it when they see us.

"Oh my goodness!" Danielle says. "Penn, what will you think of next?"

"You just never know," I say, grinning.

I lead them outside, and not too far from the lake, there's this one tree that's always been my favorite. It's tall and beautiful on its own, but with lights wrapped on every branch, it's stunning. There are three pretty benches with white furry blankets, the biggest one in the middle, and I ordered a massive bouquet with white roses and feathers and greenery from The Enchanted Florist that sits on a pillar nearby. Everyone gasps when they see the display, even Coach, and I feel my job is done.

I brought the camera on a tripod out before they got here, and I motion toward the area.

"I thought we could take pictures there," I say, when no one speaks.

"Penn, this is so beautiful," Addy says. She looks up at me, her eyes luminous. "You make everything so special." Her voice breaks as she blinks fast. "Not gonna cry. Not gonna cry. Not gonna cry."

"I love to make you smile," I tell her. "And cry happy tears," I add.

She leans up and kisses me. "I love you," she whispers.

"I love you most," I say.

When we break apart, I tell everyone where I imagined us all sitting for the picture and set the camera timer with a little remote I can hide under Jezebel's tutu. Addy, the kids, and I sit on the middle bench, and they're each holding a kitten. Jezzy's on my lap. This mother doesn't leave my side if she can help it.

She knows I've got her back.

And I think she's the tits.

Saggy, wrinkly tits, but the tits.

Our parents sit on either side of us. And right before the first picture is taken, I yell, "It's official! Our court date is on Monday and the adoptions will be final!"

At first there's a—

What?

Did I hear that right?

And then—

It's finally happening?

Oh my God, this is the best news!

Thank God for a home game on Sunday, so I don't miss it!

And I make sure the camera gets every moment.

CHAPTER FORTY

BIG DAYS

ADELINE

I feel like I'm living a dream. No, better than a dream—because this is real.

I wake up to the sound of little feet pounding down the hallway and giggle when I hear the high-pitched squeal of Winnie's excitement, followed by Sam's deeper voice telling her to slow down so she doesn't fall. But neither of them slows down. I smile in my pillow and hear Penn's husky chuckle.

"I thought they'd never wake up," he says, popping out of the covers.

He leans over to kiss me quickly, his dimples on full display, and I melt.

"Merry Christmas," he says.

"Merry Christmas. What time is it?" I ask.

"Early," he says, laughing.

"How long have you been awake?"

"Since three."

"But we went to sleep around midnight."

"What can I say? I'm excited."

The door creaks open and then Winnie launches herself at us, climbing right over Penn and landing between us like a cannonball.

"Whoa! There's a tornado in our bed," Penn says, nuzzling his cheek up to Winnie's.

Sam stands at the end of the bed, grinning.

"I tried to get her to wait until five, but no go," he says.

"Merry Christmas, you two," Penn says. "We said to wake us up when you were awake—when did you get up?"

"She snuck in my room at four," Sam says.

Penn sighs. "You mean we could've been opening presents by now?"

Sam's shoulders relax and he laughs. He's trying to be cool, but the excitement is bouncing off of him. "Sorry, Dad."

We all pause, Penn gulping hard, and he reaches out and tugs Sam onto the bed with us, giving him a big hug.

I tickle Winnie's side and then Penn's and he jerks and lets out an exaggerated whoop, making us all laugh. I launch at Sam and hug him, tickling his side too.

"You guys look so cute in your Christmas jammies," I tell them.

"You too, Mrs. Hudson. You too." Penn grins at me as he

gets out of bed and lifts Winnie up onto his shoulders, looking down at Sam and me. "Well, I'm ready. I've already been to the bathroom, brushed my teeth…checked on the felines…"

"You've been up for a long time!" Winnie shrieks when Penn bounces her.

"I'm hurrying, I'm hurrying," I say, rushing to the bathroom.

I don't mess around in there, doing only the bare minimum before rushing back out.

They're waiting for me and we go down the stairs together.

"Do you think Santa came?" Winnie asks.

"Oh, I know he did. Mrs. Claus too," Penn tells her. "It was a joint affair."

He pauses and sets her down on the stairs.

"Wait right here. Let me get a picture of you coming down," he says.

He takes one with me and the kids and then I scoot out of the way so he can get one of them.

As soon as he takes the pictures, they jog down the stairs.

"Come on, Daddy!" Winnie says. "Mama, Sam, hurry!"

"We're coming, promise," I tell her.

We round the corner and there's a collective gasp. Winnie's is so loud, I check to make sure she's okay.

The Christmas tree is perfection, if I do say so myself. The stockings are overflowing, and the floor beneath the tree is covered with presents, some wrapped and unwrapped.

"There are more presents here than last night!" Sam says, his voice croaking mid-word. He rubs his Adam's apple absent-mindedly, his voice is changing and normally, he's so embarrassed when it does that, but this morning, he's too mesmerized by the sight before him.

Winnie runs to the floppy unicorn with the fluffy mane and buries her face in it.

"*I love it!*" she says, voice muffled in the fur.

Penn was probably most excited to give Sam the skateboard he's been eyeing for a while. Sam's scary good on the skateboard and this one is his favorite skateboarder's brand. Sam goes over to the skateboard, his face all lit.

"A Disorder," he gasps when he sees that it's signed by Nyjah Huston. "How did you do this?" he asks.

"Santa must have a few connections," Penn says, grinning at him.

Sam turns and hugs him. "I can't believe you got me a signed Disorder!" he says against Penn's chest.

"You just have to wear that with it," I say, pointing to the cool helmet I found for him. "Every single time," I add.

He rushes to the helmet and picks it up. "This is so sick," he says, turning it every angle. "I love it!" He turns to look at me and I reach out and hug him. "I'll wear it every time. Thanks, Mom," he says.

"You're so welcome," I croak, hugging him tight and blinking fast.

Today's the first time he's called us Mom and Dad, and yeah, I'm going to be a puddle all day long.

We sit down around the tree...well, all of us but Penn, who jogs into the laundry room where the cats sleep. He comes back carrying the kittens, Jezebel on his heels.

"They didn't want to miss out," he says.

He sets them down and gives them the little toys we bought for them, and we laugh when Gizmo attacks his.

Penn points toward the stockings. "Want these now, or are we doing the big stuff?"

"Can I open this one?" Winnie asks, holding up a pink, sparkly box.

"Absolutely." I nod.

Sam looks on happily, still holding his skateboard.

Winnie shrieks when she pulls out a set of glittery fairy wings and a matching tutu. "Fairy princess!"

"You've always been a fairy princess," Penn tells her.

He hands Sam a box and Sam's mouth drops when he opens the new headphones. "These are—these are so cool. I can't believe it," he says, shaking his head.

Penn sits down beside him and ruffles his hair. Then he hands me a huge box.

"Me?"

"Yes, you." He smirks.

Inside is a luxurious blanket. I hold it up to my face and sigh. "So soft."

He gives me a sweet smile, his eyes heating with promise.

I give him a sweater and a beautiful decanter set that he loves. He gives me a robe that makes me feel like a queen, stunning earrings, and an adorable floppy flamingo.

It's Penn's turn to get teary when we give him an album filled with the pictures he's been taking.

Sam and Winnie are beside themselves with every present we give them, so excited and so grateful.

When they give us each a leather key chain with Mom and Dad on the front, there are more tears. And under the little leather flap that opens up, there's a picture of the four of us together.

"This is the best," I cry.

We go through the stockings one at a time, and it's Just. So. Fun. Seeing Christmas through Sam and Winnie's eyes—and Penn's because he's just as excited—makes me happier than I thought possible.

There's one little box left in my stocking and I pull it out, eyes wide at Penn.

"Open it," he whispers.

Inside the box is a delicate chain with dainty charms—Cupid's arrow, a unicorn, a skateboard, a football, ballet slippers, and an infinity symbol. I laugh when I see the last two—a slice of pizza because Sam will always say he wants pizza if asked. And last but not least, a flamingo.

I bite my lip. "Penn..."

"You like it?"

"It's perfect."

"You are." He leans in and kisses me slowly, his hand sliding into my hair.

"What an amazing day," I whisper.

He nods, leaning his forehead against mine.

The rest of the day is a blur of noise and laughter...and a little snoozing on the couch. Friends and family start pouring in by late afternoon. The house is bursting at the seams with pure joy.

At some point, Penn taps his glass with a spoon and stands. "Hey, can I say something?"

Everyone quiets down.

"I have an announcement," he says. "Well...*we* have an announcement."

He looks at me and Sam and Winnie, and there's so much love there, it almost knocks me over.

"We are extremely happy to tell you that, come Monday..." His voice catches for a second. "Sam and Winnie will officially be Hudsons."

Everyone stares at us and then the room erupts into cheers. Sam laughs and Winnie claps her hands.

"You all know me," Penn continues, rubbing the back of his neck. "I didn't think I was cut out for this. I resisted all of it. But these two?" He looks at Sam and Winnie. "They taught me otherwise. They taught me how to love big. And this woman right here…" His eyes find mine. "She made me believe I could have it all. She showed me how to love with my whole heart. I don't even recognize the man I was before because once I met Addy and fell in love with her, it took over every part of me. So, this whole family thing? It's all thanks to her." He lifts his glass and winks at me. "Literally."

I bite back a smile as tears blur my vision.

Our fake marriage may have started out as a means to an end, but there's no doubt in my mind that what we have is the real deal.

"I love you, Adeline Hudson. With everything in me, I love you. And I love you, Sam and Winnie Hudson. The three of you are the best Christmas gifts I could ever get."

There are lots of sniffles around the room.

And then we lift our glasses.

"To Sam and Winnie," Penn says.

"To Sam and Winnie," we all echo.

It's a good thing there was a game yesterday—the Mustangs won, woot woot—because otherwise, I think my husband would have driven me crazy waiting for Monday to get here.

As it is, he has been a *handful,* but at least the distraction of the game helped.

We take the kids out of school an hour early on Monday afternoon, and the nerves are high on the way to the courthouse. When we arrive, Winnie holds my hand so tight my fingers go numb.

We walk inside, and I'm touched to see our friends and parents lingering outside the courtroom. Even Sutton is there, grinning like a proud uncle, and so is his beautiful wife, Felicity.

"Aw, you guys," Penn says. "I can't believe you all came."

"Of course we did," Henley says.

"We wouldn't miss it," Weston adds.

David shakes Penn's hand and pulls us both in for a hug. "Let's make this official."

When we take our seats, I start second-guessing everything. What if they don't approve us? What if something goes wrong? But when I see the judge, my insides relax. She's an older woman with warm eyes and a kind voice. She looks at Penn and me, then Sam and Winnie, and smiles as she begins the proceedings.

David asks us a few questions and then the judge does, and it's all easier than I expected.

"I don't usually say this," the judge says, "but this is an exceptional case. Seeing the way these relationships came about…Mr. Hudson, the way you've been involved in Sam's life consistently over the years, and then the way Winnie came into your lives…well, I'll just say that this is one of the easiest decisions I've ever made."

She stamps the paperwork and then hands out the two new birth certificates.

"Congratulations," she says.

I stare down at the papers, my breath catching. Samson Cole Hudson. Winnie Mae Hudson.

Sam looks up at us, his eyes shining. "It's real?"

"It's real," Penn says, his voice thick.

Sam hugs Penn, hard. And Winnie wraps her arms around my waist. I bend down and lift her, hugging her tighter. Penn looks at us, tears in his eyes.

"We did it," he says. "They're ours."

I nod, tears slipping down my cheeks. "They're ours."

"And you're mine," he says, leaning over to kiss me.

CHAPTER FORTY-ONE

CLAW DAGGERS TIMES THREE

PENN

I didn't even want a pet. That's what I tell myself every time Gizmo launches himself at my face like he's an alien torpedo.

I mean, I'm an NFL player. I don't have time for pets. Between practice, travel, the actual games, and wanting nothing more than to spend all my time with Addy and the kids, I barely have time to breathe, let alone take care of three mischievous balls of wrinkly skin and attitude.

And yet…

Jezebel purrs on my lap, her leathery little body curled up like a question mark. She's the one who got me into this mess. This mother with giant ears and two-toned eyes who looks like she's been dropped from the mothership, gazing up at me way too trusting.

Labor changed us.

And now, on a rare afternoon off, while Addy's still at work and the kids are at school, Jezebel and I sit and watch as her three kittens terrorize the living room like little furless demons. Gizmo and Shadow are doing parkour off the back of the couch, while Elsa is hanging from the curtains like a tiny, naked Tarzan. I lift Jezebel up and we walk over, carefully lifting Elsa's claw daggers from the curtain.

"That's a no, little miss," I tell her. "No curtain climbing for you."

I toss a toy at her as I sit back on the couch, and Jezebel starts purring again when I scratch behind her ear.

"You're killing me, Jezzy," I murmur. "They're old enough to adopt. That's the smart thing to do. What any reasonable person would do."

She blinks those weird eyes up at me and purrs louder.

"I know. I'm not sure I can do it. Break up a family. Separate siblings from each other…just give them to random strangers?"

She closes her eyes and stretches luxuriously like she couldn't care less. But she'll be hating on me if I go through with it, wondering where her children are.

Gizmo launches himself off the couch and slams into my chest.

"Oof, seriously?"

He meows and starts pawing at the neckline of my shirt, climbing his way up my shoulder on a mountain expedition.

Shadow and Elsa skitter across the floor, chasing each other and rolling into a heap.

"They'd be so sad without each other," I tell Jezebel.

Her tail flicks.

"Addy and I have our hands full. Between the football season going strong and Addy trying to finish her time with the Mustangs in the best possible way…we don't need three more living beings depending on us for survival, Jez."

She opens one eye and flicks her tail again, as if to say, *Well, that's a you problem, isn't it…*

"I know. I know. It is a me problem. I'm just not ready." I rub my hands over my face, groaning. "I'm just too soft, huh."

"Way too soft," a voice says behind me.

I turn to see Addy standing there, wearing one of my old sweatshirts and a teasing smile. Her hair is piled on top of her head in a messy bun, and she looks so effortlessly beautiful that my heart does that jolting flip it does whenever I see her.

"Not always," I say, eyes heating as I look her over. "In fact, not feeling soft at all now that I see you."

She giggles and sits down next to me, pulling her legs up onto the couch. Jezebel stands, stretches, and slinks over to curl into Addy's side. Shadow and Elsa follow like magnets, jumping up and then settling next to her. Gizmo, still perched on my shoulder, lets out a loud meow and rubs his snout against my ear.

"They're kind of hard to give up, aren't they?" Addy says softly, running her hand down Jezebel's back.

"Impossible."

Her gaze flickers to me, and for a second, there's something guarded there…like she's trying to figure out how to say something.

I sit up straighter. "What is it?"

"I have some news," she says finally, her voice quiet. She breathes out a laugh and shakes her head. "I don't know why I'm nervous. It's good news."

"Okay," I say, reaching for her hand. "Now I'm nervous."

She shifts closer, until we're about an inch apart. Her eyes are shining.

"We're pregnant."

My brain short-circuits. Pretty sure my heart stops for a second and then slams back into gear at double time.

"We—what?"

She's smiling now, but her eyes are wide and still nervous. "Pregnant. You're going to be a dad again...to a baby this time." She grins at Gizmo nuzzling my ear. "A human baby."

A sound leaves my throat that I don't think I've ever made before. I place Gizmo on the couch and surge up, hauling Addy into my arms. She lets out a startled laugh as I lift her off the ground and spin her in a circle.

"OH MY GOD!" I yell.

I'm laughing. She's laughing. Jezebel stands on the couch, bowing her back. The kittens scatter, meowing indignantly.

I press my mouth to Addy's neck and then to her cheek, feeling the happiest kind of terror flood through me.

"We're pregnant?"

"Yes!"

I spin her again. "Holy—Addy, this is—fuck, what is this life?" I cackle.

And then it hits me that I'm swinging my wife around like a sack of potatoes.

"Wait, am I hurting you?" I come to an abrupt stop, lowering her carefully to the floor. "Oh, God—are you okay?"

She laughs, still breathless. "I'm fine."

"No, but seriously. Are you?"

She puts her hand on my chest. "Penn. I'm okay. We're okay."

My hands are shaking when I cup her face, my thumbs brushing her cheeks.

"A baby," I whisper. "We're gonna have a baby."

She nods, her eyes shining.

"I thought we were going to keep trying and trying, and here you go, getting pregnant right away. No fair!"

Her face falls into my neck as she laughs.

"I love you," I say hoarsely.

Her smile softens. "I love you too."

I tug her to the couch and Jezebel climbs on Addy's lap, looking extremely unimpressed. The kittens are already chasing each other again.

"You know…" Addy rests her head against my chest. "If we can handle this chaos, we can probably handle a baby."

"You think so?"

She nods. "I do."

"Yeah, but…" I swallow hard and look at her out of the corner of my eye. "Maybe we should keep the kittens still… you know, for practice."

She laughs. "I'm not surprised you want to keep all of them."

"You're not? But I was so anti-teenage mom."

"Until you met these babies," she says.

Gizmo scales my arm and flops back onto my shoulder. I swear this guy thinks I'm his personal pillow. And scratching post.

"You know what this means, right?" Addy says.

"What?"

"We're about to be very outnumbered."

I kiss her forehead, feeling her smile against my chest.

"Switching to a zone defense," I say.

She laughs.

"We'll figure it out," I say.

"Yeah," she agrees, her voice soft. "We will."

Shadow pounces onto Elsa's tail and she lets out an indignant squeak, chasing after him and knocking over one of Winnie's toys in the process.

"We're so screwed," I say.

Addy laughs. "Yep."

I wrap my arm around her, feeling her warmth, the steady beat of her heart against mine. The mayhem around us. The overwhelming magnitude of everything we've just signed up for.

"The kids will be so happy to have a baby brother or sister. We're gonna be just fine," I say.

"I know," she whispers.

CHAPTER FORTY-TWO

MOST VALUABLE

ADELINE

The energy in the hotel suite is electric and we haven't even left for the NFL Honors ceremony yet.

The whole family is in Santa Clara, California tonight. The kids are hanging out in Margo and Jeremy's suite, where they'll watch the ceremony airing live.

I'm standing in front of the floor-to-ceiling mirror, smoothing down the bodice of my red evening gown. It's strapless, with a sweetheart neckline that hugs my chest before cascading down my body. I feel like a goddess in it, which is only reinforced by the way Penn is watching me from across the room.

Or maybe *gaping* is a better word.

He's already dressed in a tailored black suit that fits him perfectly. His tie is slightly loosened, the top button of his crisp white shirt undone, and his hands are in his pockets as he leans casually against the wall. His eyes are simmering as he watches me.

"You're not even trying to be subtle," I tease, turning to face him.

"I couldn't be if I wanted," he replies, his mouth tilting into that dangerous smile. "Jesus, Addy. You're trying to kill me in that dress."

I laugh softly, but my heart races when he pushes off the wall and stalks toward me. His hands slide to my waist, his touch sending heat through the fabric of my gown.

"There's no way I can focus on anything tonight with you looking like this," he murmurs, his voice low as he kisses his way down my neck.

My toes curl as my head falls back. "Well, you'll have to," I say, breathless. "It's kind of a big night, Mr. MVP finalist."

He hums, his lips brushing over my shoulder. His mouth is hot and soft, and the scruff on his jaw makes me shiver.

"That's the last thing I'm thinking about. You know what would help me focus?" he whispers against my skin.

I tilt my head back and meet his gaze in the mirror. His pupils are wide, his mouth hovering near the sensitive skin just below my ear.

"Penn," I warn.

"Come on," he coaxes, his hands sliding down my hips and cupping my ass. "We've got time."

"We really don't.

His mouth curves into a lazy, wicked smile. "Do you mean it?"

I hesitate, my eyes on his mouth and he spins me around, pressing me against the wall. His mouth crashes down on mine and I melt into him, heat unraveling through me in a dizzying rush. I hang onto his hair as he deepens the kiss, his tongue sweeping over mine.

"Penn," I gasp as he lifts my dress.

He turns me back toward the mirror and hikes my dress up around my thighs, his hands sliding the lace down my legs.

"Do you want this? Because I feel like I can't go another second without sinking into you," he says.

"I want this," I groan. "But we're going to be late," I pant, as his mouth trails down my throat.

His eyes meet mine in the mirror.

"We'll be fast," he promises, as he slowly slides his fingers between my legs.

I gasp, bending forward, both hands on the mirror in front of me. "Fast isn't exactly your strong suit."

His chuckle is low and dirty. "Let's see if I can surprise you."

He does.

And we're right on time.

An hour and a half later, we're sitting in the theatre, my hand tucked in the crook of my husband's arm, as we wait for the MVP announcement.

Penn smells like soap and his cologne, but every time I glance at him, I see the faint flush of color on his neck and the gleam in his eyes that tells me he's remembering exactly how we started this night.

I straighten his tie, smoothing the lapels of his jacket.

"I have a good feeling," I whisper. "And I'm already so proud of you."

He kisses my forehead, lingering there for a few seconds. "I love you so much."

The announcer steps onto the stage, and the crowd goes quiet. I'm too nervous to hear much of the opening monologue, and thankfully I don't have to wait too long. A massive screen lights up with the faces of the five MVP finalists. Right in the middle is a huge picture of Penn, the way he looks on the field…or when he's worshipping my body—all serious intensity. My face heats and I fan myself with the program. Weston is standing in front of Penn's picture and I smile over at Sadie.

The buildup is intense, each teammate saying great things about the player they're representing. When it's Weston's turn, he steps up with a wide, proud grin, looking down at Penn.

"I've known Penn is the best for years. I mean, the guy's got a poster of himself in our training facility—which, by the way, he did not put up himself, but he absolutely enjoys seeing it every day."

The crowd laughs.

"In all seriousness, Penn works harder than anyone I've ever met, and he's got the kind of heart that doesn't just make him a great player, it makes him a great friend, teammate, husband, and father to his two kids."

Another cheer goes up at those words. We've gotten so many gifts in the mail and phone calls from players all over the country who are excited about Sam and Winnie.

"The Mustangs are lucky to have Penn Hudson on the team, and I'm luckiest to call Penn one of my best friends."

Penn's face is tight with emotion when I glance over at him.

The announcer takes the mic again once all five men have spoken.

"And this year's NFL Most Valuable Player is…"

I grip Penn's hand tight.

"Penn Hudson!"

Our whole section erupts. Penn kisses me. Rhodes whistles. Henley pounds Penn's shoulder. Bowie hugs him. Elle, Sadie, Poppy, and Tru are bouncing next to us.

Penn makes his way to the stage and hugs Weston before taking the trophy. He looks down at it for a long moment, then glances toward me and smiles.

"What a year…" he says.

On Friday, we have time to have an amazing dinner with everyone in San Francisco, but on Saturday, I'm in work mode. The whole team is dialed in, but the vibe is surprisingly relaxed.

I spend the day setting up my last big spread as the team's dietitian. I've got protein-packed smoothie bowls topped with fresh berries and granola, honey-sriracha chicken skewers, sweet potato fries, and that's just the appetizers. The whole grain chocolate chip cookies drizzled with almond butter are especially delicious.

"Addy, are you sure you want to retire?" Rhodes asks, mouth full of chicken.

"Well, I have to go out on a high note," I tease.

"You're spoiling us and we can't get used to it," Weston says, pouting. "*But*, we're happy for you…"

Penn and I share a look. We haven't told everyone that we're pregnant yet, and it's so hard to keep it quiet!

The game is brutal.

The action has been nonstop in this year's Super Bowl game.

I'm glad I have the food to focus on because I'd be biting my nails otherwise. Tied with thirty seconds left, Penn is the one to get the ball into the end zone and they *win the game.*

I scream and jump up and down with Toby in the kitchen.

"Go! Go be with him!" he says, shooing me out.

The team swarms the field and I run out there. Penn breaks through the huddle and takes his helmet off, hugging me hard.

"We did it!" he yells.

"You did it," I tell him.

He kisses me, and I hang on for dear life.

"It's you, Addy," he says. "You're my good-luck charm."

CHAPTER FORTY-THREE

CONFESSING ALL THE THINGS

PENN

I've known we've had a lot of screen time lately in our friend group. The guys have been on my ass about it, joking that Addy and I are basically living in a rom-com.

Which, okay, fair.

But we've settled into this crazy, wonderful life. Married. Parents to Sam and Winnie. And now…

A baby.

Which is why we've gathered everyone at Serendipity.

Greer and Wyndham are behind the counter, scooping ice cream like pros. The place smells like sugar and chocolate, and the pastel walls are glowing under the warm lights. The shop is technically closed, but when I asked Greer and Wyndham if we could rent the place for the night to have this little party, they acted like that was ridiculous.

I want them to hear the news too, so I'm happy they're part of this.

Once everyone has arrived and has their ice cream of choice, the place is packed out with our family and friends… our framily, as Bowie calls us. There's a quiet roar as everyone chatters with each other. The kids are laughing and getting more hyper as the sugar high sets in.

"All right, you guys," I say, dinging my sundae dish. "I know you're probably sick of my little announcements…"

Henley leans back in his chair and smirks. "Always gotta be center stage…"

"Well, this time Addy's center stage," I say, squeezing her hand. "We're having a baby."

There's exactly one full second of stunned silence before the room erupts into chaos.

"What the—"

"Shut up!"

"Are you serious?"

"Oh my God!"

Sam is the first to hug us and Winnie is right behind him. Henley jumps to his feet. Tru shrieks, clutching his arm. Rhodes yells and pumps his fist in the air, while Elle bounces in her seat. Sadie and Weston are laughing so hard they're almost crying.

Bowie just sits there, looking stunned. Poppy gasps and Becca beams and yells, "Baby brother or sister!"

Greer and Wyndham clink their shake glasses.

"I knew it!" Greer says, laughing. "Did I not call it?"

"Yes, ma'am, you sure did," Wyndham says.

We're tackled with hugs and congratulations and it takes a while for things to die down again.

Tru holds her hands up, her face lit like she's ready to explode. "This is the best news!" she says. Then her smile turns sly. "And…we have some news too."

Our heads all whip toward her.

Henley grins. "We're pregnant."

"What the hell is happening?" Rhodes says, wiping his eyes.

"You're kidding," Elle says, clutching her stomach.

Rhodes clears his throat. "Actually…" He slides his arm around Elle's waist. "We were waiting to tell you this…but… we're having a baby too."

"WHAT?" I yell.

"This is like a pregnancy flash mob!" Sadie says, wide-eyed.

Weston glances at her and she gives a slight nod. "Well, since we're all confessing things…"

"Shut the front door!" Addy yells.

Sadie grins. "Yep. We're pregnant too."

We all lose our freaking minds. The kids dance around and we all pound each other on the back and hug and laugh and cry. Tru is laughing so hard, she's doing one long wheeze.

Weston is the closest one to me, and I hug him, leaning back to look him in the eye.

"Would you have ever believed this would be us when we first met?" I ask.

"Not a chance in hell," he says. "But I wouldn't change it for the world."

"Me either."

And then Poppy gasps and lets out a long moan. Her eyes go wide, and she presses a hand to her belly. "Ohhhh," she moans again.

Bowie's next to her within a second. "What is it? What's wrong?"

"I think—" Her face twists in pain. "I think it's happening."

"You're kidding." Bowie pales.

Greer drops a spoon and it goes clattering across the floor.

"Oh my God," Elle shrieks.

"Everyone to the car!" Weston yells.

"We can't all drive her!" Sadie argues.

"I've got it," Bowie says. He looks ready to pass out, but he starts moving her toward the door. She winces and grips his arm, shuffling alongside him. He looks at Tru and Elle and then around the room. "Can one of you take Becca home after this? I'll call Mrs. McGregor and my mom when we get to the hospital."

He looks at Becca and Poppy talks softly to Becca, who's nodding.

"I see you when baby comes," she says.

Poppy hugs her and then Becca hugs Bowie.

"Do you need us to take Jonas? We can take him too," Sadie says.

"That would be great. Mrs. McGregor can put him down for the night while we—oh shit, Poppy…" Bowie looks at Poppy in horror when she doubles over. "Tell me what to do."

"Get me to the hospital," she says through gritted teeth.

"Right. On it," he says, blinking rapidly.

She grips his face with both hands. "Now," she says softly.

That snaps him into gear. He moves her a little closer to the door.

"Oh no...ahh. My water just broke," Poppy says. "I'm so sorry, Greer and Wyndham!"

"That's what bleach is for," Greer calls. "Don't you worry. Go have that baby!"

"Whew, I feel woozy," Bowie says.

"Not today, Fox," Poppy says, grabbing him by the collar.

Weston yanks open the door, and Bowie and Poppy stumble through it. We tell them to drive safely and let us know when the baby arrives...and if there's anything we can do to help. When they leave, it's suddenly quiet.

Addy and I stand there in the doorway, shell-shocked.

"Did that just happen?" she whispers.

"I think so." I wrap my arms around her.

"I cannot believe this." She looks up at me.

"Five babies," I say, waving my hand. "A baby tonight and then four all at once. What kind of baby epidemic is this?"

Addy starts laughing and so does everyone else. Pretty soon, we're all in a state of hysteria.

"It's going to be absolute pandemonium," I say, holding my stomach. It hurts from laughing so hard.

"Imagine when they all hit puberty at once," Elle says.

"And start driving..." Tru adds, looking horrified.

"Aw, maybe they'll ride to school together," Sadie says. "And share clothes."

"Oh my God, what if they date each other?" Elle says, eyes wide. "Aw."

Rhodes has Levi on his shoulders and he bumps my shoulder with his. "You don't mess around, Penn Hudson." He smirks. "I like this look on you."

I let out a long exhale and give Levi a high five.

"Thanks, man," I tell Rhodes. "I never knew what I was missing. Now I can't imagine how I survived without them."

I tilt my head toward Addy and the kids. I shake my head and start laughing all over again. "All these babies. What the fuck?"

"Our Single Dad Players meetings are gonna be *lit*," he sings.

"Yeah, about that name…"

Not even two hours later, we're back home when Bowie sends a text to the group chat.

> **BOWIE**
> He's here. Elias Hayden Fox. Poppy's doing well. And Elias is healthy and perfect and freaking huge. 12 pounds, 8 ounces, 22 inches long.

A picture comes through and he's adorable.

> **RHODES**
> Good God. Poor Poppy. And that's amazing. Another little Fox to love. Or should I say, big Fox? He's so cute!

> **HENLEY**
> That is one fine boy. So happy for you guys.

> **WESTON**
> That was so fast! Wow, he's perfect.

> **BOWIE**
> It was too fast for Poppy to get an epidural. She is my hero.

> He reminds me so much of Jonas! I can't wait to see him. Give Poppy our love and get some rest. Love you guys.

BOWIE

> Love you too. I'm still reeling about all the baby news. Excited our new slew of kids will grow up together too.

HENLEY

> I still can't wrap my mind around it. Best day ever.

WESTON

> Yeah, Penn is right. There's definitely something in the Luminary coffee.

I'm chuckling as I crawl into bed. Addy smiles up at me. "What is it?"

"Did you hear from Poppy?" I ask.

She holds up her phone, showing me a picture of Elias.

"Isn't he just the best?" She sighs.

I lean over and kiss her before working my way down to her stomach. I slide my hand over her stomach and place soft kisses there.

"It's hard to believe there's a little baby tucked away in there," I say.

"I think it hasn't fully sunk in," Addy whispers. "But I can't wait, Penn. Every day with you and Sam and Winnie…I feel like I'm on this huge adventure where I can't wait to wake up in the morning to see what life will bring. I'm ready for whatever comes our way."

I smile up at her. "Me too. As long as we're together, I'm ready for anything."

EPILOGUE
LEGACY

PENN

Luminary smells like another day in paradise, rich coffee, sweet syrups, and the breeze coming in from the screen door. I walk back to the meeting room where the guys are already seated around the round table.

"It's so quiet in here," I say.

"You're the one who brings the noise," Rhodes says and then he laughs because he knows he's just as loud as I am.

"I'm not sure I'm alive," Bowie says groggily. "Elias has his days and nights mixed up."

"Whew, that's rough," Henley says. "That's how Gracie was."

"It's commendable that you showed," Weston tells Bowie. "We could've rescheduled."

Bowie shrugs. "I wanted to see you guys, and it might be months before Elias sleeps through the night, so…I may as well get back in newborn mode."

"In other words, we need to get all our sleep now," Rhodes says, pointing around the room.

"Message received," I say. I lean forward. "I have something to bring to the table…unless there's something we need to talk about."

They shake their heads.

"Bring it," Henley says.

"Yeah, what is it?" Weston asks.

"Single Dad Players. It doesn't work anymore. The name. I mean, you know it *never* worked for me, but…" I tease.

"Yeah, yeah. You've had plenty to say about the name," Rhodes grumps. "But it's legacy."

"What would we change it to?" Weston asks.

I hold out my hand. "That's what I think we should decide today. Something that fits who we all are now."

"You think we can come up with something better?" Henley asks.

"Absolutely." I grin. "Let's come up with some pitches."

"Dad Players?" Weston says, wrinkling his nose.

"Sounds weird," Henley says. "And a little gross."

"Yeah, it's a no," Rhodes confirms.

Bowie finally lifts his head. "What about Dad Squad?"

Weston perks up. "That's not bad."

"Team Dad?" Henley says.

"Sounds like a bad reality show," Rhodes says.

"Dad Committee?" Henley tries again.

Bowie rubs his face. "We're not a committee."

"Dad Crew?" Weston offers.

"Boy band," I say.

"Okay...what about something more sophisticated?" Weston says. "Like...Dad Collective."

"Sounds like a commune," I say.

Weston sighs. "Dad Syndicate?"

Rhodes gives him a dead stare. "What are we, the mafia?"

Weston shrugs.

"We could go with something simple," Rhodes says. "Like just...The Dads?"

There's a pause.

"I don't hate it," Bowie admits.

"But it's kind of boring," Rhodes says.

"Or classic," Weston says.

I look down at my caramel macchiato and space out for a few seconds, thinking about all the things I love about these guys, the range of topics we cover when we're together, and how I know I can count on them for absolutely anything.

"What about...The Brotherhood?" I say. "That's what I think of when I think of us. You're the brothers I never had. The brothers that I've claimed for life."

There's a weighted silence as they all take it in.

Bowie sniffs. "I like it," he says hoarsely.

Weston nods, reaching out to squeeze my shoulder. "Me too."

Rhodes smiles at me from across the table. "The Brotherhood. I think it's fitting."

"The Brotherhood," Henley repeats. "It works."

I slap the table. "It's settled. From this day forward, we

are no longer the Single Dad Players. We are The Brotherhood."

Weston raises his coffee cup. "To The Brotherhood."

We all clink our cups together.

"Now," I say, pulling out our Single Dad Playbook. "I don't know why, but it feels wrong to change the name of this." I wave the book. "But I guess since this one is almost filled up, it might be time to rename our book too. The Brotherhood Playbook?"

"It'll always be The Single Dad Playbook to me," Henley says.

The rest of us nod and then glance around the table.

"Lots of great memories here," Weston says. "Whatever our name, let's agree to always make more memories together."

"Agreed."

I flip open the book.

I see one of my entries and grin.

Is parenthood really just faking it till you make it?
Because I feel like I still don't have a clue,
But I sure as hell act like I do.
~Penn

I feel this way more now than I did when I wrote it.

Levi will think something is disgusting.
Unless he sees it on my plate.
And then it's the most delicious thing in the world.

I want to always be the gateway to him finding things he loves.
~Rhodes

I tap the page and look up at Rhodes. "That's profound, man. Be the gateway."

He grins. "You're doing it already with Sam and Winnie…I see you, man."

My chest swells with pride and more than a little relief that I might be getting something right.

There's a moment in time
When we discover the power of
The Dad Look.
Your kid is about to do something risky.
You lock eyes.
No blinking.
Raise the brows.
Insert The Dad Look.
Unless they're Gracie, they stop what they're doing.
The rest of the time?
That's why Band-Aids and mops were invented.
~Henley

I laugh out loud at that. "Must be a girl thing because the looks I try on Winnie just make her want to do it more."

They laugh.

"She's hilarious," Weston says.

I didn't really get to be the cool dad with Becca.
There was too much glitter in my scruff.
And my hair got lots of ponytails…
That kind of thing.
Which I wouldn't trade for anything.
I love being a girl dad.
But Jonas saw me throw a football
across the yard the other day,
And he plopped down on his diaper butt
and clapped so hard.
It's the coolest I've ever felt.
~Bowie

"Ahh, that little guy is gonna have an arm on him," Weston says. "He's all about the ball."

Bowie nods. "He is obsessed with playing ball…any kind."

Wanna know how I've realized I'm getting old?
I'm leaning into the dad jokes.
*I can't **not** say things like:*
It's nacho problem.
Eggs can't take a yolk.
Who's the sheep that can sing and dance? Lady Ba Ba
And the worst part?
I LAUGH AT MYSELF.
I'm calling it a rite of passage.
~Weston

. . .

I close the book and pass it to Weston.

"That is solid work right there, guys," I say, still laughing.

Henley stretches. "We're starting to sound like professionals."

"We've had practice," Rhodes says, grinning.

"We're heading for a new chapter, boys," I say. "Are you ready?"

We all click our coffee mugs together.

Ready.

EPILOGUE

SAM

Six years later…

I'm stuffing a suitcase with too many hoodies when Mom's sniffle from the doorway makes me pause.

"Mom," I say, without turning around, because if I see her face, I might cry myself. "You're not crying again, are you?"

"No," she says, her voice wobbling. "I'm fine. I'm just… really proud of you."

Dad clears his throat. He's been doing that a lot today—hovering nearby, trying to be helpful, and then disappearing when things get too emotional. He comes back with his face red and splotchy, so it's no secret that he's going off to cry too.

Winnie is sprawled across my bed, her face buried in my pillow. "I don't think I'm going to survive this."

My little brother Atticus sits near her on the bed, rubbing her back. He hates it when any of us are upset.

I sigh. "I'm not leaving forever. I'm just going to college. And it's not that far. I'll be back to visit lots."

"You say that, but once you get to school, you're gonna be all about the girls and sports and..." Her face curls up. "You'll never come home again."

"Not true," I tell her. "I promise I'll be back."

Dad rubs the back of his neck. "And you'll FaceTime a lot?"

"And tell me everything?" Winnie adds. She props herself up on her elbows and glares at me. "You *better* FaceTime me."

I sit down next to her on the bed. "You think I could stay away from all of you?"

Winnie's mouth wobbles and she launches herself to me, clinging to my neck like a little monkey. I wrap my arms around her and pull Atticus in too. I'm going to miss them so much.

Mom and Dad come over and hug us. I look up at them and my throat tightens.

I feel the way I have since the day I moved into this home...so damn lucky.

There was a time I didn't think I'd ever have a family.

I was nine when I met my dad. He wasn't my dad yet, but looking back, it was inevitable. I was in foster care, bouncing from house to house, convinced that nothing would ever work out for me. The world felt big and cold, and I was just drifting.

Penn showed up to tutor me. He was tall and kind of intimidating, but when he sat down and smiled at me, I could tell he was genuine. I didn't know if I could trust him at first.

I was used to people pretending to care and then disappearing or hitting me or withholding things from me.

But he stuck around.

He made me feel like I mattered. He showed up. Every time. Without fail.

He told me I was smart. That I was capable. That I mattered.

Until he made me believe it.

And when Mom came into our lives, it was like she filled all the empty places in both of us with love. I didn't know anyone's heart could be so big.

They've never stopped making me feel like I belong. Like I'm wanted.

I clear my throat and hug Winnie and Atticus one more time before gently prying them off of me.

"Okay, I better keep packing."

"Do you think you have everything?" Mom asks, looking anxious.

"Maybe I'll leave something on purpose, so you'll have to bring it to me."

She grins. "Okay. That sounds like a good plan."

"You don't have to trick us into visiting you," Dad says. "We'll be there all the time, if you say the word."

"He doesn't want us around all the time, Penn," Mom says.

"Yes, I do," I say quickly.

"You'll be home for Christmas?" Winnie says.

"Of course."

"And Thanksgiving?"

"Yes.

"And my birthday?" She presses her hands together.

"I'll do my best."

"And my birthday?" Atticus asks, bouncing on the bed.

I ruffle his hair. "If at all possible."

"You're going to do so great, Sam. You know that, right?" Mom says.

I swallow hard. "I hope so."

Dad rests his hand on my shoulder, grounding and steady. "You're the most capable person I know," he says quietly.

"You're biased," I tell him, trying to lighten the mood.

"Completely," he says. "But I'm also not wrong."

I feel that familiar swell in my chest that I've felt since I was nine years old. So much love.

Dad pulls me in for a hug. "I love you, buddy."

"I love you too."

Mom joins the hug, squeezing me tight. Winnie huffs and wedges herself between them, getting in the middle, and Atticus isn't far behind.

"We're a mess." I laugh, my voice cracking.

"We're your mess," Dad says.

"Always have been," Mom says.

"Always will be," I say softly.

Want more Penn and Addy?
https://bookhip.com/GJSRGPC

Keep reading to get a sneak peek of what's coming next! Goldie Whitman and Milo Lombardi meet and instantly clash in *Take this Heart*, book 1 of the *Windy Harbor* series.

COMING SOON
TAKE THIS HEART

**Chapter 1
Beautiful Devil
GOLDIE**

Minnesota is in my bones.

Apparently, the *cold hands, warm heart* myth was debunked by scientists, who said how toasty your body is has a direct correlation to how nice you are to others.

I beg to differ.

On some winter days in Minnesota, it doesn't matter how nice you are—you, your hands, and the rest of your body parts are going to be cold.

But the cold is familiar, like a cantankerous grandma who pinches your cheeks too hard but knits you colorful half-finger gloves because she knows you love them…Grandma Donna. The kind who always smells like Vicks VapoRub and who, no matter how much you eat, thinks you don't like her food because you didn't have three helpings…Grandma Nancy.

I've missed that. The mercurial seasons. The lakes—there are more than 10,000, no matter what the license plates say. The fact that (some) people say "doncha know" without irony…both Grandma Donna and Grandma Nancy.

It's not always cold; in fact, in the sweet days of summer and fall, you can almost forget that winter is around the corner. But the consistent 70-degree sunshine in California was delightful, as were the palm trees and delicious food and people whose whole personality was yoga pants. Traffic, I didn't enjoy so much, and after I had a horrible car accident on the 405, something inside me shifted. Eternal sunshine didn't seem so important anymore. I wanted roots. Comfort. The kind of sky that makes you wonder what craziness is rolling in next.

So I came home.

I'm an interior designer by day—farmhouse kitchens, cozy cabins, the occasional baby nursery—and I paint by night. Oils, mostly. I've worked nonstop for the past four months getting ready for my art installation at MIA—the Minneapolis Museum of Art—a place I never imagined showing my artwork. I've thrown everything into it. Late nights. Early mornings. Meals scarfed in front of half-finished canvases. I love creating, that feeling of bringing an idea to life. I get some of that creativity out through interior design, but that's breathing life into someone else's ideas. It's the most rewarding feeling when I paint a piece that's all me and watch it transform with each layer of paint.

For a long time, any form of creating energized me, but the exhaustion is catching up.

The last thing I feel like doing right now is attending a

gala at the Walker Art Center. I love the place, but a room full of intimidating people on a night when I just want to be painting at home? No, thank you. But I've heard I need to put myself out there and get acquainted with the art community if I want to be part of it.

I miss Addy like crazy. We met in California. She was my roommate in college and remains my best friend, the one person who always knows what I need. FaceTime calls are never enough. She lives in Silver Hills, Colorado, with the love of her life, Penn Hudson—who happens to be a pro football player and is *the* running back of all time—their kids, Sam and Winnie, and a baby on the way. Oh, and she also houses a family of Sphynx cats whom I get almost daily pictures of…insert full-body shudders here. They're super sweet if I just don't have to look at them.

I've made a few friends at work, but I don't see any of them here yet. So I'm clutching a glass of champagne like a security blanket and sipping more than I should on an empty stomach.

I smile at people I don't know and compliment a woman's earrings, wondering how long I have to stay.

"There you are." Luna puts her arm around me. "Come on, I'll introduce you to a few people."

I sag into her. "I'm so glad to see you. I needed to see a friendly face."

Luna has taken me under her wing. She's the one who got me into MIA, and she thinks I will need to quit my job and paint full-time after my show. That's the dream. We'll see.

She flits around confidently and introduces me to so many people, I don't retain the names, and then she's called away to talk to someone else. I'm near an exhibit that's caught my eye, so I tell her I'll catch up with her.

The exhibit is intriguing—it's an architectural model of a

park with sculptures integrated with nature. I study it for a while, but when I realize that it's actually a proposal to rehaul the sculpture garden I love across the street, I frown.

"You don't like it?"

The voice is low and husky, and when I look up, I struggle not to gasp. The beauty of the man in front of me is…wow. Holy buckets. I swallow and try not to appear as shaken as I feel. His black hair falls over his forehead, firelight eyes cool and assessing beneath thick curly lashes. Perfect lips. He's also *tall*. I'd put him at 6'5" like my youngest brother Dylan.

He blinks and tilts his head, like he's waiting for my response.

"Oh. Well, it's an interesting concept, but is it really meant to replace Spoonbridge and Cherry? That sculpture is iconic! It's been part of the landscape of Minneapolis since before I was born. Why would anyone want to bulldoze it or anything else in the sculpture garden?"

He's smirking until I say *bulldoze*, and then his eyes narrow.

"I'm sure it wouldn't be bulldozed, more like moved to another location," he says.

I turn to face him and shake my head. "Part of the beauty of it is the skyline in the background. It would be a travesty to move it." I nod toward the model and make a sweeping gesture with my hand. "*This* is a travesty."

He snorts derisively, and now, I'm really annoyed. I cross my arms over my chest and stare back at him. He's *snorting* at me now?

"Art is evolving," he says. "We preserve it, yes, but we also make room for the new."

"And you think *that*," I point at the sculpture replicas in the model that are admittedly very cool, even though I will never admit that now, "is worthy of booting out the old, I take it?"

He steps closer and leans in, his breath skittering over my skin. "Yes, I do."

When I look up at him, we're about an inch apart.

I poke his chest. "*You* are what's wrong in America."

Poke, poke, poke.

He arches an offensively perfect brow, and if it's possible, moves even closer. "Is that right? And how does wanting to move a few sculptures make me so wrong?"

It's hard to think straight when he's this close and smells so good. Like cedar and honey.

Those eyes make me want to cuddle up to him and enjoy the fire.

Focus, Goldie.

"We don't appreciate history here," I say—somewhat breathlessly, but I soldier on. "We build things and tear them down when we're tired of them. Massive structures that cost millions to build become rubble if someone gets tired of it and wants to put something else there. It doesn't even have to be better, just new. Different. Why can't we appreciate our rich history and preserve it? At least the beautiful things?"

"Like Spoonbridge and Cherry," he says dryly, his lips lifting as he mocks me.

"Like Spoonbridge and Cherry," I say emphatically.

"Why not let someone else enjoy it for a while?"

"Why mess with perfection?" I volley back.

I had no idea I felt this passionately about Spoonbridge and Cherry, but it *is* really cute.

"Perfection?" he scoffs. Scoffs!

"It's the principle of the thing!" I say, louder than I intended.

He rolls his eyes and takes a step back, crossing his arms over his chest.

"Wonderful! You've met Milo," Luna says, appearing at my side.

Milo? Ugh. Even his name is cool.

Luna beams up at him. "The man of the hour."

"Man of the hour?" I say under my breath. *Man of the hour, my big, fat toe*, my brain shouts.

"Yes! He's the architect who designed this model. What do you think of it? Isn't it incredible?" Luna says, grinning between Milo and me.

I feel unsteady and then hot all over. My eyes narrow again, and I look around Milo to find the museum label next to the park model.

Milo Lombardi.

Oh my God. *The* Milo Lombardi? I can't believe it. World-renowned architect. Ridiculously talented.

Ridiculously *hot*.

Hmm. They say Satan was pretty too.

"She thinks it's a travesty," Milo tells Luna, while still staring me down.

I tilt my head as if to say, *you're not wrong.*

Luna gasps and turns to gawk at me. "What are you—"

"There's someone over there I need to see," I say, pointing behind them.

Milo nods—smug and with the kind of confidence that suggests he invented air. And maybe also a little smug because he sees right through me and knows I want to get away from him as fast as I can.

I walk away and grab another glass of champagne, downing it.

A few minutes later, my phone dings and I look at it, happy for something to distract me.

. . .

DAD

It's pretty quiet. Everyone okay? Take a pic of what you're doing right now, so there's proof of life.

TULLY

<photo of his hockey jersey crumpled up in his locker> Pretty sure I saw you in the stands so you know I'm alive. Lol Love you, Dad.

CAMDEN

<photo of a Food Network-worthy meal> Love you, Dad.

^ I don't recognize anything but the mashed potatoes. <Photo of me in front of a nude sculpture of a woman> The closest you'll get to a naked woman tonight. Love you, Dad.

TULLY

That's what you think.

That's what I KNOW because I don't want to think of my brothers around naked women, thank you very much. Hi, Dad. I love you.

DYLAN

<photo of him holding a surfboard and standing next to a woman who looks like a model> The picture speaks for itself, Golds. 😉 Love you, Dad.

NOAH

<photo of him and Grayson eating Taco Bell> Love you, Dad!

> What about me? Does anyone love me?

TULLY

Can't you feel the telepath waves of twin love?

> If I had I wouldn't have asked.

NOAH

Grayson wants his Aunt Goldie to hurry up and visit. You are loved.

CAMDEN

I just texted that I loved you an hour ago in another thread. But I'll say it again.

> ...waiting.

CAMDEN

OMG, the kitchen is backed up and I am texting my sister how much I love her.

DYLAN

You're needier than me, Golds. 😉

> And you know you're all here for it. Love you guys. I'm at the Walker tonight and would much rather be with you.

DAD

<photo of the sun going down over Lake Superior.> I love you all so much. Hanging at the lake. Homesick for all of you.

CHAPTER TWO
CURATED

MILO

She called my work a travesty.

I've heard worse. Hell, I've read worse in published reviews. But not from someone who looked at my work with what I thought was such admiration. And then the way she looked up at me. There was a spark that crackled back and forth between us.

I'd noticed her before she said a word. There'd been a moment, before anything was said, when I thought she understood what I'd built. That she caught the layered vision of it all.

But that spark turned into acid when she spoke.

Now, she's halfway across the gallery, standing beneath a sculptural light installation and looking like she owns the place.

She's in a deep emerald green dress, the fabric off one shoulder and clinging to all the right places. Her long blonde hair falls in waves down her back. Even the way she holds her glass of champagne looks proper. She has the aura of someone important. She never introduced herself. Just dropped her opinion like a bomb and then walked away without an apology.

Wait a minute.

She just took a step, and instead of heels to match her fancy gown, she's wearing black Dr. Martens.

That makes me smile.

Who is this woman?

I lean against a marble pillar, bourbon in hand, trying not to let my eyes drift back to her.

Futile.

I look.

God, help me. She's gorgeous. And infuriating. She's laughing now, her head tilted back just enough to let the man at her side believe he said something clever. He didn't. I know because I've met him before. Seth Patterson. He's a lightweight in design. Paper-thin ideas. No substance.

He leans closer to her and she steps back half an inch, graceful, practiced. She's good at this.

It's only after she takes another step back that I see her hand shaking just a bit. Maybe she's not as calm and collected as she seems.

I want to step in and save her from the lackluster and uncomfortable conversation I know she's having with Seth, but she called my work a travesty.

The gala is louder this year. Or maybe I'm just noticing more. The clinking glasses and carefully curated laughter—it's sitting wrong on my skin, like a cat who's petted in the wrong direction.

My model sits in the center of it all. This was actually a passion project. I've put all my efforts into designing a beautiful library in Duluth for what feels like forever and needed something else to focus on during the weekends or the nights I couldn't sleep. What was just passing the time became something I now love and believe in.

Elevated on a white platform beneath spotlights, the installation looks pristine. Every detail precisely constructed.

But her voice echoes over it all. *Travesty. You are what's wrong in America.*

Hell, I'm sure there are more scandalous things I've done than this park model of exquisite artwork and skill. I could dip her over the model and show her a thing or two that would truly be outrageous.

In fact, it'd almost be a travesty *not* to dip her back on the installation and show her just how wrong I can be. So wrong that it'd feel so right. The way she stared up at me, her big brown eyes with the gold specks gazing up at me with desire, her tongue sneaking out to wet those cushiony red lips, made me certain she wished I would.

I almost respect her honesty. Because she didn't critique the materials or the execution. She critiqued the lack of soul, specifically my very own dark and twisted one.

And I have to admit that what bothers me most is that she struck a nerve. I've loved Spoonbridge and Cherry for as long as I can remember. She's also right that it's a part of the Minneapolis landscape that will be missed, but isn't it worth it if more people around the country are allowed to enjoy it for themselves?

I circle the gallery, greeting board members and donors and answering questions from junior curators and well-dressed influencers. My practiced smile is in place—it's second nature by now.

But my eyes keep tracking back to her.

***

We run into each other again near the back wall, where one of the smaller installations is failing to impress anyone. She turns as I approach, almost as if she felt me coming.

"Milo Lombardi," she says, sipping her champagne. "Still brooding?"

I arch a brow. "Still spewing venom?"

Her eyes flash. "I thought you'd be off collecting compliments from the press."

"Thought I'd take a break. Let someone else enjoy the sound of their own voice."

She lifts her glass in salute. "How generous of you."

There's a weighted moment of silence that hangs.

She tilts her head, looking past me to my model.

"They love it," she says bitterly. "You're going to get everything you want, aren't you?"

I follow her gaze and then stare at the long curve of her neck as she spits daggers at my work. "Not everything."

She turns back and meets my eyes, her cheeks flushing. "Meaning?"

"No one gets everything they want, do they?"

Her eyes narrow. "I'm sure you're not lacking."

"You don't seem to be either."

"True. I can't complain."

"You make it a habit of wearing Doc Martens with your evening gowns?" I smirk.

A strange expression crosses her face, but she recovers quickly. "I do now."

I want to ask what she means by that, but instead, I say, "Well, it says something that you've stayed all evening…for me."

Her eyes flash. "I didn't stay for you."

"Didn't you?" I point at the banner that has my name on it and she rolls her eyes.

"You're impossible," she says.

"You're worse. You make a lot of assumptions."

"And you think you don't? Trust me, I didn't even notice your name. But I *have* worked with a lot of men like you." Her eyes flicker over my face with accusation.

"Men like me?"

She turns now, fully facing me. "Talented. Celebrated. Used to being the one who gets the last word."

"You think I don't listen?"

"I think you don't like being wrong."

She's not wrong there.

I take a step closer. "You hovered over the installation like you were falling in love, right until you gutted it in one sentence."

She lifts her shoulder. "I never said it wasn't beautiful. I'm just not willing to sacrifice history for it."

"You really think you're the only one in this room who understands intention? Don't you want to be part of progress?"

"When it matters, yes."

The silence between us sharpens.

I can't decide whether I want to kiss her or walk away forever. Both, I think.

Before I can say anything else, I hear my name, and from the way everyone's turned to stare at me, I think maybe it's not the first time I've been called. I'm too busy watching this obnoxious woman, watching me.

Luna clears her throat at the mic and smiles at me.

"Friends, thank you for joining us tonight to celebrate the intersection of community, art, and innovation," she says.

I tune in and out, too keyed up while standing next to this woman.

"...transforming the way we think about public spaces..."

"...a visionary who's brought something truly unique to our city..."

I hear the woman groan next to me and turn to glare at her. She looks at me with innocent eyes. Little minx.

"What is your problem?" I say under my breath.

Just as Luna says, "And now, please welcome Milo Lombardi."

Applause circles through the room.

I step forward, moving to the low stage near the model and blinking beneath the lights.

I give the speech I prepared. It's smooth, a nice mix of humble and polished. I wonder what the beautiful woman is thinking the entire time. I need to get her name before the night is over. When I finish, the applause is louder. A few of the board members shake my hand, pausing me mid-step. When I look back at the corner where we were standing together, she's gone.

***

I find her on the rooftop terrace. I tell myself that I came up here to get space, not that I was hoping to catch a glimpse of her again. She's there, overlooking the sculpture garden, Spoonbridge and Cherry a touch of whimsy for the towering Basilica of Saint Mary in the background. She's not overshadowed by the splendor behind her, not in the slightest. I've never seen a woman more beautiful than her, and for a second, I allow myself to enjoy the view.

She turns and meets my eyes.

"You again," she says, but her words have no bite this time. "I didn't come up here for company."

"I didn't come up here for you," I lie.

She looks away. "But you're staying."

"Maybe I like the view."

She looks at me over her shoulder, the corner of her mouth twitching when she sees my eyes on her. "Are you always so insufferable?"

"Maybe," I say, stepping closer. "But you haven't walked away."

Her breath catches and then her jaw tightens like she's angry with herself for not moving.

And then we're not talking anymore. Her mouth is on mine. I'm not sure if I started it or she did.

The kiss is sharp-edged and heady, a rush to all my senses. Her hands fist in the lapels of my jacket, and mine slide to her waist, pulling her against me like I've wanted to since the moment she insulted me in the gallery.

She tastes like champagne and defiance, and I'm half drunk on the combination.

She pulls back slightly, breath ragged. "This is such a bad idea."

"Probably the worst," I whisper, and kiss her again.

It's reckless. Irresponsible. A dare to wreck my world. Yet I keep going. I'd do just about anything she asked right now.

She pulls away long enough to mutter, "I don't know what to do with you."

I brush a strand of hair from her cheek. "You don't have to do anything. Just stop hating me for five seconds."

She stares at me for a beat and then her lips are on mine again, soft and urgent. Nothing else exists. Her body melts against mine, her fingers fisting my hair.

When she pulls away again, I want to chase her mouth, but instead, I grin. "You kiss like you have something to prove."

She freezes. "Excuse me?"

I frown. "I meant—intense. Fiery."

"Something to *prove*?" she echoes, voice rising. "That's what you got out of that?"

I close my eyes, sighing. "That came out wrong."

She laughs, but it's hollow. "Let's just go back to admitting this was a *bad* idea."

"It didn't *feel* like a bad idea."

She moves past me.

"Come on. Don't walk away. Stay, please—"

But she doesn't stop.

I stay rooted to the rooftop, watching long after she's out of sight.

Will they hate each other or will sparks fly between Milo and Goldie? Or both...
Preorder Take this Heart here...
https://geni.us/TakeThisHeart

ACKNOWLEDGMENTS

I have more love and gratitude than I know what to do with for all of you!

I can't believe this series has come to an end! At least for now. 😊 I've loved every second of writing about these characters and this town, and I'm so grateful for all of you who have found these books and loved them too. Thank you for reading my work. I appreciate every review, every share, every beautiful graphic, every kind word about The Single Dad Playbook!

Extra, extra love and thanks goes to:

Georgie Grinstead, we did it. Thanks for seeing this vision with me and helping me pull it off.

Christine Estevez, I seriously don't know what I'd do without you. I love that we're in this together.

Natalie Burtner, you are sunshine and the most helpful person ever and also super pretty.

Katie Friend, you're a rockstar with THE BEST comments and feedback.

Kira Sabin, you did it again. You created a watercolor masterpiece.

Kess Sabin, when I have the most random art subject requests and you laugh and say you love it and then create it —there is nothing better.

Emily Wittig, thank you, cover goddess!

Dear VPR team, you're the best! Nina, Kim, Valentine, Charlie, Christine, Sarah, Josette, Meagan, Kelley, Ratula, Tiffany, Jill, Jaime, Amy, Stephanie, Megan, Emma, and Jess, thank you for EVERYTHING!

To the Lyric team, Kim Gilmour and Katie Robinson, you've been so wonderful to work with this entire series!

Connor Crais and Vanessa Edwin, so grateful you brought your magic to these characters in audio!

To The Seymour Agency, thank you for believing in me!

Laura Pavlov and Catherine Cowles, your sprints helped me get these books DONE, and your friendship gets me through LIFE. I could write pages of thanks to each of you, separately and together, but know that the love chain has my heart forever.

Claribel Contreras, thank you for always pushing me in the best ways. I love talking to you about everything and nothing.

Tarryn Fisher, my girl, I just love you. I can't write a book without thanking you—because of the love and because you didn't let me give up.

My family and friends who are like family: Troi Atkinson, Phyllis Atkinson, David Atkinson, Tosha Khoury, Courtney Nuness, Christine Bowden, Steve & Jill Erickson, Savita Naik, Destini Simmons, Terrijo Montgomery, Kell Donaldson, and Jesse Nava, I love you and am so grateful for your love.

Anthony Colletti, you are a gem.

Kalie Phillips, hearts forever.

Winston, please live forever.

And last but in no way least, my family. Nate, Greyley & Kira, and Indigo, your support and excitement for every milestone I reach means more to me than I can say. I wouldn't be able to do this without all of you. Also, I've learned that I can never do another signing without you again! 😊 I love you with ALL my heart.

ALSO BY WILLOW ASTER

The Single Dad Playbook Series

Mad Love

Secret Love

Reckless Love

Wicked Love

Crazy Love

Landmark Mountain Series

Unforgettable

Someday

Irresistible

Falling

Stay

Standalones with Interconnected Characters

Summertime

Autumn Nights

Kingdoms of Sin Series

Downfall

Exposed

Ruin

Pride

Standalones

True Love Story

Fade to Red

In the Fields

Maybe Maby (also available on all retailer sites)

Lilith (also available on all retailer sites)

Miles Apart (also available on all retailer sites)

Falling in Eden

The G.D. Taylors Series with Laura Pavlov

Wanted Wed or Alive

The Bold and the Bullheaded

Another Motherfaker

Don't Cry Over Spilled MILF

Friends with Benefactors

The End of Men Series with Tarryn Fisher

Folsom

Jackal

FOLLOW ME

JOIN MY MASTER LIST…
https://bit.ly/3CMKz5y

Website willowaster.com
Facebook @willowasterauthor
Instagram @willowaster
Amazon @willowaster
Bookbub @willow-aster
TikTok @willowaster1
Goodreads @willow_aster
Asters group @Astersgroup
Pinterest@willowaster

Printed in Dunstable, United Kingdom